The Last Summer of Mata Hari

The Last Summer of Mata Hari

BY EDWARD HUEBSCH

Crown Publishers, Inc.   New York

Inquiries should be addressed to
Crown Publishers, Inc., One Park Avenue,
New York, N.Y. 10016

Printed in the United States of America
Published simultaneously in Canada by
General Publishing Company Limited

Library of Congress Cataloging in Publication Data

Huebsch, Edward.
      The last summer of Mata Hari.

      1. Zelle, Margaretha Geertruida, 1876–1917—Fiction.
I. Title.
PZ4.H8865Las   [PS3558.U313] 813'.5'4   79-14576
ISBN 0-517-53306-5

Book Design: Shari de Miskey

For

B.G., who generously gave me the subject,

and

B.L.H., who provided all else

"All points of view about reality are untrue, including this one."

Nagarjuna, c. 100 A.D.

"Fact rests on theory."

Goethe, 1749–1832

"History may be no more than the myth of the civilized."

Sir Isaiah Berlin, 1976

The Last Summer of Mata Hari

PARIS MISTRAL
2 June 1917

The press officer turned out to be a liar.

Ordinarily not worth a shrug. One expected military tribunals to hold accused persons incommunicado and then make fatuous excuses to the press. In this case, where the abused prisoner was a friend, Leclerc's cynicism had been severely tested. Week after week, all requests for interviews, including his, had been fobbed off despite the intense agitation of the public. Now this latest mendacity, so rawly unfair, had Leclerc ready to explode.

The other newsmen and photographers, heckling and shoving, forced the press officer to retreat backward up the long flight at the rear of the Palais de Justice.

Even without this frustration, they were in a savage mood. All Paris had tossed through a steamy night, only to wake to a stifling dawn, the city tented by a mistral up from Africa, dissolving outer world to inner and inner to a swarm, delusive, primordial.

". . . You were going to make her available for photographs at six sharp . . ."

"Provisionally, I said."

"And for interviews at six-thirty! Where is she?"

". . . Circumstances permitting . . ."

"Your ass permitting! Is she here?"

"I don't know."

"You mean, she hasn't been brought here from the prison yet?"

"I don't know . . ."

"Is there anything you do know?"

Leclerc's voice hung in the thick air. The pudgy captain gave him a sickly grin. He pulled back yet another step. The others opened up a path for Leclerc, deferring to his personal interest in this case.

". . . Hello, Leclerc."

Leclerc had known the man when he was on the city desk. Military service had ripened his potential for toadyism; and authority had only made his ineptitudes more offensive.

"Are you telling us," Leclerc demanded, "she won't be allowed to see us before the court session today?"

"I think you can assume that, yes."

"Then what about the afternoon, after court ends?" Leclerc pressed.

"I don't know."

"You mean, they have made no plans on that—it's still up in the air?"

"I haven't been informed."

"So you're saying we can expect them to keep the muzzle on her!"

"She'll get her chance to speak in court."

"Have they instructed you to be a moron," Leclerc vented his disgust, "or is it your very own achievement?"

"I'm saying I don't know if they discussed it, and when they do, I'll let you know."

Leclerc pushed his way down the stairs and, letting his

fury ebb, went to watch some pigeons swing shoreward from a flight over the Seine. The birds circled and landed beneath a tree, butting each other. Disoriented, he thought, like me.

Strictly speaking, he was free to leave. The trial itself would be covered by *Figaro*'s regular court reporter. He'd come only for a color story. But if they were keeping her wrapped in security, what could he do? If he attacked the military tribunal, the newspaper would suppress it, citing the higher interests of the Republic in time of war. Even if his editors let it by, the censors would kill it.

He came around the building and halted.

In the avenue an angry crowd fumed over the sidewalks, battered against the police cordon, viciously thrust into the courtyard and up the stairs of the Palais, bowling over court attendants and storming into the courthouse. It was a replay of a revolutionary scene of the last century, only this time the citizens were out for the blood of a single woman, a crime of passion on a mass scale.

The poison had been brewing all spring.

The Government itself, Leclerc knew, had supplied the heat. Ever since the failure of the spring offensive, it had encouraged citizens to come forward and denounce their neighbors who might be guilty of spreading "Boche disaffection and defeatism."

Among those hailed before the military courts had been a citizen who had complained in a café that the grounds at the bottom of his coffee cup were mainly mud.

Then the firing squads at Vincennes went to work. Their targets, several hundred of them, were obscure people. Minor employees at military installations and war factories. Tried, found guilty, their shadows fell across the adulterated coffee cups, heavy as silence.

From the moment of Mata Hari's arrest, the newspapers automatically played the role of accuser. Before any announcement of official charges against her, they had her deep in the sale of military secrets to Abteilung Three of German Intelligence, a relentless seducer of otherwise stalwart French officers, her bedroom activities responsible for that storm of intestines, gory muck, barbed wire, which, on the editorial page, they politely termed the stalemate on the western front.

All right. But this spectacle on the streets—this public lust to obliterate the woman—you couldn't explain that by talking about press smears, or heat, or even war misery.

He knew what they were feeling; he himself had had the urge to annihilate her.

For he, no less than they, had a sense of personal betrayal as though what she had done, or was supposed to have done, had been aimed at all that was trusting and vulnerable within him.

They—and he—could remember another day on these same streets when they had fallen in love with her with the same mass passion.

It had been May Day. A sunny day of peace, marvelously right for a parade. The city had basked in its willed refusal to think of history, past or present or future. Peace was eternal, like the gold franc. Paris marched or watched the marchers. No groups or factions for this day. It was the essence of the rite of spring to hope, and what sectary does not expect that one day the opposition must see the light, his light?

Along the avenue, as part of the parade, there appeared a team of work horses pulling a large municipal garbage wagon. The animals were fancifully caparisoned and the truck itself had been splashed with bright paints. A mountain of refuse, some overflowing, had been arranged to make a most appealing bouquet, broken machines and mashed mannequins and a revel of junk transformed into a surrealist cornucopia.

Connected to the wagon by streaming ribbons, dancing as at a maypole, were many of the artists of Montparnasse, all in the thrall of a tall young woman in the driver's seat. She held reins made up of twisted veils of many colors, which then extended to wind around her body, but left free her long naked legs and bare feet, whose velvety skin had the luxuriance of a costume.

Beside her there sat a skeleton, vaguely female, made of corset stays, whose skull was half bowed under an enormous velvet hat, an exaggerated version of the current fashion, atop which there perched an embalmed trinity of small birds nested in a shrine of white satin.

From time to time, the vivacious driver, lithe and long-necked, bold in joy of herself, acknowledged the calls of the courtiers and the crowd with a wave of one of her shimmery legs, more arresting than suggestive, eliciting a quiver of homage from the morbid figure at her side and the jumping spectators below.

Though the artists had intended only a display of impudent lyricism, the crowd was moved by something far more pertinent than an old metaphor about turning garbage to roses.

For this parade culminated a decade of promise; the recent discovery of radium was believed to have provided a substance more magical than the philosopher's stone, nothing less than the defeat of death. The new quantum mechanics was thought to be the key to the last secrets of nature, and a fount of triumphs from the laboratories assured mankind impending release from the dark past, full of old brutalities of necessity, to emerge into civilization, bright as electricity, unmystical as the young woman's legs, coherent as her laughter.

"Look at her—she's too tall to be from India—she's a French woman, after all!"

"A gypsy, they say!"

"Don't be a fool—she's English—Lady Something-or-other!"

"Look at those hands—she knows how to drive a team—not just one of those dolls!"

"Think she'll unwind her veils for us?"

Leclerc had been caught up in the crowd's delight. At the time, he'd scarcely heard of Mata Hari, whose debut as a nude dancer had created a sensation among the elite at the Guimet Museum. But such cultural fireworks did not penetrate to the burrows frequented by a young Paris reporter. As he ran beside the wagon, he had not the least inkling that he would soon be calling her Tha, writing feature stories about her, stories that would be so important in her career, so decisive for his own.

All he wanted was a closer look. He made out a wide-set face, with a glowing, peasanty sort of strength; noticed that the generous mouth that framed the husky laughter subsided in a melancholy line. Yet when her bright glance touched him for a moment, he had the illusion that she was communing solely with him, inviting him to throw off guilt and fear and rise to joy in himself, after her frank fashion.

"Not like those other actresses," someone said nearby. "The way she laughs, she means it."

"She's not afraid of anyone," another said. "One look at her and you can see things are going to be different."

As the rubbish wagon crossed the city, the wildness that had greeted her daring dance in the museum took hold of the streets; Paris, seeing in her flesh a sign, exultantly shouted its readiness to indulge itself in the new age.

A cornucopia, to be sure, but dispensed from the mouth of a cannon, requiring their bodies to ingest its largesse, more surrealistic than even the bizarre imaginings of Montparnasse.

And that accounted for their savagery today.

For whether guilty or innocent, she was a witness to their illusions, of their own careless confidence, to which they had sacrificed their sons and lovers and husbands. Without those complicitous May-dreams they might not have died, or at least gone differently to their deaths. Now, in a paroxysm of self-reproach, they wanted to expunge the image of the woman who had reflected all those rhapsodic, childish hopes, and by one stroke absolve themselves at last of innocence.

"I want to see the whore get it, with my own eyes!"

"She fooled us all—the cunt!"

"They'll stuff her purse at Vincennes with something really hot!"

Leclerc struggled to pull away from the crowd, haunted by the memory of that historyless day, the image of those invincible dray horses and the vivid driver whose generous laughter still sounded above the rancorous baying of the pack around him.

"Hey, Leclerc, aren't you going in?"

His colleagues were coming toward him, barring his escape. Of course, he could remind them that trial coverage wasn't his assignment. But these were treacherous days. They knew him as her friend. They would be watching him for signs of sympathy for a spy, a dangerous traitor. He had many rivals. Pointless to lay himself open to stray denunciations.

"Sure," he called, "help me through."

They forced a path for him. In their midst, Leclerc felt followed by Tha's dark eyes, a trace of sorrow behind their usual warmth and affection, so that he bent his head and charged forward, though nobody blocked his way.

The Matron, working over the embroidery tambour, her lips pursed, filled the windowless room with her virtuous loathing.

On the floor, nestled in a brown wrapper, lay the disputed wine-colored gown, the dove-gray pumps with their flashing silver buckles, the short ermine jacket, the glistening satin underwear, all in an offendingly luxurious heap.

Days ago they'd promised to bring from her apartment things she could wear in court. She had specified a simple blue frock for her first appearance, fearful of summoning up in the minds of jury and public new visions of her as Salome reborn.

Instead they'd produced this lavish costume she'd been wearing at the time of her arrest, an indictment in itself.

But if she went up there in her prison smock, she'd be accused of making a false appeal for sympathy; the press would describe her as the arch manipulator, playing on the feelings of the crowd, wicked Circe to the end.

Legs drawn up, Tha rested her chin on her knees, compelled to watch the steel stab through the stretched cloth. She had tried a dozen ways to breach the Matron's taut righteousness, but nothing had worked.

This was the third holding room this morning. They had taken her from her solitary cell in St. Lazaire prison to one airless closet after another to await the van, itself one more coffin. Perhaps a merciful trial run to accustom her to the real thing.

"Matron," she decided to try again, "this room, where is it?"

"In the Palais de Justice, of course."

"But where? Under the courtroom? Under the front courtyard?"

"Somewhere in the basement."

"But you work here . . ."

"A crazy question."

"It's only that if I know where I am, it helps me imagine a voyage out . . ."

"Do you want me to ask the guard?"

"No." She gave up. "Childish."

She forced her eyes away from the hypnotic lure of the needle. Even in St. Lazaire, the nuns shied from her as if she were some sort of fiend. The prison, administered by the church, had a reputation for charity and kindliness. But in her case, at least, they could spare nothing more than the starched and forbidding rustle of their gowns, confining communication to gestures, shielding themselves from her evil body by their downcast lids and from her evil soul by the prophylaxis of their prayers.

Not that she blamed them.

They weren't seeing her, but the fiction that the press—and she herself—had created. Mata Hari, indecipherable mystery, deceptive as Lilith, more dangerous than the snake with which she was alleged to have danced for her most cherished lovers. It had sold newspapers and theatre tickets, and given her an unremovable mask.

During the last eight weeks, they had occasionally let her have the newspapers, and she had been astonished how the old fiction had taken new dimensions. The campaign of calumny painted her not only as the seller of secrets to the Boche, but as a faithless creature of the underworld, of ancient evil come again, from which society yearned to cleanse itself.

Only yesterday she had read a story written by her friend, Leclerc. It purported to quote some of the nuns who had guarded her in St. Lazaire. She was supposed to have bragged to them about her predicament: "I'm not worried. As you can see from the charges against me, I cast an unfailing spell on all military men. Now that I am to be tried by a military tribunal, why should my charm suddenly vanish?"

Of course, Leclerc had invented that in the image both had so lightly created. "Sin, like virtue, is its own reward" was the slogan they'd made up for her. And, of course, that image had inescapably become part of herself. Mata Hari, the scandalous; Mata Hari, the unsafe; Mata Hari, who could be counted on to deliver a frisson with the breakfast brioche.

"Must you sit like that, Madame?"

Tha looked up at the frowning face and unclasped her legs. "I'm sorry. I didn't know it annoyed you."

"It's unseemly."

Her pelt, her provocative pelt. What had Hesse said that time in Geneva? "Your skin . . . too immediate, too rich . . . rebukes the rest of us for our fall from animal grace . . ."

"Excuse me," she said.

Pacing, feeling caged, Tha found herself trying to fight off an attack of nerves. It was too easy to fall into melancholia. The Matron's curling, disdainful lips were not yet the jury's verdict.

So far, she had done well. To all her interrogator's grilling, she had a simple reply: as an employee of French Intelligence, she was forbidden to speak of her activities without the express consent of her chief at the Deuxième Bureau, Monsieur Henri Depardieu.

Mercifully, they had not asked about Adam. At first, she thought that meant Depardieu had decided that Adam, not having been an eyewitness, was of no interest. Later, she ascribed the lack of questions to their fear that, in bringing Adam into the case—a combat officer, frequently decorated, finally blinded in action—they would risk swinging public opinion to her side. Finally, she realized that the events that triggered her arrest were going to be left unsung; they yearned only for silence.

But those conjectures aside, she knew that Adam had reached safety in Scotland, shielded, she hoped, from the trial and all its echoes. In St. Lazaire, she'd forbidden herself to think of him, for each reverie ended with her falling apart. Nevertheless, the daydreams surged, and she found herself with him again, sharing his few short leaves before he'd lost his sight at Vittel, his long stride making her pant to keep up, a lean giant with a rough black beard who drew the stares of men and women alike, his eyes glittering with the fatigue of the trenches, the dust of war on his shoulders, in every gesture of his expressive hands. And from those daydreams, she'd plunged to fathomless depression.

That way, she knew, was to play into Depardieu's hands and seal her doom. After her last teary collapse, she had taken a vow to banish Adam from her mind; now, at the moment of her trial, she must not give way to her desire for him, or it would let them destroy her in the courtroom.

Think of other victories. Of Sita.

For a while, it seemed that they would arrest Sita too. Sita, tiny and ageless, had been her savior in Java and had been with her ever since. And they had brought Sita in for questioning, trying to pit them against each other. But Sita had easily avoided their traps. She had played the role of simple old peasant retainer to perfection.

In fact, by using Malay phrases, ostensibly only random interjections in her replies to the examiners, she had conveyed to Tha her plan for going to Holland to seek to protect Tha's little daughter, Banda, from the effects of the spy trial. The child had been taken from her by her former husband, Colonel McLeod, as a reprisal for the divorce. He could be counted on to use the trial as a justification of his hatred and further embitter the child's life with his vindictiveness.

By now, Sita would be at The Hague. Her plan was to go to Tha's old friend, the Dutch premier, Van der Gelder, and enlist him in removing the child to a foster home, free from the taint of publicity and her father's malice. If anybody could bring that about, it would be Sita; and if any human could give back confidence to the child, her choice would be Sita.

And there were others out there who would not abandon her. Like Bob Maxwell, the blond young American with his big horn-rimmed glasses and his shyness and diffidence that made each utterance almost a stutter. He not only knew the truth, but he had managed to convey word through her lawyer, old Clunet, that he would not desert her, no matter how much pressure the Americans or the French put on him. She had once made fun of the American's undeviating morality. Now it would be his sword against his enemies and hers.

Clunet himself had been sheer luck. The famous defense attorney had appeared out of the blue, offering to defend her. Maître Clunet, a small man with an aureole of white hair, was nearly eighty. He was widely revered for his brilliant defense tactics in the Dreyfus case, and, even though he had not practiced for fifteen years, was still sharp and lively. That he had volunteered to help her was a miracle; and if one, why preclude others?

Even Jules Chardon, the Foreign Minister. At the moment, it might be to his interest to bury her. But Jules knew the truth, too, and Jules was no simple careerist. It was his pose that he cared for nothing but his political reputation and his wife's money. Tha depended on his enormous ego to show her he was superior even to his own corruption and come to her aid.

And the many men she had known, the many she had loved. Too many, her critics said, to love. Nonsense. Had she known twice as many, she would have enjoyed each. Men were to be cherished, their possibilities made one's own. To pass over any act of love was to reduce one's own life; giving less and expecting less from any person was a small death.

Adam had been puzzled about that, their first day together in Paris. She remembered his lean dark face, frowning high above her, as he tried to fathom her defiance of convention. She had told him about a saying in the Vedas, that even when you embraced another being, you only touched fingertips in passing, real beauty escaping on the wing.

He had listened, unconvinced. She might quote from Buddhist texts, which she had learned in Java, but she was like her friends in Montparnasse, an incorrigible aesthete, beset by turning life into art, questing for beauty in ash pits.

It had been part of their first feverish exchanges, not meant so much to explore each other as to make sure that they could depend on some genetic bolt that had, almost behind their backs, slid home. Their talk was only a way of testing a bond already made, of making their own intuition appear reasonable and reasoning, while both knew it was all irrelevant, all decided.

There had been a Zeppelin attack that night, but they had ignored it to pace the darkened streets of the city, avoiding the patrols who were supposed to enforce curfew even on a lanky battle-stained major and his girl, prowling around in a trance.

She had tried not to look at him. In their first meeting, his face had struck her as being almost preternaturally handsome, its hard aquilinity, its intense planes having a dizzying effect. She had hoped to preserve her equilibrium by concentrating on what he was saying, ignoring his physical aspect. But she could not manage the trick. Her eyes would be drawn back to his weary and ardent face, and she would feel she'd stolen something, something forbidden, leaving her more disturbed each time.

Suddenly, they were in a cul-de-sac that terminated in a small building, which turned out to be the Hotel Impasse des Anges.

They continued to float, straight from the street into a huge double bed. Neither was aware, nor could they recall later, the intervention of any hotel clerk or hotel registry. It was the street one moment, their bodies nude and pressed together the next.

Into that delirium there came the sounds of a bugle, playing the All Clear, counseling all citizens to relax their fears of the Zeppelin and get to sleep.

Though the call came from some nearby fire station, its notes seemed to originate under the pillow. As the notes ascended, they came up to demented climax, and as the notes went down, they withdrew from ecstasy, through distinct and exquisite plateaus of satisfaction, defined by the music itself.

The next morning, passing the fire station, Adam had decided to thank the bugler. She had stood in the quiet street. In the distance there was a red glow of some fire started by the Zeppelin. Here there was light, an entity unto itself, a filter through which all colors and objects passed, to be purified and intensified, made almost palpable. For the first time, she understood what her painter friends called the quality of light, or, more simply, Paris light.

Adam came to find her, lost in reverie, watching a concierge water some plants across the street, her eyes lit by the reflection from the high arcing spray.

"Adam," she had surprised herself by demanding, "you must survive."

He was so tall, his head so far above her, that she could

not quite see his expression. He seemed to squint against the brightness, shielding himself from the coruscade as the water struck the pavement, spewing crystal beads.

"I'll get a writ from the Kaiser."

But she wouldn't let it go. The light encircled her. "You don't understand. I thought my life was all right. But if you are lost, I will be in a desert, everything will turn to sand. You have to get out of this war, promise me!"

He was silent for a moment. "Let's not tempt fate, Tha."

"But I want to," she had cried into the luminousness. "For once in my life, I want to make my own fate!"

His arm came around her shoulders. "Oh," he said, "is that all? In that case, I promise!"

They entered the light. Behind them the bugler came out to reprise his nocturnal serenade. The other firemen appeared in their underwear tops to call out amiable but skeptical blessings. It was, they knew, their nuptial.

Was she being punished for that? For overreaching herself, wanting happiness, craving permanence—through another life that she had tried to make the reason for her own, the ultimate arrogance of the weak?

But that would assume there was divine retribution in the world: that one got what one deserved.

If there were, she and Maxwell and Adam and Sita would be out celebrating peace with a million soldiers on the streets of Paris, while Depardieu and Chardon and the Kaiser would be in here, suffering.

No. There was no divine justice. The scalds of her childhood in Holland, the wounds inflicted in Java, had taught her to expect only the arbitrary, only the disordered. People believed in fate to shield themselves from the havoc of conflicting wills, the ruinous evasions of death, which some called the way of the world. Even in her present predicament she hoped she was not so sick as to hide from reality, or take refuge in providence, divine or otherwise.

Adam had challenged her cynicism from the beginning. He had accused her of turning her back on society. He mocked her for calling the community paradise well lost, while seeking to regain paradise in the individual. He could not understand how she could balance such contradictions. "No wonder you became a dancer," he had said, scoffing lightly, at a time neither had realized what their differences would lead to.

Yet, it had been his way (Once, when she had tried to soften his bitterness against the war, he had retorted hotly, "What you call the grinding of axes, I hear as the sound of life.") that had brought her here.

Often, during the nights in prison, the irony had haunted her that she who had fought so fiercely to free her life from the animosities of groups had become the slave of circumstance, the victim of externals.

Looking back, it all seemed inevitable—like floating from the cobbles to the mattress in the Hotel Impasse des Anges. Sometimes she had the impression that the street on which she had been born in Holland led directly to the death cell in St. Lazaire, without deviation or intersection, separated by only a few paces. And, if she persisted, a further step would take her to Vincennes.

Yet did she want to undo what she had done? She told herself she regretted nothing. Was that only emotional loyalty to Adam? Suppose they offered her the chance to live in exchange for a confession that corroborated their falsifications, would she repudiate what she and Adam had tried to accomplish? But they wouldn't. They had no need of that. All they had to do was see to it that the jury came in with a verdict of guilty, and then tie a ribbon around her at Vincennes. That was her predicament, and no amount of sickly speculation could change it.

Suddenly she was shivering. Standing in the suffocating little chamber, her body was icy and she had to hold herself with her arms.

The Matron looked up, with derisive lip. "If you're going to be sick, there's a pot in the corner."

The effort to control herself left her shakey. She tried to assume a commonplace tone, but her voice quivered. "Matron," she said, "isn't it time for them to convene?"

"They convene when they convene."

"Is there any way of finding out?"

"They'll send for you. Don't worry."

She made it back to her chair and closed her eyes, only to succumb to a picture of Adam on her lids.

Lean and unbearably handsome, Adam stood naked in the angelic hotel room, pouring coffee. His body was elongated and tendonous, restless with dark springy hair. The stream of coffee yet another masculine ropiness. Everything about him was vertical, tensely erect against the snares of barbed wire, coiling invisibly around him.

On the bed, the curled blankets and sheets were part of her, their warmth still on her skin, touching her breasts and nipples, arousing her all over again, creating a hunger more urgent than pain, yet, even in its mounting pressure, holding out the promise of that taste beneath the palate which her native Frisians called "eating the marrow of your teeth."

Let it go, she thought in despair. Or go insane.

She brought up her legs again, clasping them to her, trying to form them into a new defense against arousal and anxiety. But this time she separated her knees and lowered her head into the well of her smock and began to chant the mantra that Sita had taught her in that shadowed room in Java, the mantra from which she had taken her name as a dancer.

Softly, softly. Mata Hari, Mata Hari, eye of the sun. Take courage from the annealing fire. See how preposterous you are in terms of its light that paints false faces on time and space at once. Laugh, as Sita taught you to laugh, speak within the infinite spew of energy, a firefly adrift in a lighthearted pandemonium.

They had branded her with a reputation as a sinner. Now she would earn it. She would commit the one transgression for which they would never forgive her: she would live.

On her back she could feel the Matron's horrified, uncomprehending stare. Bend to the center. Mata Hari, Mata Hari. Sing the sin of being alive. See how absurd you are, cringing here, as if your life depended on winning the Matron's approval. Deep within her, silent laughter belled her soft incantations.

"M'sieu Maxweeeel! M'sieu Maxweeeeeeel!"

The screech of the concierge and the shriek of the doorbell went piercing through his skull. He struggled up, reaching for his robe, almost tripping on the empty bottle of armagnac on the floor.

He took one step before consciousness broke through his grapey mist. This is the morning of her trial, he nauseatedly realized. The morning I wanted to avoid, by boozing away half the night, drowning myself in my own futility, helpless as an infant when I should be Paul Bunyan kicking away institutions like rotten stumps on my way to her rescue.

Weakly he padded down the hall, damp and sweaty and sick to his stomach, the little revolver Tha had given him thumping his thigh through the thin material. He had kept it close, even in the course of his alcoholic flight, reminding himself that the Deuxième Bureau, for all its reputation for suavity, could convert itself into a blunt instrument. So far they had got at him deviously, by way of the American Embassy and U.S. Army Intelligence, but that didn't mean they'd refrain from methods that were more direct and deadly.

He did not remove the chain on the door while opening it, to squint aslant at the patriotically lightless landing. The concierge immediately made a demonstration at having to give up sleep to these inconsiderate allies.

"Hi, Prof."

His visitor, he saw, was no thug from the Deuxième Bureau, but only his alleged pal, Major Ralph Beck, emissary of U.S. Army Intelligence.

Max wiped his damp palms on his robe and lifted the chain, trying to ignore the bruising pressure of the armagnac at the base of his skull. He even managed a soothing word to the concierge.

Beck stepped into the foyer.

In spite of the sirocco he looked fit and comfortable in his summer tans. A onetime football player and a former grain dealer, Beck had apparently been inured by Chicago to the humidity of Paris.

Even minus his gelatinous hangover, Maxwell would have felt limp and unhealthy in the major's company. He made a vague gesture and led the way into the spacious living

room with its gaudy Napoleonic furniture. From time to time
the apartment owner came for a visit to remind Maxwell he
was only the probationary curator.

Beck made the same remark he had made the last time.
"Wow, you got a real museum here, Prof."

Max groped for the handles of the French doors and
went out to the balcony. It was breathless out here, too. He
gripped the iron rail, determined to conceal his daze from his
cornhusking compatriot.

"Glad you got me out of bed," he lied. "I forgot to set
my alarm."

Beck fanned himself with a long yellow envelope. "A
steamer," he said. "You oughta sleep in the raw. Or don't they
allow that in Princeton?"

Maxwell looked down into the garden, four stories
below, fighting dizziness. "Cable?"

"Yup. Better get your glasses, Prof."

"It's all right, Beck."

He reached out and tore a sliver from the end of the
oversized envelope. He was sure the message had already
passed through Beck's hands. He had to force himself to focus,
grateful for the army's block capitals.

> RECOMMEND MERGE YOUR UNIT AND ARMY IN-
> TELLIGENCE BEST USE OF TALENT INCLUDING
> YOURS PLEASE ADVISE SIGNED HOUSE

The final turn of the screw. That "please" testified once
more to the Southern manner of Colonel House, vanquishing
even cablese. Clearly the word "recommend" had been used for
the sake of kindliness, to make it seem that a choice was being
given him, not an order.

But beneath the honeysuckle, a crusher. His unit was civilian. It had been organized to research economic data about
the French at war. Colonel House, despite his title, was no military man but the President's political helpmate and international adviser. Yet, if Max obeyed that cable, he would be
sworn into the army, and he could kiss good-bye the last chance
of any independent effort to help Tha save her life. Once they

got him into uniform, they could easily transfer him out of Paris, or, if he proved intractable, throw him into a guardhouse somewhere. One did not have to be a professor of history to know how often that had happened in the past.

He shoved the paper into his pocket, conscious of the revolver, more a talisman than a weapon. "Seem to have taken the words right out of your mouth, Major."

"As I told you yesterday, it's either that or home, Prof."

"Little as you can say for Princeton," he said, the base of his brain throbbing, "it does teach you to retain simple thoughts for all of twenty-four hours."

"Yeah. They want me to take back your answer."

"I'll need time to consider."

"Can we cut the shit, Max?" Beck demanded. "I'm only a flunky, but what you got there is an order from the top assistant to the President of the U.S. of A."

"The question is—am I the military type?"

"You may be the highbrow—a friend of President Wilson himself—but I've got to tell you they got it greased to ship you out at seventeen hundred today."

"Quitting time—does that translate for us civilians?"

Beck took one step toward Max, then, with effort, swung away to peer into the opulent room. He was obviously under orders by Intelligence to be buddy-buddy. "Okay, Max," he said, "ride me all you want, but they sent me to get your answer. What do you say we have some breakfast?"

"To tell you the truth, Major, I'm nursing an after-armagnac."

"Know just the place," Beck said. "One jolt sets you up. They call it coffee."

"Another time."

Beck shifted his body, while his eyes searched Max's face. "I don't get it. You're supposed to be a brain. How can a guy like you go overboard for a damn demirep?"

That would be the essential question for U.S. Intelligence. They had fixed categories: males, and academics who wore trousers. And nice women, and Mata Hari. He had confounded them, even gained status. As a dupe of Mata Hari, he had at least acquired testes. He could even detect envy in Beck's tone.

Max decided to live up to the official analysis. "From what I've been reading in the papers, nobody is immune."

"But hell, man, a cunt for the Boche!"

"I read that in the papers, too."

Beck regarded him with pity. "Still gone with gonads, eh, Prof?"

Max shrugged.

"She must be something," Beck said, watching him.

Max was on the verge of telling him that he had never even exchanged a caress with Tha. But that would only cause them to reclassify him; they might even use the tag from the Princeton yearbook, " '03, Robert Maxwell, genus epiphyte, draws sustenance from the air."

"I just want to consider it, if you don't mind, Major."

Beck shook his head, almost sadly. "I guess you know they're going to step on you like a bug, you go on like this, Prof."

"Nice of you to warn me."

The major blinked and gave up. Max followed him through the remnants of empire to the door. Useless to work himself up over U.S. Army Intelligence. His real adversary was Colonel Edward Mandell House, and beyond, his old Princeton mentor and leader and now the commander-in-chief, Thomas Woodrow Wilson. But with that pair, something more incisive, evidentiary, and politically persuasive than intuition would be required; and in that arena, for the moment, he was disarmed.

At the door, Beck could not desist from browbeating, all in the name of patriotism. "Let's say the dame got you on the hook, but there's a war on, and you'd figure a man with all your knowledge would want to put that first . . ."

Max thrust his hands into the pockets of his robe. His right hand gripped the handle of the tiny revolver, but he rejected the urge it sent along his nervous system. Instead, almost automatically, he resorted to the dry parody he used to silence students who became too crassly stupid to be endured.

"Why, Beck," he said, "that's perceptive indeed, indeed! Reorder my priorities! That's it precisely. I owe you for putting it so plainly."

Beck heard only a compliment. "You know the number, Prof!"

"Thank you for coming, Major."

The kitchen cupboard held an unopened bottle. Max, pouring, saw that his hand shook. The liquid slid easily. Lacing, clarifying.

Face it, he commanded himself, you have no chance against all that weight. Probably House had mentioned the matter to Wilson. The cable suggested that. And Wilson, who had always been apart by reason of status and age, was now infinitely beyond reach. No help there.

From the window, he caught sight of Beck climbing into a command car and being driven away. Which didn't mean that the Deuxième Bureau had relaxed. They had kept tabs on each and every attempt Maxwell had made to visit Tha in prison; of the representations he had made to the French Ministry of Justice, demanding to see her; of his phone calls, all refused, to Chardon.

He felt like opening the window and shouting madly after Beck. "Listen, sowbelly, I'm an expert in recent French history. I was chosen to help Colonel House put across the President's goal of 'peace without victory.' I believed in it. I still do. Not only for the belligerents, but for humanity, including the portion called Yank. We failed. But she and I tried. Now there's her life. You do your country no favor by sandbagging me to silence her."

The unspoken outburst brought him back to the kitchen table. He poured again, the glass oveflowing, his body shaking, anger unappeased.

The problem was their damned secrecy laws. He was forbidden to speak, even to seek witnesses. They had easily blocked his accusations of collaboration with the enemy by pasting a top-secret label to their fabrications. Even Colonel House had advised him to cease spreading Tha's story, for reasons of state security. It was time for serious men to get on with the serious business of war.

He might have gone along. Except for Tha. In the last analysis, his silence would permit them to take her life. They had to do that to support their version of that night in the blacked-out rail yard, expunging it from the record and from history. Their remedy for his protests: Let him be a voice crying in the wilderness, trees supplied by courtesy of Beck and the U.S. Army. For Tha, they had in mind a more permanent gag.

He set down his glass, sobered by his perceptions of his own impotence.

Lovelorn dupe, they'd said of him. And he'd stoutly denied it. Yet, during the time of her imprisonment, he'd been seized by spells of causeless melancholy, endlessly reviewing the brief hours he'd been with her. Sometimes her face disappeared, then came back in radiant light, allowing him to observe every detail, as if she were a model waiting for the stroke of his defining brush.

At first he'd thought her beautiful, struck by the vivid dark eyes, the wide full mouth, her stature. But then he had decided that she was really only a tall, though lissome, woman, with an easy gait and a pleasant face. Later, both impressions had seemed wrong. He recalled her habit of leaning her head to one side, accentuating the long neck and its graceful curve, giving her a quality of animal awareness, absorbed in what he said, what he failed to say, helping him over and under silences. She listens beautifully, he had thought; and then, still trying to define her, came to realize that she seemed to be listening with the same tenderness with which one listens to one's own promptings, fears, hurts, fantasies, hostilities. She had invaded him, she was within. The preserve, as Puritans knew, of Eros.

And it was that state of possession he had tried to blot out with alcohol; all these insinuations were grounded in truth. He had fallen in love. Behind all his bluster about the war and history and the good of humanity, he had reacted like a schoolboy and fallen desperately for a woman who was herself deeply in love with another man; though circumstances had thrown them together and bonded them emotionally, she had never gone beyond the limits of a comrade-in-arms, tied together by common aims and common dangers.

He was sick of his evasions. He wanted to go down to

that courtroom and catch a glimpse of her again, even at the expense of inviting condign reprisal by the authorities. It was too much to hope that she would be able to spot him in the crowded courtroom; and, if she did, that the sight would give her any comfort.

It wasn't much of an action. He would never be taken for a hero; as Colonel House had told him, it wasn't within him to be Dink Stover, the legendary Yale man. Yet, for the trapped, even a squirm was freedom.

Why this persistent malaise, this hounding unease?

It had made him bolt out of his sleep long before dawn. He had told himself, Clunet, it's the heat, it's your old age, it's the worries that always crop up on the opening day of a trial.

Now as the limousine sped him to an emergency conference in the tribunal's chambers, the questions surfaced again. Why had he come to the woman's defense: vanity? boredom? senile sex?

The streets outside seemed inhabited only by mutilated soldiers and sailors and nerve-torn civilians, adrift in the sickly light. Inside, the stink of petrol. The revival of the fiacre was, he decided testily, the only benefit so far conferred by this grisly, endless, deadlocked war.

His reason for getting into the case, he had to admit, could only be characterized as colossally petty. Somebody had told him that two lawyers had refused to accept the court's appointment to defend the dancer, fearing it would damage their careers. He detested both individuals. One man had offended him by asserting in a scholarly article that he had made a procedural blunder in the Dreyfus case; the other man had described his textbook, *Privacy and Public Power*, as vastly overrated.

In spleen he began to scour the sensational articles in the press about the notorious nude dancer. He had made it a rule to avoid reading the papers, infuriated by their mixture of patriotic gore and sleazy homiletics. He must have been the last person in Paris to discover that the woman who had made her fame in the dance of the Seven Veils had been arrested for selling military secrets to the Boche, and that the present doleful position at the front—the English lay stymied at the Hindenburg line, the French exhausted at Aisne—could be traced to the lady's ineluctable vulva.

Rubbish, of course.

Yet, juicy journalism to one side, the case reminded him forcefully of one aspect of the Dreyfus affair. The charge he saw repeated in the press, obviously leaked by the Deuxième Bureau, was that the woman had elicited these military secrets from susceptible captains and majors and the like, when they came to Paris on leave from the front.

But, as the Dreyfus affair had taught, combat officers of that rank were not in possession of military secrets, large or small.

Furthermore, the woman was described as moving about at the highest levels of French and European society. Among her conquests, according to the same journals, were such as the German Crown Prince, the Dutch Prime Minister, the former French War Minister, De Massimy, the recently resigned German Foreign Minister, Von Jagow. Why, one asked, would a woman with access to such gentlemen go looking for secrets among infantry captains?

The way things operated in this field had once been defined by Lord Kitchener, the English hero, recently a casualty of sea war. Kitchener had called the Cabinet the infirmary of war secrets. "If you want to find out anything, just gossip with the wives of Cabinet members. Exceptions? Oh, yes. In the case of certain Ministers, you must gossip with other men's wives."

No less disturbing than that contradiction were the wholesale executions taking place at Vincennes and elsewhere, many resulting from hasty trials, and some without adequate review.

Though his mail had brought letters circulated by members of the legal profession, critical of this or that phase of such spy trials, Clunet had reassured himself that the Government after all was in the hands of many of the men who had participated in the defense of Dreyfus, and would not, therefore, allow the rights they had fought for then to be trampled, even now. Not only did radical socialists like Caillaux head majorities in the Chamber, but there were watchdogs like Cle-

menceau, with his independent newspaper, who were far closer
to the situation and would not permit drumhead trials to vio-
late hard-won rights that—

Query: May I interrupt, dear Maître? Splendid! To cut it
short, Clunet, you decided you must act for the higher truth. Is
that your excuse?

Answer: I was working on a revision of my textbook, and
I began to see some validity in my critic's position. And naturally I was vexed. So I called Colonel Villiers, presiding judge
of the military tribunal, to ask if I would be acceptable as defense counsel.

Query: In common language, you are in this case to prove
you are superior to your critics?

Answer: In part . . .

Query: Quite. The other part being you could not resist
Villier's pap that your presence alone would guarantee the
woman a fair trial, and silence all those who carp at security in
time of war . . .

Answer: To a degree . . .

Query: The nude photos, the lubricious drawings, the sa-
lacious hints of her nymphomania, they had nothing to do with
your getting into the case? Speak up, old widower, we are all
friends here . . .

Of course there had been conjured up in his mind the
image of a siren, full of deep and secret lusts, holding out a dark
invitation, dark as the kohl that shadowed her black eyes.

But the woman who came down the bleak corridor,
wearing a faded prison smock, was tall and athletic, only the
slight sway of her hips reminding him of certain Andalusian
dancers he had known in his youth. Her smile, her manner,
were direct and candid.

"Maître, I'm honored—ready to cry—but you must understand, I have deeply compromised myself. I have acted as a
double agent, at the request of the Deuxième Bureau. They
have their reasons for wanting me out of the way. I am afraid
to confide in anybody, even in you, Maître, whose name I have

often heard. If you take my case you will run a risk of becoming the Bureau's enemy—"

That afternoon, he had phoned Villiers to accept being named as her defense counsel, remembering the warm press of her hands, the appeal of her strong face, admitting to her fears and her vulnerability.

Later, everything confirmed his belief she was speaking the truth. She related how she had been recruited by the Deuxième Bureau shortly after a Zeppelin attack had caused a fire in an orphanage in whose work she had taken an active part, both in person and as a financial supporter.

"We were all in a terrible state, not knowing what to do first. This man, Depardieu, turned up, organized everything. He was superb! I had no idea of his official function. I was very grateful to him. Then he said that if I was really a friend of those war orphans, I would agree to work for his Bureau. It only meant going to The Hague and Berlin, simply collecting gossip. He warned me that Berlin would notice my activity and approach me to do the same for them in Paris. I must accommodate them. I would be paid, of course. But I would be serving France, the homeland I had adopted and that had adopted me . . ."

The dates had verified her story. Ten days after that fire, she had left for The Hague, traveling via Spain and England, thence into Holland. Later on, just as she said, from Holland to Germany. On other occasions, the route had been through Switzerland. The very freedom with which she had moved through the countries locked in war could only be explained, as she averred, by the fact that both belligerents considered her their employee.

Of course, the French had been careful to disguise their payments to her. "They would have me appear in public with this or that famous or wealthy person, and the papers would immediately suggest I had taken a new lover. Then a check would come from this man, allegedly for my favors. I can give you a list, but I doubt any will tell you the truth."

But, in counterbalance, no payments could be directly traced to Abteilung Three; monies made into her Swiss account by the Germans had always had some sort of cover, the sale of assets in Holland, or the effects of furniture and clothing in Berlin, or for some piece of jewelry, previously the gift of a paramour. Clunet was confident he could use the prosecutor's own evidence to show that the Deuxième Bureau was her employer—even if not her sole employer—the heart of the case.

And his confidence had been bolstered by the reluctance of the prosecution to come forth with an indictment. The excuse, of course, was that the Government did not wish to expose other agents to danger. But Clunet sensed, behind this, that the woman had information that embarrassed the Bureau and people above the Bureau, and that had been the reason for her arrest, as well as for the plethora of accusations leaked to the press, but which the prosecutor, in private conversation, dismissed as fabrications.

He directly posed the question to Tha: "Do you have knowledge that threatens the Government?"

"Yes."

"Have you been questioned about it?"

"About everything else," she had told him, "but not that."

"Then I don't want to know about it either," he had said. "Unless it appears on their indictment, we will demonstrate your reliability as a depository of their confidence. Agreed?"

"Very much."

Finally, they'd produced their indictment. There were eight counts. The first seven dealt with charges that referred to 1915 and 1916. Even their phrasing indicated those alleged events had been known to the Bureau for a year or two years. They could be shown to lack urgency—certainly not sufficient cause for taking a life.

Only the eighth count referred to this year:

"Having, in Paris, in 1917, had intelligence with the enemy power of Germany, with the aim of furthering the enterprises of the enemy."

How conveniently vague.

It buoyed up his original analysis. If the interrogators were steering clear of that eighth count, they would not want to press it in court. If he could box them into the first seven, he would give assurances to the tribunal that the accused, by her discretion, respected her duties to France. The other counts could be minimized. He must be guided by the fact that this was a capital case; his objective was not to prove her innocence or even convict the Government of dirty hands, but only to prevent, by casting doubt into the minds of the jury, the spattering of her blood on the old stained grounds at Vincennes. . . .

"Sir, can I help you, Maître?"

Amiel, his young clerk, grinned through the opened door of the limousine and held out an arm to assist him. Clunet shoved his briefcase at him and laboriously extracted his aged, slight frame from the deep cushions. He stood for a moment, getting his bearings. Once the rear of the Palais had been a garden. Now it was a moonscape of cobbles strewn with oil, pressed flowers of evil.

"Have they brought Madame from prison?"

"Before I arrived, sir."

"This conference, what's it about?"

"I don't know, Maître. I've been busy with the Head Matron trying to track down Madame's dress."

"Dress? What dress?"

"The one she's to appear in, sir. The Matrons claim they can't find it."

"These Matrons, I know them. They don't feel alive unless they're cruel."

Avoiding the stairway, they entered the building at the ground level and Clunet took back his briefcase, struggling for breath in the sluggish air. "Have you read the newspapers this morning?"

"No, sir."

"They have an amazing new story. They say the Boche themselves betrayed Madame to the Deuxième Bureau, because they found her a financial liability. Hence they sent a cable to her in a code they already knew to be broken, in order to force the Bureau to arrest her and relieve them of her expense. Any part of that make sense?"

"No, sir."

"Have you had a chance to read my opening statement?"

"Yes, Maître."

"Anything disturb you?"

"Nothing, sir."

"For once be insolent."

"It puts them on the defensive. They will have to show why, if they knew of her alleged activities, they took no action against her for so long. I am certain it will tell with the jury. It tears the whole fabric of their case that she was never their agent."

"That's not to puff an old man?"

"It is true I am afraid of you, Maître. But not that afraid, sir."

"Good. Now go to the prosecutor. Tell him unless a dress is immediately forthcoming, they will have to drag Madame up to the courtroom."

"Drag her? Surely they won't be that stupid."

"Only if we coax them."

He was rewarded by the boy's laughter and urged him to go ahead. Alone, standing at the foot of the marble stairway, he gathered strength for the climb. The boy had been assigned to him by the court—straight out of the Sorbonne, and so deferential. Clunet had first suspected him of being a plant by the prosecutor. He must teach the boy to assert himself more.

Emerging from the stairwell to the rotunda was like coming from a monastic cell into the eye of a hurricane.

Bodies swirled around him, hot with anger, crying out curses at the gendarmes and court attendants who were seeking to keep them from entering the main chamber.

Batons were being used by the gendarmes, and people began to scream in pain at the clubbing; others raged to revenge themselves against these guardians of the law.

Two stout women, shouting imprecations, came charging by, shoving him against one of the pillars, sending his briefcase along the floor, only to continue belligerently toward the courtroom, oblivious to his distress.

Wincing, he hung there, feeling the column's heat. It seemed to come, not from the sirocco, nor even from these goaded people, but from distant battlefields, shoveling their millions to feed the fire storm of war, threatening to waste the world from end to end.

This is what I did not want to see, this is my unease, the source of my malaise.

Long before his involvement in this case, he had blocked the savageries of this war from his view. He had told himself that the hallowed devices of French justice, the respect for persons and law, would be preserved above the conflict, that men of reason would never be unhinged even by their country's sufferings.

In his heart of hearts, he had known the truth. The men who once fought alongside him to save Captain Dreyfus from the vengeance of the superpatriots had turned superpatriots themselves, fomenting hatred, flaunting their bloodlust as French character, this indistinguishable from their portrait of the menacing Huns, instigators of this murderous pack let loose in the great courthouse. They had stormed in here not for a trial, but for the preliminaries to a sacrificial slaying, ancient and ferine, and it was their howls, not laws, that would prevail.

The France he loved had vanished. All his assumptions had been invalidated by mass murder beyond his comprehension. His confidence in his case was only another example of his defection from reality, of his refusal to see that men had been stripped to brutes, prided themselves on it, were prized for it.

In his cowardice, he had let himself be sucked into a process that could only serve the war machine. Out of pique and flattery and a twinge of eroticism, he had let himself believe nothing had changed, and so exposed the woman to extinction. This case could never be like the Dreyfus affair. In those days, the people, though conflicted, saw the social compact as respect for life. Now that same compact made the anointment of murder its most sacred rite.

In the distance he saw a friendly guard, slicing through the riot to rescue him.

He tried to straighten up. He must find strength to confront the realities, to confess to Tha that his strategy had been based on reaching a reasonable compromise, when in this maelstrom reason and compromise were seen as enemies. He would give her a chance to change their defense, or to dismiss him altogether.

The guard had retrieved his briefcase.

"Thank you, thank you."

"Come with me, Maître."

He leaned on the man's arm, conscious of how old and feeble he really was.

Despite some nervy driving, it took Max almost an hour to reach the courthouse. At various jammed intersections he had swerved into the oncoming lane, and then, to the enraged and whistling gendarmes, pointed to the letters painted on his door: *Economic Research Group, U.S. Government.* Somehow, they let the madman get by.

But of course there had been stretches where no insanity would help; because of war shortages, old nags and battered wagons had been rescued from the scrap heap and pressed into service, throttling traffic by day, and, at night, with their ceaseless thunking, echoing the not-too-distant clash of arms, invading dreams with the sounds of battle.

On the run from his parked car, he rounded the corner before he encountered the barrier of the crowd. Heaving, squirming, they were being forced back from the Palais by gendarmes using their batons. Though some elements of the mob were engaged in a running fight with the flics, others seemed to have made a holiday of the clash. Somebody had a long pole from which hung a nude mannequin, one-armed, pubic hair painted on, a Venus that jiggled a lewd step above their heads. Some vendors hawked packages of the cigarettes, named Mata Hari, featuring a drawing of her as a stock houri. Though these cigarettes were a staple in Europe, they were unloading them before hate made them unsaleable.

Struggling to get through, encouraged by the rumor that there were still seats available in the courtroom, something tugged at the edge of Max's vision. Across the street. A knot of gray men, grayly watching. The Deuxième Bureau. True managers of this blood sacrifice to Mars. On hand to see the rituals enacted.

From the group a figure emerged. A man of average

height, wearing the average gray suit and unremarkable hat. Depardieu. Unmistakably, even through Max's unreliable vision. Frequently, Max had tried to imagine the man with mother, father, sister, wife, child—only to come up blank. Though no man could be one-dimensional, Depardieu appeared to have squeezed out all ambivalences until he was one invisible essence in service of a soulless state, an allegorical person.

Depardieu raised a hand to the brim of the felt and put two fingers to it in salute. The act held no warmth, no personal recognition of Max, no animosity. It was a notation for a dossier. It recorded the fact that, in spite of all warnings to stay away, Max was still acting in defiance and interesting himself in the woman's cause. At the same time, it dismissed his tiny spurt of daring, since it confirmed their estimate of him, no longer an opponent, but a weakling, acting out of emotion, to be dispatched at their convenience.

Enraged, Max watched Depardieu turn on his heel and merge with the gray group in the doorway's shadow. Ironically noted, and pitilessly dismissed.

Grabbing at the wooden barrier, Max struggled to disengage himself from the crowd's surgings, his sense of humiliation. He had to recover. More paralyzing than the contempt of a Depardieu was his self-contempt. It had been easy enough to be contrite this morning, to confess how deeply he felt about Tha. But on what airy tablet would that ever be inscribed? How could his action in coming here do anything but make him an object of ridicule, even in his own eyes? It was a deeper weakness he had to deal with. He had always stood aside from the direct thrust of life. As the only and sheltered child of aged parents, as the honor student concealing his loneliness in abstractions, never permitting his scattered affairs, after some early jiltings, to occupy the center of his attention, let alone the nucleus of his emotion; and then, choosing history as his subject, to become a professional second-guesser, god of his own puddle, awash with artifacts, documents, funeraries.

Now he was in history to his eyebrows. Tha had dislodged him from his cloud and dumped him into the actual—which turned out to be as blurry as small print without his glasses.

In that murk, he had to depend on passion to select the issue and light a pristine goal. That would be like a man proclaiming he was certain of the single raindrop that had caused the flood. He was asking himself, like all other hapless strivers, to leap from detachment to illusion and call it freedom. And he had to do it now, as the sage of Eli advised, or never.

At a public telephone he called Beck, rehearsing his deception as each clerk answered, until finally the major himself came on.

"What gives, Max?"

"About that coffee. Still on?"

"Bet your ass."

"I mean, I thought over your question, and I believe I've come up with an answer you'll like at least well enough to discuss it."

"Know the Rue Du Bac? Number 25."

"Half hour?"

"Cinch."

"Major, if I was choppy . . ."

"Hell, when it comes to cognac heads, you're talking to a Zeppelin."

"Much mercis."

With tassels for the cornhusker. From now on, he'd stall. First, he'd insist on finding the right slot in the army for each of his subordinates. Then he'd shuffle papers, lose files, drag a bureaucratic club foot. Meanwhile, he'd begin a surreptitious but systematic hunt for witnesses to corroborate his and Tha's version of what had happened.

On his way back to his car, he saw the gray squad still huddled in the doorway. Max lifted his hand in salute. Probably Depardieu would not be there to see. Just as well. The kind of battle he had in his mind was best joined in mutual disavowal.

Colonel Villiers, the presiding judge of the three-man military tribunal, had the annoying habit of moving from desk to window and back again, as he read from his paper, so that

Clunet had to strain to hear him each time his back was turned.

"I have prepared a release to the press. Please feel free to interrupt me as I go along."

Clunet cupped an ear. The other two officers sat immobile on a leather couch. The prosecutor overflowed a nearby chair. Slightly to the rear sat a portly attorney representing the press council, the combined organization of the French newspapers and journals.

"In the case of the Republic of France against the woman, one Margaretha Geertruida Zelle, native of Holland, divorced from a certain Colonel Campbell McLeod—"

Clunet tapped the wooden arm of his chair. "Shouldn't that be rephrased? Wouldn't it be more neutral to say 'former spouse of . . .' and so on?"

"Delete divorcée, that what you're after?"

"Yes."

Villiers went to the desk and scratched with a pen. ". . . hence sometimes also known by the spurious title of 'Lady' McLeod . . . yes, Clunet?"

"Can I suggest, 'sometimes known under the professional cognomen, Lady McLeod . . .' "

"Very well," Villiers said it through his teeth, "but more generally known to the public as the performer and nude dancer, Mata Hari . . ."

Villiers seethed up at Clunet challenging another intrusion. This time, however, Clunet decided to let the words pass, though Villiers still obviously intended to indict by identification.

". . . charged with espionage on behalf of the Imperial German Reich directed against the French Republic in time of war, constituting high crimes, jointly or severally punishable by death . . ."

Let us have a splash of blood, Clunet thought acidly. Let us keep faith with our sons.

". . . This tribunal, having decided by unanimous vote to invoke the Official Secrets Act, press and public will henceforth be barred from these proceedings."

The press councilman jumped first. "I must make an observation!"

Villiers thrust the corrected copy at a clerk. "Have that retyped," he said. "That is why you are here, Bovard."

"A mistake, Colonel!" The attorney waved his hands in the air. "A mistake, I insist. I don't care what intelligence matters may be involved. In this case, we must have an open trial!"

"Can't be done," Villiers said shortly. "Too many people would have to be exposed. I assure you we debated long and hard."

Clunet held himself back. Not yet, not yet. Let Bovard carry the argument. Let him get Villiers into it, deeply.

"I am thinking," Bouvard said, "of the effect on world opinion. I am sure I don't have to remind the tribunal of the injury the Boche did their own cause when they executed the British Nurse Edith Cavell after secret hearings. Must we do the same to ourselves?"

Villiers hardly waited for him to finish. "Look closer to home, Bovard. Look at the scurrilities of the press," Villiers slashed. "They have made a public trial impossible. It is partly to shield the accused from that press, on whose behalf you are here, that we close the doors. Would you want us to include that in our statement, Bovard?"

"Colonel," Clunet said.

Villiers swiveled to him. "You don't agree, Maître?"

"Of course," Clunet said. "Indeed, I would follow your trenchant logic to its end."

"In what way?"

". . . If the premise is a poisoned atmosphere . . . we who are suffering from the sirocco today . . . how much more are our judgments enfevered by this war. Are we not obliged to wall this case from those flames, until the temperature goes down and we return once more to cold justice?"

"You are suggesting postponement?"

"For the duration."

"You are free to make that motion, Maître," Villiers said. "We are considering now only the language of our simple statement to the press."

"So am I," Clunet spoke quickly, "and of the reasoning behind it. Let those pleas be heard in open court by the jury, let my argument for postponement be heard by press and public, and, by our example of tranquility, spread it far and wide."

Villiers came around the desk, standing over him. "I speak for myself, and I hope for my colleagues. We seal off this case first for the sake of our sons at war—so that the enemy may not use our procedures to his advantage. And once that obligation is met, we are tranquil that we shall meet all others."

"In that case, will the tribunal grant me permission to make a statement to the press?"

"Maître"—Villiers permitted himself a personal tone— "the request amazes me. You and I went over the rules concerning your conduct, the obligations of secrecy and confidence. I had supposed I had your full concurrence . . ."

Clunet felt himself trembling. "Withdrawn."

Clunet saw him swing to the chief clerk. "Have our statement read to the press, and then have the bailiffs clear the court."

"There may be a riot," the clerk said.

"Quite likely," Villiers said. "We will have to meet that responsibility, too."

Clunet stood up. There was a pain across his back. He tried to catch Villiers's eye but the man avoided his gaze to turn and face a viewless window. It would be easy to say there were precedents for this action. But his foreboding in the rotunda made him read a new significance into it, a new danger. More urgent than ever for him to consult with Tha.

Impatiently, he signaled Amiel to come across and give him his arm.

Jules Chardon, Minister of Foreign Affairs in the Ribot Cabinet, continued to make out a bank draft to one of his wife's priests when the call came from the clerk at the court informing him of the decision to hold the trial in secret.

Jules replied in circumspect monosyllables that concealed his relief. Poor Tha. No doubt she still hoped the people who had once applauded her could be won over. But the press had done its job. Under the circumstances she'd be spared exposure to the crowd's venom. A point in his favor. He blotted the check and came around the desk to give it to the young cleric.

"Thank you, M'sieu."

"Thank you, Father."

He walked the handsome priest to the door. He was conscious of the young man's pale, almost pasty complexion. It made him feel defensive about his stubby frame and pock-marked, stubble-shadowed face, as though his vitality was the mark of Cain. Fortunately marriage had cured him of being a jealous husband, though unfortunately not of being a jealous man.

"It will go to the war orphans' fund," the priest said. "I will send a full accounting."

"Render it unto Madame," Chardon said. "I am only her cashier."

The young man's eyes slithered genteelly away. Elaine had never doubted that her chief attraction for him was her dowry. One did not have to be her confessor to hear that. Only within earshot.

"Madame looks radiant today," the priest said. "I am certain that the holiday in the country will complete her recovery."

"One hopes."

"God willing," the young man offered as an afterthought.

"God willing."

The maid, summoned by his bell, came to show the young man out. Chardon waited until he heard their footsteps on the stairs before starting for his wife's bedroom. He had to make sure there were no more excuses. Today, God willing or unwilling, she'd be on that train; the closed trial eliminated certain hazards—but not Elaine.

In the bedroom, two maids were busy packing. Clothes were heaped on bed and chairs. But he could not see that any particular progress had been made in the last hour. A mirror showed her dressing in the bathroom.

"What time is it, Jules?"

He waited for her to emerge. She wore a suit of purest white, setting off her brown hair and chiseled face. Dazzlingly beautiful and, to him, staggeringly dull. Doubtless the young men in black robes with whom she surrounded herself gave her a setting for her purity. Probably some fell in love with her. He could not blame them for a virtue he lacked.

"You have less than forty minutes."

"Did you give Father Étienne his check?"

Chardon nodded. Elaine sat on the edge of the bed and pulled her stocking tighter to the supporting elastic. He could see her pink thigh, the perfect slender calf. It would, in any other woman, have excited him. In her, it raked him raw.

"You'll be relieved to hear Tha's trial will be in secret. After a week, nobody will be mentioning it at all."

Her delicate blue eyes filled with unhappiness. "What are you saying, Jules? That after all my preparations, it's no longer necessary for me to go down to the country?"

"Of course you must go."

"Secret trial or not," Elaine said, "I will know what she is going through. My nerves will suffer, just as if the whole world were watching . . ."

"That is why you must go."

"I hate the country. I don't know why I'm doing this for you!"

Wearily, he turned to the window. Her phobias were legion. He could make a list: lust, sweat, dirt, dirty jokes, urine, excreta, odors of armpit and crotch, reck of rut, smegma, earwax, flaking of skin, all diseases mentioned in materia medica. It took all her priests to help her wage her battle against this despoiling array, though they could not prevent her periodic collapse into drugs and alcohol. Her sweet Savior had nothing in common with the Man he had embraced growing up in the foundry town on the border of Lorraine. That One was stocky and stained by toil like his father. But it had been one of the first lessons of Paris, each arrondissement had its own deity, sometimes hidden, along with the cashbox.

"If only you knew how my nerves ache, you would come with me . . ."

Irritated, he swung about. "You know I can't."

"But you just told me the trial's secret, there's no need to worry . . ."

"I have my duties here."

She ran her hands the length of her stocking, cherishing

her slender firmness. "But I'm afraid to be alone. Who knows what I'll blurt out?"

He bit back anger, sending a warning glance toward the two maids. "I have repeatedly told you, Elaine, there is nothing for you to blurt. It is all your sickness. As the doctor says, you must complete your recovery in the country air . . ."

"He knows nothing about me," she insisted. "I'm no better off than I was the first day of my breakdown. I feel her presence, demanding my testimony . . ."

"Has she asked for it?"

"They have her locked up."

"She has a famous lawyer. Has he come here to demand anything of you, for her?"

"He's an old dodderer."

"Well," Chardon snapped, "when he dodders in here, I am sure you can tell him everything you imagine you know."

Her aim, of course, was not to help Tha, but to force her way back to the center of Jules's life by keeping this threat over his head. That had accounted not only for her breakdown but for its prolongation. She had reacted in hysteria to Tha's arrest, and for weeks thereafter he had had to sedate her, keeping her away from doctors and priests alike, while she wildly accused him of being a traitor along with Tha. She would come out of her drugged lassitudes to scream that he was now using violence to keep her silent and become his accomplice.

In vain, he tried to explain the larger background, the complexities of policy for France in time of war. He was amazed to discover, after all the formal dinners she had had to attend, after the countless discussions that swirled through this house and almost all the houses they visited, that she could understand so little about him, or the war, or the world.

"But of course I have been in touch with the Germans," he had patiently elaborated. "Last year, they tried to negotiate a peace through the Austrians. Surely you must have gathered that. For a time, last winter, it seemed we would come to terms, but it was not to be. . . ."

"But you denied it! I saw it in the papers. You said it was all rumor, just as you say I am all imagination!"

"Of course I denied it," he tried to soothe her. "People

are dying. They don't want to give up their lives for anything less than a certainty. Nobody wants to go to his grave to achieve some makeshift compromise of a treaty clause. You have to be duplicitous. You enlist people for good against evil, as if they were opposites like life and death. In that way, you pay your respects to the dead, while you show respect for the living by seeking a mixture, the compromise as before . . ."

"Then why, Jules, are you afraid to have me testify?"

"Because the longer the war goes on, the greater the number of dead, the more bellicose the demand for absolute victory, total surrender . . ."

He took her clammy, flaccid hand and tried to rub some of his grittiness into it. "Those who were with me in my compromise efforts yesterday will gladly call me a traitor today. That is why I must be so very careful . . ."

Elaine closed her eyes, shutting out his appeal. "But she came here that night, looking for you. With that American. And that was just before she was arrested, wasn't it?"

"It was."

"Why was she looking for you, at that hour?"

"I've already told you . . ."

"I don't believe you."

"Why is it so hard to believe? The Deuxième Bureau was trying to arrest her. She came here seeking my protection."

"Why with the American?"

"They were together that night."

"But if that's all there was to it, why can't I testify?"

"Because it means bringing me into the case. And if I'm linked with Mata Hari, the public will assume I was her lover, another source of secrets that she traded to Berlin. I'll have to resign. I'll never recover politically."

"I don't believe you, Jules."

"You're sick," he would say, "you need to rest."

At first he had supposed her motivation was jealousy of Tha. He had tried to mollify her by satirically down-playing that relationship, describing his first meeting with Tha in terms of farce. He had encountered her while out riding in the Bois de Boulogne, that familiar erotic turf. After using a ruse to achieve an introduction, he had accompanied her to the stables only to find the famous dandy, Count Esterhazy, waiting for her, taking her off in nonchalant possession.

What he carefully avoided mentioning was the sense of camaraderie he and Tha had later developed. It seemed that each time they met, Tha was acquiring a new lover, or he some higher governmental responsibility. They had a laughing compact to consummate an affair at some "perfect moment." They had adopted as their model a certain premier who had summoned a famous courtesan to his deathbed to administer the ultimate kiss, whereby his soul was sucked straight to heaven. Jules had declared that the prospect of Tha's performing such last rites for him had reinforced, with iron rod, his determination to become premier one day.

But Elaine remained unmoved by his explanations. "I assure you, I am not jealous of her, in the least. How can one be of that sort? Still, she's going to die, and you're going to let her, even though I know you are in this with her . . ."

He began to understand that her neurasthenia sensitized her to the change in their situation. She immediately saw that Tha's case had made him vulnerable, even though she could not corner him in a lie. Instinctively, she had pushed aside his evasions, exulting in her new power to destroy his career, and, hence, him—an advantage she had no intention of giving up.

Fortunately, his instinct had held him from revealing the full truth to Elaine. He thanked his stars. For if he had, he knew she would exploit it, not just for this period, but for the rest of his life, making him dance around her, male nurse to her imaginary ailments.

He still needed this marriage. Her money had not only won him his first seat in the Chamber of Deputies, but had a great deal to do with his rapid rise at the Quai D'Orsay.

His career was in jeopardy. The strengths that had brought success now threatened to undo him. His principal political asset had always been that he came from a family of foundry workers who had moved to a town on the French side of the border, after the Germans, in 1871, took over the provinces of Alsace-Lorraine. That not only made him a hereditary patriot but also equipped him with easy bilinguality and gave him a sympathetic insight into the lives of many families di-

vided in their loyalties between the two countries—people who
saw the war as a great calamity for Europe.

And that background had made him the logical person
to conduct the secret negotiations last winter, when it had
seemed that Austria was ready to make a separate peace, deserting her German ally, only to broaden into general negotiations, with the Germans participating. And then it had all
come crashing down. The Germans, who would never have
gone to war for Belgium, were demanding to stay there; and
the French Cabinet, which would never have dreamed of making the recapture of Alsace-Lorraine the reason for going to
war, now refused to make peace unless those provinces were restored. His own position in the middle was being eaten away.

That involvement in clandestine efforts at peace, of
which the Mata Hari affair was the last offshoot, had exposed
him to greater and greater dangers. To bring his name into
that affair would give his enemies the opening they needed,
perhaps driving him from politics forever.

As he had tried to explain to Maxwell, what had happened was the kind of secret it was best not to disturb until the
war had ended. A historian could unearth it only after it no
longer had the power to alter the course of the war, testimony
that the forces that had succeeded in burying the secret had
been the stronger ones, leaving history to ride the smooth tracks
of inevitability, as always.

Maxwell, unfortunately, had rejected the irony, and
seemed to have chosen to be indignant. Very American, Jules
thought, but a continuing danger, another historian determined to celebrate the individual and his moral strivings as if
somehow these might yet invalidate the laws of history.

Which, of course, meant that he could not relax his
guard against Elaine. And he must not ride roughshod over
her, as he was often tempted to do. While Tha's trial was in
progress, Elaine would insist on being a threat. But time was on
his side. The trial would end. The affair would be succeeded by
other events, other scandals, and his matrimonial flank would
again be secure. In playing a game of power with Elaine, he
had no doubt about who would prove to be the abler
competitor.

"Jules!"

Chardon started up from his thoughts to find Elaine frowning at him.

"Well, Jules?"

"I'm sorry, I didn't hear you."

"I asked you, since the trial is now closed, doesn't that mean the press and public are kept away?"

"Obviously."

"Anything that's said in court is secret, then?"

"Of course."

"Then, if I testify, no one will know. And the same for you."

"Are we back on that again?"

"It takes away your last excuse."

He advanced to her and grabbed her wrist. The maids did not even glance at them. Elaine arched her body away from his, but there was fear in her face.

"Why must you be so stupid?"

"Let me go, Jules!"

"I know you're ill, I know illness affects your mind, makes you sound like a simpleton. Five minutes after you get to that court, the press will know about it, the premier will have a call, the knives will be out for my throat and every friendly throat at Quai D'Orsay. The censors might keep it out of print, but it would be in every café, which is infinitely worse. And because the case is secret, I would never have the chance to explain my reasonable side in public."

He released her wrist and pushed her toward the bed, shouting now. "I want you to get ready, get these things together, so you can go down to the country and regain your health and your intelligence!"

She fell back on the bed, whimpering, yet inwardly pleased to have aroused his fury and made herself the focus of his attention.

"I can't possibly make that train now."

"There'll be another. I'll phone up."

"How long will it be?"

"I'll look into it, I said."

"I mean, her trial."

"Weeks, months. You'll have a good rest."

She found a piece of clothing and carried it to one of the maids. "It will be dark when I arrive. The house is always so clammy there at night. I wanted to air it out. Perhaps I should delay until tomorrow."

"Absolutely not!"

"Please. Don't shout."

"Father Étienne insisted you must go to the country," he lied. "They all agree it's absolutely essential. I'll call the depot."

He strode past the lowered heads of the maids and did not look back at his wife. Even in the country she would continue to be a menace. He would have to go down there from time to time and appease her with a display of fright, and of her power.

At his desk, reaching for the phone, he glanced down at the batch of pink dispatches from the Foreign Ministry. They held a prospect of hope. The Americans were here now. Soon they'd be launching an offensive in the Argonne. There might be a quick victory. It could even happen before Tha's trial came to an end. And in the atmosphere of victory, Elaine's power would evaporate and he would have room to maneuver. Men now afraid to show their sympathies for Tha would come out of hiding. And he with them. At the moment, there was too much at stake. For his career. For his country. He couldn't collapse into bad conscience and whine like Elaine because life unfolded itself by an excremental process.

Closing the checkbook, he saw the name of the church. He must go, he thought, and light a candle for Tha. As soon as he clapped Elaine into her compartment, he would seek a taper and renew his own purposes. He could count on Tha to be realistic. Like him, she would celebrate not only the flame but the wick's destruction.

He gave the operator the number of the depot.

"The dress," Clunet said. "The one you wanted. It was here all along, of course."

He held out the small package. She was a long time taking it from him. Her eyes were lustrous, but focused on some image far beyond him. He had a sense of having intruded on some private domain which it was indelicate for him to see.

"The dress. Yes. Thank you."

Reluctantly, he decided to bring her out of her chimera with harsh facts. "Not that it matters now, Madame," he said, "for the problem is no longer spectators, but their absence. The tribunal has decided to hear the case in camera . . ."

She came out of it, black eyes focusing on his face. "A secret trial?"

"Yes, Madame."

"But you said the press and public were making a huge outcry, that they could not close the doors!"

"I was mistaken."

"But then . . . who will see what is happening . . . who will know I'm telling the truth?"

He waited for the words to die away in her throat. Clearly she did not understand the present temper of the crowds; she was still relating to them in the old way, the adopted daughter of the city, her extravagances and Parisian optimism an eternal pair, like river and bridges.

"None but the jury," he said, sighing. "And with them, we'll have to combat the sanctity of the army, of the men at war . . ."

She tossed back the long black hair. "And that will be hopeless, Maître?"

He hesitated to bear down on her with the full and crushing consequences of the tribunal's action; permitting the press to continue their campaign of unsupported calumny, while keeping her locked in with jury who would be subject to a fusillade of government witnesses and documents, which they would never have adequate means to investigate and contradict, until even his challenges became testimony of her guilt.

"I believe we will have to change our tactics . . ."

"Of course, as you wish."

He spoke down to the floor. "As your counsel, I have no right to press you to reveal things that you consider to be to your disadvantage . . ."

"But I—"

"I mean," he overrode her protest, "we have both agreed not to probe the events immediately preceding your arrest . . ."

She came up to her feet, a head taller than he. "But you agreed, it was not to my interest. Even they have avoided it."

He nodded slowly. "I did. Another mistake. I think it is our only hope now . . ."

"To embarrass the government? To bring them all down on me as enemies?"

He faced away from her, picking up the tambour the Matron had left behind, plucking at the stitches. "But think of the alternative. We assert you are an employee of the Deuxième Bureau. They say you acted for Abteilung Three. If you are telling the truth, why did your employer suddenly turn on you?"

"Nevertheless—"

"Please, Madame, consider the jury in its current mood. We are asking them to believe that a vital agency like the Bureau doesn't know how to protect the interests of France."

"I realize all that, Maître."

"As an attorney, perhaps I realize something you do not. I mean, Madame, that it leaves us without a point of attack, it puts us in a defensive posture, and the consequences are graver than I care to contemplate."

She held his eyes and then turned away to busy herself with the cords around the package he had brought with him. He saw her long neck curving, the movements of her shapely arms that had performed in the dance of Shiva, so supple, even the elbow rounded in a shining sheath of flesh.

He sighed into the silence. "But you see, don't you?"

"Yes."

"Then how shall I defend you?"

Her voice was low. "You will prove I am not a threat to them."

"How?"

"By letting me be silent."

"What if they come forth with their version of these events you won't speak about?"

"Even so."

"What if they say your recent trip to Berlin was for Abteilung Three, not for them?"

"We'll let it go."

"And that your return here from Geneva was at the direction of German Intelligence?"

She lifted her shoulders. "All that."

He took a step closer, yearning to stroke the hair of her bent head. "But you still say you were acting for France?"

"Yes."

He turned away and went back to the seat, short of breath, dismissing legalistic arguments as soon as they came into his mind, knowing they could not prevail with her.

"And this silence—how can it protect you?"

"They consider me a threat. You must help me reassure them that I am not, that by my acquiescence to their charges they have nothing further to fear from me, that if I was once a threat, I am no longer . . ."

"But how will the jury hear that?"

"I am thinking beyond them," she said, "to the Minister of Justice, and the Premier and the others in the Cabinet, and not only here, but elsewhere . . ."

"And they will save you?"

"Only they."

He could not bring himself to look at her. "Madame. The charge is treason. The penalty, execution by firing squad."

"We will cheat them, Maître. You and I together will show them they don't have to destroy me—because I have voluntarily erased their secrets; that I am no threat to them, now or in the future. . . . I can't wear this." She had uncovered the pale blue frock and was studying it with regret for its symbolic innocence. "I'll seem a fraud to the jury."

"Madame . . ."

"Tha," she interjected.

"About this threat . . . can't you confide in me?"

"I do more. I trust you to take me as I am."

A smile played about her lips, not denying the gravity of her situation, but lifting the responsibility from his shoulders to her own.

"But don't you see how you open the way for them to find you guilty?"

"But don't I see," she said, mockery directed at herself. "I know how much I am asking you to do for me. *'Hagende Hun-*

ger, Fragende Frau, macht uns alle kaput.' "

She had come to his side and she took his nervous hands in her two warm ones. "Yes, Maître, I am a beseeching woman. Please don't desert me, even though I know it goes against your grain . . ."

In that old German proverb about the destabilizing power of a woman in need, she was asking him to shake free from the shackles of logic and throw himself into the sea of feeling and intuition, of reliance upon individuals, in which she had cast her life and made her being.

"They will say I am senile," he groaned, unable to surrender openly. "They will say I have let infatuation carry me to the point of infantilism . . ."

"If they say that"—she laughed, lightly touching his hair— "then they insult both of us!"

He looked up into her warm face, lit by humor, realizing that she had known all along of his buried response to her, that she welcomed it, not only because it flattered her, but because it opened the way for a deeper attachment to him.

"One more thing . . ."

"Yes?"

"I think you ought to dismiss me."

She paled. "Maître!"

"Yes," he said, "not only because I misjudged the temper of this court, but because your best strategy is to delay, to prolong, until the war ends, or at least there is a shift to our side . . ."

"Absolutely not!"

"You can tell them I'm incompetent, and I will very gladly support that."

Again she tossed her long black hair back over her shoulders, and it was a gesture of dismissal. "You are indispensable. You will shame all the men who knew me to come forward and be my character witnesses. Nobody will dare to turn you down. And that will count more for me than all their alleged documents . . ."

Quickly she moved away, going toward the pile of clothes on the floor. "They'll be waiting. I'll have to dress . . ."

He started for the door, but her voice intercepted him.

"Maître, why don't I go in this?"

She was lifting the wine-colored dress from the floor. She turned to him, holding it against herself. It had plackets of some silver material in which there were woven leaves. She smoothed it against her body, rich and Venusian, triumphing over the septic cube.

"I mean," she said, smiling, "if I start in with this, how can I help but look humbler each day in the eyes of the jury?"

Her lips invited his complicity—not only to share her jest, but to dare the gods of conformity, brushing aside the deadening strictures of society to reach the individual members of the jury, confident of the compassion of the single human being.

"Ah, Madame," he half lamented, and fled her radiance.

Yet he knew, even as he retreated, that he had cut his moorings. This would not be a legal case in the manner of the Dreyfus affair, but an appeal for humanity, aimed not only at the jury and the military tribunal, but at those above, the men in power, relying on them to rise above the brutalities of war. In that challenge, he would have to trust her judgment and respect her mystery, consoling himself that at least no other advocate would serve her with greater devotion.

GENEVA GENESIS
27 February 1917

"Kuprin? Café. Bottom of the street." None so pithy as a Genevese landlady about a tenant. "When he's not here, he's there."

The émigré world charted, Tha thought, as she returned to Sita in the fiacre. In the city that liked to call itself "the world in a nutshell." Poor Kuprin, prisoner of two husks.

This search for a translator had been going on for weeks. Almost from the day of their arrival in Geneva, they had been trying to locate somebody who would read aloud to Adam from various Polish and Russian periodicals. They had expected that the Geneva classified columns would be filled with offerings by refugees from those torn countries, but, of the few, none had the requirements Adam sought.

Though Adam considered himself wholly French, he

was in fact a native of Poland and never ceased to concern himself in the affairs of that country and the events of the eastern front. His family, the St. Reymonts, had emigrated to Poland as a result of the great French Revolution. His mother's family had an identical history, though the Baroness St. Reymont, who clung to her estates in occupied Poland and had differed from her late husband in things great and small, insisted she had no interest in anything Gallic, the name being yet one more misfortune of her marriage.

For a time Tha had been diverted from her hunt by the greater urgency of finding a house to live in. Weeks had evaporated before somebody told her about a small employment agency located on a lakeside street. After a prolonged interview she'd finally extracted a list of prospects and returned to Adam, whom she'd left at a bench to enjoy the sunshine.

"Kuprin," Adam announced when she had concluded reading out the biographies of the candidates. "Impoverished Russian student in exile! Sounds exactly like the man!"

"No phone."

"Farewell Kuprin."

"Never mind," she'd said. "Kuprin it will be. I'll personally hunt him down in his lair . . ."

Suddenly the lakeside around them rang with shouts.

She had to describe the scene to Adam. People were running along the strand as a bloated body twisted toward the shore, bleached and puffy and ghastly. The Swiss police blew whistles and tried to get through the crowd to take charge.

She shivered. The corpse was female.

"Let's go." Adam pulled at her arm.

But she had held fast.

Something about the distended face seemed familiar. She searched her memory, trying to shrink the woman's features back to normal size, and from some recess identified her as a masseuse she'd employed in Paris, about whom there'd been whispers that she was some sort of police spy, though what services she performed remained obscure, somehow vaguely obscene.

"What's wrong, Tha?"

"I know her."

"Come away. You're shaking."

Later, she had read to him the account in the newspaper. She had been right about the woman. The Swiss police were blaming unknown intelligence agents for the murder. They even speculated that the porcine masseuse had played fast with her paymasters, and had been made to pay the established price for such duplicities.

"Now," Adam had demanded, "aren't you grateful to me for forcing you to quit all that?"

"On my knees."

She leaned over and kissed him quickly, to blot out her lie.

"That is the posture"—he grinned—"that every Pole demands of his true love. Now, my own, rise on your elegant shafts and find Kuprin for me!"

But other things had intervened, and it had not been until today that she had been able to put all other things aside to pursue the elusive Russian.

The face of the fiacre driver appeared upside down in the window.

"Madame, there's four cafés. Look!"

Each dismal corner had its own hole, equally uninviting. For a moment she was tempted to give up her quest. But she had promised Adam.

Sita gathered her tiny delicate frame toward the edge of the seat. "I'll go."

"Wait." Tha began to gesture toward each of the four directions, chanting, "Star of East, Star of West, Star of the one you love the best . . ." She gave herself to the childish singsong, bringing back a memory of the tiny street in Leeuwarden, its white-crossed windows guarding their games. The triumph of interiors: a street in Holland. "If he's not here, don't take his part . . ." Sita's laugh tinkled, always eager to be chimed by playful wind. "But choose another with all your heart."

Her forefinger pointed to a café whose only distinction was that it was closest. "Kuprin"—she struck a pose—"be in there! The stars command it."

A wintry sun etched dignity into the threadbare street. In a shopwindow cobblers doubled over, tacking the light under quick hammers. The next place, a tinker's, showed a pile of metal junk. A rack offered dusty tools for sale. She slowed, connecting Adam's clever hands with those of the cobblers.

I should buy those carving tools for Adam, she thought. He senses form. He'll love them. But. But from me? No—he was still too full of pride to accept direction from her. Let it go, she admonished herself, be content with your errand.

In front of the café three boys were spinning small penny tops, chipped and dented, their colors grubbed. She started around when one boy looked up. In a silent instant, she saw his face turn cold and hostile. Suddenly she was aware of her arrogant Parisian toque, her sweeping furs, her butterfat Roman boots striding their bleak pavement. Useless to explain that this finery was meant for this afternoon's session at the horse auction, always a dress-up affair. The other pair retreated, abandoning their toys to her advance, letting them flop in agony to their small planetary end. I am, she thought, chaos come again, wrapped in sables. Oh, well! Oh, hell!

A short stairway went down to a semi-basement café. An awning hung from a bent frame above its steamed windows, a sardonic eyelid. The name of the place, once painted on the canvas, had faded to a serpentine trace that fed on its own tail.

But she ignored these warning signs and entered, only to be told, by a sharp visceral stab, that even if luck turned up Kuprin, it would also desert her in the same stroke.

For she knew at once this was not only a strange, but dangerous, roost. Around each table were gathered male birds with hot beady eyes. Whatever their plumage—whether the Melton double-breasteds in an advanced stage of molting, the vulturous Russian army greatcoats, the leather jackets feathered at wrist and elbow, or mere plucked sweaters; whether crested in shiny bowlers or peaked astrakhans or sparrow tops of gray workers' caps—they were all birds in passage, tensed on their expatriate perches, waiting for a distant peal to set them off, a storm wind to carry them home again.

And these beady-eyed creatures, Tha knew with dread certainty, were under the scrutiny of even more beady-eyed bird watchers. In London, in Paris, in Berlin and Moscow. Eyes ready to decode every flutter here to determine how the wind blew across Russia, how fires might be fanned in Poland.

And she had wafted in, bird of paradise, at the moment she most desperately needed protective cover, involved in deceiving not only Adam, but Depardieu in Paris and Abteilung Three in Geneva. Her stray flight would soon be transmitted to her masters, here in Geneva, in Paris, in Berlin. Yet to show the white feather now would only cause the net to be drawn.

She maintained her strut to the bar, where the proprietor arranged glasses around a huge samovar. On the counter there were sandwiches of thick brown bread, each on its own plate, but stacked in leaning towers, in a way she'd never seen before.

"I'm looking for a Monsieur Kuprin."

"Second table by the window. There, next to the bald man with the fur collar."

She threaded her way through, conscious of their quick glittering appraisals, though they did not abate their full-throated polemics. From the various German and French phrases, and from what Adam had told her, she could piece together what they were thundering about. Only recently, the Germans had installed a Polish king in the portion of that country they had conquered; meanwhile, each day brought new rumors of an overthrow of the Czar's government in Russia, with the battered army refusing to obey orders of a princely premier. One did not have to understand more than one word in a hundred to feel the beat of all their rhetoric: would they be gathered home again, or another wind sweep them to even more distant exile?

She hovered unnoticed. "Monsieur Kuprin?"

They had the Duma pinned to the small table, prodding it to pieces with merciless beaks. Some shouted that the members of the Duma, no matter what their politics, would have to be puppets of the Allies, financed by Paris and London, to arouse new war fervor on the frozen fronts. Others, as sharp, read the latest votes in the weak chamber as an augur of peace and homecoming.

She stood before a bearded young man in a soiled jacket, who only half rose to greet her.

"Monsieur Kuprin, I was given your name as a translator," she said. "I'd like to—"

"Which language?"

His brief survey of her ended in a scowl of contempt.

"Russian and Polish."

"For publication, or simply literal?"

"Actually, neither." The debate continued steadily around them. "I want you to read in those languages to a blind friend, Major St. Reymont."

Hooded eyes came up from the circle.

"Read? What?"

"From periodicals. The major, who is part Pole, is anxious to keep abreast of the news . . ."

"St. Reymont," Kuprin repeated, "would he be related to the Polish novelist by that name?"

"I believe, distantly."

Kuprin glanced toward the fat bald man and waited for a nod of approval before he answered. "My place or yours?"

"I can't say yet." She tried not to show her embarrassment. "You'll have to come meet him. I mean, Adam is . . . difficult. If you get on, you're hired. Of course I'll pay you for the trouble in coming." She dug into her purse and produced a card. "This Saturday. We're having a housewarming. Would you come, please?"

As Kuprin examined the card, the fat bald man in the fur-collared coat said something to him in Russian and the card was passed to him. There was a laughing colloquy before the translator turned to Tha. "My friend loves parties. He wants to know, is he invited too?"

The fat man was smiling at her roguishly. She could not be sure if he had identified her as Mata Hari, but she was certain that others had, and that the room would buzz with it two minutes after she had gone. She had stumbled into this predatory aviary, and the only course left to her was to be bold. "Of course." She smiled. "How can a house be warmed without some Russian guests?"

This time there was laughter all around the table, and some further exchanges.

"My friend wants you to know, Lady McLeod," Kuprin

said, "that he is Yuli Martov, chairman of the Bolshevik Party in Russia, exiled. He says if he goes to your party he will be considered a traitor to his class. He wonders if you will not also compromise yourself by your invitation?"

Martov's dark merry eyes challenged her. On one side of his bald skull there was a round white spot, which made him seem oddly piratical.

"Tell you chairman," she said to Kuprin, "tell him my reputation is beyond damage . . ."

Martov rose, giving up the pretext of not understanding her. "Ours, too, alas. So we will drink to our future at your party. I thank you—in the name of exactly half the central committee!"

His bow, full of mockery, was aimed at the other men. He waited for their laughter and then, dismissing her, resumed his diatribe, voluble and darting, provoking a storm. Other tables, as if waiting for Martov's cue, shook to their own tempests. Tha marveled at their vivacity. Adam had told her about the sullen men at the Russian front, numb with misery, paralyzing a country with their bottomless woe. But in this room they had been transformed into an inexhaustible fount of dialectics. She must ask Adam to explain that contradiction. She rushed up the steps, grateful that the hostile top spinners were no longer on guard.

From inside the cab, she called orders to the cabman to take them to the Red Cross Hospital. Her crisp tone did not deceive Sita, who put out a small hand to grasp her clenched gloved fists.

"Couldn't you find him?"

"He's coming Saturday night."

"Then what?"

She shrugged. "You know the saying. Half of Switzerland lives by intelligence, the other half by counter-intelligence."

"You'll be reported?"

"Without question."

Sita's face, combed with fine wrinkles, turned to the back window, narrowing on the vanishing café.

"But they know nothing, Tha . . ."

"Would you say this was the time to call their attention to me?"

"But you only went for a translator."

"Truth," Tha demanded again, "in the middle of my fairy tales?"

"Then make the café part of it," Sita said. "You went there to get a message from Lord Ashley. Depardieu'll be enchanted . . . you know he will . . ."

Fables—born of realities.

Adam had been furiously insistent. "I don't think attaching yourself to a blind man can last, Tha. But I know it must not even begin until you break with that Bureau and this insane war."

Depardieu had been succinct. "Quit? But how can we be sure that's not a cover to work for them? How will they know it's not an excuse to work for us? No, Madame, we would have to destroy you. Until the war is over, be advised and forget it."

She had returned to Adam, swearing her fidelity to him.

To appease Depardieu, she had invented a rendezvous in Geneva with Lord Ashley of the British Foreign Office, a man whom she'd encountered only in large gatherings in London. Ashley, however, was in charge of the Greek desk, and she knew Depardieu hungered for information about the maneuvers of his British ally in neutral Athens.

Depardieu, delighted, had congratulated her for persuading Adam to go to the Red Cross Hospital in Geneva. "A perfect cover, Madame," he had said. "Not only for the Ashley operation, but for the future. We will have many other assignments for you in Geneva."

Beside her, Sita turned from her inspection of the rear window. "You can rest easy. Nobody is following us."

"I didn't expect there to be!" She knew her irritation was misdirected, but could not help it. "And you know that's beside the point, Sita."

Sita refused to be dampened. "Poor Lord Ashley, how we drag him down!"

For once Tha could not rise to the merry game. To Sita, deceiving Depardieu was a pure delight. Sita had once compared the Bureau to a convention of fakirs in Java who would scoff at one another's tricks, and then chase some miracle man, falling all over themselves in holy awe. Sita's private name for Depardieu was "Monsieur Kamarupa," Astral Body.

But Sita's fun in the excusable lies to Depardieu left aside the inexcusable ones to Adam. Adam had put his trust in her. It was Adam whom she loved. And Adam was blind.

"But you had to give in or be killed!" Sita reminded her gently, taking her hand. "You couldn't help doing what you did."

"I could have let him go."

But Sita shook her small head stubbornly. "But you couldn't, Tha. And can't. And never will!"

It was true and it was degrading. She had to have Adam, at any cost, by any strategy. In her, the parable of the halt leading the blind had taken to the low road. She had fallen from a professional liar to a compulsive one; the fictitious Mata Hari had become real. She was belly to ground, and there she'd have to grub from now on.

Nevertheless, guilt could be borne, a kind of tithe paid by the haves to keep from becoming have-nots. But what she could not contemplate was losing Adam. Even so simple an errand as finding a translator threatened that loss—a loss that she could not endure. Outside the fiacre windows, the citizens of Geneva went briskly about their workaday activities, oblivious to the burning plains of Europe. She found herself resenting them, their unfeelingness, bitterly aware that she was working off on them her own betrayal of Adam.

Once, in Leeuwarden, a gypsy palmed Tha's penny and told her, "You will take a road one day that will lead you not to your destination but to your destiny."

The road near Compiègne, that day, was made almost impassable by frightened people, and smoke from smoldering farmhouses billowed across it, creating its own barrier.

Peasants cursed her for driving the wrong way. They wanted to get away from the guns, the front; they were fleeing with carts and animals and belongings and children, jamming the roads to Paris.

She was coming from the city. Somebody had phoned to tell her about the senseless long-range German artillery barrage that had leveled villages twenty and thirty miles behind the front.

"I hear there's a great deal of looting up there. You ought to go and look at your place before they make a shambles of it."

Impulsively, she had climbed into her car and taken the road to Compiègne. Of the few things she had in the world, the château was one for which she allowed herself to have a deep feeling. It had been the parting gift of the gentle De Massimy. And it was beautiful in itself; a small, low-lying structure, more of an overgrown farmhouse than the pompous title of château suggested, it lay on a rise overlooking the river and a garden filled with the sounds of water and insects in perpetual play, weaving an invisible web for the sunshine.

She began to lose her way. Even the narrower country roads were choked with panicked farmers. Repeatedly, she made detours, hoping that she would be able to follow the river to her destination.

At a turn in the road, a dusty major and two soldiers refused to move out of her path, ignoring her horn.

One of the soldiers climbed on the running board and ordered her to stop.

Beside the road stood an incapacitated army truck. It was piled high with vegetables and fruits. Amid this provender, there sat two sturdy provincial whores.

The soldier explained that they had been out on a "foraging" expedition when their truck gave up. They were compelled to commandeer her vehicle to take them to the closest military installation, so they could return to their front-line unit.

The major looked gaunt and bearded, extremely tall and inexpressibly weary, his dark eyes burning with fatigue. Yet, even under the dirt and stain, she had the impression of an intense personality, conscious of the apocalypse just a few miles over the smoking horizon, dueling with it, even in this moment of withdrawal.

The trio conferred. Their solemnity struck Tha as comical. They could not decide which hunger among the men had priority, sex or food.

Reluctantly, they dug in their pockets and paid off the two prostitutes. Soon, the rear of Tha's car bulged with sacks of onions, potatoes, grapes, a basket of precious eggs. The two soldiers rode the running board. The major took his seat beside her, breaking his silence only to provide her with directions.

Behind them, the two women waved good-bye from the abandoned truck.

One of the soldiers on the running board recognized her and began excitedly to reminisce about the time she had appeared in theatre in his native city of Marseilles. He had been one of the crowd outside. There had not been enough seats and a row had started. She had come out, costumed in her seven veils, to calm things down. He remembered how she had traded jokes and fended off some of her leering admirers.

The major, however, did not participate.

Tha could see she was not being rebuffed. He was too exhausted to take in anything that did not immediately relate to the war. For him, she was nonexistent, part of the breakdown of the truck, while his energies must focus only on carnage, on survival.

He stood beside the car for a moment, after he and the men had unloaded their possessions. "We are in your debt," he said, and turned away.

She drove off, abandoning the idea of visiting the château. Too late, it occurred to her that she had not learned the major's name, nor those of his men. She looked back to catch a glimpse of them, stooping to their sacks, drawn into their own world, bodies animating for a moment the long casualty lists she saw every day in the newspapers.

His goatish smell still pervaded the car. The major, she realized, had been almost mythically handsome, a replica of the traditional male figure representing the dark and fiery south for a girl in chilly Holland, the masculine face she had crayoned into the margins of school texts.

She could not shake the feeling of deprivation as she drove back to the city. I am as forlorn, she thought, as that pair left behind in the truck.

"Oh, Tha," Sita said, "I almost forgot. There was a

major. So tall he could not fit into the doorway. He claimed he met you, but I packed him off. Another devil who thinks you are mistress to the whole army!"

Three months had passed since the drive to Compiègne. In the interval, Tha had traveled to Spain for the Bureau, assigned to find out what changes, if any, were contemplated in the Spanish policy of neutrality, but only uncovering, to Depardieu's chagrin, the secret dispenser of French funds.

"This major—a long handsome face?"

"Yes . . ."

"Did he give you his name?"

"Oh . . . I suppose . . ."

"You didn't write it down?"

"Something French," Sita said, shrugging. "I was sure he was lying!"

Fortunately, Leclerc answered her appeal and made inquiries through his sources in the army, to phone back within an hour, giving her the addresses of two hotels which had been requisitioned as leave quarters for combat officers of field rank and above.

Confident, she had the taxi drop her off at the larger of the establishments, only a few streets from Place D'Iena.

But the young private on duty at the desk was dubious. "We have lots of tall majors with dark beards, Madame."

Trying to be helpful, he buzzed several rooms, using the identification Tha had provided, but none had been on the road from Compiègne.

The private, sorrowing with her, suggested she come back in the morning, when most of the officers would recover from a Paris night with an army breakfast.

On the way out, unappeased, she wandered into the courtyard, looking up at six stories of windows. Suddenly, remembering his silence, determined to break it, her voice rang out in the deep well.

"Scavenger of Compiègne!"

She could see the windows opening and men thrusting their heads out, looking down at her, amused by her insanity.

"How about me? I was once on a train that went past Compiègne!"

Their taunts provoked her to louder appeals.

"A major—gatherer of scallions—near Compiègne!"

More heads. Volunteering any sort of vegetable, offering to come right on down and stray with her in the fields. Their recognition of her as Mata Hari aroused them to greater efforts. She let them dump lewd invitations on her, parrying them, demanding they help her find the one man in the whole of the army, in all of France, in the entire universe, whom she wanted to communicate with, ending his silence, and, in some deepest aspect, her own.

Later, Adam was to relate to her how he'd been in a shower, and then heard the shouting from the courtyard, as if a small riot was in progress.

At the window, a towel wrapped around him, he looked down at a woman in a mauve silk dress, which in the shadows seemed to make her as nude as himself. The word Compiègne came up to him, and only then did he recognize the upturned face, framed in heavy dark hair, the rescuer he had vainly sought out earlier that day.

Tha, holding her place amid the hoots and jeers, saw a towel come fluttering down.

And above it, the dark bearded intense major.

She ran to catch the towel, short of breath, excited beyond herself.

That excitement became Paris, as they strode the streets, incorporating the darkened city within them, to give them sufficient space for their feelings, avid for its different twists and turns, each one of which they must immediately explore and appropriate.

Later, they had stumbled into the Impasse des Anges, which seemed to have been waiting there for them since the dawn of time. And still later, the spray of water and music, echoes of their coming together.

Leclerc was on the phone.

"I'm devastated by the news," he said.

"What news?"

"Haven't you seen the papers?"

Her fingertips pressed painfully on the instrument. "No . . . not yet . . ."

"The lists . . ."

"Adam?"

"Among those wounded . . ."

Half hysterical, her questions came in a babble.

"That's all I know," Leclerc said. "I thought you'd have been notified. Let me try to find out something more."

She hurried Sita out for the newspapers and threw herself into badgering the military for information. They had been obtuse and unhelpful, and she began to pull strings, calling on old friends who now occupied lofty berths in the military establishment.

Leclerc phoned back with one part of it. "His division was at Vittel," he reported. "They're being very secretive about it. There was a poison-gas attack. Apparently, the casualties were heavy."

"But you're sure he's only wounded?"

"So far as I can put it together."

"That's the truth, swear it!"

"Yes, Tha."

Hours and hours went by, and though there were dozens of calls, nobody could penetrate the brass redoubts to add to or confirm the first scant report.

Then, about midnight, Adam's English friend, Duchess Caroline of Cambria, now occupying some liaison post with British naval headquarters, came on the line. Caroline was one of those hoydenish, large-boned females of the English establishment, her hair close-cropped, her mannerisms fashionably brusque and masculine.

"Tha, child?"

"Caroline!"

"I don't know that I have all that much," Caroline said, trying to sound cheerful, "but since I promised to call you back with anything, that's what I'm doing, so don't really put your full weight on what I'm passing on—"

"Please, Caroline . . ."

"No, I mean it, your medical wigs are even foggier than ours—"

"What do they say?"

"It appears his eyes are affected . . ."

"Did they say how bad?"

"Oh, that's when they really spout Sanskrit! I cursed them. But still, it didn't get through their miserable mumbo jumbo."

"Where is he? Can I go to see him?"

"I hardly think, at this stage," Caroline said. "Is there anybody looking after you? Shall I come by?"

Managing to utter some sort of thanks, she hung up, determined she would not leave the telephone until somebody told her where Adam was, and she had been granted permission to be with him.

The tent was enormous—the kind one saw at carnivals or circuses. It lay in the middle of a suburb close to Vittel. All around it were the remnants of flattened bungalows. A fat black hose ran from a hydrant, coiling over the broken ground, and disappeared under the tent, seeking a staff.

The driver of the military vehicle pointed to a flap halfway down the length of the tent. "There'll be an orderly. Show him your pass."

At the far end, ambulances were backing up to a low canvas annex to the main tent, and men in blue cotton shirts unloaded the litters. Neighborhood dogs foraged in the rubble. The tent, waving in the wind, was a bellows, giving forth a vile putrescence combining chloroform, antiseptics, and rank laundry boiling in lye.

In the screened-off section, an orderly examined her document at length. The pass had been signed by a general. It had taken days and weeks to procure. Caroline had run from one end of Paris to the other, promising everything, only to discover that "everything" was the one item in oversupply in the city at war. Then, by accident, she had run across a general who remembered Adam's father, the late Baron St. Reymont, and that memory opened the gate.

"We don't allow visitors," the orderly said.

Tha kept a leash on her anger. "However, I have permission."

"Is that the signature of the general," the orderly asked, "or did somebody else sign for him?"

"His."

The orderly examined her. "Wait here. I'll see if I can get him to come out."

Tha waited in distress. Beyond the thin separation of the canvas screen, she could hear the sounds of men moaning and screaming, the clatter of surgical instruments dropped into porcelain trays; in here the stench seemed to crowd upon itself in solid suffocating layers.

The orderly returned alone. "This way," he said.

She followed him among the cots, trying not to look to the right or left, yet conscious of the men following her progress, then coming to a section where the men had bandages about their eyes.

Adam sat on the edge of his cot. His head was bandaged like the others. He was engaged in a conversation with the man in the next cot.

"Your visitor, Major."

"Ah," Adam said. He waved at the man in the next bed. "Captain Manon," he introduced. "A fan of yours. Saw you perform in Lyon. You said Lyon?"

"Yes," Manon said. "I'll go . . ."

"No, not at all," Adam said. He turned stiffly to Tha. "Went all the way to the top, they say."

"Caroline did."

"How's Caroline?"

"Fine."

"Send her my best."

"Yes."

There was a silence. Again Manon offered to leave, and again, even more pointedly, Adam insisted that he remain, that the conversation was just a friendly one. "Nothing private, Manon."

She wanted to reach out to Adam, but could not.

"I suppose they wrote up Vittel in the papers, so you know all about it," Adam said.

"Not really."

"Would you like to hear about it?"

She murmured assent, half choking with humiliation and hurt.

His report could have been rendered to a battle commander. From time to time he turned to Manon, asking for verification, or for additional details. "I assure you, it was all avoidable. The fumes must have affected my brain before they got to my eyes. I should have run like hell. Still, compared to the men whose lungs took it, we're in clover. Isn't that the way you view it, Manon?"

"Sort of, Major."

A length of rope hung from an eyelet in the canvas. Adam twisted it about one fist, then about the other, then finally bound both his hands together.

He finally offered her the sheathed fists in farewell, careful not to allow her to touch his skin. "Manon says he's followed your adventures for years and it's his favorite reading, and we're going to ask one of the orderlies to read us about your next scandal!"

She stood at a loss, turning from Adam to the other men, helpless before their bandages, their obstinacy, their false cheerfulness.

"Adam . . ."

"It was most kind of you to have come, and be sure to thank Caroline and that general what's-his-name. Shall I yell for the orderly, or can you make it out on your own?"

Tears sprang to her eyes. "Adam . . . when will I see you again?"

He waved the bound hands at her. "Any time they let you," he said. "We are at your disposal at any time, Madame."

Feeling disemboweled, she stumbled out, trying to make herself believe that this display of obstinacy and pride would pass, that it had to be an initial reaction to his maiming, a protective shield, which he would put aside later.

Adam, my love, she silently cried, I'll wait, please let me wait!

But waiting had only made it worse.

Even after Adam's removal to an army hospital in Paris, he maintained his impenetrable surface courtesy. When she went at visiting hours, he was always careful to have his roommate or some other patient on hand, keeping the atmosphere cool and distant.

She poured out long letters, one after another, piling up the words he would not let her utter in his presence. But he did not reply. And if, during her visit, she referred to them, he would compliment her on her writing style, and select a phrase or two for his roommate's appreciation.

Frequently, he summoned Caroline to share the visiting period, demonstratively responding to the English woman, shunting Tha aside.

After one such session, Caroline had taken her to a café. "Damn him," Caroline swore. "Years ago, I really chased him, but he wouldn't have me for the breeze! I'm aware I'm being used to make you cut and run. I should stop him, but I can't say no to Adam, never could. In some strange way, he's reverted to being an impossible Polish aristocrat. I'd help you, but I can't help myself!"

Even Sita tried. Using the excuse of taking him some of his favorite Indonesian dishes, which he had so relished during his leaves prior to Vittel, Sita went to the hospital, determined to penetrate his defenses.

But on her return, she admitted defeat. "He's a remarkable man," Sita said, dejectedly. "Even before this, he was bitter about this war. But he will miss it, he says, because there he found men compassionate, made so by fear of death. It always drew him back then, and would draw him in again . . ."

She shook her head in dismay. "He says war also makes passing romances seem great and eternal. But now he will live without such illusions and he expects others to be normal and distracted, in the old way, again . . ."

It seemed bitterly final.

Two days later, the hospital administrator phoned. "Madame," she heard him say, "may we call on you to help us with Major St. Reymont? Of all his friends, we consider you his closest. For his sake, would you do me the favor of coming to see me?"

She'd run, to grasp the straw

The administrator, a young man with carroty hair and

a pleasantly disheveled manner, acknowledged his failure to cope with Adam.

"We can't budge him. We have urged him to apply for a voluntary transfer to a facility in Geneva, recently established by the Red Cross. It is designed to care for victims of gas war, men from both sides. The staff comes from neutral countries, experts in their fields. In our opinion, the major would benefit from their surgical talent. He refuses to go. He's convinced it would be chasing an illusion, and would open him again to a self-destructive melancholy, against which he has fought so hard, as you must have observed . . ."

She nodded, though Adam had concealed that struggle from her, along with everything else.

"Of course, Madame," the administrator conceded, "some of our doctors agree with him, and we can't make promises. Yet, the senior surgeons here recommend a transfer. We know how much influence you have over him, and we hope you will share our point of view . . ."

She half expected the young man to dismiss her, as she tumbled into a confession of her own failures with Adam. Her own need was so great it took her beyond embarrassment or niceties. "If only I could meet him outside this hospital . . . which I'm sure is his armor against me . . . I'm sure I could reach him . . ."

The carrot head, a very practical one, thought their purposes could be joined.

Mistinguett, the musical comedy star, was their solution.

Tha had long admired the tall and elegant singer, who could imbue even a mediocre popular song with a penetrating sadness. She had often gone to listen, comparing her to the singers of the little cafés in the faubourgs, where they sang not of loss, as Mistinguett did, but of being lost themselves. Alone, Tha tentatively tried to combine those emotions and find a new sound, dreaming of one day making a new career, singing these songs, perhaps to the lyrics of Apollinaire.

"I'll be glad to help," Mistinguett said. "We'll invite

some of the wounded of the major's division. I'm certain he'll accept. You can turn up among the entertainment committee."

From the start of the war, Mistinguett had devoted herself to hospitalized soldiers. Her château—a lavish place, surrounded by cottages, not like Compiègne—was opened to provide them a weekend in the country, while the most prominent entertainers came to perform and to spend time with them. Tha herself had frequently served on such committees, but it had taken the administrator's prompting to make her see how one of Mistinguett's affairs could be used to find a new way to Adam.

Late that Saturday, she caught her first sight of Adam, among a group of army men surrounding the comedian, Devalier, presently in a wheelchair himself, but going on in his old way, making them all his straight men.

Watching Adam in that convivial group, apparently so content, she shrank away. She began to blame herself for being a hypocrite. Instead of acknowledging her horror of his blind eyes, milky with scar tissue, she had tried to conceal her aversion. No wonder Adam despised her!

At the buffet dinner, however, Mistinguett insisted she make another try, shoving a plate of food in Tha's hands and directing her to take it to Adam.

Pain whitened his face when she announced herself, but then he quickly recovered, accepting the plate, resorting to a detached, self-deprecatory grin.

"I try not to eat in public," he said. "You've no idea how hard it is to locate your own mouth, except with your thumb."

"I'll feed you."

For once, her voice sounded natural.

He looked up. "Good."

She fed him, describing the food. Again, her words came out planlessly. Unconsciously, she slowed her movements, trying to evoke her own presence from an interior darkness.

"Good," he repeated.

Abruptly, his manner changed. "Sita tell you what I said?"

"Yes."

"I tried to answer your letters. But everything I put down sounded self-pitying, or outside me—heavy, like cobblestones everybody's walked on. I'm too bitten for anything . . . but shutting up . . ."

"Adam," she said, in control, "I've made every mistake. But I'm not an enemy, not a stranger, either, and I won't be shut out . . ."

His face twisted. "Well, you want to be my protector, and that's probably worse, or worse for me, and if you go on prolonging what can't bring anything but misery, you'll become my enemy . . ."

"Then tell me what I can be?"

He handed back the plate. "I've spent a good part of my life shaking off my mother. Now I'm in a new sack, it's tempting to take a substitute. But then I remember how painful it was to be dependent on someone, so tempt me no more, Tha, and be my friend. I'm really exhausted by this outing, and you must excuse me . . ."

Abruptly he turned and called to one of the nurses to help him to his room.

Mistinguett came to her side. She stood beside Tha, both of them tall, able to look over the heads of most of the diners, watching Adam go off with the nurse.

"You know where his room is," Mistinguett said.

"Yes," Tha said.

"Excellent," Mistinguett said, and went to entertain her other guests.

The opening of the door brought a grumble from the darkness. "Yes? Yes? What do you want?"

She began to undress.

Her scent pierced his double gloom. "For Christ's sake, Tha, aren't we miserable enough now?" he demanded.

She found her way to him.

His breath came in labored gasps. "Back off, Tha." He was half pleading. "Let me breathe."

She held his hips. "Breathe, but staccato!"

He laughed, and she felt his hands over hers, half holding back, half guiding him to her. They were in a universe at once familiar and strange; because of his intense concentration, he lingered over each caress, discovering her through his hands and lips and exploring her as a first-found world through shoulder and thigh and groin, releasing her for a voyage through hypnotic calms, then summoning her to sudden surging existence.

He lay under her, sustaining her, then establishing his own rhythm, until they were locked in a time that controlled them both, connected by some caudal interchange of the blood.

Then, because of her anxiety to prove he need not fear her domination, she began to rush her responses, unable to hold back the throb of engorgement, and letting go, too soon, too soon.

Later, aroused from sleep, she knew his tongue awake at her center, reaching up, sending fire along the tendrils of her senses, to her throat, back down her spine, twining, gathering a thousand filaments, tightening about her vulva, back to the quick of his kiss. His darkness was illumined and both were within it; his shaft became one with her palms, her mouth, a whip that joined her breasts and thighs, a succulence growing from the bottom of the sea, drawing and scraping and sweeping her through a wave of orgasms—crests and troughs driven by the same deep oceanic pressure, succeeding to each other without interval, yet shaken by each separately, freeing her at last to her submarine drift, caressed by soft green undergrowth that linked her to him.

Toward dawn, she awoke to find him still within her, but deep in sleep. She kissed him, letting him roll apart, careful not to awaken him. Slowly she let go of herself to sink to the bottom of some sandy pool, secret beneath the ocean floor, yet filled with sunny air, a grotto beneath the ocean of their lovemaking. She lay nestled in dunes that were shaped like the corona of his maleness. Sleep, when it came, brought her to the heart of the universe.

The sluicing of water drew her again to the surface.

Adam was showering.

After a moment, he came groping back along the wall, toward the bed. She checked her impulse to help. He fumbled at a chair for his underwear and clothes.

"I'm awake," she said.

"I know."

She watched in silence, wanting to touch the ridge of his spine articulated against his long back.

"So now you know," he said, mocking himself, "on top of all my other infirmities, I'm easy to seduce . . ."

"Since we're making confessions," she said, "I'd like to make one too."

"Sorry," Adam said. "Since they chucked me out of the seminary, I'm not allowed to hear them."

"I've lied a lot to you, Adam."

"Go in peace, child."

"To begin with, I let you believe my father was a Dutch official. The fact is, he had a hat store, went bankrupt, and deserted my mother. I was thirteen."

"Very sad."

"I also claimed I was a schoolteacher. In fact, after my mother died, I was sent to become a nursery-school aide—a scrubwoman. But the headmaster seduced me and I was kicked out."

"Poor Tha."

"I went back in disgrace to my godfather's farm. I was fourteen and too tall and very awkward. I considered myself ugly. The farm boys jumped me and I let them. I hoped somehow I would find courage to die."

For the first time, he paused in his stubborn efforts to dress himself.

"I don't see what it has to do with us!"

"I do! I've fed you this false idea of me, desired by all, arising from a bed of roses, except for a slight marital detour—which let me pick up the title of Lady McLeod. A joke."

"Well, fine."

"McLeod has no title. He's a Scot mercenary in the Dutch army. He ran an ad for a bride to take to Java—actually to seduce girls desperate to get away. I discovered he liked to beat his women. I let him, on the condition he marry me. By the time we got on the boat, I was pregnant with my son."

"Son? You only told me about a daughter."

"Gabriel. Born in Java. Knifed to death at the age of five. In reprisal for my husband's brutalities toward the people there. I tried to kill myself. But that day, a new servant came to the house. Her name was Sita. She bound my wrists. And taught me Mahayana Buddhism, made it possible for me to live. After McLeod was transferred back to Holland, I tried to run away with my daughter, Banda. McLeod had a court grant a divorce and award him custody of Banda, whom he teaches that I'm the slut of the world."

"All right, Tha . . ."

"Wait, please. I ran to Paris. Somebody gave me the address of a woman who had a riding academy. She had no job for me. I cried so hard she let me sleep in the office at the stables. She thought I might be tall enough to work as one of the statues in a café tableau vivant. The man asked me to dance. I only knew the dances of Java. He watched me and sent me to one man, who passed me to the Museum Guimet, which wanted to exhibit native dances. They had me appear as Mata Hari, so I'd sound authentic. The next morning, for reasons I still don't understand, I was famous, and just as miserable as the day before . . ."

"A happy ending," Adam said. "Don't forget the poor box on the way out, Madame."

"Don't be obtuse, Adam. The enchantress, the ur-courtesan, never existed. Lovers, yes, but inwardly the same orphan of Leeuwarden, until I ran into an officer on the road to Compiègne, too weary even to spare me a word."

Adam shrugged and ran the tip of his cane across the brass rungs of the bed in a dismissive clanking. "All of a sudden, you're such a worthless item, not even a blind man would have you as a gift! Do you really think I'm going to swallow that, Tha?"

Before she could reply, somebody knocked at the door.

It turned out to be the administrator, and Adam welcomed his interruption.

"You find me," Adam said, "in the clutches of a most artful lady."

The administrator managed to misconstrue. He hoped Adam had a good night. "I'm sure," the young man said, "you've had second thought about going to Geneva?"

Adam turned to Tha and shook his head. "The design behind the design?"

He pushed the administrator away, and, holding to the wall, swung into the corridor. She ran out after him, bearing his cane, holding it out to him.

He snatched it from her, striding down the hall, brandishing the cane like a sword. She found herself half raging at him, "Yes, I want you to go to Geneva! And I want to go with you and never leave you! What I told you about me is true! It's not you who will depend on me, but the other way around! Why will you let that idiotic pride ruin our lives?"

Adam raged back. "I'm blind, but not altogether stupid. You're famous! Sought after! These are your years! If you began in the stables or wherever, more reason to have the best now! Ask any man here, any man in my situation, and he'll tell you the same thing, this can't work with us!"

Men coming from their rooms, attracted by their gusty debate. Many of the officers, of course, had known Adam for several years, and they lost no time in offering their opinion. Many supported him. Just as many derided him.

"Don't be an ass, St. Reymont," one man shouted. "You won't be the first to be carried by a woman. You may be outsize, but she can take you on!"

Adam shouted back that aside from his comrade's tenderness toward 75's, he was otherwise a dolt.

Carried out of the building by their passions, Tha found herself in the backyard, among the clotheslines. To prevent Adam from decapitating himself, she had to seize his arm and forcibly guide him along the corridors made by the sheets.

"Even before this happened," Adam said, "I knew there'd be no future for us. I'll never inherit, unless I go back to Poland and my mother, which I'll never do. Look, Tha, we were an accident. A wonderful one. But I'm a grown man. It's time to go back to your rich and famous lovers . . ."

"There aren't any!"

"Tha, Tha, let it go!"

"Not one!"

He swirled into a post and she had to pull him away.

Adam stamped on, more sardonic than angry. "All those men I've read about, nonexistent. Let's see, about the time I met you, it was Camaro, the Spanish ambassador. Then there was the Scottish Duke of Argyle, and I know he exists, because I saw photos of the two of you in the papers!"

"Cover stories!"

He scowled derisively. "For publicity!"

"No," she blurted. "I have no need of that, now. For the Deuxième Bureau. Pour la patrie!"

He came to a halt. "Oh, please, Tha."

"Well, it's true."

He shook his head, and she reached out and took his hand and ran it over her face. He let the scrutinizing fingers search there for a long moment.

"And they let you talk about it?"

"Streng verboten. Geschossen verden."

He withdrew his hand, letting it trace her neck and shoulder. "All those covers—chosen for you, not by you?"

"For the last two years," she told him. "Shadows to deepen shadow. If you take me with you to Switzerland, it won't be a sacrifice—but a release, something I wanted to do but had no reason for doing, until you gave me the reason, but which I can't do unless you help me . . ."

He stood quiet and thoughtful. "Will they let you out?"

"They'll have to."

"Why?"

"You're a war hero. I'll tell them I want to spend my time with you."

He reached for her face, with both his hands. "If you mean what you've said, if you really want to shake their crazy games and insane murders—that's a starting place, we may have a chance of making us work."

"That's all I ask."

He drew her face to him and kissed her, and then they went back to stand in the backyard, facing a group of veterans who had come out to the balcony and now called on Adam to tell them the outcome of the battle.

"Truce!"

He waved the cane at them and took her arm, and the balcony contingent rained down an ambiguous storm of cheers and jeers.

Depardieu arranged the meeting with his usual care. This time, they were to come together in public by virtue of their association with the home for war orphans. The occasion would be a fund-raising event at the velodrome, featuring bicycle races by schoolgirls from all parts of the city.

He was already in the box when she took her place not only to the applause of the children in the home, but, with an enthusiasm that surprised her, of the young people in the audience.

"You've become a symbol of emancipation," Depardieu said. "When the war ends, you must go in for politics, provided of course women have the vote."

"I was thinking of a more personal emancipation."

"So they tell me."

"I'm sure you won't miss me," she said. "I don't think I've helped win the war, or even helped lose the last one."

Depardieu palely smiled. "The same could be said for—or against—me. But as I know you to be a practical woman, I have arranged for a substantial payment to be paid to you through the Lazard bank. We will cover that with gossip about an affair with Lazard . . ."

"I don't think you understand."

"St. Reymont?"

"Yes."

"I hear it said, you're in love with him."

"Yes, very much."

"You're afraid he won't tolerate . . . your travels?"

"Didn't they tell you about Vittel?"

Depardieu nodded. "I'm sure we can combine both efforts, your devotion to him and to us. We would provide you with more mundane reasons for traveling—contracts with theatrical producers and so on, a revival of your career, books about you and the like . . ."

"But the objects would remain."

Depardieu lifted his shoulders. "Ah, he would not have to know, and, of course, the objects would be of no emotional consequence to you . . ."

She leaned forward, watching the youngsters straining toward the last laps of their race. "I could manage it, yes. But I prefer not to. It would be deeply distressing. I want you to release me."

They rose, applauding the end of the race. A girl approached the box and Tha took time out to hand her a trophy and to pose with her for the photographers. When she came back to the box, she found Depardieu slumped in his seat, arms folded.

"I suppose you consider me hidebound."

It was the first time he'd ever exposed a human face to her. "I never considered you at all, only myself."

Depardieu yielded another grin, less pallid than the last. "I don't encourage it as a rule. But I have a wife and two daughters. Even a few friends. And I allow myself to say I have the imagination to enter into the experiences of others. But I must still turn you down."

"But you yourself told me at the beginning that most of this is a waste; intelligence has never won a war or lost one; that it is a comfort to politicians, to make them think they are controlling history, instead of the other way around . . ."

"Philosophically, I meant."

"But why hold me for a few scraps of information . . ."

"One scrap may be a vital scrap," Depardieu said. "And even if that should prove to be an illusion, yet it is indispensable to us, as excess is in love, Madame."

She scowled out at the flashing wheels. "But if I feel this way, how can I help but fail?"

He moved to sit up, his arms still folded. "I have to take that into account. But what of the alternative? Suppose we let you drop out? Suppose you go to the Abteilung and make the same request? They would want assurances you are not giving us their secrets. They would seek to extract new ones about us, to test your sincerity. We, in turn, would have you under surveillance. We would have to draw the conclusion that you are operative and dangerous. We would have to destroy you. Unless, for the same reasons, they do it first. I have seen it happen. If you reflect a moment, you will see that it is best for me to take no official notice of your request, but to continue as you are, with such help as we can give you to ease matters with your brave major . . ."

She fell silent, paralyzed by the lethal logic of paranoia, held fast in the trap of mirror images. She knew she could say nothing to shake his belief that humanity said one thing and did another. She was the prisoner of his assumption that French security must rest on the solid foundation of distrust. The bedrock of his policy was that people were vile, here and abroad, now and for all time.

Beside her, Depardieu sighed, slid down in his seat again, and pretended to become absorbed in the activities of the young racers.

Only when all the prizes had been presented, and they were alone in the tunnel on the way out to their cars did Depardieu seek to soften his dictum. He was a senior civil servant, he averred, whose thankless role it was to sift competing claims, political or personal, and decide on the true interest of France. One thing power could not abide was neutrality, which had to present itself as a challenge to authority and its purposes, in its own way more pernicious than betrayal or opposition.

"I know I can count on you, Madame," he said, "to continue with us, until all this is well behind us."

They walked the rest of the tunnel without exchanging another word.

"Our passports," Sita said, "did you bring them?"

She felt Sita tugging at her sleeve.

The fiacre had halted. A young Swiss soldier stood beside the open window. Beyond, at the intersection, a cordon of soldiers had put up a barrier of sawhorses. All passage had been slowed for an examination of credentials.

The memory of the tunnel still lay hollow within her, and she momentarily panicked, searching for the documents in her purse.

The soldier could not have been more than seventeen. He was trying, however, to play his role, and made a serious face as he bent to the paper.

By now, this had become a familiar Geneva routine. The military saw spectres everywhere. Last week they had sprung from doorways to demand identity papers, fearful that the country was about to be seized by infiltrators from France. And the week before, they had overturned lorries, searching for German saboteurs apparently hiding in potato sacks, the advance elements of a Hun invasion.

The soldier held out the papers. "Dutch, I see."

"Yes."

"Neutral like us."

She nodded.

"Well, it won't last. The Germans will march into Holland, and the French will try to grab us."

"Really?"

"Count on it. The war'll be here any day now."

It seemed malignant to puncture the boy's grim warrior stance. "Thank you for the warning."

The boy saluted and waved the driver ahead.

Sita managed to keep a straight face until they were beyond the crossing. "At last! A military secret worthy of Monsieur Kamarupa!"

She doubled over, shaking with laughter, and this time Tha could not resist the gale.

LAZARD DEBIT
27 February 1917

Dr. Harris, the American psychiatrist, pouncing out
from a corridor, liked to grab her upper arm and launch into a
discussion about Adam.

She could never be quite certain which satisfied him
more—his surreptitious feel, or his strictures about his least co-
operative patient.

"Lady McLeod!" The American reached for her with a
soft hand. "I got your housewarming invitation!"

"Hope you'll be there."

He slipped his fingers up closer to her armpit, so that
when he swung her arm, he came into contact with her breast.
He had the infantile notion that this stratagem was so subtle it
passed unnoticed.

79

"Major says it's a beautiful place you've found up there."

"Very."

"And you've started your breeding plans."

"A yearling or two," Tha said. "But we still have to find some stock."

"Excellent, excellent!" Dr. Harris declared. "I wish all the men lived outside and engaged themselves in civilian pursuits. I believe it would cut my case load in half." His moon face beamed close. "And, of course, to have an active partner—that's worth more than anything."

"Adam's the experienced breeder," Tha said. "I'm only along for the ride."

"Still . . . a fortunate man!"

She tried to pull her arm from his damp grip, but could not bring it off gracefully and relapsed, letting him guide her down the corridor.

"Did the major tell you we have had another communication from his mother?"

"No."

"The baroness has actually had an attorney threaten us with a lawsuit unless we release her son to her care forthwith . . ."

Tha shook her head. "Incredible."

"Utterly. Yet the major told me something I find almost as hard to believe. He alleges that his father passed on syphilis to his mother, from which the father was later cured, but left her chronically ill, chronically vengeful."

"Why is that so hard to believe?"

"He likes to pull my leg," Harris said. "I'm American, and all Americans are naïve."

"Don't such things happen in your country?"

"We like to say they don't." Harris flushed momentarily. "But if it's true, that would explain a lot about her and the way she behaves . . ."

"Even if he made it up," Tha said, "it would still explain a lot, wouldn't it?"

The overfed face bobbled in agreement. "I'm just trying to find objective verification . . ."

No point her guying the American. Adam would be doing a splendid job on his own. He was scathing about psychiatrists. He claimed to have dealt with their precursors as a student in a Jesuit seminary. The healers, in black robes or white jackets, located Man's fall in the psyche, an infirmity for which one confessor offered his superior faith, the other his superior will; as penance, kneeling was superseded by recumbency. A more comfortable posture, Adam conceded, but still the same old echo chamber for the heart's long cry.

Though the story about syphilis was new, Adam had described the bitterness between a philandering, wandering father and a woman who found her great satisfactions in her inherited land and her three thousand tenants. The baroness still insisted Adam had been stolen from her by his late father, under the pretext of putting him into a French seminary; in spite of the passage of time, she continued to berate the deceased for Adam's refusal to return home. Only recently, there had arrived from the baroness a bulky package that turned out to be a white marble bust of the lady, which he might enjoy until the maternal link was restored in the flesh.

Dr. Harris made a face. "His mother is not the factor. That's not my immediate worry . . ."

"What then?"

"One of the nurses tells me he's had a visitor . . . a professional mountain climber . . . a man called Gordi."

"An old friend, Arturo Gordi, yes."

"That may be"—Harris continued to knead her arm—"but, according to the nurse, the major was making plans to climb one of the higher peaks here . . ."

She felt her heart skip. "There must be some misunderstanding . . ."

"Not according to the nurse."

"I mean," Tha said, "Adam's an alpinist. They often climbed together. They must have been reminiscing and the nurse—"

"I don't have to point out the connection between the continuation of his eye inflammation and the self-destructive impulse behind this climb—"

"If true."

"If merely contemplated," Harris said. "Doesn't it tell us . . . his real state of mind?"

"But he's been so cheerful!"

Of course, she knew that meant little. Adam went to lengths to hide his depressions from her, and their constant activity since coming to Geneva had given him another convenient screen. Adam, since leasing the farm, would go off by himself, on the grounds that he wanted to familiarize himself with the rooms of the house, or the path to the stables, and be absent for hours. Yet, after these spasms, which she respected, he would return, at least composed enough to resume his mask of composure, making her ache with admiration and love.

At the door of the gym, Tha halted. Dr. Harris continued to grapple her arm.

"You'll look into it, won't you?"

"Yes."

The gym had once been the grand ballroom of this converted hotel structure. Huge chandeliers and gilt columns still divided the space in Cartesian symmetries, but had to vie with the sweaty horde of invaders working out on exercise mats, tumbling, skipping, panting at pulleys and rowing machines, grunting over irons, as if they were performing a parody of the waltzes that had seemed, not so long ago, as immutable as the design of the parquetry.

In a far corner a section had been roped off. There the blind, stretched out on cots, took heat-lamp treatments. Heads swathed in damp towels, they were engaged in a bitter and silent struggle against infection and its threat of enucleation. This surgical scourge, Adam had confided to her, was the final and greatest fear of the blind, even among those whose sight was beyond the faintest hope of restoration.

Coming in each day to pick up Adam, she had to make an effort to conceal her queasiness. At the men losing themselves in the narcosis of exercise. At the towel-masked souls, caged in a hell brighter than heaven. And then force herself to smile, fearful that her guise would slip, and Adam would penetrate to her deeper treachery and turn his back on her forever.

Harris located him first.

"How they dote on him," Dr. Harris said enviously.

Flanked by two giggling young nurses, Adam was making his way through the cots. They pretended to help with the
fastenings of his formal military tunic, meanwhile tickling his
naked torso.

Half smiling, half frowning, he held them off with one
large hand as if they were children. In the intense light, his
scarred eyes only emphasized his inner energy and inner strife;
as if, in some strange way, his beauty had needed the flaw of
blindness to complete it.

"I dote too," she said, pulling away. "Shouldn't I?"

Harris looked abashed. "I didn't mean that." He put his
guilty hand in his pocket. "See you Saturday night. And thanks
again for the invitation . . ."

"Looking forward."

The doctor padded a step away and then swung back.
"Oh, you won't mention me, about that mountain climb. I
don't want him to think of me as a policeman. You can say it
was the head nurse. Mind, Lady McLeod?"

"No."

One more lie, she thought. Dear Adam, conspirators are
we all, and all of us are protecting you from yourself!

She turned again to Adam, slowly picking his way
among the mats, disdaining the safer path of following the
walls. The same obstinacy made him balk at sitting on the
commode when urinating. Instead, Adam would grip the bowl
between his knees, firing away, not always accurately, but
erect. Ecce homo, ecce Adam!

In the sea of bodies, two boxers, swinging away at each
other, slammed into him. Adam recovered his balance, but not
his direction. He moved now at an angle, which would bring
him, not to the door, but to a wall.

She knew better than to go to his aid. Though her body
strained to guide him, she held her place. Adam, off course,
tapped his way toward the wall, near where some men were
climbing thick ropes suspended from the old ballroom balcony,
in a relay contest between "lungers" and "blinders." Bells, af-
fixed to the underside of the balcony, had to be struck by a
climber to signify the completion of a mount, for the benefit of
the sightless.

Suddenly a ball was thrown up and struck the bell

above the lunger's rope. The blind competitor, accepting the sound, slid down in defeat.

Cries of outrage, some in mockery, some edged, sent the crowd into a scrimmage that transformed in seconds from fun to rancor. The nurses threw themselves into the confusion, trying to cool the more gladiatorial.

She ran forward, seeing him in the middle of the scuffles, fearful of his being somehow injured in the melee.

"Adam, this way!"

Much taller than the others, he cocked his head to one side, amused at the angry uproar. "Who says we aren't ennobled by our suffering?"

"Please come . . ."

He held back a moment to enjoy the scabrous abuse and rich profanity before he let her take him through the milling men.

At the door, he paused. "The nurses said Harris was with you . . ."

"Touched and gone."

"What am I guilty of today?"

"The usual. You're an enfant terrible."

"I hope you told him that's my model and I'm gaining on it."

"Next time."

Adam pulled at his tunic. "This damn Napoleon suit! Really think it's going to make an impression on the brood mares?"

"Irresistible."

At her insistence, he'd fished out the elaborate military jacket for their visit to the horse auction. Some impulse to compete with the glistening thoroughbreds made people put on finery. Adam's jacket, purchased long ago, hung about him loosely.

"Cadaver." She slipped a hand under his tunic. "Ribs of Adam." She could feel him quiver. "Those nurses set you off or just me?"

"Harris mention my mother's latest?"

"Briefly," she evaded. "Button you?"

He yielded, intent. "He wants me to write her a letter—

something filial—to prove I wish to be normal mentally and physically."

"He wants you to get well." They were alone in the corridor now, and she pulled him close, wanting to feel the warmth of his center. "More important, I found your Kuprin for you."

"Does it make sense to submit to all that browbeating—all in the sacred name of mother love?"

"Get Harris off your back, at least." She concentrated on the tunic. A confrontation over the baroness would only be a substitute for a direct clash between Adam and herself. "I think Kuprin's a revolutionary. His friends were. The café was filled with spies."

"Bother you?"

"No, no!"

"Then why are you so tense, Tha?" He grasped her hand and forced her to stop fingering the complicated embroidered fastenings. "I can feel your whole body. Ever since you came in. What is it?"

He'd always been sensitive to her moods. Sometimes, since his blinding, she felt he lived inside her skin, his raw nerves his second sight, so that she had to lie, not only to him, but to herself, keeping her own treachery behind her back, unacknowledgeable to herself.

"What did you see Arturo Gordi about?"

He held her hand tight. "Is that what it is?"

"Yes."

"That what Harris told you?"

"Yes," she said. "Though I'm supposed to lie and say it was the head nurse. Are you really going to attempt a climb?"

"I would," Adam said, laughing. "Gordi won't, damn him!"

"Praise Gordi."

"Turned me down, and he calls himself my friend!" He released her hand and let her put the tunic together. "I told him that Brymer, the English alpinist, once wrote he did fine snow-blind. Gordi says Englishmen go up and down mountains on their good opinion of themselves, but his people depend on God, ice axes, and good eyes. He says if he heard of any other guide giving in to me, he and his cousins will take care of him. So, you can relax."

"Ready." She took his arm, careful to let him use his stick and motivate himself. Her diversion had worked, and she had a momentary retrospective shudder at how close he had come to guessing her betrayal.

"Kuprin looks fierce and independent," she said. "He promises to come to the housewarming, so you judge for yourself . . ."

Sita, running toward them from the lobby, poured out a stream of agitated Malay.

"What's she saying?" Adam demanded.

"Oh, hell! The press! In the lobby! Sita thought you might want to duck out and let me deal with them . . ."

"Afraid I'll embarrass you again?"

"You'll only blow up at them, the way you did in Paris. . ."

It had been a test of their truce. The press, of course, had its bathetic formula: Mata Hari, the great lady of the European boudoir, giving up her sybaritic life to devote herself to a heroic but otherwise obscure, blinded French-Polish officer. They had her cast as the angelic patriot and Adam as pitiful cipher, lucky to be a victim.

It had done her no good to protest that Adam's paternal ancestors came from one of France's oldest and most patrician families; that his mother, the Baroness Moura St. Reymont, belonged to a clan of no less ancient lineage, that for centuries both families had given Poland some of its leading citizens. The reporters had swarmed about Adam, wanting him to go down on his knees and tell the world how grateful he was for her attentions. And he had swung his cane.

"I'll behave this time," Adam said. "Thanks to Dr. Harris. I realize now that I'm your chosen beggar!"

He tapped his cane on the floor and with the other hand rattled an imaginary tin cup, in defiant, almost sacrilegious burlesque of his own condition.

Tha tried to shush him, and when she could not, she linked her arm with his, and, laughing, followed Sita toward the lobby.

"The Paris papers say—"

"Can you deny that—"

"Lazard, the banker—"

". . . A serious damage to the Lazard prestige . . ."

"Are the previous reports in error, Lady McLeod?"

They were duplicates of the Paris wolf pack, only seedier and preponderantly male. In Paris, the women correspondents would conspire to give her breathing room, at least until she could sense the direction of their thrust, even though they too would ram it home.

"Paul Lazard—gave an interview about me?"

"Is he a new interest, Mata Hari?"

"New . . ." she decided to fence. "Oh, war ages everything."

"Lazard insists he never gave you a large sum, or any sum."

"Since he's a banker," she held them off, "one knows he is careful about money."

"He stated that if you had asked him for money, he'd have refused."

"There—the recipe for his success!"

The pulse in her temple began to pound. She wondered what exaggeration of Depardieu's had triggered this imbroglio. These reporters, obviously, hadn't any inkling of the real source of the stories about Lazard largesse or they wouldn't be asking this kind of question. She would have to keep bantering, until they revealed some more. She felt Adam, at her side, stiffen with distaste.

"Lazard says he's convinced you consider all men as mere money and admiration machines."

She could feel Adam's edginess, as he gripped his cane with both fists, half stooping over, his head bent to the floor, doing his best to shut them out.

"Paul said that?"

"I can quote exactly if you—"

"It has the sound," she plunged into this diversion, "of those Wedekind plays about the immoral Loulou." She was conscious of the reporters beginning to close a circle about her, separating her from Adam. "A femme galante . . . who considers all men alike . . . would be a drab in bed and everywhere else."

"Is that an admission, Lady McLeod?"

"Of course, if the subject is finances," Tha said, hoping to keep the questions on this more general plane. "I must be silent. But if we are discussing immorality—"

Some of them laughed, but a woman edged in with one of those grayish wartime notebooks. Clearly, she did not intend for Tha to escape her quicker pounce.

"We are told," she purred, "you paid your lease on your farm here with a draft from the Lazard bank, and that you settled rather sizeable debts in Paris with checks also drawn against Lazard Freres . . ."

The nerve began to jump painfully. "Isn't that what a bank is for?"

"From Lazard's bank, not Lazard?"

"Yes."

"Just a coincidence?"

"Unless all Lazard's depositors are friends of Paul's."

The senior wolf, a man with a stiff collar and a Calvinist frown, was on the scent of blood. "Are you disclaiming your previous statement in Paris that Lazard was your patron?"

"I never made such a statement."

"He must have thought so . . ."

"I said Paul was a generous man," Tha said. Obviously, Lazard had been nettled into some kind of statement, caught off balance by interviewers. "I wasn't measuring his generosity to me, particularly."

"Then where did the money come from, Madame?"

"Oh, a generous source."

"Can you name it?"

"I prefer not."

The man swung to Adam, irritated. "Can you shed any light on this, Major?"

"Sorry," Adam said, his head still bent toward the floor.

"You don't know the mysterious source?"

"Must I?"

"But you must have heard Lady McLeod's interest in Lazard . . ."

She found herself struggling for breath. Part of her lie had been to tell him she'd secured funds by putting a new mortgage on the house at Compiègne. If she had mentioned Lazard at all it had only been in that connection.

"But of course I did," Adam lied.

"That didn't bother you?"

"Wedekind says every Loulou needs to be justified by her burden. Why should it surprise you, every burden needs a Loulou?"

"Is that the new morality, Major?"

"Old," Adam said, "as pimping." He lifted his head toward Tha. His face had gone pale. She was certain that he had already drawn the correct inferences, that he knew the real source of that money—and the falsity of her oath to break with Depardieu.

"The main thing to be is realistic. A man in my position is only alleged to be in the dark, isn't that so, Tha?"

She felt a stab of pain, of apprehension of loss, and they came swarming at her, sniffing at the contradiction, no longer to be denied their victim. They wanted to know how she felt about seeking patrons to finance her charities to a blind war hero. Had she pangs of conscience? How different was she from the self-centered Loulou condemned by Wedekind? Did she think she was too clever to be caught in her deceptions? She felt herself losing control. They knew nothing about her, she flung at them, less about fidelity. Dullards and bookkeepers might keep accounts of love, expecting it to be measured like a long-term gilt-edged bond, preferably locked in a steel vault. But in her life, you went from day to day, giving to each moment and each person what you had to give, always a debtor.

"Once a friend, Count Esterhazy, took me to a duck shoot—which is a glamorous way for Hungarian males to get drunker than usual. I was in a blind and I overheard them accusing me of being a nymphomaniac. Esterhazy said I was in much worse trouble, I was a nympholeptic. I didn't know how wise he was because I had to look it up; and now that I've bared both breasts I'll leave you to run for your dictionaries and come another day."

As she fought her way from them, refusing to answer any further questions, Sita came to her side. Adam had gone back into the hospital, she said. Frantically, Tha made her way down the corridor until she heard the sound of Adam's voice, easy and relaxed, punctuated now and then by bursts of feminine laughter.

She halted at a doorway. In the nurses' lounge, Adam sat on the edge of a desk, surrounded by the young women of the staff, regaling them with his ribald experiences as a seminary student.

Most of his tales had to do with an epic struggle waged by the women of Dijon to take the virginity of a willowy novitiate from China, one Chen Hsiang, over the combined opposition of the student body. Tha often felt that these tales reflected a greater student interest in Boccaccio than in the Bible, yet Adam would always come up with some surprising new episode in the battle to save Chen Hsiang from damnation.

At a pause in his recital, she heard her strained voice suggesting they would be late for the auction.

He lifted his face toward her. Under its convivial smile, there lay the pale pinch of betrayal.

"I'm busy."

"I'll wait."

"Don't. Don't bother."

He swung from her, to resume his entertainment.

She stood stricken, reading her humiliation in the upturned faces of the young nurses. Her eyes scalding, she ran for escape.

BRIDGE ON THE RHONE
27 February 1917

"Sita, stay here. Look after him!"

They plunged down the steps of the hospital. The fiacre still patiently waited at the curb.

"Where are you going, Tha?"

"Nowhere!"

"But where?"

"To the city," she said. "It doesn't matter. See that he's all right."

Somewhere, at the periphery of her vision, she was aware of a governess, in white, standing beside a lacquered black pram. It seemed to her that the woman waved, but in her obsessive desire to get away, she assumed the gesture was meant for somebody else.

"Will you do that, Sita?"

91

"Of course, but what about you?"
"Never mind," she said. "I'll be all right."

She leaned over the bridge railing, without recollection of her plunge down into the city.

Beneath her, water and wind ranted against the piers. Across the lake, the excursion boat cut through the stagey winter light on its run to Yvoire, trailing showy plumes of white water. Along the distant shore, the castles and châteaus seemed one-dimensional, Gothic backdrops waiting for her to perform her act of watery immolation and be swept away with the rest of the effluvia.

Along both railings, bundled figures, faces hidden behind scarves, seemed tied to the river by their fishing lines. Each afternoon, these elderly Drogheldas of both sexes delved hopelessly for their suppers, prodded by scarcity and inflation. They held their posts until darkness drove them away empty-handed, cheated by a distant war and upstream factories that had poisoned river and lake.

The right company for me, she thought. Except they have been defeated by others, while I am my own victim.

In Jakarta, long ago, Sita and her friends had embraced her at a time she wanted only to die. They had taught her that the only stronghold was impermanence. Through them she began to see how she had tried to base her happiness on the life of her small son, that her yearning for an unchanging existence could only lead her to destroying others, or being destroyed herself.

Slowly, they had won her to their own humorous skepticism. "All views of reality," the sage had written, "are flawed. Including this one, of course."

While they taught her their incantations and their oms, they coaxed her to see them as reflections of flux; dharma was a pun, a wise saw, the crock of ages. Since no one could escape the ripsaw of experience, the only relief was to grasp the cosmic joke, to tune the whine of the wounding blade to the high pitch of laughter. And perhaps, by chance, to hear the language of the unutterable in the lives of all about her, who, like herself, by the free fall of the present into the inevitable, yet cried out to make their own destinies.

Slowly the liana of their words had bound up her wounds. She had ceased to hate McLeod, and even those who had taken her child's life; she had not been urged to forgive them, only to stop hoping other people or other things would provide her with a refuge from change, accident, the swerve of time.

And yet, like every despised whore in a Wedekind play, like every plagued female in a romance by De Kock, she had reached out for Adam as the exception, the fixed object that would be her rock of ages, defiantly holding out against the abiding truth of flotsam.

But what now?

She had battered down his defenses only to be revealed as a liar. Thanks to Lazard, Adam knew how she had taken advantage of his darkness and betrayed him. His misery over his condition, the depressions he suffered, would now be cruelly heightened because of her selfishness and folly.

Yet, in spite of all that, she could not let him go. She was Loulou. She wanted to have and to hold, what she had held and had, and which had satisfied her as nothing before in her life. In beseeching him to depend on her, she had become dependent on him; she had tried to make him a fixed object and had become fixed herself.

The wind bit under her furs. Below her, in the rolling water, her face appeared for an instant and then vanished in a plague of light, beckoning her to follow.

Behind her, a voice—a deep female voice, almost as husky as her own—made itself heard above the river's rage: "You led me a fine chase, Madame . . ."

Tha whirled.

A pace away, the governess stood watching her, smiling in condescension. It was the nursemaid with the black pram, a white cap on top of blond wavy hair, a white cape above a spotless white uniform.

"Frau Eva!"

"Frau Eva, *sicher.*"

In the seventh week of the war in Europe, on a quiescent sector of the Belgian front, two inexperienced patrols—one German, the other French—collided, exchanged untidy gunfire, and quickly withdrew to their respective lines. The brief engagement produced a single casualty. Sergeant Hugo Evard Zeit, aged twenty-two, caught a bullet in his windpipe. By the time the patrol got itself together and sent out a party to collect him, Sergeant Zeit had turned irrevocably purple.

Later on, it became traditional to say that from the ashes of Hugo Zeit there had risen the phoenix of his widow, Frau Eva, a soaring spirit no one had ever suspected in her.

Until the first spring of the war, Frau Eva had been a cashier in a small private bank in Metz, and had been considered, and considered herself, a spinster. Though blond and attractive, with an ample, almost matronly body, she had remained aloof from men, avowing that none had excited her.

But the preparations for war, and then the coming of the war, had stirred Eva, flushing her out of her placid rut, thrusting her into contact with many men in uniform, including Hugo Zeit, her junior by eight years, but a tall and handsome man, blue-eyed and blond as herself, and, in many ways, her male counterpart.

Married five days after their first meeting at a canteen dance, Frau Eva took leave from her job, rented a room near Hugo's training camp, and lived the frenzied, transported existence of a war bride. When Hugo was posted to a reserve division, Frau Eva drew a great breath of relief and went back to the bank in Metz. Nobody could have anticipated that Hugo's arrival at his new outfit would coincide with a request for replacements on the Belgian front, and that the division would decide it was easier to ship out the newcomers than to upset its training program.

Shortly after her husband's body had been returned to Metz for interment, Frau Eva applied for a job with the Alsace station of Abteilung Three. She had been engaged as a secretary. Nobody took any particular notice of her radiant smile. It seemed the mien of a war widow, bravely concealing her sorrow. Not until after she began her relentless climb and became the first woman ever to supervise a German intelligence station did people begin to see in her the beatitude of an avenging angel. By then, of course, it was known that Frau Eva considered the coming of war as salvation of her country and its folk, calling them to a destiny that would keep Europe from being submerged in a cold and heartless commercialism—most disgustingly exemplied by the franc-worshipping French, but imitated by some who called themselves German.

As rivals fell from grace or became corpses, Eva continued her rise. Volunteering for dangerous clandestine work in Belgium, she was credited with apprehending a group of English women involved in underground resistance to the German occupation, including the English nurse, Edith Cavell, whose subsequent secret trial and execution became, for *The London Times*, the benchmark of Hun bloodthirstiness.

Frau Eva, her smile more exalted than ever, occupied a resplendent office at Marshal Ludendorff's supreme headquarters. She saw in the marshal that warrior figure, who, like her dear Hugo, would set an example for all men—stern and tender. Assigned to watching the watchers, her influence was feared even in faraway Berlin, the headquarters of Abteilung Three, which considered the hunt for unreliable elements to be not only its function, but the nature of the business itself.

For Tha, Frau Eva had been a figure in the distance, met in passing, to be passed by rapidly. Yet that reaction had puzzled Tha. On the surface, at least, Frau Eva seemed an appealing German matron. And it was not just her physical appearance, but her positive, outgoing manner, the kind of bank cashier who had a bright and pleasant word for all the customers, while dispatching business with brisk efficiency.

But the fear she generated was real. Tha could not help but compare her with Depardieu. In France, the phrase *la patrie* combined mother-father not only in language but in ideal. The perfect functionary was neutered, the style methodical, judgments expected to flow from logical premises, and all personalities and exceptions reducible to categories.

But Frau Eva had a different model. *Vaterland* was the warrior father, so close to death that he had the strength to be tender to his children; a parent who defended emotion and intuition and the certainties of the blood, from which came inner strength and inner discipline. Frau Eva allowed herself to flame—unlike the soulless and materialistic Allies, wedded to commerce and greed—secure that her Teutonic instinct would unerringly lead her to serve the father who protected the nation, and would soon be the guardian of Europe and the world.

Tha, still deep in her introspections, stepped backward, feeling the bridge rail cold against her spine.

Frau Eva brought the pram closer. "Didn't you see me?"

"Not really . . ."

"But you looked right at me, outside the hospital."

"I was thinking about something else . . ."

"I thought you might be trying to avoid me."

"But I had no idea you were in Geneva . . ."

"If you had"—Frau Eva smiled—"would you have given us some advance notice of visiting that café this morning?"

"But I went to find a translator—"

"Yes, yes," the German woman interrupted, not harshly, but impatient to get on with the matter. "A reasonable cover. But what do your friends in Paris want of that species of Russians?"

Tha's mind raced through the possibilities. By tonight, Frau Eva would be reading the Geneva press. It would carry the story about Lazard. It would create a mystery about who had given her a large sum of money. And just as Adam had drawn the correct conclusion, so would Frau Eva. The least dangerous way to dispose of the question was to acknowledge that she had been sent by the Deuxième Bureau. She would confine Depardieu to his Lord Ashley's fancies, and feed Frau Eva and the Abteilung Russian fables.

"Oh"—she shrugged—"to find out which ones Berlin is buying."

"Then?"

"That's all."

"Overbid us?"

"I have no such instructions."

"A pity," Frau Eva said. "I came in a trot, thinking you'd be on an important assignment. They wouldn't use you for trifles."

"Sorry."

"This man, Kuprin—part of Depardieu's stable, too?"

"No, I'm using him only to penetrate their circle."

"Beginning with Martov?"

"You're well informed, Frau Eva."

"Your Depardieu's an ass. Martov may have the majority of adherents, but he doesn't count. There's only one who interests us. The one they call Lenin. As far as we can make out, his chief activity is to go to the library and study Hegelian dialectics. I take it that's not your field, Madame?"

Tha laughed. "Is that the only way to him?"

Frau Eva studied her and shook her head, smiling. "I know how successful you have been, Madame, but with that one, I'd have to say you would fail."

"Not my first."

"Still, we shall find some use for you."

The infant had begun to cry and Frau Eva bent down and took the child in her arms, cooing gently. "How is it, Lady McLeod, you've been here weeks and you have yet to get in touch with Von Tremke?"

Tha felt her stomach contract. "I phoned the consulate twice. He seems never to be in. And he never answered. I thought he must have reasons for not wanting to see me."

"Shall I tell you the reasons?"

Tha nodded, watching the woman coax the child into a smile again.

"Your friend Von Tremke"—Frau Eva did not conceal her contempt—"has jumped, taking the station funds with him. Along with many documents which he imagines will keep him not only safe but rich. That is why I am here and not with Ludendorff."

Tha pressed back against the railing, feeling a chill run through her. "Does that mean I will be reporting to you, Frau Eva?"

Frau Eva nodded. "I've installed myself in Von Tremke's house. This is his youngest. His wife is a hysteric. I never had a high opinion of Von Tremke. We'll catch up with him. We've already settled a masseuse in whose apartment he had hidden certain papers. I assure you I won't leave here until I've done the same for him."

Again the swollen body rose from the depths, to float grayly on the lake, as on that day with Adam. Tha expunged the picture, trying to cope with the more threatening reality of this motherly woman, now so solicitously rocking the child whose father she meant to murder.

"I'm sure you will, Frau Eva."

"Yes." Frau Eva straightened up. "But we must find a use for you. Initially, of course, we will have you feed some false information to Depardieu about the Russians and us."

"Obviously."

"As I said, I thought you would be on something more important, so I haven't thought about it yet. But we will work out a plan, never mind."

"At any time."

A wail broke over them, echoing from bridge and river. Deserting their lines, the fishers began to run past, rushing toward a woman who was leaning far over the rails and pointing down at the water, her anguished cry reaching an ever more disturbing pitch.

Swept along by the crowd, Tha saw something white and hairy come to the surface of the churning current. The woman continued her strangled screaming, but she was saying something that sounded like "Hansie! Hansie!"

The object, which had bobbed up for a moment, swirled in the vortex at the bridge support and was sucked down and out of sight.

The crowd gathered around the stricken woman, trying to calm her. "But it's my fault!" the woman wailed brokenly. "Mine, mine. I knitted a coat for him. Because of the cold, don't you see? It's been so cold. And when he jumped up on the railing, thinking I had caught something, the coat made him lose his footing! My fault! I killed him. Don't you see, because of the cold?"

Trembling, Tha pushed her way out of the crowd, now solemnly surrounding the woman and offering small gestures of consolation on the death of her pet.

Frau Eva pushed the pram toward her, visibly shaken by the woman's loss. "Poor thing," she said. "And that poor animal. The things we do to ourselves . . ."

They walked a moment in silence.

"You jumped so," Frau Eva said. "I had not thought of you as a jumper, Madame."

"Nerveless?"

"No, debonair, always uninvolved . . ."

"That's twice I've disappointed you today."

"About Martov," Frau Eva said, "on second thought, perhaps he can be of value. Let us have his view about Lenin. He'll probably offer nothing beyond the usual Marxist cant, but worth comparing with others. Will you do that?"

"Of course."

"And after you have had your housewarming, then we'll get together and find something worthy of you."

"Is it safe to call you at Von Tremke's?"

"A note in the letter box."

Frau Eva's gaze went out over the lake, calculating. "I've been in awe of you. I mean . . . the way you work—or have been allowed to. But with me, I warn you, no laxity. Even though you were born in Holland, you must feel yourself part of our German destiny."

It was both judgment and dismissal. Frau Eva adjusted her cape in one decisive motion of her shoulders, grasped the handle of the pram, and started away. Garbed in white, armed in purpose, she moved back to the city, ready to engage it, at war again.

All along, Tha had struggled to hold back her fear. But now it passed quickly, leaving her purged and sober, determined to find in herself the will to survive. In dealing with Depardieu, it had been possible to rely on cleverness without manifesting deep devotion to his cause. But with Frau Eva, Tha would be under constant, ominous inspection. She knew Eva held her in contempt as rootless and degenerate, cut off from the deep emotions and the consuming violence of Europe. And, as such, a bit of fluff, readily expended.

There had to be a way out. She would take Adam to Holland. There were scores of people she knew in Amsterdam, ordinary people, far removed from the fevered world of intelligence, citizens who would never recognize themselves in Frau Eva's portrait of the "folk." Of course it would be difficult to find a hiding place for Adam. His blindness would make him conspicuous, his great height would serve to identify him, his sardonic, haughty manner would be a constant source of exposure. Among the flower dealers, she had a friend who was blind and could be counted on; through him she'd met others who, though sightless, had found occupations in the Bourse, taking orders by telephone, transmitting them. And there were blind coffee tasters and wine experts, who might train Adam in their crafts. If necessary, she'd find work at a factory in the outskirts of the city, live apart from Adam and visit him only in safe places at safe times. But above all, she would fulfill the oath to Adam to extricate herself from this war and her paymasters; together they would survive and postpone Sita's wisdom for another day—dharma's habitat.

The crowd accompanied the wretched woman along toward the bank. Tha had the feeling that the animal had been sacrificed in her place, diverting her from her suicidal impulse, a grant of time to gain sanity and resolve.

Gratefully she made the ancient gesture of humility to the gods of river and lake. Her palms turned upward, center fingers joining to form the yoni, the cupped palms the lingam, male and female thrusting in rich disorder, symbol of unlimited energy and life.

She would go back to Adam and plead the loathesomeness of necessity or be abject or whatever else to get her way, until he forgave her lies and other weaknesses and they were safe out of this, on their way to Holland.

"Adam!"

She ran through the foyer of the chalet, Sita behind her. At the foot of the stairs, she looked up, repeating her call, never really believing he would be here.

"But I heard him tell the jarvey to take him back here," Sita insisted. "I'll ask the tenant, maybe he knows."

At the hospital, she had found Sita in tears. Shortly before, Adam had come tearing out, and commandeered the fiacre. He had coldly refused Sita's help, and been driven away.

Now, in the silent house, Tha could only speculate that if he had come home, it was only to collect his things. Yet, this was contradicted by the fact that the bedroom closet still held his uniforms, and his bureau had not been touched.

"Stay, Sita. Let me."

Outside, the wind blew sharply. Deep shadows furrowed the winter fields. There was a threat of snow.

The cottage of the tenant farmer lay several hundred yards up the mountain from the chalet. Smoke came from its chimney. The tenant and his wife had been resentful of the rich foreigners who had leased the property, openly contemptuous of their breeding schemes as the activity of idlers and dilettantes.

Doubtless, her inquiry would encourage fresh sneers. Still, if the fiacre had driven onto the property, they must have seen it.

She had covered half the distance before she heard the barn door banging in the wind.

"Adam!"

He came leading the colt, gentling it, having saddled and bridled the animal. He led it out, against the panic of her shouting, calming it, bringing it to rest.

"Adam!"

He swung up, tall and easy, the habit of a lifetime. She knew that he had accustomed the recently broken animal to him, but, always before, he had ridden in her company, and under her close supervision, even though she tried to make it seem that he was on his own. "Adam!"

Though he must have heard her, he leaned forward, giving the animal its head, letting it gather speed over the rock-hard field. She found herself running after him, in a hopeless and senseless chase, his name echoing endlessly, a cry of dismal abjection.

She came, panting, to a halt.

In horror, she saw him put the mount to full gallop. A tall hedge bordered the field. He was familiar with it, since they had explored every section of the farm, mounted and on foot. They'd even jumped the hedge. But she'd always been at his side, shouting to her mount, giving Adam time to pick up the cue from her, so that he could anticipate the unseen obstacle.

He was moving his hands to the mane of the colt, sensing the approach of the barrier. Tha yearned to take his place, her thighs contracting to the colt's flanks, easing it to the jump. But the animal had been trained to forego its instinct and accept its rider's. It would expect that Adam would shift his weight forward. Without that signal, it was now blind as its rider.

Ten feet from the hedge, the animal refused.

Adam was thrust sharply forward. Only his long arms let him keep a precarious grip on the colt's neck and twist his body to the abrupt change of direction. Before the motion was complete, he had recovered his stirrups.

But then, he was lost.

The yearling, no longer trusting its guide, took the bit and, circling repeatedly, began to rear, determined to throw its rider. Adam needed all his senses to keep the animal from running on its own, but, deprived of sight, lacked the edge in timing so that the colt quickly gained the upper hand, and caused a spill.

Dragged on the ground, Adam wisely abandoned the reins. The colt, tossing its head, streaked for the barn.

Adam climbed slowly to his feet. For a moment, he stood doubled over, then came to his full height, grimacing, struggling for breath. He heard her steps running over the hard ground and he grinned. "Now do you see why they put me in the infantry?"

She was trembling. "If I make you do things like this, then you're right to leave me. Adam, listen, just once more. I'm miserable. I was afraid of Depardieu. Perhaps too frightened. But I promise—it will be your way. I'm not going to put a gun to your head because they put one to mine."

"Why? Do you think they'll change?"

"We'll get out, in spite of them," she said, catching his sleeve. "We'll go to Holland. There are places in Amsterdam where we can hide. Separately, if we have to. Miserably, I suppose. But the war must end soon, and then we can come up, and by then, they'll forget me."

"More frightened of me than of them? That it?"

"Both, both! They have a new woman here for the Abteilung, Frau Eva. She's deadly. But I'll get away, if only you'll give me time—and help me by believing me . . ."

He pulled free of her. "Is that all it is, Tha? Why can't we see where we are? Or I am. I should have let that colt break my neck."

"No, Adam," she begged. "If you want to go free, you can. That's a lie, but at least give me credit for telling you it is."

Adam laughed, but his scorn included himself. "You can't help it, Tha. It's this thing behind your lie. You have to dominate. You'll say you won't make me the hump on your back, but you will. And if we go on, I'll let you. Look, a man in my brigade said he saw you dance, but all he could remember was your eyes. Crazy! A nude dancer, but he remembers the eyes, seeking out each person in the audience, to subjugate, to make him a part of you . . ."

"That was a performance, not me . . ."

"You may think so. It was a mistake to come here, but my mistake, above all." He was silent a moment. "The Germans say, *Hass seight sharf.* Beats eyesight. I hate butchers. You laugh and take their money. I'm in this world, not in your Vedanta. You want your way and I want mine, and even the good Reverend Harris can't help us!"

"I never asked you to stop hating them!"

"You put it differently: sorrow and rejoice over their indecencies for they are ours. But yes, Tha, you want me to be absorbed in you—give up my hatreds that are me, and I won't."

The wind cut at them. She could not evade what he had said, a truth she had acknowledged on the bridge, and which she must not now conceal. She wanted to possess him; to bind him to her; to relax his hatred of the world in his love of her. Yet every offering of her love for him, no matter how sincere, could only appear to him as another chain, so that he felt compelled to demonstrate he would never be dependent on her, even if it meant self-destructive tests like climbing mountains or blind steeplechasing. No doubt, a contest like this would have taken place between them even if he had not been blinded. His blindness only locked them tighter in a spiral which, as he had prophesied amid the laundry, could find its vanishing point only in mutual hatred and mutual destruction.

"I can't give you up, Adam."

"Echo, here—yet I have to, and you have to, Tha."

They walked in silence, surrounded by the cold. At the barn she reclaimed the colt and asked Adam to help her unsaddle it and brush down its wet flanks. They both sought refuge in the task, weighed down by their need of each other, the love that kept them flying to each other, and then apart, as contradictory as the old magic phlogiston that by being added to a substance had the effect of diminishing its weight. Yet, the same chemistry promised a bonding of their differences, unstable, perhaps, but wondrously fulfilling.

When they finished, they went slowly toward the house. The sun had gone out of the sky, and the wind sharpened its bite. At the door of the distant cottage, the tenant's wife stood watching them, arms folded, and Tha imagined a dismissive scowl on the woman's face.

"You want time," Adam said, "and so do I. To gather strength—to cut loose."

"But in the meanwhile, you'll stay?"

"For what it's worth, Tha."

A reprieve. If Adam could not help striking at her to prove himself, neither could she cease to be the out-at-the-elbows starveling of Leeuwarden, trying to anchor herself in his total and undeviating love. Yet, if they could both limit those drives, there was hope of reconciliation.

She tried to joke: "All I ask, she said, lying."

His soft laughter preserved their equilibrium of frustration, and then they bent again to fight the wind.

PARTY OF REDHEADS
3 March 1917

The day before the housewarming, snow fell playfully, turned serious in the middle of the night, and, by the morning, the road up the Gastpod had become impassable.

Near dawn, she heard Adam leave his bedroom. He now slept apart from her, stayed longer at the hospital, found pretexts to avoid her at the farm. One of his strategies was to rise early and preoccupy himself with chores at the stables or connected with the farm, until it was time to take a cab to the hospital. She lay awhile, his voice coming up faintly along with that of the tenant, as they stacked wood for the fireplaces for the party, but she fell back asleep in spite of the racket they were making.

When she came down for breakfast, the house seemed sickeningly hot. Adam, on his way to feed the stock, paused to console her about the snowfall. He had gathered the wood and started the fires, but unless their guests came by skis, there'd be no party tonight.

Tha went bleakly to the window. Great drifts blocked the country road, axle deep. Though the storm had ceased, the wind scuffed up the snow in capricious arabesques, only to slam it down in gross lumps against the fences. The sun had come out, full and strong, but a temperature rise during the day would melt the snow and isolate the chalet even more.

Dawdling over coffee, Tha finally got out her list and the telephone directory, preparing to warn her guests not to attempt the journey. Since some could not be reached by phone, she'd have to hire young men in the neighborhood to deliver messages by hand.

Numbers jumped, and she kept making mistakes. She remembered that Kuprin was not on the list. Since he too had no phone, she would have to send a messenger early so he'd have time to forestall Martov. Everything seemed botched, all her dreams about Geneva collapsed into a shapeless snowdrift.

To her surprise, the tenant's sullen wife came in to take on the role of savior. "We have a carriage sled in the barn," she volunteered. "You can borrow others from people along the road. Your guests can drive to the bottom of the téléphérique and they can be picked up at the top by the carriage sleds and brought here."

With that, the day sprang to life.

Several young men from the nearby farms eagerly hired themselves to deliver her notes with the new instructions for her guests. Sita took charge of the telephone. The tenant appeared to confirm that road crews were at work clearing the lower road and that the téléphérique was operating normally. A half dozen carriage sleds materialized to form a friendly crescent in the driveway.

At noon, women arrived to prepare the food, filling the kitchen with bustle and talk, bringing with them two stringy old men carrying small octagonal accordions, frequently mended at the folds, whose music, accompanying the cooking and cleaning, could not help but drive gloomy spirits to lower domains.

The hubbub lured Adam from his lonely routines, and the farm women elected him to be chef de cuisine. He let them set him to work shucking peas and grinding pepper and passing judgment on the sauces. One of the women had a treasury of peasant jokes and challenged Adam to come up with their Polish equivalents. And he gladly obliged. Between Adam, who had spent his childhood in country kitchens like this, and these Swiss earthlings, an intimacy sprang immediately to life, something both he and they took for granted.

Tha, looking in, discovered him laughing, his face slightly flushed, the women dancing flirtatiously around him, drawn to him not only by his looks but by the indefinable appeal of his solitariness, heightened now by something boyish and unmediated. It was astonishing to see the women flounce their skirts and flash their breasts, confident they would set up a current that must reach into Adam.

Like the women, Tha was tempted to touch him. But she faltered at the last moment, handing him some bowls and making some inane observation. Adam, mistaking the source of her remoteness, told her to cheer up; if the party was half as much fun as its preparation, she'd be the toast of Geneva.

All at once it was evening.

Tha, answering Sita's call, came in to survey the raftered two-storey room that ran the width of the house, combining both drawing and dining chambers. On a long table, serving pieces and glasses glitteringly reflected the fire; mountain flowers had been scattered on the lintels and in the corners, tiny snow flowers in delicate greenery, and they made it seem that the country had crept indoors, subtly forming a garland with flowers painted on the wood of balcony and staircase, inviting Adam and Tha and the women and all the guests to let themselves belong tonight to the magic mountain.

As irrationally as she had deciphered doom in a snow flurry, now her hopes rose maniacally, all difficulties dissolving in the horticultural rainbow, Frau Eva and Depardieu spirited away by mountain elves, herself and Adam entwined with the peasant chorus of the kitchen, beyond the need of complex reconciliations, simply together.

Sita came to her and kissed her. "You were right to

come here. No matter what happens, you must choose and follow your own path."

Tha, throat aching, took the small woman into her arms.

Pressed cheek to jowl in the téléphérique, bellied and bottomed in the carriage sleds, their blood set racing by the crisp night wind, the guests arrived at the front door, festive, randy, ready for anything.

Tha gave up trying to identify them or even greet them. The list, prepared by a Parisian friend, drew mostly on the artistic set, to which Tha had appended hospital obligations, neighbors, and a sprinkling of the horsey crowd.

A few of the arrivals, as she had expected, were intruders, pushing in for a closer look at her even with her clothes on. What startled her was the libidinous behavior of the Geneva gentry. By tradition severely prudent, they had not only brought uninvited friends, but seemed to look upon the party as a revival of those days when Anabaptists had danced naked and agape in the streets of Geneva and almost rediscovered the back door to heaven.

She found herself embraced and cosseted and bussed, not for herself, but as if the coming of Mata Hari to Geneva heralded a bacchanal, her great affair with Paris born again in the dancing wintry air on a night voluptuous with peace.

Seeking momentary respite, Tha joined the farm women struggling with mounds of coats and caps in the foyer, only to find they too had been buffeted by the erotic storm, which they translated as winter madness.

"Lady McLeod!" The voice came from the doorway. "May I introduce my friends?"

Stamping snow from his boots, Martov steered a young woman ahead of him, a woman whose amazing auburn hair, piled in glowing natural waves, framed a face at once falsely actressish and genuinely intellectual. Less to do with her makeup, Tha surmised, then her self-awareness, almond-shaped green eyes flickering everywhere, alert to the response of an invisible audience.

"Madame Inessa Armand," Martov said. "It is possible you have met in Paris . . ."

"Actually"—Inessa smiled—"a group of us went to hear one of those subversive singers at a faubourg café. But you probably have forgotten, Lady McLeod . . ."

"Of course, Inessa"—politeness made the lie easy—"I often go. My secret ambition is to sing like that some day . . ."

Martov deftly spun his rotund body to admit a couple a pace behind him. Inessa, too, side-stepped, with a curious suggestion of a curtsey.

"Madame Lenin and Comrade Lenin," Martov announced. "I took leave to bring along my old prison mates and staunchest adversaries."

This second woman, too, had red hair, only hers was dull and combed back into a severe knot. Square-faced and heavy featured, her wrinkled skin gave her an air of bleak austerity. Only later did Tha glimpse the scar under her high collar, evidence of an operation for goiter, the disease that had aged her so prematurely.

The woman thrust her hand out with disarming directness. "I am Krupskaya," she said, using her name as a title, but without hauteur. "I hope Martov knows what he is talking about when he assures us we will be welcome, since he alone asks us here."

"But please come in, Madame."

Tha felt her hand briskly seized and her body pulled toward the short man. "My husband," Krupskaya said, "likes to be sure."

Oddly, another redhead. Partly bald, his fringe, moustache, and poignard beard were a shade darker than the woman's, yet fiery enough.

He held his ground, until Tha had come to him. He had mastered a trick: by slightly elevating his eyebrows, he could make even a woman as tall as Tha feel herself being looked down at, subliminally reduced.

"I come in place of poor Kuprin, who is down with a cold," the small redhead said. "It's become a badge of our exile, passed from one displaced nose to another. However, for this occasion, perhaps I may be allowed to supply your Major St. Reymont with the latest from his country and ours . . ."

"Lenin reads twenty journals a day," Martov intervened. "Right down to the hair oil ads."

"Particularly the hair oil ads," Lenin grinned. "Alas, as misleading as the rest."

For the first time he allowed his eyes to engage Tha's directly. They were brilliant and lively, but guardians of some inner irony, some element of high intelligence, to be conveyed not by speech, but only by secret glances for the favored few.

"Still, one hopes to make a song sufficient for one's supper."

"Adam will adore it."

She took charge of their coats with the help of one of the farm women, remembering Frau Eva's description of Lenin, wondering if his coming here could be as casual as he and Martov had made it appear.

"You'll find him by the fireplace in the big room . . ."

Lenin took charge. Leading the way, he linked his arm with Inessa's, followed by Martov, leaving Krupskaya to bring up the rear, looking straight ahead, but somehow avoiding the sight of the French woman and her husband, only a pace ahead of her. A soldier marching to her duty, Tha thought, refusing herself even the diversion of jealousy.

The bells of the carriages kept tinkling up the mountain, and new guests poured in. For a time the kitchen was in a panic, certain that the overrun would cause a food shortage and turn festivity to catastrophe.

Somewhere in the swirl of sound and bodies, Tha caught glimpses of the group around Adam at the fire. Adam, intent, was leaning forward, dark among the redheads, their voices carrying in Polish and Russian and German and French, with Krupskaya sometimes being called upon to supply a word for Lenin's halting Polish, while Martov occasionally enriched the linguistic stew with a Yiddish *mot juste.*

At some point, the two grandfathers emerged from the kitchen with their squeeze-boxes, though their chief contribution was to increase the noise level. Finally their screechings drove Inessa, in self-defense, to the piano. Titian hair falling to the keyboard, she played with professional brio. First, some snatches of Beethoven, for Lenin, who stood and applauded. Then popular songs for the guests, and finally, for Tha, some of the faubourg melodies.

In the kitchen, Tha grinned as Inessa swung into one of the less-haunting tunes, humming one about the brave vet who was given a state subsidy to provide him with a wooden member.

> *In his carrying case,*
> *Laurel, palmwood, pepper tree,*
> *Satisfaction a guarantee,*
> *Dear veteran, give us a taste of orange wood?*

The notes brought back a café in the rough neighborhood of St. Denis, and with it, memory of Inessa. An actress, definitely! Daughter of some English actor! Whatever revolutionary novelties Lenin might be presenting the world, in his choice of mistress he was very much in the conventional mold; rise up like a public servant, but lie down with a thespian. But then, as Tha had observed, politicians were, whether by day or by night, old stagers all.

Out of the corner of her eyes, she saw Dr. Harris bearing down on her, paw outstretched. Fortunately, her place in the pantry permitted her a quick shift, and she merged with the crowd until she found sanctuary in the deserted foyer.

On the table near the door, some of the guests had deposited their gifts. They would, she surmised, be the usual tokens, in gaudy gift wrappings. Among them there stood a small bronze. At first glance, it seemed to be the usual curio-store version of the goddess Siva, multi-armed and multi-legged. Yet something about it compelled a closer examination.

Her fingertips traced the delicate carving; discovering that the flow combined male and female in a single torso in a subtle unity that she had almost failed to see. "The one we are and are not," they had taught her in Java, "the one we must and cannot be."

Often, in her dance, she had found her body expressing

a female configuation through its opposing masculine movement, receptivity suddenly a form of assertion, penetrating and
being penetrated, each element passing through and beyond
the other.

But because that had not been the tradition of the
dance in Indonesia, she had rejected the impulse as an expression of her Parisian and contemporary experience, modern and
neurotic and expressing some debility within her. Yet here,
under her hand, was thrilling evidence of an older form, which
must have been suppressed, or kept from her, and which she
had so unconsciously reproduced out of the dynamics of motion and body.

A small card was attached. "To Mata Hari, in appreciation, Hermann Hesse." The name meant nothing to her.
One more on the list of strangers.

"Most unusual," a thin dry voice said. "May I look?"

A man in his thirties, pale and slight, eyes deceptive behind bifocal lenses, reached out for the statue. She watched
him fondle it, almost as she had done, with a sense of awe.
"Probably old," he said with academic nicety. "Probably
genuine."

"Would you happen to know who Hermann Hesse is?"

"You mean—you don't?"

"Don't tell anybody, but no."

The man managed an ironic smile, his hand lingering
over the subtle figurine. "Hesse is a German novelist. He used
to be as famous as his friend Thomas Mann. But now that he
has broken with Kaiserism and the war and made an exile of
himself, nobody mentions him—I mean favorably, not even
here."

Tha wondered over the gift. "Can you point him out to
me? I'd like to thank him."

"Never met him," the man said. "I'm told he was once a
patient at the Carl Jung Institute where I practice. I'm Étienne
Carnet, Dr. Étienne Carnet. I had a referral from your Paris
analyst and I decided this was the time to meet the famous pa-
troness of orphans—"

She set the image back on the table, tightening. She had
no analyst in Paris. The referral, like the mention of orphans,

could point only to Depardieu. Carnet was to be her new control.

"I've been wondering how long you'd take. I suppose we should set up an appointment."

"My calendar is at the Institute."

"If that's the way to do it . . ."

"I prefer it," Carnet said. "This party of yours is an astonishment."

"And to me."

"I mean," Carnet said, "one might imagine the Kuprins or the Martovs out for a binge, but the Lenins—that deserves footnoting, doesn't it?"

Kuprin. Martov. The connections. By this time, Depardieu would have been informed, via some bird in that café, and the word sent to Carnet, who had come posthaste to find out what the Germans wanted in that aviary. This time, she had her bait ready: Frau Eva had been kind enough to supply it.

"My German friends claim Lenin is one of the most important men in Europe. I never heard of him until I got here to Geneva, where they seem to know so many things we're ignorant of in Paris. . . ."

"We can appreciate that from their point of view," Carnet agreed. "I suppose they have to see farther east than we do—"

He stopped there, half turning toward the gift table, as Inessa appeared at the end of the hallway and came toward them. Carnet addressed himself to the figurine, using his index finger in clinical precision, marking an anatomical chart.

Androgyny, he lectured, harked back to bacilli, just as the Fall of Man reflected the sexual separation in the cell, an unexpected and mysterious descent that turned us all into Humpty Dumpties, whom not even the heroics of Dr. Freud and Dr. Jung could mend.

"Excuse me, Tha . . ."

"Inessa."

"They're having this fierce discussion in the kitchen," Inessa said, "and your Adam asks you to join them."

Tha introduced Carnet. "You'll excuse me, Doctor?"

"You won't forget our appointment?"

"Count on it."

"Then don't let me keep you from your most important guests."

She took Inessa's arm, and the doctor's derisive smile haunted her down the hall.

More like a magician daring an audience to catch him out, Tha decided, ducking in among the packed, rapt group in the kitchen.

Lenin stood behind one of the long tables, challenging the guests to fire questions at him. Sipping a beer from time to time, making a point with a flourish of a slender length of sausage, he glanced down at the watch he'd placed on the board, to remind himself that the trick of argument, no less than that of politics, lay in timing. His bright eyes savored the contest, his body pirouetting at each thrust, then standing still to admire his own counterthrust.

As she made her way toward Adam, Tha felt plummeted into the obsessions of the war. The everlasting war. The apparently valid aims and ethics of both belligerents; German culture posing as the defender of humanity from English mercantilism; England declaring itself the moral savior of the world, snatching it from the jaws of Teutonic barbarism; the French, while fighting alongside English, Italian, and Russian monarchs, stoutly waving the flag of the Republic.

Making the partisans of both sides reach to grasp these dizzying contradictions, held above their heads like balloons, puncturing each one with sardonic relish, Lenin guided them down from the ethers of European rivalries and nationalisms, along the slopes slimy and hideous with bowel-bayoneted soldiery, into the pit of world revolution, tantalizing them all the way with hope of peace.

Adam edged along the bench, making room for her. He broke off a piece of his sausage. "Polish," he whispered. "Gift of our friends . . ."

Krupskaya, on his other side, had to whisper a pedantic emendation. "It comes from a factory next door to us. The stench must reach to Poland. Could that be how it gets its name?"

Somehow, the words coincided with one of Lenin's dramatic pauses and carried through the room, which came down in relieved laughter.

Lenin put down his beer. His brows knitted, as if she had deflated his argument.

"Complaints, Krupskaya?"

"Forgive me, Ulyanov . . ."

"But you make my point." The sausage was a rapier tipped toward the boisterous room. "Recently, a brilliant young friend, Bukharin, came to visit—and of course we apologized for our neighbors. But he took one delighted bite and told us we were discarding our own dialectic. He reminded us that from such noxious material, shaped by intention, comes the movement of history. The offal negated by the casing, both by the link, hence the advance to the next stage—even though Krupskaya or I may wince at the first step in the process."

"Cringe," Krupskaya corrected. "When I go out on the street, I am the historical absolute pursued by all the mongrels in Zurich!"

Martov had been staring moodily into his glass, not joining the laughter. "Nevertheless, Lenin, doesn't your thesis turn us all into the offal of history?"

The poignard beard jutted toward Martov. Tha had a sense of the pair locked in primeval contest: the round, circumvalent personality, clumsily advancing on a darting spirit, losing him when it seemed certain he had him in a bear's embrace.

"We let Hegel speak of history as a god," Lenin said. "We demystify it, humble sausage makers."

"But you say this war strips us of morality, our enemies force us to expediency; but how and when do we break the link between intolerable means and noble ends?"

"When we are in power, Yuri."

"What tyrant doesn't wave that knout in his fist?"

"When we take power, we will have ended the contradictions between the classes, and with it, the need for expediency, so that morality can reassert itself."

"Does that mean we can only have morality when there is no change? When can that be, Lenin?"

Impishly, Lenin turned to the room with an exaggerated sigh, as over a favorite but refractory student. "Let me translate," he said, taking the guests into his confidence. "You may think Yuri and I are arguing about ethics. Not at all. We are contending over the future of Russia. In a fortnight— around Easter—the war-weary and hungry masses in St. Petersburg will come out to the streets for bread and peace. Wouldn't you think that for once we have resolved Martov's question? That at last we can employ noble means to a noble end?"

Beside her, she felt Adam lean forward, anxious to catch some resonance she would not hear; his body taut to respond to a pull, some attitude beneath the argument which he related to his own turmoil.

"You agree?" Lenin asked, with an air of amazement. "All in agreement! I must become a citizen of Switzerland!"

The audience, having had a taste of him, waited for the balloon's sudden bursting.

"Now on top of all those salutary ingredients, I add yet another. The Czar himself, our Nicholas, is sending his agents to encourage the demonstrators. Nine rubles a man. Isn't that the rate, Yuri?"

"Nine."

"You will ask, what brings the Czar on the side of angels? Well, he seeks a provocation. A pretext to break with the Allies. The people are opposed to war. So Nicholas will crush this demonstration, using it to tell his Allies he must make a separate peace with the Germans—and thus save his throne! True, Yuri?"

"I am convinced of it."

"But wait—I have more tasty items! Agents of the English Allies are also nobly at work in St. Petersburg. They too are paying men to shout for peace and bread. Ten rubles! Their goal, of course, is to overthrow the Czar, establish a government under Kerensky, and continue the war. Yes or no, Yuri?"

"Quite."

"Well, with everybody so ethically unsullied, what is to be done? How can we prevent these spotless means and impeccable ends from turning us into what Yuri just called the offal of history?"

Martov growled into his heavy chest. "No ethics now, Ulyanov, if you please. I want peace and I will settle for the peace *and* the Czar. You will not. You will get revolution *and* more war."

"But the question is: shall the men go out on the streets or stay at their benches?"

"Stay."

"Let Kerensky lead the revolution? Do we weaken the demonstration so that the Czar can crush it?"

"Tell the people they are cat's-paws."

"They know that," Lenin shot back. "But whose cat's-paw—the Czar's or Kerensky's or ours? I say, the storm first, explanations later, take the rubles of the Czar and Kerensky, and into the streets!"

"The principle—on some other day, the truth?"

"The principle—power!"

"We the liberators are the end, the masses are the means. In short, the revolution upside down."

"The principle is men in motion, to which no absolute of morality can be applied."

"But without such a fixed position, how can we judge the direction?"

"I will settle for less, Martov," the small man said, with the first touch of weariness. "That is, the party . . . must ride the storm, created by the enemy, over conditional ground, to problematic ends . . ."

Krupskaya half rose, her gray skirt flying out, in alarmed cover. "You mean, Ulyanov, our enemies attempt to ride the masses, while you and the party will be elevated by them, guiding and also being guided by them?"

For one brief interval, Lenin's face revealed an almost agonized patience, only to mask itself again in smiling irony, bidding all those present to be of, and yet above, the noisesome business of the world, linked by the past, but unlinked by con- sciousness and logic.

"As I am by you, Krupskaya. As tonight we exiles have

all been, thanks to the attention of this fine company . . ."

He had brought it off, and the disdain was safely buried once again. Tha watched him take a sip of the beer, mostly for punctuation, before he slipped his watch into his vest pocket, with all the practiced gestures of a performer letting the applause roll over him.

"We have a train to catch back to Zurich. We have enjoyed our encounter with you and with history, which we can no more shake than our shadows . . ."

He came around the table and approached Adam. "You're coming to the téléphérique with us, Major?"

"Yes." Adam rose. "Yes."

Lenin gave him his arm. "Splendid."

Adam, turning to Tha, seemed pale with excitement. "I'll have one of the young neighbors look after me."

They gathered themselves for their exit, more or less as they had come, except that now Adam was steered between Lenin and Inessa, while Krupskaya and Martov, demoted to diplomacy, said a word or two to the guests before bringing up the rear.

Near the door, Dr. Carnet observed the procession through his deceptive bifocals. The psychiatrist was caught by the odd union of Adam St. Reymont, the intransigent individualist and aristocrat, suddenly arm in arm with the Russian gospelizer of the coming century of the leveled masses. Earlier, Tha had heard Lenin say that history was always a misalliance of glory and abomination, and if you sought one, you would always get the other. Now, linked with Adam, he seemed to be illustrating his own paradox.

For a moment, Carnet's gaze locked with Tha's. Between them they recognized the contradiction; and then both shrugged, helpless before the insoluble puzzle.

But the guests were swirling around Tha. They wanted their drinks refilled, or they claimed her attention for themselves and Geneva, and Tha had to let go one riddle to give herself to a series of lesser but more urgent ones.

Somebody remembered the téléphérique stopped at midnight, and Tha watched her guests go pell-mell for their coats and hodge-podge and piccalilli into the carriages, anointing her with moist kisses, vowing love until the last clock ticked in Geneva.

Finally she stood alone at the roadside. The carnival cries faded down the mountain. The grandfatherly musicians, stiff-kneed with the effort to appear sober, touched their caps to her and wandered home. From the house came the racket of the farm women, making sure not to waste half-empty bottles and glasses, merry but waning.

In the crisp night, snow and stars joined in blithe radiance, indifferent to her problems and her hopes. For a moment, in the kitchen, Adam's warmth for the Russians had seemed to include her. Now, in his absence, she had misgivings. Apparently the visitors wanted something from Adam; they had come to see him, as Carnet had suspected. But even if the Russians enlisted Adam in some activity of theirs, it might only strengthen his resolve to leave her and find some new independent place for himself, part of his plan of estrangement.

Starting back to the house, her coat draped around her shoulders, she caught sight of a lone figure on the slope above the tenant's cottage. In the light of the stars, it took some moments for her to decipher his strange gyrations.

Prone on a child's sled, a man was propelling himself by arms and legs up the incline, then descending with a whoosh, only to swerve and keep himself in a tight circle. That accomplished, he began to flail up the mountain again.

A drunk, she decided. No party could be complete without one. It would be the appropriate climax of her potpourri night to have to struggle with some strange madman.

Absorbed in his antics, he took no notice of her approach. She was virtually on top of him and he still did not cease his fishlike exertions.

"Hello," Tha said. "Hello, friend?"

He went on thrashing.

"Time to leave, sir."

"Soon."

He labored to fin himself up the hill.

"Everybody's gone," she pursued patiently. "You'll miss the téléphérique."

"As soon as I tunnel through the mountain."

"Won't that take time?"

"Not with black magic."

"Why not use it to catch the téléphérique?"

For the first time, he turned from his labors and looked up at her. His face was tanned and puckish, the tall dome of his forehead set off by large gold-rimmed spectacles, now clownishly spattered with snow.

But of all his features, she saw only one: the color of his hair.

"Another redhead! Magic, indeed!"

He removed his comic spectacles. Piercing blue eyes studied her. "What's magic about that?"

"I'll explain," she said, "if you promise to go home."

He shook his head in protest.

"But you came when I called. We're scheduled to whirl through the mountain—and discover ourselves in the light at the end of the tunnel. How can you desert me now?"

She couldn't help but be amused. But she said, "Some other time."

He breathed on his spectacles, surrounding himself with his own small cloud, a creature of another world. "Do you think, would you say, we'll look as fantastic as we do now?"

From that drollery, it was an easy leap:

"You gave me that bronze!"

He nodded, almost gravely.

"Why to me?"

"Intended for you."

"But—it's so valuable—and you don't even know me!"

"Waiting to give it to you," Hesse said. "Ever since I saw your photo with the silver figurine of Saint Mathias . . ."

"But that was—before the war—ages ago!"

"Still have my clipping. Worn to shreds. Still makes me laugh, Mata Hari."

She shook her head, overwhelmed by the strangeness of this man and his quixotic homage. "But it's another world, gone, destroyed!"

"Not at all—I'm here." His eyes, bright and laughing, transported her back to a moment she imagined everybody in the world—except herself—had forgotten. A moment that had almost ended her career.

Not long after her debut in Paris, an impecunious photographer had persuaded her to pose with a small African figure carved in ebony. The idol, majestically crude, was a
vertical rod from whose center there sprang another rod, black
and rigid and horizontal, of the same thickness as his body, half
his height.

The publication of the photo had brought down right-
eous thunderbolts. Politicians, churchmen, educators, hurled
first. Demonstrators appeared in front of the theatre. Furor. A
gamut of straight-laces. Future engagements canceled. From
being the resplendent nude, darling of pagan Paris, she was
suddenly turned into a degraded debauchée, defiling hearth
and home. Her fame, a product of the sensational press, over-
night became infamy.

Then the mail brought the tiny silver figure of Saint
Mathias. The accompanying note informed her that it was traditional to bestow the gift on girls in Brittany at their church
confirmation. Saint Mathias, in all respects but color, was an
exact replica of his ebony brother.

She had summoned her photographer and smiled into
the camera the way girls were supposed to smile on confirmation day. Even donned white, though the collar showed an ex-
panse where, suspended from a chain, nestled the sanctified
phallus.

And that photograph had been the tocsin of a coun-
terattack on the bluenoses. The boulevard wits led off by posing the hypothetical question of why the fellow left the warmth
of Africa to endure Brittany's rigors. A balladist replied.
Mathias had come north to save the menfolk from the wicked,
insatiable Widow of Brittany. He had vanquished the widow,
who, in revenge, called on the Devil to punish Mathias by ossi-
fication in the act. For his bout with Satan, Mathias was made
the guardian saint of young girls, warning them against the
widow.

Parisian lyrics had been abetted by Parisian avarice.
Thousands of the silver pendants appeared in the boutiques,
spread to the stalls, and from there to the faubourgs and provinces. And her photo, making her the invincible consort of
Saint Mathias, had seemed to the artists and people of Paris a

flash of the future, free from punishments, immune to thunderbolts.

"Not gone," Hesse said. "Never will be."

He spoke out to the starlit night, as if he had just had Saint Mathias's own assurances.

"How can you be so sure? When I asked people tonight about you, they said you are hated. Because you don't celebrate killing and mud. Maybe there never was anything else, and we made up childish games, not to see it."

He ignored her speech. "I'll pull you up half the hill, and you pull me up the rest, and we'll ask the old man of the mountain for an answer . . ."

"I'm serious!"

"If you are, you'll pull!"

She examined him again. He wore a corduroy coat and a woolen shirt, both open at the throat. His red hair was a wild crown, stiff and bristling. For all his high brow and finely pointed face, he seemed a creature of the out-of-doors, the itinerant of a country road, with a pack on his back, selling charms from farm to farm, which, once he left, would no longer be talismanic, but just gaudy trinkets.

"Very well." She took up his challenge. "But you first, Hesse."

He waited for her to mount the sled. Though he was slender and not quite so tall as she, he seemed to enjoy his task, grasping the rope, bending foward, his body light and lithe. She heard him began to sing, partly a chant, almost as if it were a work song.

> *Om ist Bogen*
> *Das Brahman is des Pfeiles Ziel*
> *Das soll man unentwegt treffen . . .*

The words were familiar enough. They had their counterparts in a dozen languages. She had heard it first in a Malay version, sung to her in the tropic air by a friend of Sita's. *The Void is the bow / Essence is the arrow's target / Do not cry out / When pierced.* Bliss could never be hunted. It was slippery with the

slipperiness of being—a shadow whose existence manifested itself only when tripped over.

"That used to comfort me," she said. "No more."

"Have you read my books?"

"Not one."

"You're in all of them. I saw you dance in Berlin, but I
had already imagined you in Delhi. I put you into my stories. If
they destroy you, what will I do for a heroine?"

"Pity both of us."

"Do you still dance?"

"No."

"Why not?"

"The war," she jabbed. "Besides, dancing in the nude is
no longer a novelty."

"It never was. That's not what we came to see."

She remembered Adam's accusation of erotic domi-
nance, and she struck out at that and at Hesse simultaneously.
"I'm not sure I ever was a dancer. Colette wrote I can move but
not dance."

"Colette," he laughed, "is a fine novelist, which is to say,
an idiot when she leaves her own garden." He had begun to
pant. Great lungfuls of steam rose to join him with the Milky
Way above them, at the same time inviting it to reach down to
them.

"Colette is myopic. You moved with the ghost of the
times, helix of belly and thigh and vulva. When you moved,
that was the dance and we saw it for the first time."

Tha shrugged. That might explain Colette or him; her
fame, like her present condition, still seemed beyond the grasp
of his description. "Whatever," she said, "I no longer have it."

"My friend Cocteau wrote to me he heard you sing.
Street songs. He says one day you'll be more famous for that
than for your dancing!"

"They do it better in the faubourgs."

"A cellar voice. He says when the men come out of the
trenches, they'll want you to sing for them."

"Even if the note is fear?" she asked. "Fear—not because nothing matters, but because you shrug because nothing
matters."

He lost his footing, came up, breathless, avoiding her question. "See—I'm determined to go through the mountain."

"My turn?"

"Not yet."

She wanted to thank him for his kindness and change the subject. Yet he had come with his gift and she knew that, under his talk about Cocteau, there was the aim of deeper communion.

"Your lover," Hesse asked, "the blind soldier, can't he help?"

"I make that impossible."

"How?"

"By being in this war—like everybody else—grabbing while you can before everything is destroyed."

"And grabbing stops the fear?"

"No!"

"The only way not to fear is not to feel?"

"Yes." She nodded tightly. "Now, my turn!"

She forced him to stop. In silence, they exchanged places.

She could not disguise her distress, for it seemed to her that he had invaded a part of her she wanted to keep only for her own inspection.

"How do you know so much about me?"

"I don't."

"But those questions."

"I've lost everything—wife, sons, friends, books, house, country—does it surprise you I've been on the same street as my heroine?"

"And you're not afraid?"

She heard him laugh behind her, as she bent to the hill, the rope tight in her palms. "You make it difficult. I thought I could make love to you and solve everything. But here you are, asking me to be the old man of the mountain!"

"Nothing less!" Her voice rang out over the silent hill, attended by mute stars and dumb galaxies. "You didn't get me to drag you up the hill to seduce me!"

His sigh was an exaggeration. "Low intentions and high altitudes. I should have known I would fall in between!"

She laughed at his evasion. The physical exertion was a relief. She lengthened her stride, half running as the crest came in view, welcoming the rasp in her chest, substituting the raw pain for her exasperation with Adam, herself.

At the top, her last energy expended, she flung down the rope. Hesse rose and came to her side. Only the sky was above them. The stars stayed put. Except for the silence that moved out there, it seemed all decoded and designed, a domestic rug with holes in it.

Hesse scanned it for a sign. "What goes up, the oracle said, must come down."

"That's all?"

"Together."

"No magic?"

"On the way down, we'll perform it . . ."

"How?"

He guided her back to the sled. She assumed the front seat, feet on the crosspiece.

"You say fast, thoushaltnotkill, faster, faster, as we go."

Puzzled, she asked, "And then?"

"Then you say it backwards. Then you tear it apart. Kill thou, not shalt. An improvement. Kill shalt, not thou. Still better. Thou kill, not shalt. Liberation. Over and over, until it is not a commandment, not words, not the world or you, but conducting the stars to the beat of your own blood, the colored rings of your own retina thrown out like hoops in a circus fair at a distant planet, sure to miss, sure to catch, while we shout it all the way down the hill."

"And then no fear?"

"If it seems to remain, I'll teach you a poem I wrote at the age of five. It is about nits. In praise of nits."

She came into his arms, wanting to be part of his airy acceptance of the contrariness of the void, and the unpredictability of human possibilities, so reminiscent of Sita's, so much like her own vanished beliefs. She leaned back, her body between his thighs, feeling his heat, and then he thrust off, sending them skiing downward, he roaring at the top of his lungs and forcing her to vie with him and outdo him, rendering and rending the most sacred of all human injunctions, their voices flung at the stars, their warmth carving a tunnel in the cold mountain, the carpet raveling and the stars released from all patterns, their bodies pressed in the quicksilver union of the ecstatic sculpture, a whirling cartharsis of disassociation.

Just short of the main house, they came to rest.

He helped her up. "Nits?"

Exhilarated, she shook her head, her body still attuned to dervish abandon. Her hands were icy and she thrust them to his neck, for warmth, for touch, for gratitude. "We should make love in the snow, and say it so fast it becomes real."

"Not if you mind your tenant and his wife watching us."

She swung to the dark cottage, but could see nothing. "They must have gone away."

"Besides," Hesse said, "your soldier's come home."

"Adam? When?"

"While you were hauling me."

"Why didn't you tell me?"

"I'm not the man of the mountain. Only Harry Hesse."

Involuntarily she took a step back toward the house, but caught his look of quizzical incompletion and came back to him, to join her mouth to his. His lips were cold, but the inside of his mouth burned and there was a sweet taste to him. She moved slowly against him, as once she had danced, awakening him.

"You gave me more than I deserve."

This time she ran for the house. She felt heartened, not only by Hesse's flattering ardors, but because he had recalled her to her own possibilities. Perhaps there was still time to retrace her steps, reminded that it was possible to prevail over the pressure of war, and refuse to succumb to either covetousness or despair. She must make another start with Adam, struggling for a new balance in herself, restoring each other to freedom.

At the door, she paused, watching Hesse ride the sled down toward the téléphérique and slowly disappear from sight. Still aroused, and without guilt, she went in to look for Adam.

"Tha?"

"Yes."

"Have a drink with me."

He was seated on a small stool near the fire, bare feet stretched toward the flame. Beside him lay a damp heap of boots, socks, coat. He had a bottle of champagne in his hand.

"How'd you get so wet?"

"Walked up the road."

"No carriage?"

"Sent it back. I fell down once or twice. Fine! Can't you find a glass?"

She tried to imagine him coming up the hill by himself, the cane beating against the fences, breasting the drifts. His face seemed demonic, his eyes half closed against the fire, and she couldn't decide if it was the drink, the bout with the hill, the Russians, or all three.

"I heard your guests! Yelling! Charged up like me! In spite of everything, a housewarming!"

In spite of. "Yes, it was."

"Those Russians—that Lenin—a fist of a man."

"Combative."

"Don't underestimate him," Adam said. "I did at first. Because of his poor Polish. But there's damn little he doesn't know about Poland. He was an exile in Riga. He's friendly with my cousin, the novelist, Wradislaus St. Reymont. Aren't you going to drink?"

"I've had enough."

"I have a mountainous thirst."

"Do, for both of us."

Adam tilted the bottle. "He tells me the Germans are using the St. Reymont novels to control the Polish peasantry, set them against both the factory owners and people of the ancien régime like my dearest mother, or even dreamers like Wradislaus or me. The one called *The Peasants* is now required reading for staff officers. He calls my cousin a Tolstoyan, still harking back to feudalism of a benevolent kind. He even knows things about me, things I haven't thought about in years. Even that I was once a Callip."

"A what?"

"Callip. Short for Callipolists. The elite, in Plato's *Republic*. Leaders chosen, not because of land, or family, but on merit. A group of us, before the war, used to get together. Caroline was part of that mob."

"Caroline—the same one I know?"

"She hung about, mostly for screwing. The talk bored her. There were others. The Duc de Guise, who is some sort of cousin, my father used to say. Your friend, the Dutch Crown Prince, and, from time to time, bloods from Prussia and Bavaria, oh, everywhere, we sat around hoping Europe would get sick of its tradesman, in and out of office. Then the war came. And that ended that."

"Lenin knew all that?"

"Even names I'd forgotten."

"Sounds as if he filched your police dossier."

Adam's brow wrinkled. "Is there one on me?"

"On everybody."

Adam dismissed the idea with a wave of the bottle. "You have a bad case of Depardieu."

"Is that all he did—reminisce?"

"Far from it."

Tha moved around him. "I thought not."

"If you're going to take that tone, Tha," he said, "let's drop it."

She watched him take another pull, and reached for the magnum. "I think I'll have a swallow, Adam." He stretched the bottle to her. "I'm jealous. Seeing somebody else get you high."

"You should have heard him!" Adam brightened at once. "He says the war will end soon."

"How? With his sticky bread riots in St. Petersburg?"

She drank and gave the bottle back. Adam rotated it in his palms. "Tha, that's rot. But there are other ways. He quoted Napoleon. About the press. What gunpowder did to the aristocracy, print is going to do to the bourgeoisie."

"For example?"

"I can't go into it yet."

"Why not?"

"He asked me not to. It's premature."

"You and he have a private way of ending the war? God, Adam, what are you saying?"

Adam rose. He clasped one of the legs of the stool in his fist, waving it. "I know I'm being used. He calls me a *lumpen aristocrat.*" He wavered a step away. "But if he uses me for his ends, I'll use him for mine!"

She took a seat on the hearth, uneasily watching his uncertain ambulations. "I suppose he didn't mention being in the pay of the Germans?"

He swung about, startled. "Where'd you get that?"

"Intuition."

"Also known as Abteilung Three?"

"No—just from what I sense. But Depardieu's man, Dr. Carnet, showed up tonight. And he wants me involved with them. Adam, don't go near them!"

Adam held out the stool, lion-tamer, keeping her at bay. "Kismet. You tell me about it. Why can't it work for me?"

"I only ask you not to stir yourself up, all for a big crash."

"But I feel this strongly. I resisted coming to Geneva. But you made me. Then, instead of a translator, Lenin turns up when I can't think of any further reasons to hang around. On the planet, I mean. And now I see a chance to do something— something I've been aching to do since the first shell went over my head and killed two men eight feet behind me. Can't tonight be my Kismet for one goddamn time?"

"But there were choices all along, weren't there? And there's one now."

"Let me tell you about that first shell . . ." He was pacing, hardly listening, inflamed. "One of those two men was a mean bastard. He would sing when he heard about another poilu getting it. He'd sing, 'He's gone to where there's no red wine, he's gone to where they don't drink champagne!' " Adam almost slammed into a chair, and turned and came toward her again. "How I hated that bastard. Yet, how guilty I felt he got it instead of me. Now—why can't I prove I was meant to survive them . . . and Vittel . . . that it all had a purpose?"

She could see that the wine was getting to him, and that her opposition would only stir him to an anger more intense than his euphoria.

"When is all this supposed to happen?"

"Soon!" He slammed down the stool on the hearth. "Tha, believe it! Or let it alone!"

"Can't I ask a question?"

"No! Yes! The answer is, I don't know. Maybe never. Dr. Harris will tell me I'm getting even with my mother, or my father, or somebody. And you chant Abteilung and Depardieu, but my answer is, it's like in the trenches; there's always somebody left to apply the law of averages. This time, me!"

"All right, Adam."

"Tonight"—he waved buoyantly—"it's on to Gilead, and to hell with you. I'm going to get sloshed on all that champagne you bought for your party, and I'll make the house fly until dawn . . ."

She came to his side and reached up and kissed him. He did not recoil. For the first time since their wounding fight, she felt his body graze hers. But she knew that his mind and emotions were winging, that he had already left her on the ground.

"Good night, Adam."

"A great housewarming, Tha."

"Let's hope."

Sometime after she got into bed, she could hear him singing at the top of his lungs.

Champagne makes loose women tight!
Wine into water and water into wine,
There'll be a miracle tonight!

His voice faded into her dream. It was one of the few dreams in which a color appeared. Bright red was the piping in the hat of a young Dutch sailor. She encountered him on a country road, while running from McLeod, who was out searching for her, trying to beat her into submission, refusing to give her a divorce, barring her from seeing Banda. The sailor was on his way to his ship. As soon as she saw the sailor, she ran to him for protection. He misunderstood and threw her down in the field and raped her. She went down to the canal to bathe away the dirt. He returned, apologetic and gentle, naïvely saying he had known only whores. She relented. They made love in a wheat field. He had blond hair like Frau Eva's and eyes that were bluer than Hesse's. They went back to the canal and he bathed her and later they found each other in the water, which ran thick and muddy and warm. She dove to the bottom and when she surfaced, he was gone, leaving behind only the hat with the red piping.

A loud crash awakened her.

In the living room, she found Adam sprawled comfortably on the hearth. A table and chair had been overturned. She fetched a pillow for his head and used the piano cover to put over him. Kneeling to kiss him, she was overwhelmed by her love for him, even for his ridiculous hopes about the war. Deeper than their divisions were their affinities, their excesses, their dreams.

But she could not go back to sleep. Instead, she climbed to Sita's room and woke her. In the darkness, they began to plan the escape to Holland. Sita would go first, immersing herself in the numerous Indonesian colony in Amsterdam, using it as a base to make quiet contact with Tha's old friends, and with their help find a room in an industrial suburb for her, and another for Adam. Sita, cross-legged on the bed, eagerly recited the names, the steps. The road had led to the mountain and the party; now it was moving on to other destinations, as Sita had always hoped. She would go as soon as Tha secured a visa for her, and even envisaged the day Banda would join them.

Back in her own room, Tha felt weary, but too excited to sleep. She would let Adam's millenary fever run its course, and when it did she would effect her plan. Not only the practical plan she'd concocted with Sita, but the one Hesse had evoked—the one that might yet let them live, in spite of the horrors, more horrible for being celebrated as triumphs of civilization and progress. Somehow, she and Adam would escape, forging their own Kismet.

ZURICH TRANSFER
6 March 1917

The card had a black border and bore the Imperial German crest. In sedate script, it set forth the time and place of the private interment of Baron Joachim von Tremke, attaché of the Geneva Consulate.

From the instant her fingers brushed the embossed double eagle, a shiver of apprehension ran through her. It was not an invitation, she knew, but a command. Frau Eva wanted her on hand, not to mourn, but to applaud, and be warned.

The Geneva newspapers had all featured the story of the attaché's suicide. It had apparently taken place on the night of the housewarming, though Von Tremke's body had not been discovered until days later. He was found in an obscure apartment, bullet in his temple, gun in hand. Police authorities disclosed that on the desk there had been a notice recalling Von

Tremke to active duty with his old regiment on the eastern front. Beside the notice lay a brief note to his wife.

Adam couldn't help but be curious about the invitation. It had been delivered by special messenger from the consulate, and the man had waited for her receipt and reply.

Tha tried to put a good face on it.

The funeral would provide her with an opportunity to meet Frau Eva and wangle a visa for Sita to leave for the Netherlands, via Germany. She would intimate to Frau Eva that she had been unable to pierce Lenin's defenses; and she would tell Carnet the same story. Of course, the Lord Ashley invention, which had been her excuse for coming to Geneva, would now have to be terminated. She would tell Depardieu, via Carnet, that Lord Ashley was being threatened with divorce by his wife and had refused to come to Geneva. "I'm sure I can get us out to Holland," she had told Adam. "But it's going to take a few weeks."

"Fine—but let's see how things develop first."

"Of course, Adam."

Ever since the housewarming, he had been preoccupied with the Russians. Kuprin had turned up and the haggard student was a daily visitor. He not only read to Adam from the newspapers, but served as his secretary.

Adam had launched a correspondence with his aristocratic friends far and wide. Though he made no effort to conceal this from Tha, neither did he share it with her. He would fall silent when she came into the room while he was dictating. Clearly his letters were going to his old Callip associates, but what she heard sounded like light, personal stuff, with only a slight reference to the possibility that the war would end soon, the killing stopped, yet stated as a general hope, rather than a specific goal.

Nevertheless it was obvious Adam was on tenterhooks, waiting for a message from Lenin. He would stand on the road, impatient for the sounds of Kuprin's arrival. The translator would accompany Adam on long walks. Clearly Kuprin was acting as conduit for Lenin and Martov. About these conversations Adam, still smarting from her skepticism, remained secretive.

She drew what solace she could from his improved mood. He seemed to have overcome his spasms of suicidal depression. And she responded to his cheerfulness, concealing her own terror that his high-stakes partners would leave him in ruins, a certain victim of self-destruction.

Perhaps by coincidence the hospital reported a marked improvement in the condition of his eyes. Dr. Harris predicted Adam would soon be able to undergo surgery, and that recent surgical successes gave every reason to hope for a distinct gain over his present vestigial vision.

As usual, Adam scoffed at Harris. The doctor was generalizing from a few instances, and even in those cases there'd been reason to hope from the start. Yet, in an unguarded moment, Adam confessed to Sita that the idea of replacement of his infected eyes by artificial ones had depressed him more than he knew; now the abatement of his infection, and hence the removal of the threat of enucleation, made all the other torments of his blindness somehow more bearable.

The morning of the funeral, spring came prematurely to the Gastpod. The change of seasons occurred in the space of hours. The morning sun poured fire over the eastern peaks, and melting snow tore gashes in the frozen ground. Suddenly, in these wounds, tiny growths began to appear as if they had been lying in wait all winter for this moment of puckish annunciation.

Tha, getting into a black dress, looked out the window to see Adam in the corral with a local breeder, who had turned up with two mares. Miffed because he'd failed to get his price at the auction, the breeder had now decided to sell to Adam at a bargain. He insisted that he did this, not out of pique, but because of Adam's war record, and because his forebears, like Adam's, had been refugees from the French revolution. Adam, amused, continued to bargain. She watched him running his hands along the body of one of the mares, to discover some new haggling point.

By the time she came down, Adam was on the phone in another room and the breeder was at the dining room table, laboring over a bill of sale. They had brought out the traditional bottle of cognac, and Tha, glancing at her watch, agreed to stay and help seal the transaction.

Adam, returning, looked flushed and triumphant, and Tha assumed it was because of his successful horse-trading.

Almost brusquely, Adam urged her to finish her drink and then walked with her to her car.

"That was Kuprin on the phone."

"Oh?"

"It's set."

"Really?"

"Tha, I want you to meet with Krupskaya in Zurich at two o'clock." He fished into a trouser pocket and brought out a small slip of paper. "We made all the arrangements beforehand. They don't discuss things on the phone. They're even more paranoiac than you."

Tha studied the paper. "I want to understand, Adam. What have I to do with it?"

"I want you to go and see her. Can't you do that for me?"

He looked like one of those angry shepherds in a church window, looming over her, holding his cane in his fist, ready to use it to force submission.

"If you wish."

He lowered the cane, then, and his other hand touched her shoulder, with gentle appeal. "Be suspicious. Ask all the questions. I'm not saying, my will be thy will."

"Aren't you?"

His mouth twisted in self-mockery. "I'm seminary trained. I have to be a pious bastard."

"But you encouraged me about Holland."

"See Krupskaya, please. And then come back and tell me if our only hope is running and more running—and that I'm a cracked bastard, in the bargain."

He released her and went laughing back to the house, calling the breeder's name, urging him to pour out fresh drinks.

As she climbed behind the wheel, she saw Sita watching from a window above, pinched and gargoylish. Poor Sita had hardly slept since the news of Von Tremke's death. She had always been afraid of Frau Eva, and the attaché's death had seemed to her an omen, threatening their plans for escape to Holland.

Swerving the vehicle onto the muddy shoulder, Tha knew that before she could do Adam's will, she must first find a way to free herself from Frau Eva's.

Everything about the funeral was empty but the coffin.

In the chapel of the crematorium, the Geneva Reichs-consul rose from his place in the front row, mumbling that, at the request of the family, the customary ceremonies would be omitted. A choral group, to which the baron had belonged, would provide a requiem. No hint that Von Tremke, as a Catholic suicide, was being dispatched in an unhallowed urn.

Heavily veiled, the widow emerged from an alcove to take the consul's arm. No children were in evidence. Nor any governess.

Tha fell in with the processional. A large pink-faced man marched beside her. The file progressed behind the coffin along a marble corridor, whose walls were lined with small crypts, each with its glistening nameplate. A smell of brass polish hung in the air.

Ahead, the pallbearers wheeled the casket into a large circular chamber domed in stained glass. The mourners disposed themselves along tiers from which they had an unobstructed view of the fire that burned behind a rose-colored glass panel and gave out a ruby light, very lively and very hideous.

As soon as the casket started on its way, the choir began. A Bach fugue had been chosen, and their rendition of it was warm, moving, and of concert caliber. Whatever the sins of the deceased, his musical tastes were above suspicion.

At an intersection in the marble hallway, attendants broke into the column just ahead of Tha, wheeling in trolleys banked high with lavish floral displays. Two large men unctuously halted the procession, and a third, with quiet adroitness, ushered Tha out of the way into the intersecting corridor, to provide turning room for the bedecked trolleys.

Not until the maneuver was in progress did Tha realize that she had been isolated, a single petal plucked from a bouquet, and that she was now in the capacious hands of the pink-

faced man, who continued to move her down the hall, away
from the mourners, effectively screened from them by the
massed floral display.

The man grunted and steered her into a room.

"*Danke, Erich,*" Frau Eva said. "*Bitte, passen sie auf.*"

Erich bowed deferentially and closed the door, muting
but not eliminating the dirge.

"Come in, come in, Madame."

The room was windowless. Circular reflectors, suspended by electrical cords, splotched light on desks and work-
benches, the latter piled with artificial flowers in various states
of assembly.

Frau Eva, behind a desk, wore her white uniform, a
black lace handkerchief flapping from a breast pocket, held
there by a little gold rosette. She had an infant in her lap and
was feeding it from a silver porringer. She used her forefinger as
a scoop in the old Alsatian way, so that the infant sucked with
each mouthful.

Nearby, a toddler played on the floor. His toys were a
scattering of the artificial flowers. Behind him a long wooden
worktable was heaped with horticulture in states of composi-
tion or decomposition; a pile of petals; a slag heap of stems; a
rash of leaves. The florist, like the undertaker, could produce
an artifact that surpassed nature, providing beauty even in
dismemberment.

"I won't keep you long," Frau Eva said. "We'll want the
guests to see you among them when they leave."

Beside the silver porringer lay a small revolver. It, too,
was of silver, chased with gold, a finely decorated piece, the
work of a jeweller.

"Swiss made"—Frau Eva took note of her glance—"but
a silly weapon for a man. Still more to take his life with. Even
so, he needed help to pull the trigger. I saved it for you, my gift
to you."

Tha contained a revulsive shudder. "Thank you," she
said. "But weapons that pass through police hands aren't
among my collectibles."

"Without your help," Frau Eva said, "Von Tremke
might still be giving us difficulties."

"My help?"

"We knew Tremke would want to sell his material to the French. We were sure he knew you were in the city. So when we located his number, I called, and used not only your name, but your deep and most appealing voice . . ."

Uttering the last phrase, Frau Eva gave an accurate and credible enough imitation of Tha, even while she deprecated her performance with a wrinkle of her nose. As an Alsatian, of course, she disposed of French and German with equal facility, but somehow she had caught Tha's Dutch rhythm as well, just this side of satire. It was the nun parading as wanton, almost effortlessly convincing.

"Naturally," Frau Eva continued, "he asked all the right questions about you, which I was in position to answer, and he nicely gave me his address. His poor widow resents our planting that army notice beside him, but we were determined to keep the Swiss police from getting into the matter . . ."

A little bubble of saliva had formed about the infant's lips and Frau Eva punctured it with her square forefinger. She sighed with a note of believable weariness. "I never had much use for Von Tremke, and his widow is a hysterical woman, but, still, one would have preferred, for the children's sake, something less harsh. But it could not be, in the short time we had . . ."

"The Abteilung will be pleased."

"Ah, the Abteilung . . ." Frau Eva stood up and extended the infant to Tha. "Would you take him a moment, Madame?"

Even the weight of the infant in her arms could not overcome Tha's sense of falsity. She watched Frau Eva take a fresh diaper from a manteau and brush away some invisible marks from her spotless uniform.

"I'm afraid," Frau Eva said, "it will take more than disposing of a greedy Von Tremke to make the Abteilung happy at this time . . ."

She seemed in no hurry to repossess her charge. Instead, she kneeled beside the tot on the floor and, taking a little brush from inside the pocket of her cape, began very professionally and even lovingly to bring luster to the child's golden curls.

"It was to be expected. Every time there's a new Foreign

Minister, the Abteilung goes to pieces. Von Jagow wanted to give priority to the war in the East. Now Zimmerman comes in and gives emphasis to the West, to the submarine effort. It is still the same war, but the Abteilung loves to indulge in hysterics, have you noticed?"

"I try not to."

Frau Eva smiled. "This Lenin, did you get somewhere with him?"

"Not really."

"Zimmerman has always opposed Von Jagow's policy of giving money to revolutionaries of that stripe. Of course it is in the German interest to make trouble for one enemy, the Czar. But that kind of trouble can spread. It can even spread to us. So Zimmerman now orders the Abteilung to destroy Lenin's reputation, before those Easter riots in Petersburg. Have you any ideas on this?"

"No . . ."

"Compromise him with Inessa Armand?"

"Would that hurt him?" Tha rocked the infant in her arms. "In certain quarters, it might make him more attractive—than buried in a book by Hegel."

"Not decisive, I agree."

Frau Eva straightened up and put the brush back into her pocket. She advanced thoughtfully, ready to relieve Tha of the infant.

"Something direct." Eva held back, frowning abstractedly at the child. "Follow me. Suppose we pass along a large sum of money to Lenin. And suppose we can make it seem the money comes from the Deuxième Bureau. Then we have the Swiss police make the arrest, for violation of Swiss espionage law. And make sure the press labels Lenin a French agent, who has sold out the Russian Revolution to the French. Even if that canard only endures during the next critical period, while our objective is to keep the Czar on his throne so he can make a separate peace with us, that would satisfy me. How does that strike you?"

Tha handed over the infant and went to the worktable. She began to assemble the flowers, hiding her uneasiness, though she couldn't yet pinpoint a reason for it.

"Will you get somebody to pose as a French agent? Is that the weak point?"

"It would be, but I was thinking of the genuine article. I was thinking of your control here, the psychiatrist, Dr. Carnet."

Tha swung around. Frau Eva had gone back toward the desk. She was by no means satisfied that she had thought through all the facets of her plan, and wanted to test each step with Tha.

"Dr. Carnet? You know about him?"

"Long, long before your little housewarming," Frau Eva said matter-of-factly. "So the problem is"— Frau Eva proceeded slowly, exploring her thought—"can you convince Carnet to make the payment to Lenin? I would think you could readily tell him you had your instructions from Depardieu, to make the payment yourself—and then throw yourself on his mercy, saying you fear the assignment and beg him to carry it out. Couldn't we count on you to establish a closer relationship with Dr. Carnet? As background, we know that Carnet is intimate with many of his women patients. . . . I take it you will become another patient?"

"Yes."

Tha carefully matched petals to a stem, grateful for having a chance to do something with her hands, to take time to appear to deliberate over Frau Eva's plan, when she had an immediate reaction of panic, of danger directed against her.

"Let's imagine I could." Tha kept her voice down. "Where would that leave me with the Deuxième Bureau? Dr. Carnet, arrested, would inform Depardieu that I had betrayed him. I doubt that I'd be safe in Switzerland or any place after that . . ."

"A consideration, of course." Frau Eva came around the desk. "Your safety must be assured, or it is no good. Hence, I think, once it is done, you must go to Germany . . ."

Tha pressed the incomplete flower in her palm and the point of the wire pricked blood. "I'm to seek refuge in Germany?"

"What alarms you about that?"

"But that's impossible for me . . ."

"Because of your French officer?"

"Yes."

"But I've looked into that. We've excellent medicine in Berlin. And as a brave officer, he will be honored among us, you can be assured."

"He doesn't know I work for you."

"Nor need he," Frau Eva said. "We will have you detained on some specious charges while visiting Berlin, and he can come to help you. There are a dozen ways to arrange it, and you will manage it skillfully, I know . . ."

From the chamber the Bach fugue began to rise; the voices combined to the complex cry of a solitary being, despairing at finding an exchange, even with the most naked of pleading agony and lament; rising to a terrifying climax that promised expiation, even glory, but no relief from utter isolation.

The three-year-old on the floor, exposed to those sounds, responded in alarm and sought Frau Eva's skirts. She stroked the child's head. "Let your German soul hear it, don't be afraid, liebschen . . ."

They would be giving the coffin to the fire, Tha sensed. Rose-colored panels would be removed, but the pallbearers would immediately screen the consummation from the mourners, denying even this moment of truth to poor Von Tremke, an appearance in transit to an apparition.

"They'll be leaving," Frau Eva said crisply. "Is there anything more that troubles you, Madame?"

"Perhaps it's a conceit," Tha said, "but I thought the Abteilung would want me for further work. Are you sure that Berlin will agree with you, in terminating me?"

Frau Eva deposited the babe in a little basket and came around the desk toward Tha. She picked up the revolver as she advanced. Her smile to Tha was warm and sympathetic. "Let me also assure you that its serial numbers have been safely erased. Take it as a memento of our efforts. I have consulted the highest authority. You will be looked after discreetly as long as this war lasts, and openly honored after victory comes . . ."

In all her imaginings about this meeting, this trap was the one that had not occurred to her, and she had to reach deep into herself to keep behaving in a normal way. To continue to voice objections would only arouse Frau Eva's suspicions. Any German agent, presented with this alternative, would certainly welcome it as an end to duplicity and to danger; the chance to live in tranquility as benefactress of Czars.

"What gave me the idea," Frau Eva said, "was the way you jumped, that day on the bridge. I thought, she is ready for it, her nerves are at the end, the famous Mata Hari has had enough . . ."

"I don't mean to seem ungrateful," Tha said. "But it is a shock . . . to think, after all this time, one is going to have to live with oneself, without benefit of masks . . ."

"A letdown, to be sure." Frau Eva dropped the revolver into Tha's purse. "We will be in touch, shortly. Of course, you must quickly launch your friendship with the susceptible Dr. Carnet . . ."

They embraced briefly, and then Tha was in the presence of the ponderous Erich in the corridor, offering her an arm, as he helped her merge with the retreating mourners.

In the car, grasping the wheel, she opened her palm, and the crushed petal fell from it into her lap. Her blood had stained the perfect pink of the cloth rose. It was a token of a triumph of real over the fake; but the memory of Frau Eva's perfect smile warned her not to exaggerate it.

Two boys, whacking away at each other with their schoolbags, descended the trolley step ahead of her, shrilling juvenile obscenities into the mild Zurich air.

On the far side of the island, another trolley had simultaneously disgorged its passengers and the two streams vied for the strip of concrete, buffeting her as she sought a neutral space, suddenly leaving her with an old man, a beached, faded Crusoe, on a bench, content to watch traffic flow in the sea around him.

Across the road lay a market square, its aisles covered in bright canvas. Women with string shopping bags ambled among the stalls, some munching fruit and candy, inhabitants of a continent lost in time.

Tha had scrupulously followed the complicated instruc-

tions given to her by Adam. She had parked her car near the
station in Geneva and purchased a train ticket to Berne. Then,
as directed, she had crossed the platform and boarded the
Zurich train, paying the conductor in transit. Two trolley
changes had brought her to this alien shore. All this seemed un-
necessary and amateurish, but she conformed, in case one of
Lenin's people was watching.

The square clock moved to the hour and two new trolleys, grinding and sparking, touched off another islandic fray.
She tried to hold aloof, as she searched for Krupskaya. The
bells had begun to ring again before she saw the Russian
woman on the rear platform of the northbound car, exactly as
scheduled.

Tha boarded, waiting for the passengers to enter the
car, making her way to the open platform at the back.

Krupskaya bent down, conducting a search of the contents of the shopping bag at her feet. She wore a kerchief
around her head, presumably to make her undistinguishable
from the other suburban wives, though it only accented her severity, more implacably intellectual than ever.

"Go well?"

Tha nodded.

"On my side, too."

Krupskaya came erect and gripped the handrail and
spoke into the wind, letting it suck her words away from them,
lost in the clangor of the trolley's progress.

"We admire your soldier," Krupskaya said. "All of us.
He is a man of deep feeling. Lenin may call him a Tolstoyan,
but he doesn't borrow his thinking from anyone."

"I know."

"It may surprise you, but I was once a real Tolstoyan.
Many of us began there. Inessa, too, though she denies it these
days, once trotted after Tolstoy, sometimes living on his farm,
just like me . . ."

"Tolstoy himself?"

"I know it seems another age, and it does to us, too."
Krupskaya smiled, looking into the distance being scissored by
the converging trolley tracks. "I was involved in helping prostitutes find a better life. I taught them to read and write. Tolstoy

told me I was wasting my time, that it was thus in the time of Moses and would remain thus. I parted with him. You take money from men, I'm told."

From another person, it might have been insulting, or at the very least, maladroit. From this woman, it was neither. She lived in a world of facts; she was simply seeking to acquire another; neutral as a measure of time.

"I have," Tha said, equally matter of fact.

"Yet you do not consider yourself a prostitute."

"On occasion."

"I don't comprehend."

"When I don't enjoy the man, or he doesn't enjoy me."

"Can one make such subjective distinctions?"

"I know wives who do."

Krupskaya squinted, absorbing the thrust. "Nevertheless, Lenin and I have good relations with prostitutes. Here, we share our lodgings with one. She insists there is no difference between selling her body to perform labor and selling it for her service. Ulyanov says, if only the wage earners saw as clearly that they are prostitutes, there would be a real advance. We both think she is one of the most intelligent persons we have met in Zurich!"

"Perhaps," Tha said, "there's hope for me."

Krupskaya would not admit the irony; the social worker firmly gleaning her crop of case histories. "I ask these questions," she pursued, "because, though we have been made familiar with St. Reymont's attitudes, yours are in doubt. Lenin says your former husband made you the victim of a brutal colonial murder. Your little son, he said. Has that made you bitter?"

Tha felt the pain of the old wound again. "How did he find that out?"

"Ulyanov is thorough."

"Adam tell you?"

"No, Lenin has researched you. You must hate the imperialists, he says."

"Once," Tha said, "until I saw that it would only continue the cycle . . ."

"You are a quietist?"

"I don't know what that means . . ."

"You let the world make you, you give up the effort to make yourself?"

Tha lifted her shoulders. The accusation was familiar and even Adam had voiced it. In a way, Frau Eva, with her accusations of aloofness, had misconstrued it. To some, it was preening; to others, a vast ennui.

"The answer to that is—I'm here."

"For St. Reymont, you mean . . ."

"Yes."

Krupskaya gazed bleakly at the retreating streets. They had passed through a neighborhood of small houses but were again coming to another commercial high street. "Lenin will be disappointed," Krupskaya said into the wind. "It is no longer enough to act out of personal motives, he says."

Several people got onto the car and some came to the platform. Among them, a proletarian with a lunch box. He sidled up to Tha, grinning and aggressive. She liked his vivid coloring, his scarf negligently thrust about his neck. But Krupskaya immediately came between them and brushed him aside with a ferocity that sent him scuttling into the car itself.

When the car was in motion again, Krupskaya said, "At the next stop, we will get off. You will find a pastry shop just off to your right. If I don't join you within ten minutes, we will have to abandon this for now."

Tha tightened her grip on the rail, conscious of Krupskaya's strained tight-lipped toleration. In the midst of a holocaust, she had demanded to be a "person"—an individual. And that was tantamount to declaring herself insensitive, even electing to be an outcast. She had been judged, but worse was yet to come. Next, unbearably, it would be her turn to judge.

The shop was dreamy with chocolate. The aroma hung tropically over the pastries, oozed lushly from the candy trays, and coiled up in thick vapors from the cups of cocoa, sipped and stirred and spooned by afternoon addicts, halfway to their dark heaven, attended by the angelic pink on the icing of the petits fours.

Her childhood had been saturated by the fragrance. On

Sundays, at traditional family gatherings, the house would be drenched in it, and on weekdays, her mother would often pick her up at school and take her to similar dens, thralled to the same satanic syrups. But those rapt, languid sessions had come to a sudden jolting end with her father's bankruptcy, and Tha found herself exiled not only from the pastry shops but from home. Outside, the winds sweeping in from the Zuyder Zee seemed aimed at her alone, cutting and disjunctive.

Yet, in her exclusion, Tha had discovered another universe. It had been there all along, just beyond the enclaves of redolence.

In that world, a different language was spoken—not Dutch, but Frisian, the tongue of the ancient Anglo-Saxons, still alive among the poor in the remote province of northern Holland. It did not take long for her to be inducted into this other, this out-of-doors nation; to be told in whispers about the last of the wild Frisian chieftains who, after long refusing to become converted to Christianity, at last was brought to the baptismal font. He had put one foot in and was about to put the second in after it when he suddenly demanded a guarantee that his ancestors, too, would go to Heaven. Though the bishops had been desperate to win over the wayward leader, they conceded they lacked power to open the gates to the unwet dead. Which was why, her street friends whispered, Frisians were known ever after as "the people with one foot in and one foot out."

"Even me?" Tha had childishly asked her companions.

"All who live beyond the Zuyder Zee," they had chanted, "none will ever be tamed!"

Once, in bed with Adam, she had told him about the relapsarian chieftain. He had roared with laughter. Her secret, at last! Beneath all her contradictions was a Frisian, with one tame leg, one wild. And they had spent the rest of the night finding out which member she favored.

Now coming into this place, with its rich fragrance, Tha felt she had left part of her in the street, that she would always be outside one sorority or another. She looked up as the Russian woman entered the shop and joined her at the little table, her face gray and stern. Krupskaya frowned at the women around them. "You may think we are overcautious. But we are watched night and day. I think we are all right in here, don't you?"

"I'm sure."

Even then Krupskaya remained silent until the waitress had filled their orders. Cautiously she leaned close to make her first disclosure. "You know of course the name Krupp—the principal arms maker in Germany?"

Tha nodded.

"Perhaps you also know that, along with Zimmerman, he is the main advocate of naval and submarine war in the West, cool to Von Jagow's undercover efforts to help us overthrow the Czar. What is not known, however, is that Krupp is planning a quiet trip to Geneva, ostensibly to inspect one of his factory subsidiaries here."

Krupskaya thrust a fork into one of her petits fours but did not bring it to her mouth.

"The actual purpose is quite another matter." She put down her fork. "We learned of their journey from a friend of ours, in the German Foreign Office. Unfortunately he has been dismissed in the new changeover from Von Jagow to Zimmerman. However, we know that Krupp is coming here to meet with the principal arms manufacturers of England and France, namely Sir Vickers and Monsieur Schneider-Creusot. In secret, as you can well understand."

Tha found herself staring. "All three? Why would they risk that?"

"All three countries are nearing the point of exhaustion. We are informed that the Three Cannons, as Lenin calls them, want to be certain that it will be safe and wise to continue the war. After all, the Three Cannons cannot destroy the economies of the nations whose blood they leach."

"You told this to Adam?"

Krupskaya stirred her cocoa endlessly. "We all agree that, if that meeting can be exposed, it would open the people's eyes to the hypocrisy for which they have sacrificed so much, so many have died. All three regimes would be discredited. The anger of the exhausted soldiers and their families would bring peace, bring it rapidly, at long last . . ."

"Not only peace—but revolution?"

The Russian woman went on stirring, her eyes filled with excitement. "Don't listen to Martov. We want peace too. At the very minimum, the scandal would require Zimmerman to resign and paralyze Krupp's opposition to us in the East. We have a broad aim, and a narrow one, but none concealed."

"And to bring about this exposure you're enlisting Adam and his Callips?"

"Precisely," Krupskaya said. "Lenin feels if we become the instrument to reveal that meeting, it would be labeled as partisan and be dismissed. But, originating with the major's aristocratic friends, the outcry led by them would make the disclosure impeccable in the eyes of the world press . . ."

Tha tried to keep the whole thing at a distance, only to be invaded by a memory of Adam during one of his leaves from the front, only a few weeks before the gas attack at Vittel.

They had gone to a little restaurant. Suddenly Adam had excused himself. The food had been served but he had not returned. She had gone outside, to find him leaning against the side of the building, smoking a cigarette. He begged her to go back and eat, not to let him spoil her dinner. But she had remained at his side. Haltingly he confessed his inability to keep the two worlds apart—the underground universe of trenches and viscera and death; the upper reaches of his love for her. Across the table, watching her, the wall had come down and his nausea had flooded in. "Each time I leave you," he had said, "I find it harder to go back. It's not war anymore, Tha. It's like a plague that nobody can cure, that sweeps their side and ours, that has no meaning and that will never end. If there was a purpose to it once, there isn't anymore. Whatever it was that made it seem right has been buried under the corpses. . . ."

They had not gone back to the restaurant. Instead, they had roamed the streets, and he had let her look into the torrent of wasted bodies that the newspapers called the battle of the Somme, the campaign of Verdun. A million had died and another million had been wounded. And these millions had been levied impartially against both sides. But those multitudes were tongueless numbers. Adam could only count the officers originally sent to the front with him, of whom not one in ten still

lived. And that remnant existed in a kind of stupor, their camaraderie a perilous bridge linking them to their past identi-
ties, to the natural order of leaves and furloughs, to her speech,
her laughter, which, in the quiet restaurant, had suddenly
seemed sickening phantoms, combining with the glint of cut-
lery and the white sheen of cloth to become a nightmare.

Now, beyond the frown of the Russian woman, Tha saw
Adam's dark face once more, now blind, reflecting that pestilence within against which he writhed to be free, yet to which
he clung, as his reality and the reality of his generation. And it
was to that division inside him that the Russians had spoken;
offering to let him remain faithful to his dead and shed them,
too—a cure worthy of a magus of old.

That became aware again of the table and the assertions
of Krupskaya. "I see all that. I see how that would fascinate
Adam. But why tell me? What difference can it make if I approve or disapprove?"

"But what we want," Krupskaya stated in her down-
right way, "is much more. We want your help. Didn't he tell
you?"

"No," Tha said, uneasily. "Not a word . . ."

"We know the meeting is to take place in Geneva. We
don't know exactly when. Or specifically where. To get that information—the key to the matter—we need someone to go to
Berlin . . ."

Tightening, Tha leaned forward, crushing the pastry
under her knife. "And Adam suggested me? Is that what you're
saying, Madame?"

Krupskaya nodded. "You are a Dutch neutral, with
friends in high places. The major assures us that you can get
into Germany . . ."

". . . Then what?"

"We have a plan. We feel you can get that information.
But what is essential at this moment is, will you commit yourself to go?"

Tha, shutting out Adam's appealing image, studied the
sugary devastation on her plate.

Around her the air reeked of Swiss complacency. In this
shop, the world of Krupp's shells and Vickers' steel and

Schneider-Creusot's explosives was a regrettable indisposition; burned lungs and blistered eyeballs and the schemes of Frau Eva and the gory dreams of a Krupskaya only a passing intestinal contraction. If one only spooned and fed in good measure, and relied on time, the Swiss god of gods, all would right itself.

"You hesitate?"

"Yes."

"Because you are afraid?"

"Because I need time."

"But it is urgent. That meeting may be taking place even now . . ."

"Even if I agreed with you," That said, "on a practical level, I'm not sure I'm the right one to go . . ."

"But that could be dealt with—if only you wanted to!"

Circling the center of her disquiet, Tha postponed the negative on her lips, and then looked up to see two teen-aged girls, nudging each other, come from the counter toward the table. One pushed the other forward and the girl squealed and then blurted, "Excuse me, but aren't you Mata Hari?"

"Yes."

"We've seen photos of you," the girl said. "Of your dance, I mean."

"We do it, too," the other said, blushing. "In our room, at night. With the seven veils.!"

"Very good."

"We're not the only ones," the first girl supplied. "Others at our school. Lots and lots of us. We have to do it behind the prefects' backs. But, after the war, we'll be like you, free to show our bodies, as free as you!"

Around them, the room had fallen silent. At the tables, the women, alerted by the enthused youngsters, had now recognized Tha and were staring at her. At the counter, the saleswomen ceased their transactions and became spectators.

Krupskaya frowned at the pair. "Women are liberated only as men are, and liberation does not come from taking off your clothes, but through struggle against your oppressors."

The backfische, overwhelmed, began to trip over themselves in retreat. Tha stood up quickly and went after them, catching them at the door. "Thank you for saying hello. Never mind what anybody tells you—don't let them take away your joy in your bodies!"

Krupskaya came to join her, lips pale and taut. "We must go," she said. She had carefully wrapped the petits fours in a paper serviette, not only those on her plate but those that Tha had left stabbed and broken.

Moments later, paying the bill, Tha glanced up at the crowd of cocoa drinkers. Their eyes were still focused on her, full of distaste and repugnance. She knew she had violated their clotted matinee, her advice to the young girls an irruption by a barbarian, unsettling and offensive.

She longed to shout at them, in harsh Frisian dialect, one of Count Esterhazy's rueful reflections: "This would be the best of all possible worlds if only fucking would remain only fucking." She refrained because they would translate that as— only vulgarity.

But she could not resist the Frisian impulse. She spoke in ringing tones to Krupskaya. "Seven orgasms in one night?" Her voice caromed off the startled gray face to the other women in the shop. "An exaggeration! The truth is, I had seven partners—so the feat could have been duplicated by any woman here!"

And then she was out on the street, leaving her abashed companion to catch up with her.

Krupskaya trudged alongside her toward the trolley stop, aware the rejection had been aimed at her, along with the other women in the shop, yet unwilling to accept defeat. "Is there some question I failed to answer?"

The everlasting schoolteacher, Tha thought. No enigmas, only problems; no riddles of the universe, only laws waiting to be discovered; instead of the strangulated cry of save me! the steady susurration of midnight oil.

"You explained it very clearly."

"Is it me? Have I sounded too harsh? Sometimes, in my wanting to achieve a result, I sound unfeeling . . . but it is only because I am impatient with the waste of life . . ."

"I don't question your sincerity."

"Then why hold back?"

Tha knew it would be useless to tell this woman that she had seen the men who held power in the world, eager as any for peace, yet squirming in their seats, frustrated by the waves of bloodshed that had overwhelmed them, and would wash over the world again, part of the inheritance of self that men could not disavow, the crime of war sanctified beyond all heresy.

"Perhaps," Tha limited herself, "I've seen too much."

The Russian woman half turned to her as they continued striding down the street. "But don't you see, history is entering a new phase, like no other before this . . ."

"How? With me, a whore, as handmaiden for the millennium?"

"I didn't mean to abuse you . . ."

"Or with the help of German secret funds which you admit you got from Von Jagow, a partnership with one tyrant to overthrow another? Sacrifice Adam for that? Or me?"

The goiter-ravaged face became gaunt. "But these are temporary handicaps, contradictions one uses for the sake of the future . . ."

"But the men of Europe—the ones I've met—say the same. Expediency now, justice later."

"But the people will have the power, they won't have to exploit one another, they will cherish the earth and those who live on it and toil on it for one another . . ."

"And how will they keep power? Won't they need sluts like me and blind men like Adam, useful today, discarded tomorrow?"

"But it will end, I know it will, if we only go forward."

"Ah, of course," Tha said, and the bitterness came back into her voice. "My husband beat me, not to enjoy himself, but to make me a better woman, and he beat the natives to teach them progress, and they killed my son to teach him a lesson in equality. Forgive me for not going back to that school."

"The major's wishes, they mean nothing?"

"Everything. And he means everything. And I don't want to help destroy him."

Silently they crossed the avenue, moving more rapidly as a trolley appeared in the distance. Tha was oppressed by

Krupskaya's deep sigh. At the kiosk, she turned and saw that there were tears in the eyes of the Russian woman.

"Let me discuss it with Adam." Tha tried to soften the blow. "Perhaps he can make me change my mind."

Inconsolably, Krupskaya shook her head. "Lenin was counting on me. I offended you. I am a bookish person. Women of the world, even Inessa, make me say the wrong things . . ."

Tha wished she could reveal herself to the unhappy woman. She imagined herself saying, "I am a spy. I must warn you the Abteilung is preparing a trap for your husband and his cause." But if she did that, they would never trust her again. Not only would it make her ineligible for their errand, but they would immediately protect themselves by cutting off all relations with Adam. The only result would be that Adam would hate her for having betrayed his dream of peace, and seal, forever, her last hope of reconciliation.

"But you haven't offended me, Krupskaya . . ."

"The truth is, I don't understand women like you. I mean, I can't live without hope. I don't see how any woman can . . ."

The trolley came screaming down, breathing burnt air. Tha gave the despondent woman a quick embrace and then let herself be caught up in the thrusting crowd.

As the machine sawed and sparked away, Tha caught a glimpse of her, her gray coat and nondescript kerchief and fraying shopping bag. But the habits of a lifetime had taken control of Krupskaya's spine and stride. She had straightened up, impelled by the action of putting one foot ahead of another, confident that by such practice one prepared for the inevitable leap into the future; and since no one knew which step would bring one to the threshold of this miracle, it was imperative never to cease plodding ahead.

Something about the Russian woman's single-mindedness left Tha smarting with guilt. As if she had come off second best, deaf to the cries of the hungry and the naked. Yet she had been one herself, in Holland, in Java; in childhood, as an evicted wife. And Adam had baptized her in the blood of the Somme and of Verdun; and pulled her down into the pit of

Vittel, from which she could find no escape. Yet how could she forget Lenin's scorn for the hungry in St. Petersburg: "But they know that they are cat's-paws!"

She knew she was. Either Depardieu's or Frau Eva's—or now Adam's and Lenin's. She wanted not to be, but that was as puling as asking release from her own passions; longing for a cure for her own divided self by magic unknown.

"Mata Hari!"

Hesse straightened up from the fire pit as she came along the garden path. Smoke, in goatish curls, gave him a shaggy coat. Beneath it, he wore a tan work shirt, paint-spattered, and baggy trousers bunched oddly at the waist.

"I spoke with a young man on the phone. Didn't he tell you?"

He shook his head. "I'm the last one to get messages. Caught me with my pants down." He tugged at his waist, revealing that his trousers were being held up by suspenders used as a belt. "Both buttons at one time. The plucking fingers of fate." He peered at her through the fumes. "Come to reclaim your sled?"

"Nothing so threatening," she said. "Only to make love."

His blue eyes widened and he fanned at the fumes between them. "Have you been banished, or are you the banisher?"

"Is there a difference?"

Hesse examined her face and then stooped to a mound of paper at his feet. He began to feed them to the flames. Some were manuscript sheets, covered with tiny handwriting, others were large sketch sheets, splashed with aquarelles or charcoal sketches, or just gnomic lines.

"Come help me burn these."

"If you turn me away," Tha said, taking some sheets, "black magic on you."

"Siva has writ," he said, tossing papers into the flame, " 'He who takes a blind man's woman must burn ere he beds.' "

She glanced down at a sketch, a delicate congerie of greens and browns. A smiling bottle hung by its neck from a scaffold, and a green sun was being dragged down into the sea by ropes attached to a brigade of bottles, and these in turn were tethered by a chain of sparkling glass to a white sun plunging to sea bottom.

A fragment of a nightmare, only initially charming and playful. She had no idea what it intended to convey, yet found herself disturbed at the idea of destroying it.

"Why are we doing this?"

"Toss."

"But there must be endless hours of work . . ."

The flickering light gave him an appealing self-mockery. He let some more sheets tumble into the pit. "My failures. They are the authentic me. My successes always jangle off key. In the fire, I imitate my Maker, my own first cause, twice on Sunday. I hope I can say nothing to dissuade you from your rash pursuit."

"Nothing."

Hesse smiled at her, and dumped the rest of his papers, and relieved her of her pile. "You have persuaded me to repress my curiosity. The bedroom is on the first floor right. Laud we the gods, the great unbuttoners!"

As they reached the house, a young man came hurrying in from the street, shouting, "Harry! Harry!"

Hesse paused. "Any luck?"

"No!"

"Where did you try?"

The young man looked vexed. "Where haven't I!"

Hesse took his spectacles from his breast pocket and put them on, studying the young man's face. "We can't give up. We have to find her." He turned and introduced Tha.

The young man was apologetic. "I meant to leave a note about your call," he said. "But I ran out right afterward." He turned back to Hesse, still fidgeting. "I'm willing to help, but tell me, where do I look now?"

"Her relatives?"

"They never see her, they say."

"Then you have to go from friend to friend."

"I'll do it because you say so," the young man said, "but I still say she's run away."

He took a few steps toward the gate, and then came back, hailing them as they moved again toward the house. "I'll need some money," he said.

Hesse searched his pockets, but produced only a few coins. He suggested that the young man try to get some money from some people inside the house, but the young man insisted they lived on what he gave them, and they would be without funds, like him. This struck Hesse as reasonable, and he turned to Tha. "Can I be a borrower?"

It amused Tha to think that she had to pay for her urgencies, and she extended her billfold to him and he took a note and gave it to the young man, who marched to the gate, full of grievance.

"Crisis," Hesse said. "A young woman who comes to clean has taken the only manuscript of my new novel . . ."

"But why?"

"To destroy it," Hesse said. "I haven't been able to work since I left Germany. Then this poured out. For once I was using words to break the prism of sentences, to escape the suffocation of 'I am I.' I know I'll never put it back together, so I decided to have a bonfire of all my previous efforts . . ."

She stopped, appalled. In her own anxieties, she had neglected to observe his, imperiously demanding he help expunge her miseries, even if only for a time. "Do you want me to go?"

"Go? No! We have a greater bonfire to make."

Laughing, he put his arm around her waist, his hand slipping over her belt, gripping her firmly. "I called and you came belatedly and I won't let you get away."

In the living room, a phonograph whirled and a young man strummed on a beautiful intrument resembling a mandolin, except that it had a bent neck. Tha had never seen one like it. In another corner, a young woman with a round pleasant face bent to file a large bronze sculpture, her movements in no way influenced by the music, the screech of the file the counterpoint of labor to play.

Hesse introduced them and waved them back to their occupations, leading the way up a narrow and twisting staircase. Young Genevans, he explained, seemed determined to compensate him for his two sons, who had elected to remain in

Germany. His firstborn had wanted to murder him, and he had discovered a like impulse in himself. So far the young people who had renamed him "Harry" had shown no signs of vaticide, and he was grateful to his new family.

The bed was still unmade.

Hesse wanted to do something about it, but she stopped him and made him help her undress. In return, he asked her to undress him, starting with his glasses, and she saw his blue eyes glitter with desire. She unfastened his suspenders, and the trousers came slipping down. He wore no underwear, and she saw that he was ready for her, but she slowed him down, making him take off her mourning dress and all the other undergarments she had worn to fit herself for her funeral role.

Nude, his body seemed smooth and sculpted, reminding her of the glabrous young males of Java, polished by the ocean. Even his face, skin tightened by desire, had a swimmer's freshness.

But for all her hot impatience, she was dismayed to find herself dry. He kneeled beside the bed, bending over her, his lips going to her navel. She had a fleeting image of Adam, on the first day they had come together, standing on the bed, gaunt, the full height of him reaching to the ceiling, tantalizing her with his cockstand high above her head, making her reach for his shaft, pulling him down, her temporary captive.

Hesse's lips and tongue moved from navel to belly, making her swell, rounding her in the center, and yet he held himself away, tracing sensation under her knee, forcing her leg to arch, until she trapped his head between her thighs. She felt herself silky to his caress and she reached out and grasped his face, bringing him up.

But if she had not been to India, he had, and he coaxed her to top him, his mouth possessed of her breasts and nipples, his hands flourishing in her thighs.

She reached to his throat, catching the cords in her teeth, and he came arching up inside her, absorbing her own coiling pressure, pulsed by the strings from the room below, the screech of the file rawly passing through her vulva, urging her to surpass its high note.

But he restrained her, prolonging it, sliding his firm

stand from her, turning her body, thrusting up from behind her, his hands lightly cupping her breasts, completing now as they had begun on the sled, gently moving her to the end of his penis, excruciatingly threatening to break the connection, then forcing her back hard on him again, and when she felt him ready to come, she grasped him to hold him and then with two harsh and triumphant strokes, strung along a fine wire of heat, brought them both to trembling dehiscence.

As they lay moist together, he used her hand to fondle her mount, reliving his enjoyment through the mediation of her fingers, she rediscovering her completion in her own hand.

"Now can I ask questions?"

"I've been accused—I accuse myself—of turning my back on the world."

"So have I," Hesse said. "Sometimes that's the only way to address it. And now you think he hates you?"

"And loves me," Tha said. "And I'm the same."

"You didn't expect me to release you from that?"

"No, just what you did."

"What you did," Hesse said softly.

They lay awhile, quietly balanced, lightly in touch with their bodies and each other, their minds discharged of all thought, waiting for desire to steal back upon them, opening their nostrils with its woodland scent, its euphoric power sweeping away all knowledge of its evanescence.

From below, there was a cession of the music, followed by new shouts of "Harry! Harry!" and it was the voice of the aggrieved adopted son.

Hesse rose on an elbow, resting and resisting their claims. "Close your eyes. Maybe we can make it pass." But instead the narrow stairway thundered with steps and the clamor came to the door. Cursing softly, Hesse slipped into his trousers and opened the door a crack.

"Teresina's here! You'd better come, she's out of her mind!"

From the door, Hesse beseeched Tha, "Don't leave me, don't you dare leave!"

She lay, crouching against the return of guilt. The memory of Adam broke through, brandishing the small stool at her, demanding release from her fettering cynicism. And, with it, the voice of a young woman, speaking in Italian, came through the darkening room, operatically unhappy.

Uneasy, Tha rose and went to the window.

A young woman stood near the fire pit, its smoke rising behind her. In her arms, she hugged a manuscript. Teary, disheveled, plain of face and plump of figure, she was a pathetic hellion, threatening to throw Hesse's pages into the flames.

Hesse stood before her, a prisoner, hands clasped behind his back, as if in bonds. From time to time, he interposed a word, too soft to halt the flow of condemnation.

Tha's small knowledge of Italian did not permit her to absorb all of the girl's recriminations. One phrase, spat out venomously, struck a nerve. "Nero magia!"

Tha felt sorry for the girl, and sardonic about her own enticement by that phrase of Hesse's. After all, it was too much to expect of a man, even a magician, that he produce a new set of tricks for each bag.

Of course, Hesse would have a defense. He would tell her that when Hesse went forth, it was Hesse who would watch him from every window and when Hesse crossed a threshold, it would be Hesse who came from the shadows to greet him; that from this everlasting circle of self, the I am I, there was no escape, not even coital frenzy.

Quickly she got back into the black dress and slipped unnoticed from the house, grateful alike to the girl and to Hesse for having restored her, if only by their imperfections, to reality and to decision.

The Reichsconsul was polite, but dismissive.

Much as he would like to oblige Lady McLeod, he said, war regulations limited travel to Germany by all foreigners, even Dutch neutrals, to those serving the interests of the German state. Her request for a visa, he regretted to tell her, would have to be processed through normal channels, and even with his endorsement that could take weeks or months.

Tha let him continue. She had stood outside on the line and sent her name in patiently, trying not to draw attention to herself, but to seem to be yet another in the crowd of supplicants. Nor did she want to startle the portly man unduly.

"I understand," she said, and went to the window.

Her breath formed a mist over the cold glass. On it, with gloved finger, she inscribed: "H-21." Aloud she said, "You may wish to check my passport with the former Foreign Minister, Herr Theodor von Jagow."

The man straightened, his manner suddenly grave. He half bowed as he ushered her along the hall into an empty office. "Please wait, Madame," he said. "I shall of course put things in motion at once."

Twenty minutes later, as she had anticipated, Frau Eva came in. In spite of her fixed smile, it was clear that she was furious. "Why this breach? Why didn't you come or phone me at the Von Tremke house?"

"Because it is being watched."

"You must be mistaken!"

"Dr. Carnet calls it his bonus from the Von Tremke affair."

"Does he?" Frau Eva said. "What else have you found out from the doctor?"

"You were right about him. He is susceptible."

Frau Eva enjoyed the triumph vicariously. "Splendid," she said. "Carnet wants you to go to Berlin?"

"Not Carnet. Lenin."

"You've succeeded with Lenin, too?"

"With Krupskaya."

"The teacher? You've bedded the teacher?"

Tha laughed readily. "Far better. She believes all whores are guilty and wish to repent. So I told her Adam's suffering had converted me to her husband's cause. And it turns out they are desperate for somebody to go to Berlin and beg Von Jagow to convince Zimmerman, so payments to them can be resumed . . ."

"And that is why they went to your housewarming?"

Tha nodded. "Lenin wants me to convey to Von Jagow new guarantees that he will work to effect a separate peace by Russia and Germany, if he comes to power. He wants new secret funds for this Easter riot. And I, of course, saw how that could tie in with your Carnet scheme . . ."

"How is that?"

"In outline, it's clear enough. I'll return with good news for Lenin that his funds are to be resumed and will soon be delivered. I'll tell Carnet I blocked the funds. After a short interval, I'll inform Carnet I've had fresh instructions from Depardieu. The French are to buy Lenin. I will take the francs you give me and have Carnet deliver them to Lenin. They'll be caught red-handed and arrested—and Lenin will be finished—"

Frau Eva's eyes showed a new respect. "Why only outline? What worries you?"

"One element . . ."

"And that?"

"Depardieu. I know he has people in the Abteilunga . . ."

"That doesn't surprise me."

"They will alert him to my visit to Berlin. And Depardieu will ask Carnet why did I go to Berlin? And, lacking a cover story, that could quickly lead Carnet to discover the French have no intention of buying Lenin's services. And that, in turn, would abort your plan, our plan . . ."

Reflecting, Frau Eva went to the window and began to pull the shade up and down, alternately blocking out and letting in the morning light. "The problem, then—keeping the Abteilung in the dark about this visit?"

"I know that's not possible."

"Then?"

"Misinforming them," Tha said, quickly. "But I'd need your help."

"Misinform them in what way?"

"Tell them you are sending me to see Von Jagow, in an effort to entrap him, to find out if he is still willing to help Lenin in opposition to the Zimmerman policies."

"Won't that get back to Depardieu?"

"Probably."

"And, in turn, to Carnet?"

"Of course," Tha said. "But it is exactly what I will say to Carnet before I leave. I am undertaking your errand, but I will act for France. In Berlin, I will block any possibility of Von Jagow's supplying new funds to Lenin."

"After which," Frau Eva said, "you receive new instructions from Depardieu . . . and so on . . ."

"And so on . . ."

Frau Eva brought the shade down again, obscuring her face. "One deception for two purposes—to the Abteilung to deceive Depardieu's agents, and to Carnet, to pave the way to bring down Lenin . . ."

"And, if you want, we can supply another reason for my trip to Von Jagow."

"No, never mind that. It will be useful to test Von Jagow."

"Of course," Tha said, "these are only suggestions. I am only trying to keep your priority—the aim being to discredit and destroy Lenin . . . but if there are other means, of course, I'll follow your lead . . ."

She could feel Frau Eva's gaze rest on her admiringly.

"I must say, Madame," Frau Eva said, "you impress me this morning. I always thought of you as emotional and haphazard. But I was wrong. You're quite thorough."

"Where my skin's involved."

The shade, released, flew to the top and set off toy machine-gun fire. Frau Eva came back in the room and took her in her arms. "One almost wishes," she said, "that this was not your final assignment."

Tha kissed her on her cheek.

Minutes later, her visa and Sita's all duly stamped, she was on her way to pick up Adam at the hospital, to take him with her to Dr. Carnet.

The clinic-home of Dr. Carl Jung turned out to be a construct of the psyche of the famous mind healer.

Years before, in seeking a refuge from the sterility of hospitals, Jung had begun to build a place where he could meet his patients, and had followed a vagrant vision, troweling stone on stone, until there appeared a lofty churchlike nave, whose haphazard walls and random changes of floor level mounted toward an altar that was the interior of the hill itself.

Later, as his fame grew and people came to him from all over the world, the structure acquired several additions and outbuildings winding about the hillside garden in a series of grottoes and caverns, where Jung's assistants counseled their clients, and which appeared to have a curative effect, restoring battered minds to some imperfectly remembered womb, part of man's effort to find a secure place for himself on earth.

Carnet, irritated, deposited Adam in one of the lesser caves and paced the garden with Tha, out of earshot of employees and visitors.

"You haven't told him about me?"

"Not even about me," Tha assured him. "I said we were coming to seek a joint consultation with you, a safer cover, it seemed to me."

"I suppose some emergency justifies all this?"

"I think so. Lenin wants me to go to Berlin, to seek new funds. I'm hoping to find out where the funds go, so we can block them."

The psychiatrist's pale face registered some clinical asperity. "I wouldn't have thought he'd be susceptible, even to your charms, Madame."

"He wasn't, isn't."

"Then how did you get to him?"

"He's vulnerable to his cause. I told him I wanted to work for him because of Adam's suffering, that I was convinced only his revolution could end the war."

"When are you supposed to go?"

"Tonight," Tha said, "but one thing worries me . . ."

"Yes?"

"Depardieu."

"You amaze me." Carnet stared at her. "He'll be the first to congratulate you."

Tha shook her head. She did not want to overdo it, but she knew she had to make the decision appear to be Carnet's, not hers. It was essential to make him feel they were partners in this operation, strengthening his confidence in her against future surprises and accidents.

"Perhaps I have been in this too long," Tha said. "But suppose Von Jagow agrees to supply Lenin with his funds, and I don't learn the channels by which they are being transmitted and I can't block them. And, let us say, Lenin is successful.

Won't we be accused of having helped the Germans recruit Russian defeatists? Won't we put our heads in the noose, for some future time, when they want a scapegoat or two?"

Carnet took a turn around a path. "But we always run that risk. Once you're in this they can always say you've worked for the other side."

"I'm only too well aware of that," Tha said. "But I still think the way to handle this is to inform Depardieu only after we've found out about those funds. Then we'd be delivering a coup, something he could boast about in Paris . . ."

"You're not very trustful, are you?"

"I don't want Depardieu for an enemy. I don't think you do, either, Doctor . . ."

The doctor's eyes were amused and detached. "A classic anxiety case," he observed. "On the outside, superconfident. At the level of the ego, all nerves and cautions. At the instinctual level, an infant expecting the entire world to love you, and when the world refuses to live up to those narcissistic hopes, anxiety, disguised as swagger . . ."

"Maybe," Tha said, "but then that corresponds with the reality, or the reality of the Depardieus . . ."

Carnet laughed. "All right," he said, "but once you return here, you really must come in for consultation!"

They had started back toward the little cave when a man's hoarse voice broke over the quiet of the garden. They halted in the path as two nurses rushed to restrain an elderly man who kept shouting that he was going to kill Dr. Jung, whom he blamed for his daughter's suicide. Jung was a sorcerer; anti-Christ; doctor of Satan; a fiend on whom the final hour had fallen.

Alarmed, Carnet left her side to help the nurses, repeating his request that she visit him on her return from Berlin. Tha paused, seeing the aggrieved parent encircled by doctors and nurses running into the garden from all parts of the establishment.

In the cave, Adam reached out for her. "Berlin?"

"Yes."

"Any suspicions?"

"Lots."

"But Depardieu?"

"Bypassed for the moment, like the Abteilung."

He ran a hand over her face. "Daughter," he said intoning like a bishop, "you do this not for them, not for me, but because it excites you to ride the world between your lovely thighs, confess to me, daughter!"

She knew his analysis had as much truth, or as little, as Carnet's, but she took his hand and kissed it with mock solemnity. "Amen, padre."

Laughing, Adam slipped to his knees, his beard running electric from belly to her source, and she imagined that in this shadowy cave they were like the pair in the fairy tale, so deeply enamored they became inextricably bound by each other's tresses.

"Blessed am I"—he touched his lips to hers—"in nomine Mata Hari, gloria mundi!"

She pressed him closer to her, her fingers to his mane, grateful that he could not see her troubled face.

BERLIN STRAITS
8 March 1917

From the train window, they looked out upon a land of women.

Uniformed female conscripts were at work in the winter fields, mending fences, repairing roads, vigorously smashing freight at the way stations, driving lorries and cars and ambulances with a zest encountered only on recruiting posters.

It was all very saddening to Sita. In France, she had castigated the women's volunteer auxiliaries as traitors to the sex, poor creatures temporarily deluded into imitating men and their base games. Soon there would be an awakening, and women of all countries no longer willing to sacrifice husbands and sons and lovers would declare a general strike of the soul and end the war. Yet here on the other side of the border, it was evident the sex was capable of permanent madness and that

Germany was prepared to fight to the last distaff.

Nor were they cheered by a Serbian couple who shared their compartment. The pair had lost three sons in the war and were on the way to visit the sole remaining boy, now hospitalized in Berlin, after having been dragooned first into Austrian service, then transferred to Germany.

"It may end in other countries," the father told them, "never in ours. Each family has been betrayed by some other. We will hunt each other like wolves in the hills. After I see my son, I will go back to get revenge."

The father forced them to listen to a nonstop recital of the events of his homeland; one story dissolved into another; there were different names, but the same rapes, disembowelings of children, of bonded fraternity loosed as insatiable blood lust. Six million Serbs had been alive when their capital of Sarajevo gave birth to the war; now two million were dead, another two million maimed, and the last two million involved in ceaseless vendetta between Serbian Croats and Macedonians, neighbor against neighbor, the hills echoing to gunfire of lost bands, preying on one another.

"It can't end," the man stated with bitter satisfaction, as if in savagery man at last found his authentic connection with his kind. "We go back in a fortnight."

The wife remained wrapped in a sorrow so dense and impenetrable that even Sita did not venture to breach it.

As the train lurched north, the delays became more and more frequent, as they were shunted aside for military traffic. Parading the cold train corridors with Tha, speaking in Malay, Sita tried to revive her hopes, blasted by women, with the prospects of their Berlin mission. She reminded Tha they had often heard mention, in rumor and gossip, of the collaborative efforts by bankers and industrialists of all the countries at war to continue their normal business with one another in the midst of war. Both knew of specific cases where French notables had secretly shifted part of their wealth to Germany, fearing a French collapse; and of duplicate transactions by highly placed Germans. It seemed to Sita that Adam was right in predicting an explosive anger, once the people knew the war was being prolonged at their expense to benefit a powerful few.

But the more Sita convinced herself of their larger goal, the more she worried over the details of their assignment.

"Suppose Lenin lied?"

"It's not in his interest to lie."

"How does he know there will be this dynamiting of a Krupp plant?"

"Because he gave instructions for it."

"But he is a Russian," Sita argued. "Will Russians do the dynamiting?"

"No, Germans."

"Why should they listen to him?"

"As I explained," Tha said patiently, "his is an international party. His word carries weight with the German party."

"Yet he is going to betray his associates?"

"Yes."

"Why?"

"Because he says it is for the sake of peace."

"You believe him?"

"I believe"—Tha chose her words—"only that he wants to bring me together with Krupp, who is a most inaccessible person, and to provide me with instant bonafides as a protector of Krupp interests . . ."

"Because you will prevent the dynamiting?"

"Try to," Tha said. "Hope to."

"I would never trust such a man."

Tha sighed wearily. She knew that Sita wanted not only a blueprint of method, and a written guarantee of success, but on top of all that, purity of soul. Yet the very opposite had attracted her to Lenin's proposal. It was direct and ruthless. It not only corresponded to Lenin's character, it was a shrewd outflanking of the obstacles ahead. And in addition to opening an avenue to Krupp, it gave her an advantage she could speedily transform into the hard facts concerning the meeting with Krupp's fellow cannoneers in Geneva.

But Lenin himself had not ignored the possibility of failure. "They say Krupp is a secretive, inward sort of man, remote from associates and family."

"I've heard that too."

"Before we agree on this approach, can you think of any other?"

She had searched her mind for fragments of information about the industrialist. But she had never met him, and knew nobody who was intimate enough with him to give her the kind of introduction she needed.

"I know he is an obsessive horse breeder," Tha told Lenin. "But that path is blocked, because he closed down his stables as an exhibition of self-imposed war austerity. I believe that's his only hobby, or the only one I ever heard him having . . ."

"Then it's my plan?"

"It provides an opening."

"Only that," Lenin had agreed. "The rest is your responsibility."

Neither had mentioned, though they had both been aware, that in undertaking this plan of exposure she was no longer a neutral, but a combatant; and that from now on she would be in a zone of combat, of death, of no mercy.

Beside her, Sita began to shiver. "Aren't you cold?"

"Yes."

"You wish I were the old Sita, laughing at Monsieur Kamarupa?"

"I love even the new Sita."

"It is too cold to stay out here and listen to your lies," Sita said. "Although it's not much better to go back to the compartment and listen to that poor father again."

But the latter evil prevailed.

Back in their places in the freezing compartment, they piled coats on top of themselves, covering even their faces. That muffled, but did not shut out, the Serb and his unending threnody.

A limousine, sent by Von Jagow, picked them up at the terminal, drove at breakneck speed through the foggy night, and deposited them at a luxurious little apartment house a few streets from the Brandenburg Tor.

But the lobby of the building was icy, the elevator out of

commission, and the aged hall porter, helping them with their luggage, spoke of these hardships in the half-boastful manner of a frontline soldier: "No fuel, no fuel anywhere, and this is the hardest winter of our history!"

Sita, limping because of the cold, lagged behind. Tha, impatient after the long trip, ran up ahead of the porter to the third landing to let herself into the apartment.

In a huge drawing room, all pink and gold and plaster arabesques, a tiny fire burned in the grate. In a wing chair, a gray-haired man sat slumped, huddled under an overcoat, chin on his breast, staring fixedly into the flames.

The pose reminded her of those flamboyant portraits of Cicero who, poison cup in hand, muses on his own downfall, wondering if what he has lost is only his invented self, or, if the public mask has become his real self after all, degutted by his own deft hand, a suicide before the first swallow.

"Tha, dear Tha," he said, still brooding over the fire, "why do you stand so quietly?"

She tried not to let him see how shocked she was by the change in his appearance. A scant two years ago he had been athrust in the great world, a heavy man with a bold and crooked nose who laughed readily as if the international political scene were being played out for his sole entertainment. Now he seemed to have become the caricature always drawn by the political cartoonists in France: the Hateful Hun, hook-nosed and lantern-jawed, prognathous, ready to devour children, a gray wolf of a man.

"Theodore, how nice to see you again!"

Too late. He had already caught all the implications of her dismayed scrutiny. "I console myself that less is more." He pushed himself from the chair and came to greet her. "That is necessary, a stage on the way to proclaiming nothing is most!"

Sita's entry gave him a chance to recover some of his customary bonhomie. He welcomed her effusively and agreed with her anathemas on Berlin's damp cold. The memory of this winter in people's bones would outlast every other suffering of this terrible war.

"Let me show you about," he told them. "There's not a hotel room in Berlin that the government hasn't requisitioned.

I've sent my assistant out to bring us something to eat. He should be here at any moment."

He led the way down the corridor toward a bedroom.

"This place belongs—belonged—to Prince Hohenlohe. Killed at the front. Remember him, Tha? Climbed telephone poles when dejected. And a collector of note . . . as you will soon see . . ."

A vast bedroom too had its tiny fire in the grate, and its precious little pile of firewood. Here the walls, from floor to ceiling, bore paintings and statuary and mosaics, all devoted to the theme of Madonna and Child. Large statues occupied half the floor space. The style ranged from Byzantine pietàs, with their sense of death as merciful mother, to the present century's lush tears over man's misdeeds, from which the viewer remained happily immune.

"His main collection is in his castle in Bavaria, piled from cellar to attic. Even so, they don't rival Hindenburg's. Our marshal is the world's leading expert—if one can use so profane a word—in this sacred subject. As for me, I visited Rome and looked at Michelangelo's mother and was struck by her resemblance to an actress of my acquaintance. She seemed young enough to be the lover of the son in her lap. Perhaps that's the point of all this, of Hohenlohe's and Hindenburg's obsession. But then I was brought up by nurses, whom I detested, so don't trust me . . ."

After Sita, teeth chattering, excused herself to go off to another bedroom and seek the warmth of bed, Von Jagow led Tha back into the living room and its small fire.

"Ever since your telegram came, I've been trying to think—what was it between us, before the war, did we ever have an affair?"

Tha laughed. "If you've forgotten, so must I."

"Please, please. So much has happened since. Schemes and counterschemes. Gossip. How are the Kaiser's dinners? Does Ludendorff roll soft dough at the table, his sign of consideration, or shatter crumbs with his thumbnail, in his autocratic mood? Did you hear how Ludendorff engineered my downfall? He told the Kaiser I don't know how to bang my fist on the table, because I am too intelligent! I, a Prussian, head of the

Berlin police, a magistrate. I don't know how to make a fist. Absurd. But the mortal stroke, the stroke of genius, was to call me intelligent. I was doomed . . ."

He gave a harsh bark, and then turned to her, appalled at himself.

"Forgive me, Tha. I ws trying to remember about us. Just before the war. Give me a hint."

"A beard . . ."

He glanced at her, still not making the connection.

"I was your beard . . ."

Suddenly the crooked gray face broke into a grin of remembrance. "Stephanie Pauker, the wife of the flower vendor!" He stood up and edged closer to the fire, stretching his hands, delighted now. "We let everybody think I was pursuing you, so I could have my Stephanie . . ."

"The flowers you sent me!"

They were both warming to the episode, out of the pre-war idyll. "I was so afraid if it came to the ears of the Kaiser I was chasing the wife of a flower hustler, I'd be denied my portfolio!" He thrust his hands into the pockets of his coat and flapped them at the fire. "Thanks to this war, a man can fall lower than a bed of roses and still become Foreign Minister!"

"It was acceptable to woo me," Tha said. "I was merely scandalous!"

Von Jagow shook his head. "Did I ever tell you the upshot, Tha?"

"Never."

"Too painful," he said, ruefully. "When her husband was called up, she felt she could no longer betray him. So I got my marching papers, too!"

"Poor Theodore."

Von Jagow came back into his seat, and suddenly the gray weariness settled over him. "Comic opera," he said. "But also very real. Recently I heard he was back home, wounded. I sent her a letter, with a check. She kept the latter and sent back the former, with a few choice words about the war . . ."

He was once more in the grip of the present time, of this winter and its cold and its countless dead, knowing that, in the eyes of many in Germany and the world, the blame for all lay on his shoulders.

"Dear Tha, forgive these elegies. Tell me what it is I can do for you, even though I am out of power, which is even worse than being powerless, as you know . . ."

But before she could begin, the bell had sounded and he was on his feet calling, "Eugen!" as a willowy blond young man with a straggly gold moustache appeared leading a waiter with a large linen-covered tray. "Supper! We must eat, and then you will tell me why you came to this tortured city, in the middle of this wretched winter, to see dismal me!"

As it turned out, Von Jagow was the only one who did any eating.

Eugen Gunther did little else but blush, which he did easily and often. The young man had been assigned by the Foreign Office to help Von Jagow tidy up his papers and ease the descent from the rarified air of power to the suffocations of privacy.

Von Jagow seemed to enjoy making the youth turn crimson, and he invited Tha to share the sport with him, as he kept recounting various myths about Tha, particularly the ones about the Dutch Crown Prince, who had so delighted in her that he had begged her to introduce his sixteen-year-old virgin brother to the joys of sex, an act of brother-love and of courtesanship still celebrated in the palace at The Hague.

Though Tha was leery of making any disclosure in the presence of the young man, Von Jagow insisted that he had total confidence in Gunther, who had been his assistant for more than six months, and who had connections in the Foreign Office that might be crucial if they were to be of service to Tha.

Only after the waiter had gone and after Tha had made her appeal without interruption did Von Jagow lay his fork on his plate and his knife on its crystal rest and turn from his absorption with food to an examination of her face.

"Can we examine the position," he said, lighting up a cigarette, "to see if I understand it properly?"

"Of course, Theodore."

"Lenin's purpose in sending you was to impress the Chancellery and Krupp with his good intentions toward the Reich, in the hope of getting new funds from us."

"In general."

"And to show us how serious he is, he sent you to warn us that there is to be a Red dynamiting at the Krupp plant in Potsdam."

"Yes."

"About which he supplied you with the details?"

"Yes, all of them."

"He has chosen me," Von Jagow said, "because he fears the Abteilung would welcome such an explosion, to put further distance between us and the Reds here and in Russia."

"Exactly."

"So the difficulty," the diplomat pursued, "is to find a way to prevent that explosion, and yet not alert the Zimmerman forces in the Abteilung?"

Tha used her fingernail to draw a line on the tablecloth. "We knew Krupp is a personal friend of yours, and we hoped you and I could go to him, and we could get a few of his security men at the plant to take care of the matter."

"I can see how that would seem an answer in Geneva . . ."

"It isn't one?"

"Don't you know what they make at the Krupp plant?"

"Munitions."

"To be sure," Von Jagow said. "But what kind?"

"I don't know . . ."

"Doesn't Lenin?"

"He didn't mention it as a problem."

"They make submarine parts there," Von Jagow said. "The place crawls with Naval Intelligence. Krupp's own security guards are infiltrated by them. Anything we told them, or Krupp told them, would be in the hands of Abteilung Three within minutes, and on Zimmerman's desk an hour afterward . . ."

She made no effort to hide her dismay. In Geneva, when Lenin had outlined the plan for her to gain Krupp's confidence, it had seemed seamless. And in rehearsing it over and

175

over again to Sita on the train, she had seen no flaw in it.

Now, the perfumed smoke of Von Jagow's oval Egyptian cigarettes consigned it to airy fantasy.

"You seem depressed, Tha."

"Oh, I went around Frau Eva, thinking I could be of help to you and Krupp. Now, if the Abteilung finds out, I'll have my hands full . . ."

Von Jagow nodded, in sympathy. "Not too good."

"To be diplomatic, rotten."

Von Jagow applied himself once more to some morsels he'd left on his knife, which he now scraped clean against the edge of the plate. "One wonders if the whole matter is worth the risk to you. This submarine offensive is based on a doctored report. We've been at it, all out, for ten days. At the present rate of effectiveness, the English and the French will be brought to their knees no sooner than the middle of the century. To be perfectly blunt, Tha, if it weren't for the danger to lives in the plant, one might reasonably ignore the whole matter . . ."

"Give it up? Go home?"

Von Jagow kept honing his knife.

For the first time Eugen intervened. "I believe one can infer from His Excellency's remarks, the entire matter lies outside his province. If it embarrasses you to inform the Abteilung, he is too polite to tell you, he should stay out of it, too. He has enough enemies as it is."

Von Jagow put down his knife with a clatter. "You have not been listening, Eugen!"

"I thought I had, Your Excellency."

"Only to superficialities." Von Jagow frowned. He pushed away from the table and stood up. "There are basic policy questions here. I have again and again recommended our support of subversion in Russia. It is essential we do not fight a two-front war. To dismiss Lenin's new approach to us would be a continuation of all the old stupidities!"

Eugen looked up. "But, sir, those are no longer—"

"My responsibilities?"

"I only meant"—Gunther turned scarlet—"officially."

"And officially, I'm deceased?"

"Sir—"

Von Jagow rose abruptly, apologizing for having to leave. "This rich food—one is used to rationing. Stay, Eugen. The chauffeur will see to me. A little touch of The Hague would do you no harm at all . . ."

Tha walked him to the door, but there, without warning, Von Jagow crumpled to the floor. She kneeled in panic, but his eyes opened and, hoarsely, he urged her not to worry. Eugen had come running and located the minister's pillbox and pressed a small white tablet in his mouth. Von Jagow, Eugen explained, had a heart condition, and brought on these attacks by his habit of eating too quickly.

Together, they assisted the diplomat to the fourposter in the bedroom. Again he apologized to Tha, closed his eyes, and assured her that he would be on his way after an interval of rest.

Despite her promptings, Eugen refused to leave. Instead, he went back to the table and began to consume his untouched meal. He was bitterly abusive, blaming Tha for having brought on the attack.

"For a diplomat," Tha said, "you say some odd things."

"But I'm not one," Eugen retorted. "I'm the last surviving son of a Hanover banker, shoved into the Foreign Office so there'll be somebody around to run the bank after the war."

From time to time he went to the door of the bedroom to have a look at Von Jagow. Slowly his hostility dissipated as he explained the present atmosphere in Berlin, the failure to agree on the terms of a negotiated peace that had led to Von Jagow's dismissal. Those who, like the Kaiser, believed in the chance of achieving a quick victory with a submarine offensive had carried out a purge of a particularly vindictive character.

"I know of a banker here who was viciously isolated from friends, family, business, because he had suggested the time for peace had come. It took the entire banking fraternity to rescue him from this social oubliette. But Von Jagow doesn't have a bank. He's a civil servant. Right now he's on the edge of suffering house arrest by innuendo. And this affair of yours could easily be the pretext for worse—"

"In short, compared to Von Jagow, I'm not worth the risk."

"That's crude," Eugen said. "But accurate."

"Thank you, Eugen."

Eugen went on eating and then stomped off to the bedroom again. This time, she could hear their voices. After a time, Von Jagow came back into the living room, while Eugen trailed, carrying the older man's shoes and hat. He had never removed his coat.

"Dear Tha, I decided if I'm to expire ignobly from indigestion, I should at least do it in my own bed."

Eugen helped him on with his shoes.

Von Jagow waited for him, valiantly trying to regain his old verbal buoyancy. "Of course, Eugen is right in one way. It's out of hand. We magnify English morality; they mythologize our discipline. We took Belgium as a military expedient, but it's cited as our crime. If I had proposed going to war to annex Belgium in 1914, they would have clapped me into an asylum. Now we won't give it up. The French do the same. They are reliving 1870. The Czar has ancestral dreams of Constantinople. Ah, I won't go on. We rehearse the past, with bullets and blood, but the past seems safer than the future—"

They all went down the stairs together, Eugen supporting Von Jagow on one side and Tha on the other. He made no direct reference to their conversation, except to reminisce about Krupp. "When I first met him, Gustav was an attaché in the embassy in Washington. A sports car enthusiast. That was before he met the munitions heiress and became Von Halbach *mit* Krupp. Gustav loved America. Ironic that he subscribes to an unrestricted submarine warfare that will help provoke the Americans to come into this endless bloodletting. Still, he can't have forgotten his days in the foreign service. He knows the value of subversion—though he fears it as a dangerously communicable disease. I think—in spite of everything—Gustav knows how to listen . . ."

The chauffeur had gone to the hall porter's place to keep warm and Eugen went round to fetch him. Von Jagow tried to cheer Tha with a compliment. "Perhaps," he said, "my mistake was not sending you those flowers in earnest, Tha. . . . Tonight was most enjoyable; you gave me the illusion of power again, and that's worth a little heartburn!''

Later, in the apartment, Sita came in to join her in the big bed. They were profligate in their use of the small supply of the cordwood, but the room remained clammy. Sita could not get over the shocking change in the appearance of Von Jagow, but refused to accept the reality of the impasse. Von Jagow, she insisted, had not changed his personality. He had long been a friend, and he would not abandon Tha.

Though Sita finally fell asleep, Tha could not. Dawn came, and, with it, fog seeped into the room. It formed a softening nimbus around the sorrowing mothers and their fallen sons. Tha hoped it might contain the poor ghost of Hohenlohe visiting his collection, and on that fantasy, yielded consciousness.

At eleven-thirty promptly Eugen came by the apartment to drive her to the Krupp factory. He had been brusque and resentful on the phone. "Congratulate yourself, Madame," he had said sarcastically. "His Excellency has added you to his overburdened shoulders."

The day before, Von Jagow had phoned to assure her that he was still seeking a solution and would let her know what conclusions he had reached, helpful or otherwise. Not until Eugen's call had there been any hint of a way forward.

Ahead of their auto, fog lay in patches, turning the city into a molting animal. Hairy grayness would be followed by bald spots, where even the sky could be glimpsed, though still gray and wintry. The streets were choked by heavy military traffic, impeded by the uncertain visibility. The side windows were covered with moisture, so she could see little except for rivulets trickling down the pane, like those ancient maps that divided the unknown with imaginary streams.

She had to keep prodding Eugen. He seemed mulish about the slightest information. She gathered that a small luncheon was being staged at the executive suite at the plant—a party to bid farewell to Krupp, who was about to leave on an inspection tour of his facilities around the country.

Tha tried to conceal her interest behind a casual question. "Oh? When's he going?"

"I don't know," Eugen said irritably. "And it's beside the point."

"So it is. Sorry. What about the Abteilung?"

"His Excellency has gone to his old friends in the Berlin Police Department to provide protection for the guests. It seems there has been a crank letter threatening them. So it's not an intelligence affair at all. In fact, you are one of the threatened guests . . ."

Tha looked out at the oblique world, feeling a guilty relief. "Wonderful!"

"About this bombing," Eugen said, "did you write down the details as His Excellency suggested?"

"Yes."

"Let me have it, please."

She took the paper from her purse and watched Eugen shove it carelessly into the pocket of his mackintosh.

"Will Krupp be there?"

"I imagine. Why?"

"I'd like to meet him."

"Why?"

"He's the richest man in the world."

"He's a monk, an heirophant of steel. Unless you can make small talk about ingots, you won't get far with him. . . . But the whole thing is really ghoulish, dynamite for lunch. I keep hoping we'll get lost in this fog."

"I can't afford such . . . sensibility."

Eugen grimaced. "Neither can I," he acknowledged. "Ignoring an invitation from Krupp isn't the better part of valor, not in the Foreign Office it isn't."

They had entered a factory area where coal smoke hung heavily. Military trucks, with their headlights, loomed like giants in their path, only to slide by with furtive, downcast eyes.

Tha leaned out of the window, peering into the murk, sharing Eugen's distaste, yet ever more apprehensive that the

fog would prevent then from reaching the factory by noon—
the hour scheduled for the dynamiting.

Ordinarily the enormous smokestacks of the Krupp
arms complex could be seen for miles. But in the fumy morning
all they could make out was a pulsating red glare in the midst
of darkness, an abscess that stayed just out of reach of the inci-
sion of their headlights.

And then they were within it, assaulted and overwhelmed, sound and light dissolving into each other. The glare
of great furnaces fused great crashes into a third element.
Spectrum stretched along the whine of steel on the lathes until
it blinded and deafened simultaneously, having no source,
close as an eyelid, lost in infinity.

Slowly their eyes and ears adjusted, and they could resolve the road leading past the gates of the factory, taking them
into a vast quadrangle illuminated by globes atop a hundred
tall poles, surrounded by long, low, blackish buildings from
which there flashed the white light of the foundries. Small
donkey engines crossed the open space, hauling boxcars toward
unseen tracks; long trucks, piled high with steel parts covered
by tarpaulin, waited to shoot the gap to the gate.

Tha could detect no sign of special surveillance. At the
gate Eugen had given their names, and the guard waved them
on to the administration building at the far end of the quad.
Uniformed porters took charge of the car and they were
ushered by elevator to an executive dining room, a spacious
chamber with glistening wood panels, cushioned from the factory's thunder by heavily padded drapes that completely covered the windows.

Once inside the already densely filled room, Eugen
promptly left her to go to Von Jagow, who was surrounded by
elderly men in the fancy uniforms of the court, though what
their emblems meant Tha had never really learned. At these
functions every group lined up according to rank; Von Jagow,
as the previous Foreign Secretary, held a status equal to that of
the Kaiser's intimates. Hence, where they stood was the summit of the room, and all grades flowed downward from the oc-
cult height.

Nor was it difficult to distinguish the senior Krupp executives. They were all in dark suits and all wore identical ribbons in their lapels, denoting war service in an essential industry. They commingled with navy and army officers of command rank and above, and their talk concerned itself exclusively with production schedules and fuel shortages and delivery targets.

Just below stood their wives, deeply involved in other trade information of equal urgency, which might suddenly decide their fate. They were keeping minute charts of the Kaiser's growing paranoia, always carefully disguised as the most amusing and delicious and harmless gossip.

Edging among them, Tha gleaned bits about the Kaiser's recent birthday ball, at which the Kaiser and his cousin, the Crown Prince of Prussia, had openly quarreled. The Kaiser had accused his fellow Hohenzollern of shirking frontline duty and being a secret sympathizer of the English enemy, in correspondence, via his brother-in-law, the Duke of Connaught, with British intelligence. As a result of the imbroglio, the Crown Prince had not only been banished from court but had been compelled to have himself examined by alienists at a sanatorium. Now the ladies discreetly worried that their husbands and sons, who had been friendly with the Crown Prince, might soon fall victim to similar allegations.

One of the executives—close-cropped and jowly as the rest—twinkled and made gestures to Tha, and she sidled past the women to join him. Eager to impress the famous Mata Hari, he spoke freely about Herr Krupp's coming tour of various factories in the Krupp domain. It had been planned a long time, though this luncheon had been rather impromptu. No, Krupp was not here yet, but he would be glad to introduce her when the master arrived.

One of the wives steered her away to beg a personal favor. Whispering, she confided that her lover, an English gardener, had been interned in a German prison camp just outside Basel. She was unable, because of her husband, to visit, and even writing had been difficult. Would Tha, on her return to Switzerland, stop off and bring the poor man a letter, some money?

Their private conference evoked the attention of a tall young man, and Tha was sure that he was one of the many naval intelligence men in the room. The matron broke off and hurriedly rejoined her group. Engaging the eavesdropper in a new conversation, Tha could see that Von Jagow had disappeared from among the court gentry.

Eugen came across to her to say blandly that he would get her a plate of food, and to mention, in passing, that he heard that Krupp had been delayed and would not attend his own party. "You'll have to collar your billionaire another time, it appears . . ."

She could see the hand creeping to the noon hour, and broke from him to start toward the window.

Halfway to her goal she was intercepted by a film director she'd met in the past, who demanded her complete attention. She had difficulty being pleasant, half dragging him to the window. From without, partly lost in the clatter of plates and talk, a whistle shrilled a five-minute warning for the lunch shift.

"We're doing *Golem*," the director was saying, "at the new studios at Neubabelsberg. And it is the new Babel indeed. The meddling! We've been cleared by the Propaganda Ministry, and the legend plainly warns the people not to worship the false god of their own creature comfort when their community and country are in danger. They say the war draws soldiers closer together than lovers. But what is does to civilians—ah, there is no shortage of enemies on the home front!"

She managed to separate the draperies with her toe while making the expected responses to the director's woes. Through the slit she could see the quadrangle fill with workers, some streaming toward the gates, others sauntering to find places at the benches by the side of the buildings, taking out their lunches from sacks and boxes. Only the donkey engines continued their uproar as the giant works slowed into silence.

"I would love to have you in one of the episodes," the director pursued her. "We could film your dance. An enchantment that keeps people from their duty. Don't you see how marvelously that would fit?"

From below, gunfire sounded, cracking out above all the

other sounds. She saw the workers beginning to scatter, making for the shelter of the buildings or throwing themselves to the ground. After a moment, two men, with large paper sacks, ran wildly toward the gate. Behind them came a dozen plain-clothesmen, firing at will from service revolvers.

"Or perhaps, if you prefer," the director went on, oblivious, accepting the sounds as normal to the factory din, "there's a scene in which the figure of Salome—"

One of the pair sprawled, face down, on the cobbles, blood oozing from his head. Some of his pursuers ran to retrieve his package while others stood over him and pumped revolver shots into his body, providing it with postmortem convulsions.

". . . with a decapitated head on the tray of a bicycle, rides past the Golem—what the devil is that, Tha?"

In the quadrangle, a second man had been cornered. It was easy to see, now that the director had pulled aside the drapery. The garish floodlights drew their gaze directly to the man's terrified face. He stood quite still as the police closed in, firing as they advanced. He hurled his paper sack at them, but it landed short of them and did no damage. Yet it halted his pursuers for a moment, giving him time to run again, seeking to use an advancing donkey engine as a shield against their fire. He moved quickly, only to be tripped up by the track, and she saw him go down on his hands and knees, crawling like an infant, as the engine bore down on him, brakes screeching, before it obliterated him from their view.

Guests had crowded all the windows, jabbering in excitement. Tha pushed her way out, hearing Von Jagow's voice sounding above the clamor, uttering words of reassurance. Some thieves, he answered, trying to steal some valuable equipment made of platinum. They had been caught red-handed by the police. Nobody need worry; it was all well in hand.

Nauseated and shaken, she found herself at the bar, knowing herself as the executioner of the two men, offered up by Lenin and Martov and herself and Adam on the altar of necessity, making incantations about the greatest good for the greatest number. Nor had the corpses been any impediment to

Krupskaya's firm trod, the gray face looking rigidly ahead, immutable in its kindliness.

Eugen joined her. He was pale. His mouth twisted sardonically. "To the victors, the spoils. The great Krupp wants to meet you later on!" He turned away as the bartender extended a tray of canapés.

Though she knew the thousands of flaring torches were meant to achieve an effect of somber, Teutonic majesty, that didn't prevent her from having a reaction of submissive fear. Burning atop the grandstands that lined both sides of the Brandenburg Tor, their smoke formed a menacing cloud over the packed thousands in the stands and the many more thousands crowding the park behind the triumphal arch at the end of the broad avenue, all waiting impatiently for the unveiling of their idols, their own ceremony of subservience.

The last preliminaries were coming to a close, as Eugen guided her to a box seat. Schoolboys, wet from sweat and fog, thrust narrow hips toward the finishing tape. Under the crowd's roar, Eugen leaned close, whispering, "There, Madame, there's your mark. Behind us!"

A frowning man of middle height, with a sharp thin curved nose, was coming down the steps. Two generals from the imperial staff, acting more as bodyguards than companions, brushed aside the greetings of those in their seats, to assist the arms maker to a roped-off section just above the level of the street.

Eugen had been drinking steadily since they had left the factory. She had encouraged his assumption that she was an adventuress tracking the spoor of the millionaire. And Eugen had lost no chance to show his contempt for what he considered her futile chase.

"Our very own Herr Gustav Krupp von Bohlen und Halbach. We take pride that he is the richest man in the world, even if he got there at our expense. Shall I start counting your gold marks, Madame?"

In the avenue, a white bearded man in a lavish cape of purple velvet trimmed with ermine began to shepherd the youthful winners to receive their trophies from Krupp. The old man was the Court Chamberlain and he lent an air of pomp and cut a more regal figure than his absent and paralytic monarch, Kaiser Wilhelm, reportedly ailing at his country estate.

With a wave of a jeweled staff he preceded the youngsters along the middle of the avenue. A military band, one of many standing in formation, struck up the Double Eagle anthem. The crowds beyond the arch responded with a roar and had to be held by police cordons from demonstrating their fervor.

In front of the arch stood seven giant forms, swathed mysteriously in muslin. They rose sixty feet, colossi in white, gathering strength from the dwarfs at their feet, their heads lost in the fuliginous mists like the legendary host of Wotan.

Staircases rose alongside each of the great figures, and then permitted descent on the other side of an inverted V. In unison, seven of the victorious youths mounted those stairs, waiting at the top for the anthem's climax, and then, at a signal from the Chamberlain, yanked ropes that released the coverings, revealing the massive wooden statues, the deities of a nation at war, the marshals and admirals of the German empire.

The sound that came from the throats about her was raw and visceral with release, as if a stone had been rolled away from the entrance to Valhalla, that at last the multitude might enter and receive the blessings of their heroes, more than recompense for all their privations and sufferings.

At once the grandstands erupted, and people poured down to the street to follow the procession of notables advancing to the carved goliaths. Pulled along by Eugen, pressed by the surging bodies, she confusedly made out the faces of the heroes, endowed with vitality and expression by the flickering torchlight. They were faces that had become Germany for the world. Hindenburg, the father figure himself, dominated the center, one great square hand tucked into the buttons of his greatcoat, booted legs widespread, unshakably rooted in northern earth. On his right stood Von Ludendorff. His smaller, sharper head seemed inadequate to the thick trunk beneath. Yet something about this lack of symmetry made him more dynamic, more fearsomely alive than all the others. Von Moltke, Von Falkenhayn, Von Mackensen, Von Tirpitz, Von

Schlieffen, also bestrode the avenue, looming up against the cavernous sky, their names like shrapnel, neither men or gods, vessels of duty, mighty rods to coerce any who fell from the line, whether from weakness or strength.

The press of the crowd carried her up one of the stairways until she stood near the shoulder of one of the great figures. Eugen handed her a long slender iron spike and a hammer, instructing her to drive it into the wood. "Armor for our heroes," he told her. "Your turn, Madame."

Already a portion of the giant bristled with spikes. Some had been driven in deep, others stood out like quills. Part of the malevolent coat to be provided by a worshipful and obedient nation. Tha managed a few uneven taps and fled down the steps.

On the street a soldier waited for her descent. He had one empty sleeve, and he presided over a large carton surmounted by a flag. Into it the folk were dumping money, watches, jewelry, furs, even their overcoats.

Eugen scattered some coins into the box and then yanked her away. "Who says we Germans don't know how to enjoy ourselves?" he asked bitterly. "Now are you ready to get drunk with me?"

On the way back to the box, they fell in with some of the younger relatives of the Krupp family. Most of the young men wore their field-gray uniforms. They seemed to share Eugen's mood, and passed a bottle from hand to hand. The tone of their celebration had a self-wounding mockery that strongly reminded her of Adam, who once told her that the last privilege of the aristocracy, being swept to the herd's elected doom, was to choose wit above illumination.

"Lady McLeod?"

Krupp stood beside her, bowing.

"Krupp," he said, reaching for her hand and passing his lips in its general neighborhood. "We are grateful you were able to join us." He straightened, and began to walk alongside her to the box. "Deeply so, Madame. Will you be staying in Berlin?"

"Unfortunately," she said, "I have obligations in Geneva."

"But I heard there was the possibility of your doing some film work here."

Tha glanced at the pale eyes, lively under a habitual gravity. "Had I known the source of that invitation, Herr Krupp, I might have thought more about it."

A faint smile touched the ascetic but perceptive face. "No, Madame, pass it by. These days, our culture is rumps and flags, waved separately or together. I'm told that if our authors and artists are doing serious work, they safely keep it concealed for riper times. And so, alas, must a more extended meeting between us ..."

"This tour, you mean ..."

"Yes, Madame."

"Will you be away long?"

"I'll have a chance to get back to Essen and my family," he said. "Von Jagow tells me your given name is Margaretha."

"Yes."

"My wife's as well. And that of Ludendorff's spouse. I would like to pledge you, Madame, one day, I'll bring all three Margarethas together so we can demonstrate our gratitude for an act that must presently pass in silence ..."

A shout went up beside them. Two of the youngsters had pinned a third to the street. One of the attackers had a hammer and one of the spikes.

"Karl!"

"But Uncle," the boy said, "we only want to make him a Reich's hero!"

Krupp advanced a step toward them and all three scrambled away. He came back, frowning indulgently. "Barbarians," he said, "but what other breed these days?"

Tha made one more desperate effort. "Since you are going to Essen, and I am going to Geneva, perhaps we can travel together?"

"How one would enjoy that," Krupp said regretfully. He struggled to alter his fixed frown into a smile of genuine warmth. "I neglect so much, so much. I can only offer, lamely, any help I can be to you in return for what you have done—not only for me but for the Reich ..."

He reached for her hand, and this time, his kiss was more than perfunctory. As he straightened up, the two generals came automatically to his side, smiling for him toward her, and helping him make his retreat, smooth as a parade drill.

Alone, chafed and irritated by Krupp's elegant evasiveness, she tried to measure her failure. In Geneva, success had seemed a human possibility. What she had not foreseen were the iron social molds that locked in even a Krupp, whom she had expected to be exempt from them.

Above her, from one of the rows in the box, she heard a malicious laugh and looked up to see a wrinkled crone in an outmoded black beaded dress that reached to her ankles, gathering scalloped layers of braided material as it fell. The old woman, wrapped in a fur, was examing her with viperish glee.

"What did you expect? A soiree at the Krupp palace? A bit of the *vrai* Gustav, God forbid?"

Wincing, Tha turned to look for Eugen and his cavorting group. But the sharp voice of the old woman came down on her querulously. "Have I given you leave to go?"

Tha still sought escape. "Excuse me, but I'm with a friend and—"

"Never mind that!" the old lady interjected imperiously. "Unlike the gentleman who just left, I am an authentic Krupp. He has to be more Krupp than Krupp, and I can be less, almost tolerable . . ."

The fur coat across her knees impeded her effort to rise. "Come, give me a hand here. I let the servant go and touch wood or drive spikes in evil spirits or whatever else is going on here today!"

Others in the box had taken notice and Tha, embarrassed, came to help the spiteful old woman into her padded caracul as the only way to stop her ravings.

"There," Tha said. "Anything else?"

"Nothing, Mata Hari," the old woman said. "Did you think you would trick me with a kindness to help you peddle yourself to that tacky nephew of mine?"

"But—"

"Run along. You are beautiful—and stupid!"

She came down the steps, waving her away with a lit

cigar. She was not quite five feet tall. Age had taken away all sexual identity, leaving a structure repellent in its harsh and unconcealed avidity, a scrawny bird of prey, her perversity concentrated in her bright eyes.

"Mathilde!" she called. "Come quickly—I'm dying for a smoke!" At a distance a plump young maid was surrounded by some soldiers. She either failed to hear the summons, or ignored it, letting herself be turned away by her admirers.

Tha couldn't make sense of that, and the old woman had now suddenly swung back to her. "I was once told that Count Esterhazy, in great ecstasy, bit off one of your nipples!"

Tha laughed. "I've heard that, too."

"True or not true?"

"Count Esterhazy is not only a diplomat," Tha said, "but a Hungarian, who reserves his rhapsodies for good cooking."

The old woman stared at Tha and reached out a hand and poked at her breasts. "I thought you would have big ones, but you have no front porch to speak of. Here, if you want to do me a good turn—give me a drag on this."

Tha, astonished, was forced to take the old woman's cigar.

"Inhale it!" The old lady was almost beside herself with cranky impatience. "And then breathe it into me! I have emphysema. It has to be purified for me!"

Tha inhaled, as the old woman opened her mouth in a greedy circle, a voracious nestling waiting to be fed. Tha had to remind herself of her own predicament before she brought her lips to the other's and exhaled the smoke.

With closed eyes, the old woman savored her addiction.

"Make you sick?" she demanded.

Tha shrugged. "A lovely cigar."

The bright flickering dark eyes lit up with humor. "A liar! Which proves you have some intelligence. I'm Natalie von Krupp—his wife's aunt. Come and have dinner with me, and we'll see what we can do for you!"

Going in search of Eugen, Tha imagined Frau Eva, coiled against one of Ludendorff's legs, waiting for her to fail, her smile seraphic.

> *It's a long long way to gay Paree,*
> *Even longer for the German infantry . . .*

Four warbling Krupps danced about a fat little streetwalker they had brought home with them. Other members of
the clan littered the floor. Some were covered with blankets,
some found warmth covering each other. It was not simply a
matter of fuel shortage, they had told Tha. The founder of the
family had decreed that money must not be wasted in heating
the palace in winter, and the absent Gustav enforced the edict
to the last sacrosanct degree.

> *Save yourself with saltpeter, Peter.*
> *Do be careful about vermin, Hermann.*

Two of the dancers were debs. They were garbed in
borrowed field grays and they strutted around the chubby
whore, booted and belted, groping at her from time to time.
Meanwhile, two cousins, in borrowed tutus and leotards, performed quite creditable pirouettes, absent, with leave of the
present company, from their male and martial fronts. Now and
then the rotund sister of the night threw out a thick ankle, in a
show of gratitude for being in such noble company.

> *Take heart, hear the dernier cri,*
> *You can be gay, and sans Paree!*

Swaying, a Krupp whelp came in with an armful of
bottles. "Uncle Gustav's very own usquebaugh! Hoarders be
warned, everything will be taken from you! This is war!" He
wandered around the room, distributing his loot, and, when
rejected, sprinkled the refusers with some of the purloined
liquor.

One young man was very intently painting the tree of
life on the shivery body of a young woman, inverting it so that
the pubic hair represented the roots, and the girl's legs were
wild twin trees, growing downward from heaven. From time to
time the girl made cutting remarks about the artist's literalness.
Her thighs were long and creamy and inviting. Periodically

some of the others came along to find an unpainted spot to kiss, planting lipstick knots, teeth-mark burls.

Unlike the others, Eugen refrained from drugs, and he sat alone with a bottle between his knees, drinking steadily, looking up every now and then to examine Tha. He had willingly come along to the Krupp palace, and it was clear to her that he was under some directive by Von Jagow to keep her in tow.

Tha ached to get away to make a search of the house, hoping somewhere to find a clue to Krupp's itinerary, but there'd been Eugen's eyes, and servants, and young people urging her to join in drug or drink.

"Mata Hari!"

From the doorway, Baroness Natalie beckoned insistently.

The old woman had disappeared some time ago, without any explanation. There had been no food, nor any hint that it would soon be served.

"Help me with this!"

The old woman had a huge platter, covered with cooked meat. That was all: steaks, piled high; in its abundance, somehow revolting.

"No more kinderspiel," the old woman said. "To business."

Escaping, Tha felt Eugen's eyes following her.

Bearing the smoking food, Tha followed the old woman along the granite imitation Gothic corridor. She had already subjected the dowager to intense questioning about Gustav's travel plans, but Baroness Natalie answered testily that her nephew's comings and goings, like everything else about him, were of little interest to her.

At intervals Tha had suggested that she be shown about the house, but the baroness had shrugged that away, too. "A dreadful place," she had told Tha. "It will only depress you."

Yet she had shown an insatiable curiosity about the details of Tha's love life. The riper, the better. She set the tone for confessions with a tale about one of the Empress's current ladies-in-waiting who forced all her lovers to get themselves circumcised before she granted them her favors, and then made a collection of their prepuces, which she preserved in perfume bottles and exhibited on her vanity table. "She has fashioned more Hebrews than the Grand Rabbi!"

A narrow winding flight terminated in pitch blackness. "Here, here"—the old woman's bony hand reached out and plucked her along—"it's only a few steps and the light switch is a kilometer away . . ."

Tha, balancing the plate, helped her push open an ornate oaken door.

Dim oil lamps, suspended from the walls, illuminated a lofty but narrow chapel. In place of windows, there were arches, paned with stained glass whose religious images were given wavering life by candles placed behind them.

In the shadows, Tha made out several figures. Some men were polishing sacramentalia, others waxing oak benches and stalls. One huge fellow gave luster to a large silver cross mounted on the wall behind the pulpit.

All the men wore army drill. On their backs were the white letters identifying them as prisoners of war. Their heads, shaven, made them seem a band of acolytes.

The baroness pointed to an offertory table in front of a smaller altar to the Virgin. It was the sort of table where women customarily left their gifts for the church. "Set it there, my dear."

Tha stood aside as the old woman knelt and then dutifully picked at beads with her taloned hands. Her lips moved in silence. The prisoners continued silently with their chores.

But if they were not taking any notice of the baroness, the old lady was examining them. Her eyes flickered from one prisoner to another, full of the same impatient hunger she had shown for the inhalation from her cigar.

"Cossacks," she whispered to Tha. "I feed them and they nourish me. Which one shall it be?"

Tha was slow to grasp the inference

"But you must help," the old lady said crossly. "I can't do it by myself. I always have one of the backfische along here to rub them up a bit. The meat isn't enough, not for my dried withers . . ."

She rose from her observances and grasped Tha's arm, pulling her past a large wooden screen. In the alcove, usually reserved for the choir, stood a bed, piled with puffy goosedown quilts.

"Afterward, you can have free run of the house, though I can tell you beforehand you won't find Gustav. Mostly he sleeps at his factories. One ought to say, with them!"

Abruptly she left Tha and went around the screen and stood observing the men, who had now crowded around the plate and were tearing at the meat and stuffing hunks into their mouths.

"Russian, you!" she said and pointed to the giant who had been so scrupulous with the cross.

Her eyes were feverish as she came back to Tha and her voice trembled with excitement. "Liebchen, help warm me, too." She touched Tha's breasts with her tiny claws. "I take it back. They are lovely. I never had much. I am a mean old witch, am I not?"

Raptly chewing, the great Cossack came around the screen. In the oil light, his head was an auric egg. The old woman took his great hands and directed them toward Tha, bobbing her head up and down, the layers of jet beads on her dress shaking. Tha felt the huge thighs pressing against her and heard the old lady's diseased lungs labor to breathe the heavy chapel airs, each breath an infantile cry of enchantment.

From the walls, the oil portraits of deceased Krupps glowered down at her, ominous witnesses to her defiling passage through the silent rooms.

Though she tried to move on the balls of her feet, the uneven stone floors frequently caught her heels and the sound went barreling along the granite hallways. She had to depend on the light coming from the windows, the torchlight from the ceremonies at the Brandenburg Tor just a few hundred feet away, creating shadows that made threatening obstacles of the massive furniture.

On the avenue, the military bands, sometimes playing in unison, sometimes alone, struck up airs that had a subtle dance beat, conveying a cozy vision of war, to be enjoyed from the jolly corner of a beer garden.

Fainter, from the room where the cubs were at play,

voices shrilled and whooped, punctuated by the twanging of a harp, struck with abandon, antiphonies that made it harder for her to control her movements, sickened by the odor of meat and the lingering smell of the Cossack on her body.

So many, many rooms. Each, like its neighbor, a warehouse of lumpish mahogany, carved with grotesque animals that crouched to attack her, not so much because she was an intruder, but because she was warm and alive.

Her fingertips encountered the leather bindings of thick ledgers. Near the window, the gleaming top of a huge desk. His study? Risk a light?

A small golden pool spread from the lamp to the onyx inkwell and widened across the inlaid surface. A leather folder. The papers inside it were covered with numbers. The center drawer, a silver letter opener, a small tin of lozenges, a sheaf of memoranda. No day book; no appointment calendar; not even a scratch pad.

In the corridor, running feet.

Awkwardly, she extinguished the lamp and swiftly retraced her steps to the door, sheltering herself against the wall, tightening against the approaching sounds.

One of the tutus flashed by, shrieking, pursued by the other. If they had seen the light, they were too involved in their own to stop.

Emerging, she found herself a half dozen paces from an aged butler. He frowned at her. Despairing, she ran by him, crying to the dancing pair to wait for her. She was conscious of the butler's frowning disapproval of their antics and hers.

Plunging on in the wake of the pair, she hurled herself up the staircase, stumbling on the unfamiliar turns. Above her, she heard a door slam and soon the sounds ceased. Below, she could hear the butler padding in pursuit.

At the landing, she could not decide where the master bedroom might be: there were double doors at both ends of the hall. She chose right, hurried by the sound of the butler's steps on the stairs.

The room was a cavern lit by the uncertain light of the torches outside. At the far end, a small bed with a prim white coverlet. Near the window, small chairs, covered in needlepoint, and a delicate kidney-shaped desk. If this was Krupp's bedroom, he wasn't a monk, as Eugen had said, but a fearful virgin.

In the center of the desk, a blotter in a leather holder. And in one corner of this blotter, a small sheet, a carbon copy, neatly typed.

In misery, she saw that she had failed to close the door behind her and, in fear of the old servant, she had no courage to turn on a light again.

Trembling, she bore her prize to the window. A schedule. Time, in disciplined segments. 8:15 Breakfast, Thinnes. An address. Names and addresses in precise order. Prince Max von Baden, Dinner. Ceremonies, Brandenburg Tor. Her own name. Final entry: *11:15 P.S.* In the corner of the page, inked secretarial initials.

Lights flooded and drained the world away, leaving her in perilous space.

From the doorway, Eugen grimaced, a bottle held in his clenched fist. "Never give up, do you?"

Her throat worked without utterance, and pain thrust a beak under her breastbone.

"Still looking for him?"

"What else?"

She could not conceal the page. She brought it back to the desk. He advanced slowly. His eyes were bloodshot and bleary. He stood beside her, examining the memorandum, and his voice was filled with scorn.

"Why did the Abteilung send you?"

"You're crazy."

"What do they want, did they send you to frame Von Jagow? They won't be satisfied until they prove he's a traitor!"

"You're drunk, Eugen."

"I warned him against you—but he wouldn't listen!" Eugen laughed harshly and went past her to the window. "But you had no trouble seeing through me, did you?"

"You?"

"I saw you watching me ever since you came here," he said wearily. "The Abteilung leaves you no choice, isn't that the excuse?" He drank again from the bottle. "They have to destroy him. We are sleepwalkers, moving toward extinction, convinced we'll be unscathed, only others must die in our place . . ."

She came slowly to the youth's side. His face was drained of color. He was staring out unseeing at the distant torches burning before the extravagant icons.

"Does Von Jagow know?"

Eugen shook his head. "They threatened to send me to the front. I am a great coward. More so, now that my brothers are dead. I do what they ask . . ."

"You were assigned to destroy him?"

Utterly abject, the young diplomat leaned against the pane. "I wanted to tell him. But I was afraid. I admire him. Everything he says is true. But I am trained to be obedient. I am a specialist in it."

"Did you report my conversations with him to the Abteilung?"

"I should have. I still should. I can't be one thing or the other, theirs or his. I am nothing, can't you see that?"

Guilt and alcohol had him locked into a paralysis of degradation. His obsessive need to confess was part of the sentence he had passed on himself, and what he wanted was not forgiveness, but, as an obedient child, punishment.

At the desk, she scrawled a note to Von Jagow, thanking him for his help and telling him that she had to leave at once for Geneva.

"Eugen, I must go. Will you give this to His Excellency for me, please?"

He nodded remotely.

"Good-bye, Eugen. I wish I could help you."

When she left, he was still at the window, miserably staring down at the great totems of the national religion.

For the first time since coming to Berlin, Sita found something to throw her heart into: packing to leave. In her eyes, all Switzerland had become a tropical paradise and the Potsdam Station was its gateway: 11:15 the time of departure.

Tha, on her part, wanted to be there well in advance. A phone call had readily established that the 11:15 from Berlin went to Basel, thence to Geneva. But that still left unknown the most vital fact of all: would he be on the train? There were several bars and restaurants in the great terminal, and one ought to serve as an observation post. Her plan with Lenin called for her to send a telegram to Kuprin informing him of her arrival in Geneva. It would be essential for Lenin to have notification beforehand so he could arrange to have the arms maker followed from the Geneva depot. But it would be foolish to risk that wire until she was certain that Krupp was indeed aboard and on his way to the rendezvous.

The ancient hall porter groaned over every valise, and Sita, trying to preserve the old man's dignity, made elaborate excuses to grab the heavy bags and run down the steps, even forgetting to complain about the icy drafts coming from the lobby.

Everything had finally been assembled below when a man in a heavy overcoat appeared and announced himself to Tha as a detective from the Berlin police force. He eyed the baggage, and then, still polite, asked that Tha accompany him.

"Why?"

"Routine identification, Madame," he said neutrally. "Won't take long."

"But I'm leaving for Geneva!"

"Have your woman take your things to the terminal. When's your train, Madame?"

"Elevenish."

"Should be done by then."

In the police car, the detective remained uncommunicative and his companion was a model of taciturnity. They drove her back past the crowds at the Brandenburg Tor, thence down the main avenue itself to the center of the now vacated grandstands.

At a small gardener's shack beside the Tiergarten, the car pulled to a stop. Several uniformed police were on hand, and, at a little distance, a knot of people, the inevitable curiosity seekers of the streets.

Before they let her in, the detective murmured something about an unfortunate event, and said he had been silent to spare her feelings.

Inside, a senior detective greeted her by name and held out a folded sheet. It was, she saw, the same one she had given to Eugen.

"Yours, Madame?"

"Yes."

"You gave it to Eugen Gunther?"

"Yes."

"When?"

"Less than an hour . . ."

"Notice anything about him?"

"He was drinking."

"Depressed?"

"Oh, the way people are when they've had a lot . . ."

"Nothing extraordinary?"

"No."

The senior rose and started for an adjoining door, but changed his mind and turned to her, hand on the knob. "Nothing to indicate, Madame, he might take his own life?"

She felt her haunches go watery. "Is that what he's done?"

The official nodded several times. "Came here, joined the lines, then jumped from one of the platforms. Drove a spike through his heart when he hit the pavement. Nothing could be done for him . . ." He opened the door a space. "There's no need for you to identify him, but you can see for yourself, if you want."

Miserably she half turned away.

"What we really hoped for," the senior said, "is some help about the motive. Even a little thing might be of use, Madame."

"Yes . . ."

"Your last conversation, what was that about?"

"My leaving."

"You weren't, by chance, leaving him?"

"No."

"Can you recall anything of the last talk?"

"We spoke of the ceremonies, of how the folk were giving up so much. We were both impressed."

"A patriotic young man, by all accounts"—the detective nodded—"which makes his act so much more difficult to fathom . . ."

Outside, there was the sound of a motorcar drawing up. The senior detective glanced at his watch and then abandoned his place by the door. He seemed relieved now that he no longer had to go through the farce of asking questions to which he really sought no reply.

The middle-aged man who came stiffly into the hutment was so clearly of the Abteilung that Tha had no need of an introduction.

"I'll take you to your train, Madame," he said stiffly. "Eleven-fifteen to Geneva, isn't it?"

She nodded, not trusting herself to speak.

The Abteilung man let her into the front seat and then went around and climbed in to take the wheel. He remained silent until they had left the Brandenburg Tor and only when they reached one of the lesser streets did he identify himself as Henried Tessman.

"Gunther doesn't surprise us," he said. "He's never been happy with his assignment. I think he was predisposed to do what he did." He shrugged, closing the subject. "But what we want to find out about is Von Jagow. How far did you get with him?"

"Not very."

Tessman kept his face to the road. "He seems to have been in touch with Krupp, did he go into that with you?"

"So I thought at first," Tha agreed quickly, "but I couldn't get him to tell me anything, if indeed there was anything."

"Frau Eva informed us you were going to test him out on certain proposals about Lenin. How did that work out?"

"Not too well . . ."

"Let's be specific, Madame. Was he cordial or the reverse?"

"To me, personally," Tha said, "he seemed warm enough. But for the rest, all he would say was that he was no longer involved in such matters and that I should go to the Abteilung or Zimmerman . . ."

"Nothing about going to Krupp?"

"Just that luncheon—which was so horrible . . ."

The Abteilung man seemed pleased. "I don't mean to sound malicious, but we all felt that Frau Eva's sending you here was a waste of time. Von Jagow must have seen through it from the start . . ."

"Really?"

"No doubt of it," the intelligence man said. "Von Jagow is much too battle-scarred to let himself be caught in so obvious a way. Of course, Frau Eva likes to think she knows more about these things than we do . . ."

"I only follow instructions," Tha said modestly.

"To be sure, to be sure."

For the rest of the journey Tessman chattered on about Von Tremke, claiming that the whole sordid affair could be blamed on the new division of authority, stemming from Frau Eva's widening influence under Marshal von Ludendorff.

Tha limited herself to curt, neutral replies. She was struck, not by the interdepartmental rivalries, but by the man's taste for simple, even rudimentary answers to complicated problems. For all their love of devious methods, in the final analysis, they remained idolaters of the obvious.

At the depot, the Abteilung man offered politely to accompany her to the train.

"Thank you," Tha said, "but that's not necessary."

"Well, Madame," he said, "have a good trip, and give my regards to Frau Eva."

She tried not to hurry, but inside the terminal, she began to run. Far down the platform she could see Sita pacing outside one of the cars. The clock showed hardly three minutes remained before train time, and unless Sita had sent that telegram, it would be too late to do anything about it now.

Sita was virtually in tears. She had been worried that Tha would not come back in time, that something had gone wrong. And she had not seen any man who matched Tha's description of Krupp.

"The only thing I saw," she said, "is that nobody got on the last carriage. It is marked first class, but it is locked. I know because I tried to get on and they told me it was all booked. I know how much this means to you, Tha, but that is all I can tell you . . ."

At eleven-fifteen whistles shrilled, and in the finest German tradition the train pulled out exactly on schedule.

In the east, a faint light fringed the mountain escarpment, a yellow promise of the warmth to come. Miraculously the train had kept to its timetable all the way to Basel, slowing only as they reached the customs point. They could see women wearing the little braided caps called basels, traditional garb on both sides of the border, giving them a sense of already having escaped the war zone.

It had been a restless, wakeful night.

At each stop, they had taken turns observing the train. Virtually all the traffic had been military; German soldiers detraining at each stop, and cars jettisoned en route.

Despite their vigilance, they had discerned no activity at the rearmost carriage. The curtains, drawn at Berlin, remained tightly shut. That in itself proved nothing, yet they sought to bolster hope with its negative evidence. And while they might invoke God and German punctualities as the sufficient reason for their uninterrupted passage, it seemed even more persuasive to call it a Kruppian dispensation.

Though Tha had been wearied by the journey and the events in Berlin, she caught some of Sita's sunny mood. The Javanese woman had brightened with each kilometer that carried them from Berlin. She even belatedly claimed that many men on board answered Tha's description of Krupp, but her inability to discriminate among white people explained why she had been so vague in Berlin.

At the border, the incursion of the German customs, making a final inspection, struck them as another nuisance, more Reich thoroughness. Yawning, they dug out their papers to wait a final stamp, slow to react to the stern request to disembark and submit to a search.

In their dressing gowns, they were marched along to a shed. Tha decided not to kick up a fuss, fearful that their train might leave without them and rob them of their last slender chance of finding their elusive prize. Tha's experience of customs men had been disagreeable. Often, on pretext of looking for smuggled goods, they had required her to disrobe, so that voyeuristic guards might observe the famous nude from behind the slits in the boards. At times, these grubby invasions had aroused her fury; more often, she had shrugged them off as the excise tax of notoriety.

A middle-aged man sat behind a desk, and Tha opted for attack. Before she undressed, she said, she would be grateful if he ordered his men to come out from hiding, so that she might grant them a public, albeit unpaid, performance.

Astonishingly, the soldier stood up and bowed. "Please come with me, Madame. There seems to be a mistake. There is no need for a search."

Disturbed, Tha followed the man around the shed. The commandant saluted a figure in the deep shadows, swung on his heel, and promptly departed.

Von Jagow's voice spoke softly across the distance. "Why do you stand there, Tha? Have I frightened you?"

She came toward him and he took her hands in his. In the semidarkness he began to speak consolingly of Eugen's suicide. He had been distressed. He hoped it had not spoiled her short visit to Berlin. He could not help feeling that the boy had, in some strange way, been sacrificed to his enemies in the Foreign Office. Or was he imagining enemies?

"No," Tha said. "I'm sure they exist, Theodore."

Von Jagow nodded dolefully. But neither mourning for Eugen nor fears about himself had made him fly down here on a military plane.

"Thanks to you," Von Jagow said, "I was able to have a long discussion with Krupp. He, too, it turns out, doesn't believe there's any chance of victory in submarine warfare. He was sickened to discover, he said, that the projection submitted by his executives in order to get contracts to build the subs has now become the official doctrine. He urged me to go to see Ludendorff with your Lenin proposals. He told me that Ludendorff and I are oceans apart about most things, but he sees the necessity of a one-front war. Accordingly, Ludendorff has agreed to provide the Bolshevik faction with additional monies. I want you to tell Lenin that these are to be made immediately available through his contact in Sweden, Herr Halecki, for these demonstrations in St. Petersburg, and means will be provided to return Lenin to Russia. It is essential for him to know that he has Ludendorff's support. All others, including myself, are superfluous. Clear, Tha?"

She nodded. She could hear the train gathering up its steam. "I mustn't miss my train."

"Of course," Von Jagow said. "But we can always get you across from here. I thought it would amuse you to know that Herr Halecki's business is that of a wholesaler in condoms. Strange device to bring about the birth of a new age."

"Very," Tha said. "But I must run."

He held her back. "In a way, I am grateful to you for letting me play one more role in the great world. There's something Ludendorff grasps about war—that its new instruments transform it, affecting not ony soldiers but the infant in the tiniest village—that these means dictate total defeat or total victory—the other side of the insight the American Colonel House gave me, warning that we Europeans can no longer afford our balance of power and small wars, but must back a great parliament of nations, or total destruction. But what neither of us understood, it puts the military in charge, no matter how we pretend otherwise . . ."

Von Jagow broke off, conscious of her distraction as she heard the train whistles sounding. "I bore you, Tha."

"No, no!"

Impulsively she reached up and kissed him on the lips. He pulled her close, holding her body tight.

"Come again, please, Tha, even if it's too late for flowers!"

Running, she shouted to Sita, who stalked the platform, and they boarded the jolting cars. Her last glimpse of Von Jagow reminded her of her first view of him in Berlin. Staring down at his feet, hunkered within his coat, he was aridly assessing the consequences of having been too intelligent, too soon.

In the train lavatory mirror, Tha inspected herself as she applied cream to her face. This ritual—Adam once called it her morning mantra—usually revived her spirits. Now it only made her feel more haggard. By now Adam would have her telegram, sent from the Swiss side of the border, and be on his way to the station, his hopes pinned on her.

Outside, in the dim dawn, the Geneva terminal came into lurching view. The train had taken on its Swiss habits, stopping and starting again every other minute.

Oh, Adam, she thought, I would turn the world for you; but all I can bring back is another masquerade of good cheer.

"Tha! Tha! Open!"

Sita stood in the aisle making frantic motions with her arms toward the rear of the train.

"He's getting off!"

"What?"

"Krupp. And another!"

Pulling on her robe, Tha ran along the aisle. The train had stopped within a culvert. Gray cement walls loomed close, bearing chalked and painted railroad hieroglyphics, undecipherable and ominous as *mene mene tekel upharsin*.

Against the untranslatable fate she raced on, struggling with the heavy doors at the end of each carriage. At the car next to the last, the aisles were jammed with French prisoners of war, officers on their way to an exchange at Lake Constance. The car stank of sweat and cheap wine. She had glimpsed them during the night, celebrating their release in sleepless carousal.

They reached out frolicsome hands, simply because she was female, and then somebody recognized her and that brought them up from their seats to form an obscene gamut. Hands ripped at her robe and reached for her crotch, and they wanted to know what she charged and whether she could take on the whole car, as it was said she had once done out of patriotism.

"We're not wounded," they cried, "but we'll give you a better time, Mata Hari!"

One youngster, somewhat greener or more gallant, ran interference for her. But when they had reached the end of the car, he turned and tried to make her sign her name on the pack of cheap cigarettes that bore her name.

"Later—"

She tore from his grasp, to gain the last car, only to find, in the next vestibule, that the door was locked, immovable.

Ahead, whistles were blowing.

Breathless, she pressed against the window. In the narrow angle, she could see a man removing luggage from a compartment in the last car, and she was sure he was one of the generals who had been a bodyguard to Krupp, though he now wore civilian clothes. But about the man who next descended, she had no doubt. It was Krupp. In the same sort of dark suit of their meeting in Berlin, his complexion pale and doughy in the dim light, a slender self-absorbed figure, he was quickly swallowed up by the recess of the culvert wall, ordinarily used as a shelter by repair crews against passing trains.

As soon as the general had safely stowed their luggage, Krupp waved a signal toward the front of the train, and the cars groaned and rattled and then leaped forward, smoke blowing backward, obscuring the bay and its occupants.

Impotently she hammered her fists on the heavy glass, her choked misery lost in the grind and crash of metal.

Moments later Sita reached her and put her arms about her, and still later, when they pushed into the prisoner car, the sportive officers, chastened by Sita's fierce countenance and Tha's stricken expression, let them go through without further demonstration.

GENEVA CROSS
11 March 1917

Adam stood in the center of the platform, his white cane planted between his outspread legs, bending forward to challenge the incoming flux. People gave him a wide berth in deference not only to his blindness but to his air of uncompromising mordancy.

Leaning from the window of the slowing train, Tha had the strange feeling of not merely seeing Adam there, but being him; of straining past darkness to reach out to her; of gripping the cane to contain the sharp thrust of expectancy.

Before the train came to a halt, she was off and running, as if in their embrace she would postpone, rather than deliver, her blow. She was slowed by a group of Red Cross officials who were on hand to process the prisoner contingent; a small stand had been set up to provide refreshments for the officers, and a three-piece musical outfit was on hand to play them welcome.

Her kiss concealed nothing.

"Why didn't you wire Kuprin?"

"Let's find a taxi," she said. "Sita's coming later with the luggage."

But he gripped her arm, hurting her. "Tell me!"

"He left the train . . ."

"When?"

"Here in the . . ."

Five yards away, accompanied by a young blond man in a beige sweater, Depardieu came striding toward her. Her French paymaster stared directly at her, but, unnervingly, gave no sign of recognition.

She was sure she had never seen the other man before, swiftly surveying his square and attractive face, unkempt yellow hair, horn-rimmed glasses behind which his blue eyes were focused on some object at the end of the platform.

"Tell me!"

She sheltered herself against Adam's height, putting her arms around him. "The mares," she said desperately, "I meant to write you about them . . . about putting them to stand . . ."

Depardieu and his companion hurried past them.

"Mares . . ." He had felt her alarm. "Yes, it's something I neglected—"

"Let's get a cab, and I'll tell you all about it . . ."

"Fine."

She took his arm, stroking it in silent gratitude for his quickness, his sensitivity to her. They tried to go at a normal pace down the platform, routinely becoming a part of the queue at the taxi rank. Machines came down a curving ramp from the street, picked up their loads, then made a sharp turn to exit on the ramp.

Screened there, she could see Depardieu and the tousled blond stranger emerge on the far side of the prisoner group. They went directly to the rear carriage, where a station attendant was already at the customary unlocking and throwing open the doors to the compartments, announcing that the train had reached its terminal.

Depardieu peered into each one, invited the other man's inspection, and then with an eloquent shrug moved on to repeat the performance at the next vacancy.

Adam heard her suck in her breath. "What, Tha?"

"Friends everywhere," she said. "Berlin, Paris, here. How go the Braille lessons?"

"Mind wasn't on it, for some reason."

"Tell me anyway."

Adam forced himself to cooperate. "From here to home." He grimaced. "But I give you permission to interrupt, if something important occurs to you . . ."

They got into the cab, and Tha gave their address, and leaned back and took Adam's hand in hers. She had slid back the glass partition between them and the driver, but she still did not trust herself to communicate.

"Or shall I tell you about the weather in Berlin?"

"I want to know all about the weather in Berlin."

The taxi slowly mounted the narrow ramp to the street level. At the opening to the street, it came to a halt, waiting for an opening in the traffic. From the curb, a dark sedan slid directly into the taxi's path, blocking them. There were two men in the front and a third in the rear of the vehicle.

Out of the shadows of the arched portal a man sauntered toward them, smiling, waving his cigarette at them.

"Lady McLeod! Major St. Reymont! What luck!"

Martov tapped politely at the glass and then opened the door. He heaved his bulk into the rear, maneuvering adroitly to occupy the jump seat, facing them. "Thank you both, I do appreciate," he said, still genial. "Just a short lift. Mind if I tell the driver?"

He slid back the glass partition and gave the driver an address. The driver nodded. Only then did the sedan with its three dark-suited men move out of the cab's path, preceding them down the busy thoroughfare.

A jovial grin spread over Martov's jowly face. He reached out and patted Tha's knee. "I hear they're having a miserable cold spell in Berlin," he said affably. "Do tell me about the weather in Berlin, Madame . . ."

It seemed to be an urgent topic.

Ten minutes later the cab nosed into a narrow alley and pulled up beside a bleak warehouse, at whose door the sedan had already parked.

Martov got out first. "Madame has changed her mind," he told the driver, doling him some coins. "She'll get out here with me. Keep the change."

Martov helped Adam get out and then offered his hand to Tha. He managed a line of circumspect chatter. He was doubly lucky that they would drop in and have a drink with him. He always enjoyed their company; more so when they brought news of Germany, so hard to come by in Geneva.

As the taxi backed out of the dead-end alley, the three men climbed out of their machine. They were all in blue serge double-breasted suits, rather threadbare, somehow too tight. They were all very big men.

Deliberately, Martov ground out his cigarette on the pavement, saying a brief word in Russian to the trio, who went to take up positions at the mouth of the alley.

Abruptly, the Russian's face lost its conviviality. "Nasty enough to discover Krupp among the missing," he said. "But far nastier to see the head of the French Intelligence. I take it, Madame, we owe his presence to you?"

"Don't be stupid."

"Come Madame, Monsieur Depardieu turns up in the company of an American, probably another agent, and they examine a train, on which Krupp was a passenger. But you know nothing about it?"

"I know," Tha said, "Krupp left that train in the yards, thirty minutes before we pulled in."

"Just like that? Out of the blue?"

"Obviously not! Somebody must have warned him!"

"But not you, Madame?"

Adam took a step toward Martov. He was coldly angry. He did not raise his voice, but that did not make it less abrasive. "Damn it, Martov, don't you see she's more upset about losing Krupp than you are, or I am?"

"Is she? You have perfect confidence in her?"

"Yes!"

"Then you won't object if we look into it, will you, Major?"

"Anything you want!"

"Excellent," Martov said. "In the yards, Madame, you said?"

"Yes."

"The train was halted, so the German could get off?"

"With another man— a German general in mufti—yes!"

"Let us hope you are telling the truth. Fortunately, we have many friends among the railroad workers here."

Martov called to the three men. Two of them guided Tha and Adam toward the sedan. The third remained behind. Adam, resentful of the man's hard grip, made a move to strike him with his cane, but Tha intervened, begging him to understand that she welcomed this inspection, that it was in their interest too.

With Martov and the bulky pair they rode in glum silence.

Their first stop was at a row house in a treeless street. A man in striped overalls came out, stood chatting with Martov, and presently came to join them in the sedan. He worked in the roundhouse and had just come off duty. Yes, he knew the engineer of the train very well; it was his habit to stop off for a beer on his way home.

The sedan circled almost to the point of origin, taking them back to the far side of the rail yards. Seen from this height, Tha was impressed with how expansive they were, the activity contained within them.

Most of the shops had not yet opened for business, but among them was a café that was active with the odor of beer and fried foods.

"Please, Madame, come with us."

Adam wanted to go too, but Martov put him off.

"If you're so certain, Major . . ."

"Stay, Adam."

She followed Martov and the railroader into the dreary little establishment. Men, in booths, were eating heavy breakfasts and drinking beer. Their guide greeted the men and went up to the bartender.

"Seen Fenelon?"

"Either in the crapper," the bartender said, "or he lit out for home. Know where he lives, don't you?"

"Sure, Jean. Thanks."

Early sunlight threw slicing shadows over the backyard, overgrown with weeds, piled high with rubbish and battered wooden barrels and cases. An uneven path, well trodden, wound through the debris to a small brick blockhouse at the rear.

The roundhouseman preceded them to the entry and stood peering inside, saying, "Hey, Fenelon, some folks want to see you." Then, after a moment, he moved inside, but only a step before he urgently beckoned to Martov.

"Bastards!" The man swore softly. "See what the bastards have done, comrade!"

Martov ran forward and Tha came more slowly in his wake, uneasy, fearing to see what the gloom held.

Both men were stooping down. A gray-haired man in the striped overalls of an engineer was sprawled on his belly, his face partly covering the raw hole, slimed with urine and excrement, now mixed with the blood that had oozed from the knife wounds in his back.

Tha tried to back away but Martov reached out for her and pulled her forward, grimly, forcing her to stand beside him, be a witness with him.

"See what one gets for serving the Krupps!"

Martov used the toe of his boot to turn the body half over, then let it flop back into its reeky pool. Blood and dung spattered over Tha's skirt and shoes.

She pulled away from him, plunging toward the blade of light at the entry.

"Yes," she flung at him, bitterly, moving away, "like those men in the Krupp factory, who were loyal to you!"

Martov came out to join her. His jaws were heavy with resentment. "The Krupps teach us how to rule—and we are their prize pupils!"

He left her a moment to confer with the railroad man, who nodded and started back to the café. Martov steered her to the alley, warning her they would have to get out before the police were notified.

"They're so damn confident," Martov said. "A murder or two, but they'll hold their meeting."

The sedan came to the rear alley. Tha felt drained and

spiteful. "You can tell Lenin he's going to get his funds from Halecki in Sweden. He can stop worrying about Krupp and peace. From now on, he can follow Ludendorff's orders."

She could see that Martov resented her news. "They're backing Lenin?"

"Via Von Jagow, from Marshal Ludendorff."

Martov put her into the sedan and instructed the men to take her and Adam home. He looked heavy and tired and very middle-aged. "One had hoped for peace," he said. "I should have known it would be the deluge first."

She remained close to Adam, both silent because of the Russians up front, enduring the long ride up the Gastpod and at last to the chalet.

On the bathroom floor her clothes lay in a jumble. Above the bloodstained boots and slimed skirts, her silk underthings were an indecency, a lacy disguise for the murderous Krupps and Martovs, the Frau Evas and Depardieus, ribbons for the cold parcels of mechanized death, end products of European national dreams.

From the bedroom she could hear Adam pacing in anger. He had translated Krupp's escape from the train as a measure of his own puny, crippled efforts against the war makers and their jackals, so that no matter how he blindly clawed, their steely power would remain without a scratch.

"Damn, damn, damn, Tha, if only I had my eyes, if only I had been on that train!"

She knew that his mood would be a prelude to action, always imminently suicidal, yet she could see no way to forestall him, divert him from the downward spiral.

"You have to get out, Tha," he had said. "Get out to your little safe cellar in Holland, now, because you're going to catch hell from all your friends. I want you to be on your way out of here before noon . . ."

She had made vague promises and fled to the bathroom, hoping for a quiet interval.

"Adam," she called, "come help me bathe!'

"Bathe? Crap! Haven't you heard a word of what I've been telling you?"

"But I have! Come and tell me more about Gordi—"

"Don't scoff. Gordi'll have you over the Italian border and on your way to Genoa. I know some people there who can put you onto a boat going to the Hook of Holland . . ."

"All by myself?"

"Tha, Tha, all you need now is to have to tote me—a damn giraffe—when you have to be inconspicuous! You're leaving. Alone. That's flat. That's final!"

She thought, so you can stay here and find incontrovertible proof that you're not worth occupying space on the globe! Oh, Adam, oh, my love. Aloud, she said, "Then help me. Not only to scrub. But I'm going to have to make up some stories for Frau Eva and Dr. Carnet, just to keep them away. You agree to that, don't you? Yes, Sita?"

Sita had opened the bathroom door but she did not come in. "Visitors," she said, low and unhappy. "Kamarupa! And he's brought Monsieur Chardon with him!"

Behind her, almost simultaneous with Sita's wavering introduction, Chardon's voice boomed out, as if addressing the Chamber of Deputies. "We are determined to see our charming friend. Any condition is the best condition!"

She went into the bedroom, calling, "Jules!"

Chardon came from the hallway, short and magnetic, with his attractive pocked face and black vital eyes, confident of her warm welcome.

"Dear Jules," she said, and pulled the wrap around her, moving toward Adam. "Jules, Major St. Reymont. Adam. An old friend, and our own Foreign Secretary. Delighted!"

Vigorously Chardon seized and pumped Adam's hand, stretching up to bestow a Quai d'Orsay kiss on each of Adam's rigid cheeks. "Major, I've heard all about you! If I'm not mistaken, the Legion of Honor list will soon have you wearing the rosette!"

From the doorway, Depardieu stood watching impassively.

"You know my colleague, Monsieur Depardieu . . ."

The gray man came slowly into the room. "One hopes, Major, that you will be kind enough to let us have a few moments alone with Lady McLeod, some nuisance about the banker, Lazard . . ."

Abruptly, seigneurially, Adam said, "With me."

Tha came around to Adam's side, seeking the eye of the intelligence man. "Please understand, circumstances have compelled us to dispense with secrets . . ."

The sallow face took that in with foxy patience. "Carnet told me about your jorney to Berlin."

"Yes. Of course."

"Any results?"

"Yes, they refused to give the Russian any funds."

"I rather thought so," Depardieu said. "Didn't I, Jules?"

"He's not so negligible as you think."

"You are still the Radical."

"I hope so," Chardon said, acidly. "I must stay abreast of the rest of the world." He turned to Tha. "You saw my old opposite, Von Jagow?"

"Yes, briefly."

"How is he?"

"Out of office."

"Is he worried that the Americans will come in on our side?"

"Very," Tha said. "But nobody pays any attention to him anymore, he says. They're too busy with their submarines."

"If we win this war," Chardon declared, "it is because they are even denser than we."

Tha laughed at the small man's bracing cynicism. "Is that what they call the fortunes of war, Jules?"

Chardon came toward her, to caress her arm, and to take Adam into his other hand. "I must tell you, Major, that but for a failure of nerve, I would have been a rival of yours. Have you ever told him, Tha?"

"No . . ."

"Then I will! I was a Radical candidate in need of funds, so, instead of pleasure, marriage. Then history played me a dirty trick, and I was elected without spending a sou!"

Chardon enjoyed his histrionics, watching his image in the mirror. Discussing his past follies made him more human, also without costing a sou. "But never mind, I'll land in the Elysée Palace sooner or later. Even Depardieu will not bet against me. What are you doing, friend?"

Methodically Depardieu circled the room, carefully scrutinizing drawers and closets. "I am waiting for Madame to share with us the important facts of her Berlin journey . . ."

Tha stiffened, keeping Adam close. "If you mean the suicide of Von Jagow's equerry, I can add nothing to that."

"I meant, Madame, your meeting with Krupp."

"Oh, Krupp."

"Yes, Krupp."

"Oh, a blank . . ." Tha said. "Part of Lenin's efforts to show his willingness to serve the Reich by betraying some bombing friends of his. Krupp was polite, but unimpressed."

"So it was only by chance"—Depardieu was sarcastic—"you left on the same train with him?"

"Really?" She shook her head in puzzlement. "Is that why you were at the depot? Is that why you passed me by? I've been wondering!"

At her side, Adam stirred. "Are you saying the German munitioneer is here in Geneva?"

Depardieu's glance lingered on Adam's face and then shifted to Tha. He lifted his shoulders, and resumed his restless search of the drawers. "I am saying, Major, I was at the depot to find out if Herr Krupp was on that train."

A tiny knock sounded at the door, and Sita poked her head into the crack. "Excuse me, Tha," she said, her voice almost inaudible, "but I heard the bath faucets running . . ."

Quickly Tha interposed her body between Sita and the circling, snooping Depardieu. "I'll do it. Thank you, Sita."

Sita came in a half step. "Let me."

"Thank you, Sita."

Alarm touched Sita's face as she backed away and closed the door. Tha could feel Depardieu following her as she entered the bathroom. She knew she would never have time to rearrange the damning heap. Halfway to the brimming tub, she swung to Depardieu.

"The man who was with you—an Englishman?"

"An American."

"I was afraid I called attention to myself."

"He never saw you."

"Sure?"

Frowning, Depardieu moved past her. "Madame, it will

overflow, can't you see?" Obeying the habits of a lifetime, he moved to the taps, bending over them, turning them off, his back toward her and the incriminating boots.

Quickly she slid a towel from the bar, letting it fall over the heap, obscuring most of it. "I almost greeted you," she persisted. "You haven't any idea how close I came. Fortunately, Adam said something to divert me . . ."

He straightened up. "Just in time!" His eyes slid past the heap to the rest of the room and then returned to her. "Nothing to worry about, I assure you."

"Thank you," Tha said, turning to go. "I was afraid you'd come here to chastise me about that."

"Rather more vital, Madame."

This time she shut the bathroom door behind her. Chardon, perched restlessly on the end of the chaise, growled at Depardieu. "Now we know the Kaiser isn't on the pot, Depardieu, can we get on with it?"

The affront sank without a trace in sponginess. "I am satisfied you can take Madame into your confidence," he said.

"Wonderful." Chardon grinned. "Did you ever hear Clemenceau declare that the genius of France is in her politicians? I'm flattered, but unconvinced. And so are all the civil servants like our good friend. . . ."

Depardieu said nothing, prowling about to shut tight the drawers he had previously opened. Chardon watched him, tempted to bait him some more, but sighed and returned to work.

"Tha, you saw that American at the depot?"

"The one in the sweater?"

"His name is Maxwell," Chardon said. "Robert Maxwell. Professor of French History at Princeton University, presently an aide to Colonel House, who is in Paris on behalf of the American President, to decide on the question of America coming into this war. Now, Maxwell is trusted by House, and no man is closer to Wilson than House. So, when you get Maxwell to go to bed with you, you will be seducing the American President!"

Tha laughed. "Jules, what a romantic!"

"Major," Chardon said, "you must say to yourself, as I

do, there are no sacrifices too great for our country in time of crisis."

Adam nodded, saying dryly, "They also serve who only stand and wait. Motto of the towel boy in a brothel."

Chardon laughed and turned again to Tha. "We realize, with Madame, that the promise is as important as the performance . . ." He came up off the chaise, walking the length of the room. "I wish I could say Maxwell is attractive but a fool. Far from it. He has written a remarkable book about Talleyrand, and a disturbing thesis about the unsolved murder of our great socialist leader, Jean Jaurès, who opposed the war. In it, he raises queries that must give our Depardieu bad nights . . ."

Depardieu showed no expression as he avoided this new barb. "At the moment," Depardieu said, "what deprives me of sleep is this war . . ."

"Unwinking is the Deuxième Bureau." Chardon preened before the mirror. "Now—you wondered about Krupp. Someone informed Maxwell there was to be a meeting here between Krupp, Vickers of England, and our own Schneider-Creusot. I don't need to tell you, such a meeting would be collusive, scandalous; but above all, it would enrage our moral American, Colonel House, and turn him against American entry . . ."

Depardieu stepped forward toward Tha and Adam. "A total fabrication, it goes without saying. We are convinced some Boche agent reached Maxwell with this story for the purpose of driving a wedge between the Americans and the Allied cause. Yet Maxwell refuses to give us the name of his informant. Even after I went with him to the depot and proved to him that Krupp was not aboard, he remains skeptical of us. He has got it into his head that we had a hand in warning Krupp to get off that train . . ."

"But you told me Krupp was on it," Tha said.

"When it left Berlin," Depardieu replied promptly. "But he could have gotten off anywhere in Germany. That hardly proves there was to be such an infamous meeting here, does it?"

Tha could feel Adam's body quivering beside her. "But

if your American has such a fixed idea, if he is a fantasist, you need not me, but your Dr. Carnet . . ."

Chardon's laughter filled the room. "Tha, how I miss you!" he said. "But we need you. Maxwell's gone back to Paris. We want you to go there and find out from him the name of his informant . . ."

"To Paris? I'm to return to Paris?"

"But you love it, Tha. And it loves you!"

"But Major St. Reymont . . ."

"Major," Chardon pleaded with Adam. "One hates to ask further sacrifices. But a short absence of Madame's . . ."

"In fact," Adam said, "I'd be glad to go back."

"So!" Chardon was vibrant, now that action lay ahead. "We are agreed! A short visit. A pleasant little game with an agreeable American, and then you can resume here, as you were . . ."

Tha turned to Depardieu. She made her resistance sound very real. "I suppose this means that I must abandon all the efforts I have put into this matter of Lenin and the Russians."

"We must ask you to leave today." Depardieu waved her question away. "I hope that it is no great inconvenience?"

"If I must."

Chardon waited to shake Adam's hand and to give Tha a parting hug. And in the show of affection, the supreme politician looking after his constituency.

"Forget Depardieu," he counseled after the Deuxième chief had left the room. "Nothing tests one's loyalty like the grating voice of the patriot. Think of it only as a service to my career. The man who brings America into the war on our side will be the next Premier. And once I'm in the Elysée, I'll see you are repaid, Tha, and you, Major."

She gave herself to his embrace, his stubby masculinity thrust for a moment to her body. Even after he had left, the air was charged with his energy, another territory annexed to cynical aplomb.

Long after the sound of Chardon's limousine had drifted down the greening hill, they did not trust themselves to speak. Sita had returned to the bedroom, to crouch near Adam for a moment, and then to remove Tha's boots and skirts to the furnace for burning.

Adam was deep inside himself, held back in his zeal for the quest by his fears of the dangers it involved for her.

The bath water had cooled. She let it flow out the drain and turned on the taps again, to fill the small room with its comforting steam.

"You can still cut for Holland, you know."

"But they're meeting."

"I know," Adam said. "But I don't want you being set out for meat."

"Maxwell, you mean."

"They want him chopped, don't they?"

"Or his informant."

"Or both, plus you."

She came back to him and drew him to bed with her. "I'm not going to Holland. I'm not going to stop. I'm not going to let them take you away from me."

"Still making our fate, Tha?"

"Forbidden?"

"Damned," he said.

"Then let's both be."

He drew her down, her desire channeling itself through him, a dazzlement that was able to suffuse his black universe. She was aware of the temptation to control him, in the name of helping the world. But above all, to have in him the security against the war in herself and the savage universe around her.

"Listen . . ." he said.

She tried in vain to hear what he heard.

"The tide cometh . . ."

Turning, she saw it: the tiny rivulets of water as it came from the bathroom over the threshhold, splashing ever so faintly, to form a little pool on the shining floor, a glittering star within a glass.

She wanted to go to stop it but he forced her down with a laugh, and the light was sucked up in their light, returning to its source.

Si j' t'encule cule cule
si j' t'encule cule cule
si j' t'encule cule cule
si j' t'encule c'est pour ton bien.

It sang through her head. The anthem of the espions. Satan get thee ahead of me. I love thee best, rearmost.

Frau Eva slowly wheeled the pram across the toy shop, pausing to allow the infant to reach in wonder for the stuffed animals and bright objects just beyond his grasp.

A salesgirl marched to where Tha stood examining the mobiles, a cascade of celluloid butterflies and coruscant bird-lings, suspended from strings, taking flight at her breath. Tha dodged the proffered help, saying that she liked to make her own wonderland excursions.

A few moments later, Frau Eva came to stand beside her; they were two shoppers exchanging banalities about the objects that fluttered between them.

"Berlin went well?"

"Objectively, yes. For you, personally, not at all."

The smile was still radiant behind some delicate glass bubbles that rotated on a silver axis, some with gold leaves slowly circling within their glistening prisms. "How so?"

"I must beg you"—Tha spoke with soft earnestness— "not to reveal that you had the warning from me."

"You have it."

Tha launched into her rehearsed lie with confidence. "Von Jagow told me in confidence there's a crisis in the Abtei-lung. He says a cabal exists which has prevented Ludendorff from gaining a proper assessment of the revolutionary resources inside Russia. They think you are part of it. A purge is under way . . ."

Frau Eva still managed her smile, though her voice reflected panic. "But I have had very little to do with Russian affairs!"

"So I told Von Jagow. But they blame Von Tremke's

failure to work with Lenin to your influence and orders."

"Those were my directives from Berlin!"

"I'm sure they were." Tha knew each soothing statement would only aggravate Frau Eva. "But you have many enemies—envious men, mostly—in the Abteilung. Von Jagow says Ludendorff is determined on a thorough housecleaning, and they've already planted these lies against you. I don't have to tell you that swinging axes do not discriminate among heads . . ."

"Has it begun?"

"It may," Tha said, sighing, "but I'm sure if you get back to Berlin, you can still save yourself. I only ask you to go about it delicately—not drag me into it as well . . ."

Frau Eva tapped one of the mobiles; pith sticks ricocheted and jiggled. Slowly her mouth set in a hard straight line, and she forgot to smile when she turned again to Tha.

"I'm grateful. I know I don't have to tell you how much."

"I only hope there's time."

"There will be."

Frau Eva reattached her sophia mask and took a firm grip on the handles of the pram. Still posing as another shopper, she made her way to the street.

Tha remained in her place for a long time. She had spent many hours considering a dozen tales to tell Frau Eva to cover her return to Paris. Each had seemed too dangerous. It was essential to prevent the Abteilung shadowing and interfering. Far better for them not to know of her return to Paris. And there was litle risk in sending Frau Eva on a chase to Berlin. It would be some time before the German woman discovered that Tha's story was groundless, and that she'd been duped. By that time, Tha hoped to uncover the truth about the Three Cannons, let it explode across the chancelleries of Europe, creating a crisis that would make possible her escape, before the Bureau and the Abteilung could find her and destroy her. And in that interval, having made an ally of the American, Maxwell, she would ask the Americans to get her and Adam safe to the U.S.A.

She came back from the other side of the Atlantic to expel a long breath, almost a sigh, setting the birds on their tethered frenzied flights, their strings twisting, endowing them with new energy to soar and dive while Tha escaped the shop.

MONTMARTRE VALE
13 March 1917

Soon, she thought, my turn to clutch and claw,

Outside the café window the flea market swarmed to the gates of the Montmartre cemetery, grotesque spawn of war.

Though the poor had always shamedly trafficked the effects of their dead here, the war had brought buyers from every quarter, not only in search of scarce clothes and eyeglasses and false teeth, but for the tang of a bargain snatched from eternity. Secondhand dealers had provided stalls and carts so that the humblest citizen might wrest a trophy, no matter how threadbare or soiled or chipped, from the German Gothas that flew over the city each night to maim and kill and burn, leaving a film of ash upon the river, the fulfillment of an ancient curse.

"Our American friend, Maxwell," she had been instructed by Depardieu last night, "has posted one of his men at the mart, as a more reliable index of our economic difficulties than our official figures. He's very perceptive. And disciplined. He'll show up there to talk to his man, Granet, at three. I have arranged for you to meet him. Please pay close attention, Madame."

It had been a mark of Depardieu's urgency that he violated his own rules and turned up at her apartment just before midnight. True enough, he had let himself in by a skeleton key at the servants' entry to avoid ringing the bell and alerting her neighbors.

He had drilled her in the steps that were to be taken this afternoon. Nothing would be left to chance. He would have men on duty around the cemetery. Everything would be timed so that she could appear on the scene to play lady bountiful; no casual encounter had ever been so carefully charted; a seduction, she had thought, perfumed by cordite.

Nor had Depardieu departed until he had been satisfied that she had versed herself in the dossiers on Maxwell, on his superior, Colonel House, and even on President Woodrow Wilson. These had been delivered to her as the train had left Geneva. Usually she skipped these dry curricula vitae; they had all the facts, none of the aberrations, the intense body heat which alone could guide her past the public mask to the private man.

She had been able to perform brilliantly for Depardieu because Adam had shown an interest in these documents and she had read them aloud to him on the way to Paris. It fed Adam's expectations to discover that Maxwell, as a young instructor at Princeton, had become the personal friend of Woodrow Wilson, then president of the university, and had aided Wilson in his battles against the trustees and their snobberies in an effort to create a more intelligent, liberal, multidisciplinary curriculum. And that these early ties had been strengthened when Maxwell had helped Wilson make a successful campaign for governor, again risking his job to uproot the entrenched politicians and vested interests that had dominated the state for generations.

"But don't you see, Tha," Adam had exclaimed, "he'll be an ally—he wants exactly what we want—even more than me—he detests these corpse-changers!"

His enthusiasm had only increased her anxieties. The portrait of Maxwell had blended with those of Colonel House and Woodrow Wilson to become monolithically unseducible. The record contained not a single trace of scandal, no hint of corruptibility, no whiff of weakness of the flesh. Besides, it was well established that Americans were fixated on virginity. They even pretended their wives, by reason of not enjoying sex, remained physically intacto. Americans seemed, from these dossiers, to have realized the English ideal: a nation of upper torsos, propelled by circumlocutions. Maxwell became a monstrous examiner, glaring down at her through Woodrow Wilson's severe pince-nez, held on by a frown of revulsion.

At noon—after Adam and Sita had gone off to the villa at Compiègne—her misgivings had surfaced again, painfully.

Putain, she had told her image in the mirror, *poule.*

Her eyes looked puffy. Her lips too thick under voluptuary paste; her body, encased in the false garb of mourning, too lush, plucked over, to use a euphemism.

The fetid vocabulary of contempt which the world reserved for women overwhelmed her: *grue, fille, trotteuse, belle de nuit, cocotte, con, Mata Houri!*

Maxwell. The name of a remedy for piles! Woodrow Wilson. Syllables like stones for a wall of rectitude; a synonym for the moral imperative.

In panic, she had shed the black masquerade for a plain gray suit. But that only increased her dissatisfaction. She must not ever attempt to pass herself off as a schoolteacher, an effort rendered absurd by her dark eyes, her long midnight hair. At the last moment, she had added a scarlet scarf and red gloves: if she had to fail, better as a tart than a dowd.

The waiter brought a small cup of black fluid, allegedly coffee, bitter enough for the most abject of mourners.

Outside, the citizens thronged the stalls and fell upon each new heaped cart. Homage of the dead to the living; just as she, today, was to be the homage vice paid to virtue.

She stripped off the red gloves and stuffed them into her purse. Wrong, all wrong.

Stupid to blame Adam, and his soaring hopes, for her crisis of confidence.

Such crises were familiar enough. For the whole of her childhood, calamities had come each day; her nose had been too big, or her complexion did not match the one described in a magazine or a romance.

But there were deeper cellars, and darker shadows that had not scurried away.

Like that, not long after fame had come, when she had longed to run and hide, feeling inadequate to the brilliant people she met each day, convinced that they despised her ignorance and dullness, that they were hypocrites when they praised her dance.

At the time, she had been living with Count Esterhazy, a brilliant cynic, who took her among people of wit and learning in whose presence she often felt lumpish and inferior. He had tried to laugh her out of her miseries, hoping to convince her that her grace and delicacy, which she had absorbed in Java, were more important than any verbal feats.

But when his assurances produced in her even greater despair, verging on breakdown, he had devoted himself to a cure. He had introduced her to the library of memoirs and biographies of the great courtesans; the exploits of famous women of ancient Japan; of the slave girl Scheherazade who charmed, not by her beauty, but her energy and curiosity; she had met Greek country maids who had become temple hetaerae, schooled in companionship that was deemed the very core of Greek culture.

To be a vestal—whether the polished Madame Pompadour or the rude Catherine Walters from a Liverpool shuttle park, still worshipped at eighty—had less to do with sensuousness than embodying what the lover saw as the unattainable, that shimmering bubble of justification for which all men and women endured the painful stumbles from one day to the next.

Like *bakhti,* as the Hindus called the liberating surrender to the invented shadow of God, the subtlest and utmost eroticism.

"Forget education!" Esterhazy had commanded when she complained of her sketchy schooling and near-illiteracy. "Facts are a parlor game—a source of fantasy. You have to touch people at a deeper level."

And he had been dismissive of sex, even of sex augmented by sadism, which extended its range but not its objective. "You have this gift, Tha, to make people feel thrillingly stretched on the web of existence. All the rest is ejaculation, bird drop."

Later, when, under his tutelege, she had begun to delve into people and their desires, so carapaced by the formulas imposed by society, she had worried that she was callously using people to gorge herself on their secret dreams.

"Craft, of course," Esterhazy had agreed with a dandyish smile. "But if you devote yourself to it, as unattainable perfection, you will make it art; cease to be harlot and become courtesan."

And when he was about to leave her to return to his duties in Austria, he had congratulated her. "For you, there will be exemption from the servitude to marriage and fashion. But, like your gurus, you will attain heaven only by having many disciples, though they will be the bravest and best."

Harsh rapping brought her out of it.

She looked up. A security man had entered the café and stood at the counter, drumming a coin on its marble surface. Her cue. Call to wiggle in the bazaar.

Outside, another of Depardieu's minions directed her, by a nod, toward a stall near the gate.

She made her way through crowds vying with one another, fingering objects in total devotion, hunting among the huge armoires, empire desks, obsolete swords and pistols for a touchstone, to find everlasting life in the next grab.

At a cart, she paused to purchase a small bouquet. It drooped and had a brackish smell. Appropriately tainted, she thought, for her sham sorrow at a stranger's grave.

Advancing, she caught sight of Maxwell. Hatless and blond, wearing tweeds, his profile made severe by the horn-rimmed glasses, yet taller and sturdier than she remembered him from her brief glimpse in Geneva.

High above her, atop the hill, the consecrated onions of the church of Sacré-Coeur glistened in the sun. She and Adam had explored Montmartre's Byzantine alleys during his leaves, before his blinding at Vittel. The Caliphate of Balzac, the neighborhood was called, and she had imagined that someday, after the war, she would buy one of the tiny, crooked houses and create a permanent place for their love, the perfect setting for the union of East and West.

The memory impaled her and she had an impulse to turn back. Her misery, she suddenly saw, had little to do with fear of failing with the American. She was violating the rituals Esterhazy had helped her to treasure; she was snaring Maxwell, not because she wanted to celebrate him as unique and individual, but for ulterior purposes which, however laudable and lofty, belonged to the whore's faceless traffic.

Yet the memory of Adam drove her on. To falter now would be to relinquish Adam. " 'Tis the strumpet's plague to beguile many, but be beguil'd by one." Once Cocteau had quoted Shakespeare to her when she confided that, in her love for Adam, possessiveness and jealousy had taken her by storm. She had fled the temples, no longer the avatar of love, but, like the crowds in this teeming bazaar, she was pawing for jetsam, for an attainable, a procurable, prize.

Maxwell had joined a small round man, who, notebook in hand, was showing him some notations. That would be Granet, as Depardieu had told her.

Nearby, some gendarmes, assigned to keep order among the competitive scavengers, moved imperceptibly closer.

Time for her entrance.

Close to Maxwell and Granet, two women began to scream at each other in their battle for possession of a small table, each holding a leg, threatening to tear it mortise from tenon. The dispute immediately involved some men, who took up the cause of one woman or the other, and these rehearsed players attracted bystanders, who quickly turned illusion into reality.

Elbowing and punching, the belligerents swarmed over the two Americans. Granet was sent hurtling to the pavement, while others in the crowd swept Maxwell away from him.

Even if she had the will, she could not have left the scene now. People came from behind to push her toward the fallen American. The flics had closed in. A sergeant had appropriated the notebook, while one of the pugilists, collared by the police, hurled accusations at Granet, still on the ground.

A few feet from her, she saw Maxwell battle to the side of his assistant, help him to his feet, and then reach out his hand for the notebook, which the sergeant had begun to tuck under his belt.

"Sorry, Monsieur," the sergeant said. "This one wants to lodge a complaint." He indicated the captive pugilist. "It will be held in evidence."

"Never mind that," Maxwell said. "Let's have the book."

"Come along to the station," the sergeant said. "This man says your friend struck him without cause. We can sort it all out at the station."

"A nuisance," the accuser shouted, thrusting a red face at Granet. "He began it all. He interferes with everyone. A *sale* American. A spy. I am sick of these Americans who get rich from our sufferings!"

Around them, the crowd joined the game, echoing the small man and the latest accusations they had gleaned from the newspapers. All the world knew the Americans were standing on the sidelines, trading with the Boches, getting fat while brave Gauls and hardy Britons died in battle.

Maxwell, smiling, showed a stubborn jaw. "The book, Sergeant," he repeated. "This is all absurd."

Tha took a step forward. She could see the American's eyes were more gray than stereotypical blue, and that he could be far from the imperturbable scholar she had evoked from the dossier.

"Sergeant," she said, "be so good as to return the visitor's property. I saw it all. These men were attacked. I am a witness."

The sergeant swiveled to her. "Excuse me, Madame—"

"At once!" She assumed a haughty, peremptory tone. "I warn you, in your own interest, do as I say!"

"If you wish to go to the station . . ."

"One would regret," she cut in, "annoying the Foreign Minister with this stupidity, but I will do so, and I can tell you he is a great and good friend of mine!"

The crowd had by now recognized her. The women who

had begun the hubbub now elbowed each other for a closer look. She had become the main show. And some of the male spectators, anxious to bring themselves to her attention, became partisans of international amity as just a few moments ago they had been zealots of chauvinism.

"They are our guests—give it back!"

"Don't be a pig, Sergeant. Mata Hari is right, you are a disgrace!"

Ringed by the now hostile crowd, the sergeant grudgingly gave back the notebook, while asserting his authority. "Nevertheless, I will have to make a report at the station . . ."

Tha nodded, and dug in her purse, extricating a calling card. She extended it to Maxwell. "If there should be further bother, don't hesitate to call, M'sieu . . ."

"Maxwell." He studied the card. "Robert Maxwell."

"In spite of everything," she said, half turning to the crowd, "we all adore Americans and know they will soon come to save us."

The crowd parted as she began her advance toward the gate. She glanced down at her bedraggled bouquet, assuming once again a solemn expression.

"Excuse me, Lady McLeod . . ."

He was overtaking her, waving her card awkwardly. "I haven't thanked you—and apologized for not recognizing you."

She made a moue of resignation. "I sometimes go in disguise, fully clothed."

"It's not that . . ." He glanced down at his feet, suddenly sheepish. "I mean—our idea of you—and you—didn't match."

"And what is that idea?"

"Oh"—he tried to laugh it off—"woman of mystery."

"For us," she took him up, "the mystery is your American girl, the inviolable virgin."

He digested that with a scholar's appreciation. "What perplexes us," he said, "is your European model—violated, but undefiled."

She pressed her advantage, beyond flirtation. "Suppose you accept perplexity? Would that solution go against the grain?"

He blinked in surprise, examining her face to read its subtext, then grinned. "Goes against the New Jersey grain."

Behind him, Granet was calling to him, being pulled along by the flics. "Damn them, Max, damn the whole lousy froggerie! They're going to take me in!"

Maxwell stood torn. "Excuse me." He began to run, and turned back, waving her card again. "I may have to call you for help—not over this—but for degraining!"

She threw him a smile of encouragement, and then took the precaution of completing the charade. Evading the crowds, she followed a small path among the headstones, until she stood alone.

The angel of silence, menacingly still, pirouetted on a slab, two supplicatory palms pressed in front of her sealed lips.

Tha deposited her bouquet. Carlotta Mercier. Aged thirty-eight. Long gone. Wife of Alexandre, mother of Amélie and Annette.

The American had reacted. But clearly, for him, she was a creature from below. Adam called the war inferno. Somebody had told her that in one of Dante's nine circles, several of her own Frisians could be found. A cold circle, it must be, for in Holland the idea of hell was a winter beside the Zuider Zee.

She could hear Depardieu's icy voice: "You will go home. In due time, you will be escorted to the police station, to serve as a witness. You will be left alone with the American in a bare examination room for several hours, while waiting for succor from Chardon. During that interval, you will be two victims of French injustice. What could be more perfect for romance?"

Two priests, black robes purifying their collars, led a small funeral procession to a nearby grave. The glances of the mourners chided her, as if her presence scandalized the shade of the mother of two.

The ninth circle, she decided, would be having Depardieu pander her through eternity, and she hurried to put the offended angel behind her.

SHADOW PLAY
13 March 1917

Twilight brought no calm to the city, or to her. Before the war, in this pink interval—after the shutters of the shops had rattled down and before the pots began to clatter for dinner—Paris would fill its lungs, bracing for the night's quick pantings. Now the streets groaned under military traffic, while the citizens, fatigued by prolonged labor, facing another night of bombers, dragged themselves homeward, their shoes whimpering along the pavements.

Ever since Depardieu's call at four, she had roamed the apartment, unable to eat or drink or find a spot to rest. Depardieu had been cryptic. The plan, he said, had miscarried. He would come by later on to explain and discuss alternatives.

She was grateful that Adam had gone to Compiègne to

meet with his aristo friends, preparing to turn back the clock, improving the future by an imaginary past.

The front doorbell began to shrill and did not cease.

Another violation, she thought. Depardieu is becoming unstuck.

Chardon, his arm around tiny Adèle D'Estrelles, leaned on the button even after Tha opened the door.

"Jules," she said, "let up."

"Soused," Adèle said. "Pay no attention, Thata. He's a monster."

She pushed Chardon, flushed, collar open and tie dangling, into the apartment. Adèle seemed the permanant waif, hardly five feet, with a childish face and immature body. She had invented the nickname "Thata" and came around frequently to complain of Chardon's cruelties, which consisted of long spells when he paid her bills but otherwise ignored her.

"Only exhausted," Chardon said thickly. "Come to console you, console myself."

Though Adèle tried to steer him to the drawing room, he shoved her aside and stumbled to the bedroom. "Where better to recover than in the boudoir of Mata Hari—the center of the center—particularly for me, the consummate centrist—"

He kicked off his shoes and flopped on the bed, full of disconsolate laughter. "All men are to the right or left of where I stand." He paused to add, "Or where I lie!" and then spread-eagled, relaxed by his verbal felicity.

Adèle came to the bedside, regarding him acidly. "Forgive him. At the Quai d'Orsay, they consider it diplomatic to laugh at their own jokes."

"Can I have something to drink, Tha? Anything."

"Don't," Adèle warned, bending over him to help him out of his jacket. "He's sure to become amorous. I can never tell with him which is the aphrodisiac, booze or politics!"

"You are a child, Adèle." Chardon waved her away. "Wine helps other men to throw off their masks, but permits me to assume mine."

"And what does that mean?"

"If I waved my cock from the top of Cleopatra's Needle,

I'd be forgiven!" He poked horned fingers at her. "But lusting after power—taboo—because it reveals too much about your colleagues!" He bared his teeth at her. "Jules Chardon, your covert Caesar!"

Adèle hung his jacket about the back of a chair. "And all the world's his closet. Don't let him intimidate you, Thata!"

Chardon lurched up on one elbow to peer at Tha. "Speak to Depardieu?"

"He's coming by."

"He tell you what happened?"

"No."

"Idiotic! Some fool police captain let Maxwell phone Colonel House, who got on the phone with me, so I had to let them go. You'd think in an important matter like this, Depardieu would have briefed those dolts! It would be something to laugh at, but it's my head. I'll have to resign. And if Clemenceau has his way, I'll do a jig before a firing squad at Vincennes!"

Adèle threw up her hands and came to Tha's side. "Oh, God, we're about to hear the latest stanza in the martyrdom of Jules Chardon. Unbearable!"

Chardon sat up, glowering at her before turning to Tha. He was sweating. "I mean it. You've guessed by now this meeting with Krupp is no German fable, but a French reality."

She knew better than to act naïve with Chardon; still better to appear unsympathetic. "I did," she said, "but is there a difference?"

"I instigated this tripartite meeting. I had Premier Briand's approval and General Lyautey's at the War Ministry. Now they're all running out on me, in fear of Clemenceau. I'm convinced Depardieu's in this with Clemenceau. Both of them think any Frenchman who refuses to turn in his grandmother for listening to Wagner is a traitor. How they'd love to abort this meeting and see me fail!"

Adèle grimaced. "You're paranoid, Jules." She marched to the door. "I'll get the bottle. Might as well be crocked if I have to listen to this!"

"Believe me," Chardon said, "I know Clemenceau. His rhetoric has a way of becoming a volley of rifle fire at dawn!"

She turned away. She knew some of it had to be brag-gadocio, centering the world on himself, exaggerating the per-secution by brutal hosts. But she had also read Clemenceau's newspaper, *L'Homme Enchaine,* and its ferocity had sent a chill along her spine, even unaccompanied by Chardon's whines. Somebody had said of Clemenceau's sheet that it was edited by sadists to test the mettle of masochists.

Chardon heaved himself from the bed and came pad-ding across the room in his socks, to stand beside her, peering up into the darkening sky. "Our Gotha pals are late tonight. Do I frighten you?"

"A little."

"I meant to." He began to unbutton his shirt. "Paranoia comes with the dispatch case. I rely on it. And on you, Tha."

"And is that why you kept me in the dark about Krupp?"

"A mistake."

He ripped off the shirt and threw it to the floor. His arms were almost as thick at the wrist as at the bicep, covered with dark hair. His undershirt was moist. Whatever might be false, that odor of fear was real.

He put his arm around her waist. "I need your help, Tha."

She forced herself not to flinch. "With more lies, Jules?"

His hand came to caress her arm, ardent and urgent. "Don't scold, Tha. We need loans from the Americans, desper-ately. So do the Germans. But we block each other. We say the Germans are on the verge of collapse. They spread the same tales about us. Schneider-Creusot and Vickers suggested this meeting in Geneva. Krupp agreed. We would cooperate for loans. Now Briand insists, in fear of Clemenceau, that we get our loans first. I must convince Krupp. Clemenceau has al-ready accused our Interior Minister, Malavy, of being a Ger-man agent. Even Caillaux, who leads his party in the Chamber, he calls pro-German! That is why we were so con-cerned about the leak to Maxwell, why we could not even take you into our confidence . . ."

"But I thought Depardieu was on your side."

"So did I, until this afternoon."

"Because a policeman let Maxwell make a phone call?"

"No, no, there's more than that . . ."

The door opened and Adèle came in, bearing a tray with glasses and a bottle. She took in Chardon, shirtless, his arm about Tha, and began to giggle. "Thata, don't tell me you've agreed?"

Tha turned to her, puzzled.

"I don't mind," she went on, gaily. She poured out half a tumbler of cognac. "I've wanted to go to bed with you for the longest time. I never had the nerve to ask. How did Jules manage, has he convinced you he's going to save your life?"

Dutifully she carried the glass to Chardon, who glared at her. "Shut up and get undressed, Adèle." He swung back to Tha. He no longer appealed, but commanded. "I'm going to have that meeting, swing those loans, keep France solvent until America comes in and gives me power. You're in this, Tha, and you're going to help me!"

She retreated within herself, warding off his cannibalistic picture of himself and the world around him, each brute ready to climb a mountain of corpses to wave his stick of power from the summit. Yet, even if she accepted that view of Europe as truly Chardon's, it still didn't mean that he wasn't telling her more lies to enlist her for his own uses.

"Oh, stop torturing her, Jules!"

Adèle was in a robe. She was carrying some veils. "I found these in your wardrobe. Are they the ones you used to dance in?"

"Yes."

"I never saw you. Dance for me. We'll shut them out, the whole vile pack!"

Tha went to pour herself a drink, still caught in Chardon's dark vision. Vincennes, she thought. She had picnicked beside the old fort with Adam. He had told her one of his ancestors had faced a firing squad there. She couldn't remember his name. They had spread a spotless cloth over the blood-stained ground and enjoyed their Sunday.

Adèle came close by, stroking her. Her waif's body looked like a boy's. "You used to make everybody forget everything. Now do it for yourself and me, Thata . . ."

"I can't, anymore."

The light slid through the room's darkness, stealthy and rapine. She could feel the cognac's warmth, but it left untouched the hollow core of her fear. Adèle had her arms about her, her dimunitive body protecting her from the scythes of light.

"If I had your body," Adèle said, moving to excite her, "I'd never share it with a man or a woman—I'd parade before mirrors, day and night."

Vincennes, she thought, how easy it would be for him to shift it from his shoulders to mine.

On the bed, Chardon had taken off his undershirt. Curly black hair matted his body at front and back. The stubby, powerful, black miner's physique, glistening like the coal in Alsace, diamantined by the blood of warring generations. He has earned his lusts, she thought.

He saw her glance and misread her desire for revulsion. He used crude German which he imagined passed for Dutch, asking, "Beast with two backs, am I?"

"Ugly," she said, also in her native tongue.

"Adèle doesn't find me so. Do you, Adèle?"

"You're a cruel bastard," Adèle said. "That's what I find you."

She bent her lips to Tha's breasts. Tha was surprised by Adèle's body. The way Adèle held herself, one would think she had neither breasts nor pelvis; now beneath the robe she could see its softness and delicacy within its slender compass.

Chardon came from the bed, watching their play, savoring it. "You haven't given me your answer, Tha. Will you take the risk, for me? Serve me, not Depardieu?"

Adèle protected Tha with her arms. "Don't do anything for him," she said. "He's mad. He'll sacrifice you to his insanity, just like me."

Adèle's body quivered between them, as Chardon approached. Her body was a soft extension of his hard manhood. His raw stink, the stink of power, covered them both, quickened by the revolving shaft of war invading the room, spinning them into the bloody vortex.

Tha let herself go, joined to them by their despairs and her own, a congerie of flesh squirming in fury to stay alive.

But in place of the crescendo of orgasm, they were shaken by the thunder of an antiaircraft barrage. The flailing light, which had brought them together, now whipped them apart, each sent into separate directions by the reverberating guns, bearing down on them, closer with each burst.

Adèle slipped to the floor, her forehead tucked in between her thighs, panting. "I wish I were dead," she moaned. "I'm so miserable, I wish they would come and finish me . . ."

The spasm passed over them. Chardon looked down at Adèle and cursed her and then moved away.

She lifted Adèle to her feet.

"Come with me," Adèle begged in fright. "We'll go to the Métro. I always go there. It's safest."

Jules went to the window as the first bombs began to fall. Though the explosions were at a distance, flame spurted toward the dismembered sky and threw a glare into the room. Adèle began to sob.

"Miles away, idiot. Be silent."

"Be blown apart! It's what you deserve."

Fire and smoke rose into the rays of the searchlights, to be cut into mendicant shadows, hounded to heaven. Against the baritone roar of the Gothas there came the thin, almost strangulated tenor of the French defensive aircraft: the familiar inharmonious duo of Paris nights.

"I'll go in this robe, Thata. Just let's run."

Tha let herself be drawn to the door, pausing only to grab a coat.

"Tomorrow," Jules said, "the American Puritan!"

"Yes, Jules."

He lifted his drink to the tumult above. "I forgive those bastards everything but spoiling our evening."

In the middle of his rueful toast, Tha heard the click of the service door. She bent to Adèle, bidding her to wait, then threw out the warning to Jules, "Our faithful Depardieu."

He whirled and nodded.

Halfway down the long corridor to the back door, the familiar gray form came marching toward her. "I saw Chardon's limousine outside."

"He's here."

"Good," he said. "I must see you both."

She preceded him slowly.

Chardon was putting on his shirt. Adèle, in her robe, huddled in a chair beside the door. Depardieu took it all in, filing it away, maintaining the conventions with the Foreign Secretary.

"I followed your instructions, sir. I went to Colonel House. I used the incident to try to compel Maxwell to disclose the identity of his informant. I pointed out that Maxwell was laying himself open to Boche violence. Colonel House agreed. But Maxwell insists he doesn't know the identity of his informant. He repeats the story that he was alerted by a telephone call, the ruse that took him to Geneva. He swears he has no further information . . ."

Chardon came toward him. "You can stop using that language. I have taken the responsibility of telling Madame the truth of this matter, and its urgency. The fact is, we are exactly where we were in Geneva, faced with a loose cannon . . . called Maxwell's informant."

"I believe I have provided a sufficient pretext for you to call Maxwell to your office. And Madame. They can meet in your waiting room, as we planned to have them meet in the police station . . ."

Chardon turned to Tha. "What do you think?"

"I think, Jules, we've badgered him enough."

"You think you can manage on your own?"

"Unless the American male responds only to abduction."

Chardon grinned sardonically. "I put it in your hands then, Madame." He turned to Depardieu. "With your permission, of course."

Depardieu lifted his shoulders. "Of course, Madame, before you put any plan into action, we will confer."

"In the morning."

She swept Adèle from her temporary hiding place and together they raced down the corridor and flung themselves into the spiral of the stairway. She knew she was far from escaping the ninth circle. Chardon had given her room to maneuver without Depardieu, but her movements would be closely watched. Still, it was an opening, not only toward the American, but to keep faith with Adam and his hopes.

Had Dante more?

The darkened boulevard was alive with citizens hurrying belatedly toward the sanctuary of the Métro station.

It was a phenomenon Tha could never understand. People refused to move until after the first wave of devastation, behaving as though the incessant raids, timed almost to a fixed hour by a methodical enemy, were illusory, harmless, unlikely to occur again.

Of course there were fatalistic nonrunners like herself; or those who only quickened the pace of a lifelong race to shelter, like Adèle.

But the majority remained immobile, unconvinced of each nocturnal visitation until the first dismal crunch shook the earth, reawakening primitive nerve cells in their tails and spines, impelling them at last to flight. Something fundamental seemed involved. Tha could only surmise that death was acceptable only in recollection, that it was screened out by her karma as well as by Adèle's illusion of a perfect hiding place. Which explained, too, why the atmosphere in the underground stations of the Métro had about it the abandon of a wake, a rollick sanctioned by the fact that death had passed them by, leaving them to celebrate in the dark.

They were not the only women who were half-robed. Many of the men, too, had jumped from their beds in pajamas or underwear, coat slung over their shoulders. Many bore mattresses with them, prepared to spend the rest of the night underground.

Away from Jules, Adèle seemed less volatile. Among Parisian demimondaines, Adèle was a rarity. A daughter of a substantial family in the provinces, she had abandoned a convent school to become a Paris streetwalker—only to discover, to her dismay, that her boyish charms were vendible only in the circles she had fled, that her waspishness was an amusing substitute for whips among the worldly and guilt-ridden, a perfect foil for such as Jules Chardon.

"Instead of giving in," she chided, "you should have laughed at him, Thata!"

"I didn't see the joke."

"He's ridiculous! Everybody knows that, except me, who had to fall in love with that Alsatian monster, who creams when you whisper Elysée to him . . ."

"But he sounded afraid—genuinely alarmed."

"If the world came to an end, he'd see it as a plot to keep him from the premiership!"

"But Lyautey, Briand . . . that has to be true . . . and Clemenceau, how can you doubt that?"

"The pigs—they don't care who dies as long as they get their loans. And I don't believe it's only loans. They'd do it through the banks in Switzerland, without Jules. The vermin are cooking a big deal. He's lying, Thata. I hoped you'd tell him to go to hell!"

"And I thought I was the cynic . . ."

"You know what they enjoy about power—chopping their pals! I don't know what you see in them. They're either eunuchs—or bastards like Jules!"

They had started down the steps to the Métro, pressed about by the converging streams of bodies. Adèle warned her that there was virtually no light down below. "If we lose each other, look for me at the far end to your right. We may have to go to sleep on the concrete, but tonight that will be Paradise!"

Even with that warning, Tha was surprised how dark it was. As she gained the platform, bodies enveloped her. Though she tried to hold Adèle's hand, they lost contact within a few moments. And when she groped again, a woman turned and let loose a stream of profanity, accusing Tha of molestation.

In the gloom, a figure bore down upon her. She retreated toward a wall, unconsciously protecting herself with her hands, covering her center.

A train boomed into the platform, its lights flashing over the crowd. Silver gleamed momentarily on a dark chest. Tight trousers rounded the man's ornament. She did not see his face.

His body backed her against the cold tile. She felt his

hands at her thighs, her skirt lifted to meet his nakedness. In the fierce contact, his hands came around her buttocks and rawly pulled her to him.

The train hissed and spat and withdrew in another shudder of power, plunging her into deeper gloom. She heard herself whimpering, but did not resist. He forced her lips back with his fingers and he entered her with abrading pain.

Convulsively, she pulled him to her. She wanted to surrender to physicality, erasing all consciousness, all other civilized rapacities, including her own designs and avowals, to immolate herself in her body, and, writhing in its opacities, writhe free.

WOUNDS OF TIME
14 March 1917

The caretaker told her that Sita had left for the market and he had last seen Adam going down to the boathouse.

Growth, lovely and fierce, covered the slope from the villa to the river. Nothing remained of the lawn; a few stunted bushes reminded her of her efforts to keep alive the flower beds all through that hot summer of 1914, right up to the sudden guns of August and the end of her own private Eden.

She paused at a path, now half overgrown, hiding a sundial and a bench, where Massimy, moving from one to the other, had struggled to tell her of his decision. He had been asked to become War Minister. He felt compelled to accept. But, in that act, he must give her up, abiding by the unwritten pact to share with the poilu his spartan life, his sacrifices.

Yet how hopeful they'd been! The war would be over in a few months, they told each other. It was no more than a family quarrel that had sprung up quickly and would soon blow away. Yes, everybody said Europe would quickly recover, it was no more than a rash that would cure itself by Christmas!

He had made her a gift of the villa "to tide her over" until peace was restored and he came back and they could take up their pleasant life again. She had paid him a last visit at the baroque mansion on the Rue St. Dominique that served as the War Ministry. He had given her the deeds and they had gone to the billiard room and played a desultory game, and then he had walked her to her car, a slender, graceful man, more interested in his hobby of archivism and information retrieval than in the arts of war, and he had made no effort to hide his tears.

That was the last time she had seen him.

Within a year he had been driven from office, blamed for all the disasters that struck his French army. She had heard that he had returned to his home in the south, an invalid. She had written him several letters, but he had replied only with brief notes of thanks. Later, she had heard he'd recovered sufficiently to take on an assignment or two for the government, but he had never made any effort to reach her.

The boathouse was obscured by shrubs. Somebody had cut a narrow path through them and the hacked branches showed ends white with submission.

I mustn't tell Adam about Chardon's schemes, she thought. It would only make him more savagely bitter about the war. Besides, if Adèle was right, all that might only be new lies to cover the real purpose of the munitioneers' conference.

Light glared up from the river.

Adam sat strangely composed in the center of the floor. Around him were the bits and pieces of his dismembered rifle. "Can't stop. . . ." He waved an oily rag. "They used to make us do this blindfolded, but I always cheated. Do we have to leave right away?"

"Almost."

"Caroline agree to come?"

"Yes."

"You explain it to her?"

"Enough."

"Tell her she's not to make a run at Maxwell?"

"I tried."

"Come and kiss me and tell me how you managed with Depardieu."

"Just barely."

"But how?"

"I argued against the bedroom approach. I made him see Maxwell will never unburden himself to a mystery with veils. The only way to win him over would be as one who shared his misgivings about the war. Which made it essential for you to come with me, a couple whose sufferings made them worthy of his trust!"

"How close to the bone!"

"At the end, Depardieu still preferred sex to sympathy, but agreed to my way . . . our way."

The last of the steel parts snicked into place and Adam grinned serenely over his handiwork. "Yesterday, when I didn't hear from you, I climbed walls. This morning, even before you called, I was euphoric. About us. About what we're trying to do. Call from above." He grimaced up at her, almost embarrassed. "See—leave me alone for a day and the Jesuits get me!"

He stood up, supporting himself on the completed rifle, in edged parody of a prophet hobbling with a staff. "Or, if Depardieu is right, God allows me to hustle you for peace!"

She took his arm, laughing, relieved not to be questioned about Chardon. "Amen!"

He squeezed her hand to him. "Which reminds me. On our way, can we stop off at that little church the Germans shelled?"

"Saint Hilaire?"

He nodded. "The caretaker tells me we used the tower as an observation post. Got smashed good, he says."

She could not suppress her surprise. "But you hate churches!"

"But today"—for one moment he dropped the quixotic pose—"let us be absurd—which Saint Aquinas tells us is a state of blessedness."

"Of course, Adam," she said, and kissed him again.

*   *   *

At the edge of the wreckage, she hung about, letting Adam tap his way through the debris.

Saint Hilaire had never been known for its architecture, but only for its antiquity. Built in the eleventh century, it had survived untouched, one of the few in France. In the past, neither its history nor its crabbed but defiant garden, its tablets scoured from breasting time, had interested Adam. That Adam should want to make a pilgrimage, now that it had been leveled to the ground, seemed strange, and yet moving, as if he could consecrate in these piles of sediment not only his own lost faith, but their mission today.

The church must have taken several direct hits. Its tower was gone, and only a small section of its rear wall still stood. Rough stones, which had sustained generations, lay scattered about, drawn molars with upturned roots, jagged and unsightly; ripped graves, showing bones, proving that the dead could die again, but proving nothing more.

Suddenly she came to a paralyzed halt.

Ahead of her, a woman in a white cape and white cap led three small children through the waste, supervising their search for holy relics. From beneath the cap, long golden hair halated in the sunlight; even the figure seemed ample and all too familiar.

Some syllable of her dismay must have escaped her, for the nursemaid turned and faced her. She was not more than eighteen, with a round and vacant face that bore no resemblance to Frau Eva's.

"It's horrible, isn't it?" the girl said.

"Yes."

She managed a distracted smile and then swung away. Frau Eva, she thought, my malevolent angel. By now, Frau Eva would be in Berlin, chasing down the story of her fate. Soon she would discover that the policy on Lenin had been changed by her own idol, Marshal Ludendorff, that she was the victim, not of any cabal in the Abteilung, but only of Tha's deceptions. Perhaps, even now, she'd be racing back to Geneva, seeking revenge. Time was growing short. She could not allow this day to be wasted. She would have to win over Maxwell before Frau Eva had a chance to retaliate.

"Adam! Let's go, please!"

He stood head bowed before the vestigial nave, not moving.

"Adam," she called again, running to him, "please . . ."

". . . Lucus a non lucendo . . ."

He was ashen. His forehead was covered with sweat, and his voice trembled. ". . . A grove made from the absence of light . . ."

"Adam, what is it?"

He reached out and grasped her wrist. His grip was bruising. "I must be in a bad way," he said, shakily. "For a moment, I thought I saw this nave . . . wax dripping from a shelf . . ."

She stared. A portion of the curved nave leaned precariously; on a shelf, several candles, melted by the heat of the explosion, formed waxy stalactites in some aboriginal cave thrust upward from prehistory, recreated by the havoc.

" . . . But there is . . ."

". . . I'll be a sinner babbling peccavis in a minute."

"But Adam, there is!"

"A blur," he said, still holding her, "half toppled in . . . ropes of wax!"

"Yes!"

Veins stood out at his temples. "Ah," he said, "to hell with it. Hysterical remission. You see it at Lourdes. Then they buy back the crutches at the back door!"

Almost angrily he began to poke his way out and she hastened to take his arm to keep him from stumbling on the obstacles strewn about them.

"But Adam, the doctors did say . . ."

"That quack, Harris."

"You must let them operate!"

"We'll be late."

"Adam," she begged, "promise me, if this day works or not, miracle or not, you'll submit to surgery."

He lifted his shoulder. "Can we get out of here, now?"

At the automobile, he paused to turn a blind stare toward the ruins, and the memory of vision born from the futile stones. "Ex-theology student. *Aeternum servans sub pector vulnus.* Everlasting sore in the breast and Latin tags in the pate. To Paris and the bed militant!"

She helped him in and she knew that he had cast aside his effort to find justification for his present hatreds in his early faith; that he would turn away from the illumination of the moment to make a new and terrible passage back into his darkness, where she could not, must not, follow, except with the lidded glance of love.

At her suggestion, they stopped at a little café. A loquacious proprietress served them tea and spoke of her husband, who had been posted by luck to a supply depot in Normandy, far behind the lines, only to check herself, glancing up at Adam's sightless eyes.

"I'm a fool," she apologized. "Nobody should talk about happiness until the war ends. Forgive me, sir!"

Something about that guuileless plea stirred Adam out of his solitude. On their way back to the car, he put his arm around Tha, trying to make her understand his disorders. Early this morning, after her call, he'd walked beside the river. On the banks, he'd heard the sounds of the water and of insects, of the sun expanding green things, echoing a dream of infancy, and he had felt new possibilities within himself, even in his blindness, a closeness to her, not because of the Three Cannons, but, as the woman had said, as a stroke of good luck, which only a fool would talk about.

"I'm even jealous of your American," he said. Half in tears, Tha took him back to the car. They rolled along the road before he spoke again. "I feel like saying to hell with everybody and everything, let them have their damn war, I'll keep my Tha!"

Her lashes were wet. "You have her."

"Then why have you been so silent?"

"Fear . . ."

"Of me?"

"Yes," she admitted, "and that I'll blunder with the American."

She felt Adam's hand move under her skirt. He had guessed that he had excited her and she laughed at being so easily deciphered. "Yes, Adam, but not now . . ."

"Just drive," he commanded.

His fingers explored her, light and buttery. She responded, desire mixing with her laughter, and turned to see his face alight with glee.

"Adam . . ."

"Tha, love."

She wanted to slow. Instead, Adam's foot came to top hers on the accelerator. The car leaped forward. "Christ, Adam . . ."

"One or the other, not both!"

The road became a swoon of sex and speed. His finger tantalized, caressed, urged, snaked deep. Her body began to quiver and she gripped the wheel trying to concentrate on the narrow road.

"Come," he whispered in manic delight, "as you go."

"Adam, you'll kill us."

"For us, nothing exists, no American, no Germans, no blunders, no faith . . . only us!"

She felt herself pulse to the demand of his fingers, caught in the middle of a wave of fear at their hurtling through space, and the rising crosscurrent of her need for fulfillment. He was leaning his head close to her and she felt his teeth on her neck and the heat of his tongue, compelling her to abandon herself.

In a blur, she saw a wagon ahead and heard herself cry in dismay, but he laughed, pressing her foot hard, trampling, increasing the pressure of his stroke within her.

Somehow the car careened and righted itself, and in that gravitational suspense her whole being came to meet his guiding hand and she could not see the road but only give herself to a blind thrust, taking her in a series of gaugeless, ragged spasms, bringing a shout to her lips and his laughing cry.

His foot relaxed, and he leaned down to her lap, drinking her in, pronouncing that, by having him and the world simultaneously, she had become his new faith and that they need no longer fear the road or their destination.

And she believed him.

BILLETS DOUX
14 March 1917

"This American of yours"—Caroline shouted provocatively across the genteel lounge of the Hotel Richmond—"where's this fascinating Yank I'm supposed to lay?"

Caroline made it a point to sound off in public places. It was a way of demonstrating to the plebeians that though they might legally occupy space around her that did not oblige her to recognize their existence.

The Hotel Richmond specialized in English guests and an aura of respectability.

In the dull brown air of the lounge, all stout leather chairs and solid oak tables and ladies in sensible travel suits, Caroline was a heresy of color: orange-tinted hair, faded officer blues of the Royal Navy Auxiliary, scarlet lips and nails, heavy jewels on every joint of every finger, an offending rainbow.

"Shut up," Adam said levelly, "and order me a drink."

"You've disappointed all these poor dears!" Caroline charged. "They were feeling good to see me drinking alone—me! no less!—in the midst of all these horny armies!"

A hundred female heads—all immaculately set in the same frozen waves—dipped low, preserving English middle-class decorum from this fishwife assault, even though the assailant happened to be the Duchess of Cambria.

Adam let Caroline give him her glass and suffered her to smack him juicily on the lips. "I thought Tha set you straight!"

"Revolting!" Caroline held her cheek to his. "I'm to give the American hots and Tha gets the toasted bun. At least you might offer yourself up by way of apology, Adam."

Adam grinned and pulled away. "Try not to draw the attention of the Western world to this table, while I explain the procedure for tonight."

Caroline sank back in her seat, grinning mischievously at Tha. "He'll even save the world to elude me!"

"The Yank's bringing his car. You'll show him the way. But afterward, you and I will leave together, so that Tha can drive with him . . ."

Caroline sighed, theatrically. "At least I'll be there for you to fall back on—which, come to think, may be an interesting position!"

"Finish up," Adam said. "Tha promised we'd meet Maxwell in the lobby. Try not to look grogged."

Caroline appealed to Tha. "How can I make him tumble, Tha? Why can't I learn the secret?"

"Poor, dear Caroline."

It was part of a social fiction that Caroline was a wanton. Though Tha knew Caroline was far from chaste, her randiness was primarily verbal. Part of it was fashionable anti-Victorianism, but it had been fueled by the current "body-snatcher" attitude, the reaction to seeing too many young men die, hurled from warm arms to cold graves between breakfast and sunset, day after day, year after year. And, in the special case of Adam, Caroline liked to disguise her infatuation for him by these comic assertions of sexual freebooting.

A hotel clerk came threading through the tables toward

them and Tha thought for a moment he was coming to say Maxwell had arrived. Instead, he bent over Caroline and spoke under his breath. Caroline broke into a hoydenish grin, fluting, "Oh, lovely, lovely. Do it right now, without delay, oh, please, I can't wait!"

After his departure, she leaned forward and for once lowered her voice. She was about to strike back at her critics— the "refined" British matrons of the Hotel Richmond lounge— prisoners of matrimony, toadies to their own wardens, reserving their stilted outrage for any female who flouted, having a candid itch, the rules of their snug, smug gaols.

"They all have husbands away at the front. They wrangle passage on military crafts to come from their cold beds in England to get tossed in Paris. But then they lose their nerve. They spend their afternoons in here, drowning in sherry and frustration. I should feel sorry for them. I loathe them. That darling clerk helped me. I've deposited identical little notes in their letter boxes. Signed by a pining gigolo, named Blaise Pascal . . . begging each of them for a date . . ."

"Pascal?" Adam laughed at the sacrilege. "Such pensée, Caroline!"

"Never mind," Caroline scoffed. "English provincials don't read French philosophers. I wouldn't—except I keep such bad company. Listen, do listen, sweetie!"

A page boy's chant came from afar, and then the boy himself appeared in the lounge, an impassive cupid, singsonging his bilingual love call, ringing a small bell.

"M'sieu Pascal, in small salon, waits for Madame. Attention, s'il vous plait. M'sieu Pascal attends Madame dans le petit salon publique. Attention, please . . ."

"Oh, enchanting!"

Caroline half rose in her seat, craning for a better view of the ladies of the lounge. They did not jump or run. After all, a decent English interval had to be observed even before an indecency. The page had turned to complete his belling round before the first matron arose, slipping toward the door, then another; yet a third and fourth. Demurely, of course, eyes down, trained not to draw attention to themselves.

"Gawd god," Caroline invoked her particular deity, "let's get out of here before I wet!"

At least a dozen wives converged on the door. They were in the full thrust of the mating pattern before they saw the trap. Behind them, another group halted in their tracks and began an awkward retreat to their seats, praying to sink through the floor.

Tha and Adam screened Caroline, helpless with repressed laughter, past the lounge that throbbed with equally repressed hostility. A perfectly British show of good manners on both sides, enabling them to get Caroline out to a couch in the lobby.

"Gad gawd god!"

Caroline, reaching the limits of her theism, chortled aloud now, long legs thrust before her, half lying back on the couch. "I'll have to find a new hotel—but it was worth it!"

"—in Australia," Adam suggested helpfully.

In the middle of their sadistic hilarity, Tha saw Robert Maxwell crossing the lobby toward them. Dark suited, wearing a white shirt and correct dark tie, he nevertheless seemed as much the young don as he had been in his sweater; he needed only a notebook to lead them to a classroom.

Tha went across to greet him, and brought him back to introduce Duchess Caroline and Adam. She had not warned him of Adam's blindness. It had an immediate effect. His glance went from Adam to her, all his previous assumptions about her suddenly shaken.

"I've told Adam about your work, Professor," Tha said. "He has a hundred questions. You're not just going to be entertained tonight."

Max grinned. "Only if you let me grill you, Major— about what really counts out here—"

Caroline took possession of his arm. "I'm to be your chauffeur. My role is to divert from all serious discussions."

Max allowed himself to be steered a step and then halted.

Through the lobby, another page, sounding his small golden bell, sang out for M'sieu Robert Maxwell, wanted on the telephone. Maxwell frowned at them, excusing himself. He was damned if he could figure who knew he was there.

Moments later, he rejoined them. He looked pale and tense. His eyes questioned her again, as he had at the cemetery, testing her at her depths.

"Emergency?" Tha ventured.

"Sorry," he said briefly. "Nothing."

She could feel him retreating behind his donnish defenses. "Caroline wants to take us to a fashion show—it's strictly illegal—we might even be arrested. I'm not sure you'll think it worth the risk to your position."

He met her challenge. "I'm not that official."

"And it may be rather—steamy."

"Steamy?"

"Oh, not New Jersey."

"Didn't we agree," Max said, "I'm here to learn?"

She laughed and called Caroline. "Our historian wants to see for himself." She went across to get Adam, satisfied that she had at least shaken the American's defenses, and that she would soon be able to put into operation her plans to overcome his last resistance.

"Don't drive too fast, Caroline—and wait for us," she said and went to guide Adam to the car.

SATURNALIA
14 March 1917

A low stage had been erected at one end of the huge loft. Models swished in lingerie and night dress of silk and satin and lace, joined to fur and metals and pearls, exultantly rococo from petticoats to strings. The models, lithe and narrow-hipped males, did not deviate from the traditional poses; what made them so provocative was their rapture in their roles and costumes, their will to express themselves in adornment.

Behind them, Tha caught a glimpse of a group of mimes. A giant figure of Mars dominated the silent dance. Across his golden face gore ran in irregular streaks, while his belly, protruding in unnatural and loathesome fecundity, sported an enormous and immaculate white shell.

At the feet of the god of battle a brood of chicks, heads covered in bird masks, were irresistibly drawn, by startling leaps and convulsive flutters, to peck away at the shell, chipping it here and there, then skittering away, only to return mesmerized to puncture the grotesque womb, ignoring the giant's gathering rage, his fists flailing at their minuscule invasions.

But the real entertainment, Tha saw, was the audience itself. Despite the presence of a number of females, most of the guests were men in French and British and Australian uniforms who were accompanied by their male lovers, released for this night to indulge their appetite for each other and for the silk undergarments, transformed from figments of the imagination to tangible, purchasable objects, defying the prohibitions of scarcity and of authority.

The evening was working out well. Almost too well.

Max and Adam had bonded immediately. From a superficial discussion of the current status of the armies at the front they'd plunged into an animated debate about war and history, about the optimism of America, about the pessimism of Adam, their exchanges deepening confidence each moment.

Caroline came back across the packed room to join Tha at the buffet table. "To hell with them," Caroline said. "They say they don't want to eat. But I'm starved."

Tha glanced at her watch. By now, according to the plan, Depardieu's men would be out there in the darkness, staking out Maxwell's car, preparing yet another trap for his innocence. She had reluctantly agreed. It wouldn't do, she had acknowledged, to shut Depardieu out of this act entirely. She not only had to win Maxwell's trust but retain Depardieu's. And the planned action, designed to increase Maxwell's faith in her, fell in with her own designs. By acquiescing, moreover, she would make it possible to get away from the Bureau's surveillance.

Yet, it would be fatal to delay too long. Those men out there, waiting beside Maxwell's car in the dark for her to reappear with Maxwell, would be cursing her, every moment increasing the danger of their being discovered. And, of course, if they could not perform, Depardieu might make her abandon her efforts, resulting in yet another abort with Maxwell.

Ahead of her, Caroline directed a waiter to heap two platters with delicacies, sighing over each choice like a starveling, diverting Tha from her anxieties.

It was, for these times, an overwhelming spread. Foods that had not been seen since the earliest days of the war appeared in profusion, embedded in creams and sauces, all in the elaborate prewar style of the defunct Restaurant LaRue that had passed into legend. Yet for all its flamboyance, there was a touch of rebellion in this fare, an assertion that men would not permit themselves to be forever reduced to fertilize the fields of Europe.

Faintly, beyond the boarded window, the air-raid sirens sounded, but nobody paid the least attention. In this company, the sound might have been that of church bells calling the faithful to vespers. If it had any effect it was to make the celebrants express their gaiety at a more intense, almost feverish, level.

Tha caught up with Caroline.

"It's getting late."

Caroline, bearing her two heaped plates, looked across the room to where Maxwell and Adam, drinks in hand, were bent head to head.

"Shall I break it up?"

"Please."

"Suppose," Caroline asked, "Maxwell accepts my invitation to get a stick at the joss house?"

"He won't."

"He came here."

"Then you'll drive Adam, and I'll drive Maxwell—and take it from there."

With a sigh, Caroline yielded the platters. "The sacrifices I make." She grabbed a handful of salad, shoving it into her mouth, enjoying her crudity as much as the food, and turned to make her way to the two men.

Tha looked for a vacant spot on the long table to discard the plates, feeling guilty at this display of conspicuous waste.

"Disgusting," a voice said at her side, "enough to make one throw up for a week, like Comte Montesquiou after he slept with Sarah Bernhardt!"

"Elaine."

Chardon's wife held a snowy plate on which there rested

a single white potato, a rebuke alike to the degeneracy of chefs and guests.

"One wraps bandages all day long," Elaine Chardon complained, "and then, this debauch. And these Uranians are supposed to be arbiters of our taste."

Tha, tempted to point out that attendance tonight had not been mandatory, murmured an innocuous comment about the food, hoping to get rid of her. Instead, Elaine remained at her elbow. "I hear," she said maliciously, "Jules chased you all the way to Geneva. Does that spell the demise of the D'Estrelles person?"

Again Tha tried to avoid conflict. Tonight, of all times, the one thing she could most easily dispense with was a public altercation with the wife of the Foreign Secretary. She could see that Caroline had reached Maxwell and Adam, and, after a brief conference, was starting back.

"Is Jules with you tonight?" Tha asked.

"With me?" Elaine's soprano was enough to provoke the attention even of the enraptured food gatherers. "Please don't add insult to injury!"

Dutifully, Tha laughed and tried to shake her off, excusing herself to reach Caroline.

But Elaine kept pace. Jules, she asserted, had a craving to see himself astride the world, hence his weakness for " 'les grandes horizontales' like yourself, Tha. I know you're not as stupid as D'Estrelles to imagine it is anything more than that!"

Adam and Maxwell were moving along the opposite wall to the exit. Tha wove through the crowd, to intercept Caroline. But Elaine would not let herself be shaken.

"Done!" Caroline called. "You go your way, I take Adam off for a sniff of white!"

"Am I invited?"

It was Elaine.

Caroline said, "Oh, buzz."

"Sluts. How can you be such sluts?"

"Luck."

Caroline grabbed Tha's arm and moved her away.

Maxwell and Adam had paused at the door. In front of the stage, the proprietor began to call for bids for his collection, reminding his audience that should the war go on, they might never see the like again, or never be on hand to see it again.

Suddenly a short man cut across Caroline's path. A dark moustache sprouted in a waxy face, marked only by black circles under his bright eyes.

"Caroline!" he said, opening his arms. "I can think of no one in the world who can do more and to whom I am less reluctant to appeal. Believe me, I vouch for this young man. He's supremely intelligent. It's a pity he's illiterate, but would you callously send him to the trenches simply because he lacks our addiction to word play?"

Caroline embraced him. "Tha"—she half turned the small man—"the ghost of the Ritz, our dearest Marcel Proust. Here is one you should know, Lady McLeod, adopted by Paris as Mata Hari . . ."

The burning dark eyes took Tha in with a sweep of approval. "The friend of my own Jean Cocteau, who tells me you will one day teach us to hear the music of our streets," he said, deftly weaving her into his single-minded appeal to Caroline, "which must predispose you to persuade our august lady we must not be snobs, the young men who wait on us, who open our doors and scrub our floors may be luckless—and who, believing in luck, may speak of an inferior?—so see him, standing by that table, Ihab Yassan—look at the way he carries himself and then tell me of natural kings!"

In the distance, an Algerian, in his colorful uniform, bent over his food, his mouth close to the platter, and slurped in Duchess Caroline's own style. He seemed brown and muscular and attractive: royal only if one stood in the forest primeval with Rousseau.

"But, Marcel," Caroline begged off, "I don't have that kind of weight, not even in our army, much less in yours."

"Dearest," Proust said, his eyes still on his young man, "tomorrow asthma and veronal will have me flat again—how his fez helps him digest—and by the time I am strong enough to write to anybody, he will be transferred to who knows what dangers, what horrors. A victim of my lassitudes and the world's dulled perceptions. I leaped, seeing you. You know everybody. Dearest, think hard, summon up a name, sweet

Caroline, so at the very least we can effect his transfer to his brother's regiment, stationed in Provence. Come with me, Caroline, we shall have a private Saturnalia, master waiting on the slave, and he will give you the details himself, I'm so hatefully inaccurate about these things . . ."

"We have to go. Please, Marcel."

"I'll see you out." He switched his tactics. "Think, Caroline. Some French relative. Even those on the wrong side of the blanket. But essential, if one fails to feel with the underdog, what is left?"

"I'll come by tomorrow," Caroline deployed.

"Tomorrow, I may be comatose or worse," Proust insisted. "I promise to be silent while you close your eyes and summon up a magic name."

In spite of Caroline's continued efforts to escape, the relentless magnanimity of the little man hammered them to a standstill. He was certain they would want to rescue "this splendid youth" from an unjust sentence of death. Even Tha found herself caught up in his appeal, each utterance gathering itself like a serpent, the coiling sinews of language more alluring than any apple, hypnotizing her for the sudden, fanged, anagogic strike, leaving her grateful for the savor of forbidden fruit.

She watched Caroline struggle to free herself from the author's powerful spell.

"I swear, Marcel," Caroline begged, "tomorrow, if you're too ill to see me, I'll get all the information to your good Françoise and I'll do something!"

"But tonight," Marcel admonished, "how is he—how are we—to get through the agony of tonight?"

They had reached Adam and Maxwell. Caroline had to make the introductions. And Proust, seeing his chance to delay her escape, brought up his howitzers of recollection.

"Robert Maxwell." He held the American's hand between his delicate palms. "But of course. The author of a monograph on the assassination of Jaurès?"

Max nodded, pleased.

"I remember. The Princesse de Noailles told me I must read it. It inspired her to sketch a portrait of Jaurès. Not handsome, she said, but a something. A force. A man of peace. She said you intended to investigate how we permitted the assassin to use a trial to escape. How does that study progress?"

"Postponed for the duration," Maxwell said.

Caroline pressed toward the exit, prodded by Tha. But the pale novelist would not give up. "Think, Caroline!" He turned again to Maxwell. "At the time, I would have said the militarists killed Jaurès. The same who almost victimized Dreyfus. But time plays tricks. Today our same militarists denounce Junkerism. They say the cult of violence is our enemy. Meanwhile, some who defended Dreyfus, like Clemenceau, for example, are more bloodthirsty than our old adversaries. We hunger to put our boot on the German neck, as the papers say. By the time this war is over, history will have so stripped us, we will all be revealed as those who, if we didn't bring down Jaurès, opened the doors for his assassin . . ."

"I wish I could agree . . ."

"Ah, you don't?"

"When this war ends, the victor will say the loser started it. That will be history; the truth about Jaurès will be historiography, a form of your art, Monsieur Proust . . ."

Proust held Caroline's arm. "Dearest Caroline, I depend on you." He gazed longingly across at his splendid youth. Then his eyes returned thoughtfully to Max. "But if America doesn't come in, how can there be a victor or loser? Or are you telling me, in this subtle fashion, that you Americans have decided at last to rescue France?"

His question, posed so innocently in his high, piercing voice, was not intended for Maxwell, but for the young officers around them.

Under her breath, Caroline implored, "Marcel, please!"

But he closed the trap about them. "But, dearest, you told me this young man is here with Colonel House. So in fact this isn't an idle observation, but virtually the official word of the American government!"

Maxwell flushed painfully. "But I don't predict that at all, sir."

"You mean," Proust demanded, "you will enter on the German side?"

"I doubt that."

"Remain neutral? Flourish on our misery?"

"If that is what it is."

Proust, having stirred up the officers around them, now turned to taunt them. "You mustn't condemn the Americans! After all, our own moral English allies, who howled at Hun brutality toward Belgian civilians, are now blockading and hence starving the noncombatants in Germany, the first victims the very old and the very young. And all the while, on our side, certificated men of honor don't show the least interest in such German deaths—credit the Americans, even if from greed, with feeding both sides!"

It was meant to provoke the officers and it succeeded. Proust, delighting in his role of devil's advocate, his voice rising in excitement, praised patriotism as a lover's passion, unreasoning by its very nature; the irony of his will to be free of chauvinism while still displaying his fidelity to friends risking their lives for France, a contradiction lost on the young officers, who were now surrounding Maxwell and demanding from him a categorical yes or no to the question of American intervention in the war.

Proust seemed to become younger as the dispute flared. His face was remarkably unlined, only the dark circles under his brilliant eyes hinting at his age and suffering. As Union Jack and Tricolor, along with odd pieces of purchased lingerie, were being waved aloft by the furious debaters, Proust, like Dorian Gray, seemed purged of age by his fine perception of his own corruption, a fortunate example that the willful child is father to the man.

Twice Adam, responding to Tha's pull, tried to get Maxwell to leave; but it was hopeless. Maxwell could not be extricated. He was deeply involved in a simultaneous defense of Colonel House, Woodrow Wilson, and the American Puritan tradition.

On the stage, the chicks, having created a gaping hole, were now elbowing one another to leap into the belly of the war god, unimpressed by its threatening fists. In the midst of this ingathering of innocents to the lord of slaughter, the proprietor mounted the stage, bellowing for silence, while the chicks jumped happily to make a nest in the immolating womb.

Police whistles came from a distance, scarcely heard.

"Please, please," the proprietor shouted, "there's nothing to worry about! They blow the whistles because they have been bribed to give us a warning! There will be plenty of time to leave. Do not add to my misfortunes. My people will show you the way to the rear stairway. Let there be no accidents, dear friends and patrons!"

Gleefully everybody began to run, joyously vying for a place in the narrow corridor and even narrower stairway. The uniformed men and their burly lovers relished the simulated cries of hysteria, the pretense of pandemonium, hands reaching everywhere, an exodus festive with proximity.

In the little alley behind the building, not only did whistles sound closer but from above came the growl of the heavy Gothas, accompanied by the servile nag of the French squadrons. The crowd broke into groups; soon singles and couples took flight into the dark streets.

For a moment, Proust held Caroline captive, forcing her to promise to visit him in the morning. Even so, he did not release his hold until pulled away by his young Algerian, while still appealing to Adam and Maxwell, clarifying his stand. "I'm torn. I want the Americans in, but I don't want our misery to touch your young men. I wish I were a prophet like my own Baron Charlus, who tells me we are now harmonized by our grief, but, alas, in peace we shall be pulled apart by our dissonant reliefs. Caroline," he added with morbid playfulness, "I will delay falling ill until you come to see me!"

Caroline succeeded at last in taking Adam away, calling over the crowd, "We're off to fly the broomstick. Sure you won't come?"

In the dark they heard Elaine beg, "You'll take me, Caroline?"

That struck Caroline as howlingly funny. "Oh, hell—tonight's the night for compassion!"

She led her charges away.

Searchlights passed overhead. The police whistles came

closer, shriller. Tha and Max began to run, grateful for the arrangements that had provided adequate warning for their escape.

At a corner, Max paused. "Damned if I know where my car is!"

"I think I do," she said, and took his trusting arm.

MAGNUMS
14 March 1917

At a corner they took shelter in a doorway, waiting for the cops to trot by at a gait dictated by their longer view of history.

Maxwell, still animated by the discussion in the atelier, wanted her to know how impressed he was by Adam. "We hear these stories about the Polish auxiliary here, allegedly posting a sign, 'There must be privates in our division,' and we fall into attitudes of contempt, and then you meet a St. Reymont. I owe him an apology."

"Adam forgives you."

"And you?"

"Am I involved?"

He studied the last of the flics whistling past.

"By other wrong assumptions," he said, "which I'll explain one day. For the present, accept them on credit."

"Then, I forgive you—on credit."

Laughing, they clattered into the silent street where Max had parked his car. The searchlights, reflecting from thick clouds, shed a phosphorescence around them, as though a swarm of fireflies had passed by, a fleeting and magical wand that granted them immunity from the attackers above.

In that agitated light, two heavy figures stooped over Max's car; its doors were open and they were half inside, involved in a search of its contents.

Max sprinted forward, shouting.

In the fading light, the two men ran, to reach a car parked farther down the street.

Headlights came up in the blackness, and the car roared. The pair were darkly visible as their vehicle lurched away from the curb.

Tha ran to catch up.

Max had flung himself behind the wheel of his car, coaxing the engine into life, intent on giving chase.

She screamed at him to stop.

He tried to push her away as she reached in through the window and clung to the wheel, howling, "You'll be killed!"

Angrily, he tried to pry her loose as his car began to move.

"No!" she screamed at him. "Underneath! Look!"

At the end of the street, the two men swung their car into the darkness of the intersection and vanished.

Max came out from behind the wheel, stooping. The brake cables had been severed and trailed like vines of steel in the gutter.

Slowly he straightened.

He confronted her, almost angrily. "But why are you helping me? I was warned. You want me out of it."

She could not see his face in the darkness, only feel his fury, directed at her in place of the absent men.

"I don't know what you're saying, Max."

"That's what you invited me for, isn't it?"

She moved away from him. "You're badly upset. I don't want to hear any more of that."

But he caught her arm and swung her to him. She could feel his harsh breath close to her face. "I was told. Even though it didn't make sense, I was told you worked for the Deuxième Bureau."

"Told by whom?"

"Do you?"

"Is that why I saved you?"

"Maybe they worked with you."

"Maybe," she said, turning, shaking loose. "But you're alive and ungrateful, which amounts to the same thing."

She strode down the street, keeping to the center of the cobbles. From a great distance bombs crunched, devouring some small corner of the city.

He was at her side. "I had that call . . . at the Richmond . . ."

She shrugged, but did not break her pace.

"It seemed ridiculous," he said. "I hadn't told anybody I was going there. Except you . . ."

She sensed his uncertainty. "Then I must have notified them! To warn you against me!" She allowed herself a short laugh. "And you are a student of our chicaneries!"

He went with her, silently. "You think she could have sent those men?"

"She?"

"My informant."

"She, he." Tha shrugged. "I saw two men trying to kill you and I cried out. So forgive me and let us say good night."

He matched her stride, supplicant now. "I trust your St. Reymont. He's been there. He hates the war. If you do, help me, don't walk away."

She did not slow. "I'm not Adam. You have to say things to me simply. What do you want of me?"

"Come with me. Confront my informant. If she's lying about you, help me expose her, get to the bottom of this. If not, I'll know there's not much hope of anything over here."

She halted abruptly. "Where is this woman?"

"I'll take you to her."

"How do I know she won't kill me, as those men tried to kill you?"

"You don't. And I don't. But for Adam . . ."

She let him wait. "On credit," she said.

The cab had been saved by the war, and so had the
driver. He sat in the open front of the decrepit vehicle and he
did not stir as they came alongside. He continued to smoke his
pipe and look up at the sky with the air of a connoisseur.

"Are you for hire?" Max had to demand.

He took his pipe from his mouth. "I miss the Zeppelins," he said magisterially. "They put on something worth a
night of sleep. These moths in the light, theirs or ours, nobody
can tell which, don't compare. They say these Gothas don't
come over to drop their bombs, but just to keep us awake. They
had that with the Zeppelins, so you can see how stupid the
Boche are, after all."

"Well, are you?"

The cabbie indicated the rear of the vehicle. "The top is
stuck," he said. "Can't pull it shut, or open. I leave it to you."

Max helped her into the cabriolet, whose tonneau was
caught in a permanent yawp of surprise.

"Hotel de l'Arcade," Max said. "On the left bank. Do
you know it?"

The old man expelled dottle with a long breath and
then indulged in a phlegmy laugh. "Now one begins to see why
you are braving a raid!"

Max frowned at Tha. "What's the joke?"

"A famous brothel," Tha said. "Didn't your informant
tell you?"

Max was nettled. "Nevertheless, that's where we want
to go," he told the cabbie.

He fell silent as the cab rattled and sputtered through
the nearly empty streets; the curfew for the restaurants had
passed, and soon all civilian traffic would be forbidden. At various intersections they were stopped by Senegalese patrols,
wearing their white pantaloons, and each time they had to
submit identity papers and be reminded that they must be off
the streets by midnight.

She decided not to question him, maintaining her air of
injury. He volunteered that his informant was unknown to

him, but that he considered her reliable, on the basis of past performance, and though he might be succumbing to a ruse, it was vital for the hope of peace—which he'd shared with Adam—to pursue this lead to its end.

Inwardly, she tried to sift through the possibilities of a trap set for her, as well as for Maxwell. Chardon had warned her that Depardieu had objectives of his own, that the stakes, beyond any struggle for power, went to the future of a war that now bled half a world, and threatened to gore the rest.

"Bishop's balls and Pope's piss!"

Roaring these votives, the old man slammed his ancient car to a quaking halt.

Ahead, the street was blocked.

Dark figures surged on thoroughfare and sidewalk. They seemed to be besieging a square black building at the turn of the road. Behind their stalled vehicle, men came tearing down the street, to join the rampage, enveloping the cab.

The old man honked, edging forward. His headlamps were old and yellow and wavering, and the mob disregarded the vehicle, moving away only when prodded by the fenders. Police whistles sounded somewhere; but they were, this time, shrill and urgent.

With a sigh, the old man pulled his brake and climbed down into the street, trying to gain the attention of the rioters. Finally he came back, shaking his head. "You have to go on foot. Second street on the right. Just on the right. If there's no light downstairs, you should see one on the storey above."

They stood for a moment, as Max paid him, jostled by the crowd that grew denser around them. "Hoarders," the old man explained. "A warehouse full of champagne." He flashed them a grin, stuffed the notes into his hacker's coat, and with the air of a man stoutly performing his duties for the Republic, he went off to join the looters.

Max wedged a path to the sidewalk across from the warehouse, where the crowd was somewhat thinner. Somebody knocked off his glasses, but he disregarded that to batter his way through, bringing them to the lee of the wall.

Near the warehouse entrance, a group of Senegalese sol- diers went through the motion of protecting private property, while careful not to interfere with the sacred right to pursue happiness. They resolved this contradiction not by impeding the traffic, but by only guiding its flow; first around them, and then keeping peace so that each man, struggling with his heavy wooden crate, containing the magnums of fine vintage, might escape unharmed.

Many of the men were in high spirits, preferring to fill up on the spot, guzzling from the plump bottles.

Frequently a case would be dropped, accompanied by satirical lamentations, and the heady exudations of the wine filled the street.

Behind Max and Tha, several trucks appeared. They were army vehicles loaded with recruits, still in their civilian clothes, being transported from some nearby processing center, on their way to their first military post.

The looters saluted them by lofting crates into the hands of the recruits. And they showed their patriotism by opening a passage so the trucks might go on their way.

Max, alert to this new opportunity, pulled Tha along in the wake of the vehicles.

The recruits crowded to the sides and rear of the trucks, dazedly accepting the drunken cheers and filched offerings. Most of them were young, very young, it seemed to Tha, and beardless and pale and frightened. They might have been schoolboys, sprinkled now with unholy water, dementedly preparing them for their baptism of fire.

Clinging to the outside of the tailgate of the last truck was a boy, not more than seven or eight.

Beyond the stakes, a recruit kneeled, urging the boy to give up and descend. His pleas were half embarrassed, half desperate. "Now," the recruit urged, "while we are going slowly. I want you to!"

But the boy ignored both pleas and commands, hanging monkeylike to a cross bar. The trucks, emerging from the crowd, were now beginning to pick up speed. The recruit began to pound at the boy's fists, finally dislodging him.

Tha ran past Max to where the boy sprawled.

The youngster, weeping, let her lift him to his feet. "My

brother," he said, wrestling away, trying to run after the truck. "They've taken my brother!"

Some of the rioters joined Tha in trying to calm the child and make him abandon his useless pursuit. Sobs racked his frail body. Some of the men offered to help the boy home, but he struck out at them, wailing, beside himself, still trying to get back on the truck.

A stout woman, a Marianne in black cotton skirts, came from the crowd and pried the youngster away from his consolers. She brusquely thrust a heavy crate into his thin arms and commanded him to go home.

Tha watched the youngster stagger away with his prize, narrow shoulders heaving against the weight and the heavier burden of sobs.

Max came to Tha's side and put his arm around her.

She felt as wrenched and weak as the boy himself. She yearned for the strength of Adam's angers to console the child not only for his loss but for his prize.

"I may be the innocent abroad," she heard Max say, "but not about you."

Without his glasses, he looked more vulnerable and boyish than ever. His arm steadied her and drew her forward. At the corner, several vans were disgorging police, armed with batons. Intent on the looters, the police charged past, and after that, the way ahead was clear.

LIVE WALLS
14 March 1917

A bald man with a round sly face hastened from the desk and made a sweeping bow to Tha. "We are surprised and honored, Madame," he said. "Our establishment is graced by your visit." He hovered about as Max announced himself. "Mademoiselle Entendu has come in only a few minutes ago. Room 203, if you please, M'sieu."

At the stairwell, he bowed again, and Tha knew that greed would get the better of discretion and that by tomorrow he would have spread it far and wide that Mata Hari had come to his house.

Max rapped at a door halfway down a padded corridor.

From somewhere nearby there were peals of laughter; and from a distance the roar of the air battle and the clangor of a fire engine.

273

"Madamoiselle," Max said, repeating his knock. "The American. Maxwell."

They could hear the laughter die away, along with a distant explosion, rumbling into silence.

"Mademoiselle—"

Frowning, he turned the handle. The door swung open. Tha followed him into the room.

A young woman lay on the bed.

A pillow covered her head.

She was fully dressed. One pump had been kicked free. The other was half off, as if she had been caught in mid-step.

"Mademoiselle," Max said.

Tha knew he did not expect an answer. She waited for him to advance to the bed and remove the pillow. The face was turned down, but bloated and splotched. Whoever had strangled her had used the pillow, so there were only slight marks on the childish neck, more childish than ever.

Convulsively Tha came to the bed and, keening, knelt down. "Adèle. Adèle."

"You knew her?"

Max was standing over her, half accusing.

She stayed on her knees an extra moment. The walls of the death chamber were live around her. It could not have happened more than a few minutes ago; and those who had committed it had waited for Adèle here, must still be here.

Swaying, she reached up and put her arms around Max, whispering into their embrace. "We're being watched." She felt him try to pull away, but she leaned close to his shoulder, her whisper soft and urgent. "Wait outside for me. If I'm to help, do as I say."

He pulled away, undecided, returning to stand at the bedside, staring down at the slender body. On the wall there were a series of framed reproductions of French landscapes; lyrical camouflage for a voyeur's peephole.

"Yes, I knew her. I warned you you were being duped!" She made her voice shrill, hoping that its stridency would reach the observers in the room beyond the paintings, careful to preserve her role as their agent. "A well-known demimondaine. No doubt in the pay of the Germans. Now paid off by the French!"

She picked up the pillow and tossed it cruelly at the body.

"I was a fool to let you persuade me to come here. There will be a police inquiry. I will say she was alive when I last saw her. I hope you will do the same. On your way out, make a pleasantry to the proprietor. I will leave after an interval. Understood, M'sieu?"

His eyes came up and met hers, locked in understanding. "Yes, understood." He waited another moment and then swung out of the room.

She waited until she heard his footsteps descending the stairs. On the wall, a leaf fell silently in a Tissot forest.

Swiftly she went down the corridor and then entered the adjoining room. A heavy man lounged in a chair. She did not know him. The other, turning from his viewing spot at the wall, was Depardieu. Coming slowly to greet her, his head bobbed dolorously.

"This business," he said.

"But Adèle . . . why?"

"We hired her to keep a line on Chardon. We knew she became involved with him, hated him for his neglect of her, but we never imagined she'd try to spoil his bid for power by going to the American with her tale about Krupp . . ."

"But if you knew she was coming here—"

"We only knew some woman was, one who called herself Entendu. In part, we owe that to you."

Tha stared.

"Oh, we had our men at the Hotel Richmond," Depardieu said, putting the matter in its proper perspective. "When the call came to Maxwell in the lobby, one of our men had the operator put him on to listen in. So we came here and waited. And then D'Estrelles turned up. We had to act—at once, before you arrived. Don't worry about an inquiry. For Chardon's sake and ours, it will be perfunctory. As for Maxwell, go to bed with him, if he insists, or jettison him. Unlike D'Estrelles, we can see our faith in you was not misplaced . . ."

It was the closest thing to a compliment she had ever had from Depardieu, and it made her rage inside. "Can I go now?"

Depardieu accompanied her to the door. "You should start considering whether you want to go back to Geneva or take up a new assignment here. However, I'm relieved you called D'Estrelles a Boche agent. It should quiet Maxwell, and we'll insist it was she who sent him to Switzerland on the Krupp matter to discredit us. We'll make the same charge to Colonel House, of course . . ."

He was no longer communicating with her, only tying up loose ends in a file, putting a ribbon on it, before relegating it to things past.

"You look exhausted, Madame."

She nodded, weighed down by the image of the body of Adèle; always a waif, living too close to her emotions, perhaps striving for this grisly death as a goal, free at last from injury.

"Thank you again, Madame."

She stood in the corridor, remembering how Frau Eva had praised her for unwitting aid in the murder of Von Tremke. Now Depardieu, if more wearily, had granted new sanction, even more unendurable than her crimes, inciting in her a hatred that was like Adam's.

They found each other in the shadows, not far from the plundered warehouse. The raid still continued and aircraft droned overhead. Far away, the fall of bombs were suppressed sobs.

She glanced back several times, though she knew Depardieu had lost interest in them; anything they did now was for him only an epilogue.

Max loped along in the darkness, seething and dissatisfied. "Who was she?"

"Adèle D'Estrelles."

"A whore?"

"Mistress of our Foreign Minister, Chardon."

"How do you know she worked for the Germans?"

"For the French," Tha said. "Like me."

He stopped for a moment, fighting his disbelief, regarding her with a scathing frown. Then, unable to dismiss her confession, he began to move ahead of her, bristling, the edge of a savage anger turned against his own gullibility.

"You mean, this whole excursion—through lace and lavender—to keep me from meeting her?"

"So they think."

"It may be sheer Americanism," he said bitterly, "but so do I."

"They are mistaken. And you, as well."

She did not want to sound weary; she knew he would translate it into contempt for him.

"Splendid," he said harshly. "She promised to tell me about a meeting tonight of the munitions kings of Europe. I trust you'll now fill me in."

"Unfortunately not."

"Why unfortunately?"

"Because I don't know if it's to take place, or where or when. I hoped to learn it from Adèle or you, and then Adam and I would make sure, no matter what you did, that the world would hear about it, and draw what conclusions it would . . . to end this horror!"

"You're doing this, not for the Bureau, but for Adam?"

"Yes."

"Honesty, at last?"

"Yes! Yes!" She was ready to implore him on her knees. "For Adam! And if you can't believe that—for me! For everything I care about!"

He balked, half truculent, half convinced. "How do I know that's not just more waterworks from the Bureau?"

"You don't."

"Take you on faith?"

"On results," she said, fighting exhaustion. "Adèle had only one source. Chardon. Now that Depardieu's satisfied you're no threat, they'll hold the meeting, and Chardon, of course, will be there . . ."

"And how do you propose to get Chardon to confide in you?"

"I can try."

"But how?"

"I'm good at lies." Fatigue made it sound almost indolent. "I'll say Adèle told me about the meeting before the Bureau silenced her. I'll assure him he's not to worry. And I'll have to bring you along as proof of my conquest, having convinced you Adèle was a German agent . . . and you'll apologize to him, for having let yourself believe a malicious German fiction."

Admiration won over his reservations. "They say a good lie rests on truth. To that extent, you've made a conquest."

They went, two noctambules in search of a cab, to take them from mid-Atlantic, where they had tentatively joined, back across Paris.

The maid began to say that His Excellency was not at home when they heard Elaine calling from inside, her voice blurry, demanding, "Who is it? What do they want of me at this hour?"

Embarrassed, the maid withdrew as Elaine came stumbling into the foyer. She wore a white housecoat, flouncy and silky as any of those they'd seen on display. She peered at them with effort. ". . . Mata of them all! Whom men salute by falling down. Why are you here? It's Jules who pursues you . . ."

She was, Tha saw, precariously balanced on a snowy peak, vertiginous and giddy. Tha led Max forward. "I must get in touch with Jules. Do you know where he is?"

"Where is Jules?" Elaine giggled. "Where Jules always is. On both sides of the fence!"

Tha took her arm. Elaine shook with laughter, almost out of control; she was at the point where even her pulse had a humorous beat.

"Elaine—I must know."

"Astraddle a straddle!" she chortled. "Left as soon as he saw me!"

"His appointment book?"

"In the study." Elaine waved blithely. "But he's a minister. He never writes anything down. He says anything he writes incriminates . . ."

She had some trouble with the last word, repeated it, then gave up.

"Cabineteer . . ." she mumbled to her own amusement. "I married a cabineteer, and I can't find the key . . ."

Tha had no trouble locating the leather-covered volume

on the desk. But it showed blank for the evening hours; and, as Elaine said, apparently was not used by Jules.

Sprawling on the couch, Elaine began to complain about Duchess Caroline. "Treats me like a footman. No. She'd lay the footman. The Armenian gentleman adored me. He gave me his best merchandise. They made me leave. She's coarse. A muledriver, with donkey's knees. You, too, Tha. Your thighs and belly are too ... too mandoliny. . . . Only I am young, tight . . ."

Tha went back to the couch and sat beside her. "Of course," she said, "and if Jules had any sense, he'd be home, cultivating his garden . . ."

"Oh, he does," Elaine said. "He's made us richer. Never a sou on me, though!"

"Elaine," she soothed, "close your eyes and think, where did Jules say he was going?"

"That D'Estrelles! I try to be her friend. I warn her. She'll get less from him than me!"

"Close your eyes."

Elaine complied, then opened them wide again. "He keeps her in a hovel. I thought he'd at least give her a villa, as Massimy did for you . . ."

"Concentrate on Jules . . ."

Suddenly Elaine sat up. "Massimy, wasn't he the Minister of War at one time?"

"Yes."

"That's where he went."

"To see Massimy?"

"No, don't be idiotic. To the War Office. . . . From Massimy to Chardon, what a fall for you, Tha!"

She lost herself in her incoherencies while Tha went to the phone and gave the operator the number that she would never forget—the prison on the Rue St. Dominique, to which Massimy had voluntarily surrendered, which had become the charnel house for France.

But a crisp military voice, that of the officer on night duty, told her that the Foreign Minister was not there, nor had he been there, nor was he expected to be there. "And I have no idea where he can be reached, Madame."

Elaine became petulant. "That's what he said! He was standing right where the American is. With his back to me. As usual!" She swung to Maxwell, still aggrieved. "You were with Caroline. Then you went with her. Don't you think I'm more beautiful than both of them?"

Somehow Max said something gallant.

"But I can prove it!" Elaine stood up and began to unbutton her nightdress. It opened in the middle. It revealed a body without flaws, that might have come, sectioned, straight from the Tegea temple. Yet it was the kind of body which Minerva, in her wisdom, always fleshed out with draperies. One detail stayed with Tha: the pubic hair was parted in the middle, neatly combed back.

In agony, Max tried to make himself nonchalant.

But Elaine would not have such neutrality. "These Americans, they are geniuses with machines, but that is the only perfection they dare to praise!"

Tha decided to take Max out of his misery. "If I thought she'd do more than tease, I'd urge you to stay. She knows where Jules is, and she's teasing us about that, with all that self-adulation . . ."

"I've more to offer than all those," Elaine said. "Eleanor, Adèle, Tha, and lots of others . . ." She looked down on her navel and suddenly began to cry. "But I don't need you. Or that Armenian. Go away . . ."

Tha decided on one more thrust. She went back to Elaine and began to rebutton her. "Elaine, let me tell you why I must get in touch with Jules. There's been an accident . . . Adèle D'Estrelles is dead . . ."

The pale face, flaccid with drugs, tried to tighten. "I never wished her any harm! Never!"

"Jules has to know, so there can't be any scandal for him, for you . . ."

"She killed herself and blamed Jules?"

"The important thing is to see that I get to Jules quickly."

Elaine began to shiver. "I'm sure he mentioned the War Ministry."

"Lyautey, Briand, perhaps Schneider-Creusot?"

"No." Elaine bent toward Tha, her forehead furrowing. "The War Ministry. Privately. In private. In a private car."

"Are you sure?"

"That must have been it," Elaine said. "The private railway carriage of the War Minister." She straightened up as Tha rose, and clung to her. "Do you think she loved him? Adèle, I mean? Is that why she killed herself, in my place?"

Slowly, Tha coaxed Elaine down the hall and into the bedroom and finally into bed. "Let yourself go to sleep," she said. "It will be all right now. Leave it to me. There won't be any danger to you, Elaine, or to Jules."

"Jules would like me to do it, to get rid of me," Elaine said. "I never will, no matter what happens."

Later, leaving, they paused in the street, attracted by a blue light coming from the communication center at the first level of the Eiffel Tower. She could hear a continuous crackle and sparking, a small universe in eruption. Cerulean enough, she thought, to serve as a sign from Heaven.

WALKING WOUNDED
14 March 1917

In the darkened living room, Krupp went impatiently to the window, knowing there was little he would see, less he could do.

Five minutes ago they had arrived behind the high wall that shielded this suburban house from the street and from its neighbors. They'd come with the clangor of an ambulance and the klaxons of motorcycle outriders, just as the French security man had said, assuring them there was no need for alarm, since the neighbors would believe the military ambulance had come to pick up the French officer who was alleged to occupy this quiet, sheltered residence.

It had been impossible to challenge these arrangements or the overcautious maneuvers that had preceded them. Clearly, Luce Schneider-Creusot was a frightened young man, unwilling to proceed with their meeting until he was certain it was secure, safe from prying eyes, impervious to political explosion.

In Geneva, the decision to shift the venue to Paris had been made under pressure and in haste. There'd been a disposition on the part of Luce to postpone the meeting, and even old Roy Vickers had expressed his misgivings.

Of course, the leak could have come from any one of them. He had reviewed his side of it. He had confided in the Kaiser, the Prime Minister, and of course, his aide, General Oppen. Of the three, only the last was absolutely dependable. The others might, for their own reasons, have decided to betray the meeting, end it before it began.

Naturally, the same considerations obtained for his French and English compeers. Both had been compelled to confide in their political leaders; both had perforce given some hint of the meeting to at least some members of their staff. In the final analysis, a secret was a known fact your enemies could not compel you to acknowledge publicly.

He turned, as General Oppen came back into the room. "Baron?"

He announced his position by the window with a cough. "They're ready, sir."

"The others, finally gathered?"

"Yes, Baron."

General Oppen advanced through the gloom. He wore a French military overcoat draped over his shoulders, and carried another one. Krupp let himself be helped into it. Oppen offered him a French officer's cap, but he thrust it away.

Outside, he noted that the intelligence people were operating, for a change, with only marginal arrogance. The motorcycles had been lined up on either side of the driveway, their headlights pointed outward, so that a lane of concealing darkness led to the rear door of the waiting ambulance.

Oppen preceded him to the door, and Krupp accepted his help to mount the clumsy stair.

In the dark interior, he had to adjust his vision again. Roy Vickers, small and stout and aged, hunched on the rearmost litter, while Luce, slender and fashionable, stood, head bent, clutching a strap that hung from the low roof of the vehicle.

A year had passed since their last meeting in Geneva. At that time, Roy's older brother, Arthur, had been alive, but already in the grip of the illness that had taken his life. Roy had always battened on his brother's ability and energy. Alone, now, he seemed to be reduced in size, having taken as a legacy only his deceased brother's advanced age.

Krupp waited for the bell of the ambulance and the klaxons of the outriders to sound before he exchanged greetings and small talk. Vickers complained of the harsh winter and the premature spring, both of which he ascribed to the activity on the western front.

Luce made apology for the delay. "The Bureau assures me the leak has been eliminated and we can proceed. They tell me the public is used to having ambulances go shrieking through the city. Though it may seem spectacular to us, we are reduced to the commonplace."

"If you are content," Krupp said, "then we must be."

"I wouldn't go that far," Luce said. "They are consistently incompetent. Chardon will join us in the War Minister's private railway carriage, which is frequently used for night meetings, and which is deemed quite safe."

Krupp decided to use that opening to regain command. "I'm told Lyautey resigned. Cold feet?"

"He's better off at the front in Africa," Luce said. "I never trust military men in these things, anyway." He glanced at General Oppen. "I don't mean you, General. You are a steelmaker, on loan to the military."

"At the moment"—Oppen waved the French cap in the narrow aisle—"to your military."

Vickers grunted from his crouch. "Better the military than our Downing Street chap. Not even Lloyd-George can cope with Lloyd-George."

Krupp heard Luce's polite snicker and then decided to end the chatter, his voice taking on a choked quality, as it always did in moments of stress.

"I must say, for my part, I welcome this chance to be without Chardon. Events have outrun our agenda . . ."

"You mean," Luce said, faintly ironic, "you are no longer the principal creditor of the Reich? They've paid you off, Gustav?"

"No, obviously not."

"I'm relieved," Luce said. "New loans must be floated. Chardon's only condition is some German restriction on submarine war, even if only in the name of food for our women and children, or some such formula. I would think that would satisfy the Americans that we weren't about to collapse, and the loans would be forthcoming."

Krupp heard out Vicker's supporting murmur, forcing himself to remain silent until the old man had droned on to the end of it.

"It's true I agree to discuss all that, Luce. But matters have gone far beyond."

"What matters?"

Krupp weighted his words. "We have to save Europe from chaos, from revolution and disorder."

"What?" It was old Vickers. "What's to happen?"

But even Luce, though suave, changed his tone. "This is not just prophecy . . . I trust."

During the long hours of delay, he had prepared a balanced and thorough exposition. But now, faced with his two friends and competitors, he decided to abandon all prefaces, and present the basic facts.

"You say I'm the principal creditor of the Reich. It's also true that the founder of the house of Krupp laid down the rule that our business was to supply Germany and anybody else with steel and arms, not dictate policy. Those two tendencies, always in conflict, have now come to a climax. The military are now in command. Ludendorff, fearing American intervention, has just decided to support revolution in Russia. He wants a one-front war for victory. The Kaiser accepts the gamble. It may be that Ludendorff can succeed militarily. That is why I have not opposed his decision. Nevertheless, I am afraid that the genie he decants in Russia will soon rule what remains of our divisions and yours . . ."

Vickers was flustered, short of breath. "That's insane! Surely, you must stop him!"

The young French magnate was quieter, more pointed. "Beyond genies and such, you must see some solution . . ."

Krupp reached for the two straps above the litter and pulled himself up, so that he came up to the level of the young Frenchman.

"Stopgap."

"But tell us, Gustav," Vickers implored.

"I want to take back a proposal to the Kaiser. You must guarantee America will not intervene. And I will guarantee that the revolution in Russia will not be supported by us, but on the contrary, crushed, in its nest . . ."

The two fell silent.

Outside, the motorcycles wailed and the ambulance bell tolled on a higher note of urgency. They went roaring around a corner. They could hear the fall of bombs, not too far away, followed by the new uproar of fire engines.

Vickers blurted first. "But we're counting on the Americans to save us . . ."

Again the Frenchman was more subtle, more at ease. "You mean," he said, "you are ready to condone this criminal action of Ludendorff's unless we agree to your proposal?"

"I mean," Krupp said, "I want you to understand the gravity not only for me or you, but for all of us."

Luce sighed. "One understands," he said. "But we in turn are captives. Public opinion is irrevocably turned toward the Americans. We could never reverse the tide politically—or survive if we try . . ."

"I quite realize." Krupp soothed them. "What I suggest, therefore, is to make it impossible for the Americans to come in, on any terms they would accept. I mean, here, in France, for you to bring Clemenceau to power, who will demand complete rule of a defeated Germany, excluding the Americans. And for Vickers to encourage the fire-eaters in the Cabinet to stiffen Lloyd-George to similar proposals, and offend Wilson and prevent American entry. If I could take that much back, I might still have the Kaiser overrule Lundendorff . . . and save us all from disaster . . ."

Luce laughed. "One always forgets, Gustav, that you began as a diplomat . . ."

"In Washington," Krupp said. "The Mecca of the moralizers. Do you know—during that near-miss in Geneva—I was tempted to let the American discover our meeting ... that would have kept them out of the war for all time!"

"Gustav!" Vickers was appalled. "What an idea!"

"A temptation." Krupp sighed. "Except that the disclosure would also bring down the Kaiser, and, worse, me with him ..."

"Yes"—the old Englishman was dry—"but what of our loans? How will you get yours and we ours? Our paper is losing value. It's irksome. Arthur would never have tolerated it!"

"Once we have dealt with the major issues," Krupp said, trying not to dismiss the old man out of hand, "we'll be able to handle the loan question, too."

Luce hung onto the strap and cursed the jolting vehicle. "I should think," he said, "we would do better postponing further discussion—until I'm sure I have a head on my shoulders."

Krupp laughed and agreed. He remembered the Bavarian adage, "Truth is everywhere, but its home is exile." He had excluded his own part in fashioning the two-edged sword of Ludendorff and Lenin. The target was agreement, and for that he'd have to win over both Luce and Chardon. He could wait. Between the threat of Ludendorff's victory and Lenin's spectre of disorder, he could outflank them both and fashion agreement from fear.

The ambulance rattled through the streets.

BLOOD AND IRON
14 March 1917

Everybody in Paris knew the war chariot

Parents took their children to view it from afar, a thing of wonder, shining out of the gray cindery vastness of the yards of the Gare du Nord, its brass fittings and black lacquered sides gleaming in the sunlight, frosted beveled panes and stained-glass windows guarding its interior, preserving the mystique not only of the War Minister or war, but of power itself, to which all must, even in the imagination, subordinate themselves.

The problem, Tha explained to Max, would be to reach it; not only would it be protected by the blackness of the yards at night, but there would be soldiers patrolling each entry, on regular duty against sabotage, undoubtedly reinforced when some important conference was taking place.

Often, in those early days after Massimy's appointment, she had stalked these environs, trying to come to terms with herself, her eclipse as a dancer and a courtesan. In those hours, seeing the distant lights of the carriage, she had imagined herself in the outer edge of darkness, without past or future, hopelessly adrift.

A cabbie, mystified by her directions, carried them from one side of the yards to another. In the middle of the black pool, she had seen some dim light over a strip of concrete and, near it, an isolated carriage. But from no vantage could she determine whether it was indeed the carriage they sought; and if it were, how they could reach it.

From time to time they passed small bridges or walkways that led down into the inky yards, but always these openings were screened by soldiers, not Senegalese, but military police, white-gloved and white-crossbanded, warning ghosts in the darkness.

Frustrated, Tha even considered calling Adam, who by this time must have returned to the villa at Compiègne, to ask him to summon a group of his hotbloods and prepare for a frontal assault.

Max, professorially, rejected that. Armies organized against other armies, but were helpless against individuals. Coolly, he directed the cabman to retrace his path around the periphery of the yard.

To her surprise, he had the cabbie drop them at a small bistro which lay to one side of a bridge. "Right here," he said confidently, peering into the street.

After the cab left, he skirted the bistro, to steps that led down to a damp urinal. He had nearsightedly made out, on their first survey, a figure emerge out of the dark, buttoning his trousers, but, as an academic, he had needed time to weigh the evidence of his impaired vision.

They stumbled across tracks and ties. Though the searchlights scanned the skies above them, the reflections did little here below. At wide intervals a globe held a weak swatch to the gloom; from time to time a signal arm poked a colored eye into the murk, only to blink shut.

Even the dimly lit strip of concrete had been swallowed

in the well around them, and Tha had the feeling they were moving in circles.

Max, a step ahead, began to run.

Out of the darkness, a dark tracery of iron formed itself—a small bridge that spanned a dozen tracks, grounded on each end in pitch.

She panted to keep up, bruising herself as she stumbled up the stairway. He half crouched against the filigree of iron struts, able at last to study the ground around them.

The strip and the railway carriage lay less than a hundred yards from them, in one of those many slight depressions in the yard. Shielded from the lower level, its brass work caught the faint light that made it seem radiant to them.

At the edge of the strip, they could see a dozen soldiers—huge elite guardsmen—shouldering rifles, marching up and down in cadent solemnity, on duty against all interlopers.

In the distance, a vehicle, its headlights shaded, approached slowly on the narrow concrete band leading out from the depot. A man descended the rear stairs of the carriage to await its coming. Passing under the slit of light from the partly opened door at the rear of the carriage, his shape was vaguely illuminated; yet Tha had no trouble in identifying the short, husky man. It had to be Chardon.

The vehicle, which she had imagined would be a limousine, turned out to be a French army ambulance, the white crosses of Geneva painted on its roof and sides, cauterizing all their expectations.

The man she was sure was Chardon marched toward the ambulance, to greet four figures and direct them toward the railway carriage. As the party advanced, the guardsmen came to stiff attention.

That first pair, wearing army overcoats, she recognized without difficulty. One was the military man she'd seen last in the Geneva railyard; the other, slightly stooped, was the current custodian of the Krupp name and fortune.

"Him," she said.

"Positive?"

"Yes," she said.

"The others?"

"At the rear, the one with Chardon, Schneider-Creusot. The old one, I don't know. The other in the army coat, an aide of Krupp's."

"Vickers, then, the old man."

"Probably."

Max came to his full height, carefully screening himself in the shadow of a girder. "Think you can find your way back to the bistro and the telephone?"

She nodded.

"I want you to call Colonel House," he said. He rehearsed her in the number. "His private phone. You'll be calling for me. Tell him. Make him come. They won't dare stop him."

She saw him take a step. "And you?"

"Try to get closer, stay with them if they move. If something goes wrong, I'll keep in touch through your friend, Caroline . . ."

She nodded, reciting the colonel's number like an om. Far above, a single stray plane soared, then plummeted far away. Her heart tightened painfully.

"Max!"

She caught up with him at the bottom of the stair. She dug deep into her purse and produced the small silver revolver that had been her bonus in Von Tremke's death.

He smiled at her offering. "Without my glasses, they'd better keep their distance."

She forced him to accept it. Her only thought was for him to emerge unspotted from the slaughterhouse she and Adam and Europe had prepared for him.

They were close together—in a way, joined tighter than any embrace—as they crouched low to the ground, laughing nervously, touching each other only in parting.

Five paces onward, she stumbled over a rail, and the beam of a lantern struck her flush in the face, a blow from which she recoiled, helplessly.

A trackwalker came plodding toward her. He stared at her in astonishment. "Looking to get killed, lady?"

She could make out his short, heavy body. He wore civilian clothes. An armband denoted his services in a war industry.

"You have to help me."

"First," the man said, "come with me."

Suddenly he swung his beam around and caught Max in its swath.

"And you," he said. "Unless you want me to beat your brains in, you're going to the yardmaster in the tower."

He carried a short, snubbed stick, and held it up before them.

Max was beside her, pressing her to comply. "Very good. We need the yardmaster. We want his help against the Boche."

The trackman growled. "What are you? English?"

"American."

"Those," the worker dismissed. "March. Both."

The lantern beam whipped them along, away from the carriage. In the distance, a dark tower was outlined against the sky, a shaded light in its control room, a tiny red star at its peak.

She could feel Max's body beside her, close again, beseeching her to accept the alternative that had been forced on them. They would have to persuade the yardmaster to let them phone Colonel House and hope that he could appear in time to reach that meeting.

From the darkness, several men appeared. Most wore the traditional clothes of the railroaders; many were in blue uniforms. The trackman enjoyed his moment, relating that this idiotic pair had a shit story about the Boche, and he would let the yardmaster sort it out.

"Oh, you're really a great man," somebody said. "Don't you know who you've got in your bag? That's our own Mata Hari, you freak."

"Who?"

"Farthead," another jeered, "go back to Cabourg. You're going to get yourself into an assload of trouble."

"Fuck off," their captor said. "If she's the shit-Madonna herself, she's coming to the tower."

Around them male voices threw out reassurances. Some assumed she had come to lay the American in a cinderbed. An odd setting, and an even odder choice, considering how skinny the American looked, but then, who were they to be choosers?

By the time they had arrived at the tower, a group of twenty or more had emerged from darkness and the word had sped ahead of them. A quiet, wizened man descended from the tower. He wore a blue uniform that had fit him in the prime of life and now hung in folds about him. The men held up lanterns while he examined Max's identity papers. He held them close to his spectacles, silently mouthing the information,

"What is this about the Boche, then?" He squinted up at Max.

"Krupp," Max said. "In that private carriage."

Around them, the men had fallen silent.

"Friend," the yardmaster said measuredly, "we have lost sons and brothers. Be careful of what you say."

"Krupp," Max repeated. "And your Schneider-Creusot, and the English, Vickers."

The men around him began to growl. "Provocator! Who sent you here?"

The old man waved his hand to silence them, and turned again, this time to Tha.

"Aren't you some sort of foreigner?"

"Dutch."

"You too imagine the Boche cannon maker is in that carriage?"

"I saw him. I know him."

"Why do they meet here?"

"Isn't it enough," Tha said, "that they meet?"

The old man looked beyond the crowd to the distant carriage. He remained above their rage and their impatience. "We will ask to inspect the carriage, as is our duty. If there is nothing, we'll turn this pair over to them. If something, you will have reason for your anger . . ."

He reached out and took a lantern and went into the lead.

The men swung beside her. The old man preceded with Max. She could hear him trying to convince the yardmaster. "I would be grateful if you would call my superior, Colonel House." But the old man shrugged that off. Max tried again, mentioning his work in investigating the Jaurès killing. "I'm known to the leader of your confederation, Martet. Others, too. Fontin, Lachelle. Please—stay away—call Colonel House . . ."

The yardmaster raised his arm, halting them, slowed by Max's appeal.

"Let me speak with the officer," he said. "No blood. We have enough of that. We shall soon see who is the liar."

Reluctantly, the men agreed.

"You two," he instructed Max and Tha, "come along, but I'll talk."

They went in the wake of the lantern.

The men behind them had fallen silent. Even the skies above were quiet, undisturbed by aircraft, no longer lanced by the searchlights, though the All Clear had not yet been sounded.

"Officer," the old man called out, "I'm the yardmaster, Capel. I've been told there's a Boche aboard that car. I will make a search, under the regulations."

"Colonel Sisson," the officer said stiffly. "Go back to your duties. I'm acting under instructions of the Foreign Minister. We have ordered an engine. We shall be clear of your yards."

"Sir," Capel said, "these are my duties. Permit me to inspect the carriage."

The colonel decided to treat it as a joke. "I assure you, old party, everything's in order, nothing to worry yourself about."

"In that case, a look should be no trouble."

"Capel"—the officer stopped being friendly—"the movement of this carriage has been authorized by the stationmaster. Follow the orders of your superior."

Tha watched an engine slowly back across the yard to hitch itself to the ministerial carriage. Smoke drifted across to them, a heavy and sullen swirl.

"Under the regulations," Capel said, "no stock may clear the yard without clearance from me."

He beckoned with his lantern and moved ahead. They

could see the engine crawling to make the join, then heard the first clang of the metal.

"Grandfather, you are making a nuisance of yourself." But there was no amusement in his tone. He spoke over his shoulder to some dark forms. "Sergeant, let them have a round over their heads. For these and the rest of them. Then secure the tower. On the double."

The rifles spoke in disciplined unison, upturned pieces flaring almost simultaneously. The guardsmen began to advance at a trot, rifles at the ready. The railroaders held their ground for a moment or two and then began to fall back, shouting and hurling clubs and stones and lanterns as they covered their rout.

Capel moved back, grabbing Tha's arm, shouting at Max. "Get out! No chance! Find a way out!"

They held together a moment, as the colonel, taking his service revolver from its holster, slowly advanced on them.

She ran a dozen yards into the darkness, and then suddenly the old man was swallowed up in it and she was alone. She continued to run, searching for some hiding place, before she realized her pursuer was Max.

Silently she reached out a hand to him and they helped each other through the rough darkness. Bitterly they saw the engine begin to overtake and pass them. It was tantalizingly close, moving slowly, its single eye dismissing them.

Behind them, in the distance, the guardsmen had recovered some of the lanterns, and were already circling the control tower. There was no gunfire, no outcry from the railroaders.

Max pulled her along, lunging to cover the ground between them and the slow-moving train, when the earth seemed to give away, and they found themselves sliding down a cinder embankment, sharp edges biting through her dress, stinging her elbows and cheek.

He came to her side. "Hurt?"

"No."

"Bastards. Where's Capel?"

"I don't know."

Miserably they watched the engine haul its dark luxurious load, slowly opening space from where they lay.

On the concrete strip, the ambulance's headlights flared, turning to follow the guardsmen back to the depot. Only a handful of security men remained within the dim compass of the lamppost, apparently waiting to see that the carriage had cleared the yard, leaving the gray place to sink into historyless obscurity.

A hundred yards from where they crouched, the carriage lurched to a halt. A figure appeared on the rear platform. He stood for a moment shaking hands with the three men, and then, attaché case under his arm, let himself down the steps and leaped into the darkness. As he passed under a light, they recognized Chardon.

She heard Max suck in his breath.

At the strip, the security men had begun to move toward the Foreign Minister.

Too late she became aware of Max's intention. He was running through the night toward Chardon.

"Max, don't!"

Numb with fear, she ran after him.

She heard Chardon's cry, and when she came upon them, Max was standing over the shorter man, seizing his dispatch case and pounding him, venting all his frustrations in each blow. She heard Chardon weakly calling on Maxwell to stop, pleading for rationality.

"Pointless, pointless! Maxwell, don't!"

Behind them, the voices of the security men sounded, seeking to locate Chardon. Max turned to her, pale with anger, beside himself.

"Tha, go. Call House. I'll stay with him. Get out . . ."

She tried to resist, but he half thrust her away, forcing her to retreat out of Chardon's hearing. He insisted on her submission. They would certainly revenge themselves on her. Through Caroline, he would send word when it was safe for her to come out of hiding. "We'll force them to arrest me, bring it into the open . . ."

She brushed his cheek with her lips, and then ran into the darkness. To the north, the engine and the curtained carriage were becoming one with blackness. Far behind her, men's voices lifted in hoarse dispute, and she discerned Maxwell's among them, sharp and insistent, his accent clear even after she was too far away to distinguish his words.

The streets kept receding. The bistro had long since closed and she had to grope her way along the embankment before the stairway came up under her hands.

She came up to the street as the All Clear was being bugled through the public speakers. The lighthearted notes, which brought her back to Adam, seemed a sardonic requiem to their hopes. As she went in search of a phone, people came up from their cellars and formed a noisy procession, spurting laughter from the bellows of fear.

IDES
15 March 1917

They were making him a prisoner of punctilio.

One of the security men had come into the room with a silver coffee service and offered to fetch up food and liquor. A senior official dropped in to assure him that Colonel House had been notified and was on his way. Monsieur Depardieu, as well, had been summoned and begged Monsieur Maxwell to be patient until, together, they might sort out the matter.

Meanwhile, a security man remained with him, holding Chardon's attaché case on his lap. It would be opened and its contents examined in the presence of Depardieu and Colonel House, exactly as he had demanded from the moment of being taken into custody. His Excellency, the Foreign Minister, had also offered to cooperate, and had agreed to remain on the premises until the colonel and Depardieu had satisfied themselves about all aspects of the affair.

Yet Max knew, behind it all, he was, in the old Yankee phrase, as welcome as a skunk at a lawn party. In the corridors there were frantic scurryings; phones rang; in the courtyard limousines came and went, needling the nerves of the sleeping city.

Three A.M.

By now, even if these people were lying, there must have been a call from Tha to Colonel House. He knew she could not have been arrested. He could still hear Chardon's cry, classic, "Tha, *you?*" bleated from the ground, before he had pulled her away. All these officials, coming and going, were evidence that not only was she still free, but they were worried about it.

He felt her on his skin. Nothing she had said. Only that all her disguises—or what he had perceived as disguises—had been stripped from her, in his presence, pressing her to a collision, through her love for Adam, with him; revealing herself and her needs with a force that had stirred him, brought him closer to her than to any other woman in his life. Like the boy with the case of cognac, he had come away with a prize with which he must learn to cope.

"M'sieu . . ."

A security man stood at the door.

"They want you downstairs, M'sieu."

Very polite. Max turned to his companion. "With my friend here."

"To be sure."

Behind the pair, he marched down a magnificent staircase, balustraded in carved bronze, carpeted in blood red. The security of the French State had made a home for itself in nineteenth-century grandeur, manufactured from its inherited Roman envy of Greek simplicity, a shaky foundation for its great pretensions.

Double doors led to an enormous Empire drawing room, which had the effect of reducing Colonel House to a wispy presence.

Strangely, the imperial scale had no effect on Depardieu except to make his gray exterior more crustacean.

"Max!" House, small and deft, came swiftly across the

great space, his eyes grave, his mouth smiling. "Fallen into the hands of the posse, have you?" He sounded Texas and drawling, but Max knew what a pose that was; like his title, "Colonel," which only meant that, in rural Texas, he had more than a single pair of trousers. "Heard about your derring-do." He had his arm around Max. "Didn't intrepid Dick Stover go to Yale?"

But the grip on his shoulder was far from light; it was intended to warn him, and yet support him. Under that avuncular manner was a man who had run the largest state in the union, and run it hard; the son of a merchant banker who had fought the big railroads to a standstill and kicked them out of the statehouse, and then went on to find his perfect alter ego in Woodrow Wilson, and elevate him to the White House, leaving others to puzzle which was the shadow, which substance.

Depardieu came from around his desk, cordial, but functionary. "I've asked His Excellency, the Foreign Minister, to join us. One doesn't want to prejudice any inquiry until we've heard an explanation—or account—from Monsieur Chardon himself."

"Most considerate," Colonel House said, all honeysuckle and rose, "in view of the hour . . ."

"I would only report," Depardieu said, "that I had that carriage stopped and searched at once. No passengers were aboard. Naturally that doesn't preclude there having been passengers prior to my action."

"Ye-es," Colonel House said.

It was gently opined, in the tone of a man with a mint julep in hand watching the evening sun go down on rich land. Max relished it, knowing that its thunderous undertones of rejection were lost on Depardieu.

"We all appreciate your prompt response to this emergency, Monsieur Depardieu."

Somehow that velvety deference appalled Depardieu. "Of course, if you wish it, sir, we can have Monsieur Maxwell make his charges out of the hearing of the Foreign Minister."

The dreamy blue eyes of the presidential adviser came to Max. "Would you, Max? Would you feel that to be necessary?"

Max followed the subtle lead. "Not at all, Colonel."

"Good."

Depardieu motioned a man to fetch Chardon. "Would you rather a secretary set this down, Colonel?"

"We're here as guests." House took his seat and hitched up his pants. "I don't only mean in putting you to all this inconvenience, but in the sense we come from far away, to observe, to learn, not to make cases . . ."

Yet, this time, Max felt disconcerted by that spacious manner. House had put himself at a distance not only from the French, but from Max, from any rashness he might have committed or would commit, in order to preserve his position as the President's emissary, representing a country "neutral in word and action." And somewhere in the room there hovered Woodrow Wilson's austere image.

"Gentlemen!"

Chardon came in briskly behind his energetic salutation. In the interval since Max had last seen him, he'd got himself another suit, still ministerially black, but without smirch or cinder, humility of blows.

Nor was there even the vaguest hint of any hostility, as he shook the colonel's hand and then did the same with Max. "A distressing night," he said, his voice ringing oratorially, "distressing not only for me, but for my country. I can well imagine in certain eyes, even those of the world, I seem to have hopelessly compromised myself and have no alternative but to resign . . ."

Depardieu watched Chardon usurp the chair behind the desk. "I wish, Your Excellency, to put my Bureau's position. We are obliged to provide security and follow your orders. If there are transgressions—danger to the safety of the Republic in time of war—it is the duty of others to prosecute, not ours."

"Well said."

Chardon bent over the desk blotter, leaving Depardieu to hover impotently beside the desk. He dipped a pen into the well and then permitted a splash of ink to drop on the blotter, absorbing himself in its spreading, ambiguous stain.

"And, in deference to the American style, let me be blunt. I initiated a meeting of our Schneider-Creusot, the staunch Sir Roy Vickers, and the puissant Baron Krupp."

Briefly House's pale blue eyes came to Max's face, cautioning him to sit back and wait. "I'm relieved, Your Excellency," he said with smooth Southern courtesy. "I confess, when they woke me out of a deep sleep, I imagined it was part of a nightmare, my young colleague here caught out with phantoms . . ."

"Considering the results," Chardon said, "I wish it were only a nightmare."

House nodded gravely. "Ye-es," he said. "I have no doubt Your Excellency had the most profound reasons for convening such . . . in time of war."

"I had," Chardon said. "Or thought I had."

He traced the outline of the stain with a pen, enlarging it, then, as in a geodetic survey map, expanded that with yet another outline.

"Or we thought we had, didn't we, Depardieu?"

"About Krupp, you mean?"

"About Krupp."

"Our information was that Krupp was our best hope."

"Exactly," Chardon said. "And that is why I invited him. To save France. Europe. The heritage we share with America."

Colonel House murmured, "Our heritage, we are obliged for it, Your Excellency."

If Chardon sensed the ironic stress, he did not pause in his artwork or in the case he was preparing for himself. "The information was that the Germans were backing Lenin and revolution in Russia so that Ludendorff would be free to embark on a one-front war, but that Krupp opposed this venture, fearing revolution would spread to Germany, and from Germany to us. Wasn't that, boldly, your information, Depardieu?"

"Yes, sir."

Chardon deliberately dipped the pen in the well a second time and this time scattered drops in a wide arc. He began to link these drops together with wavy, convoluting lines.

"As you know, Colonel House, I'm a miner's son. I have seen such passions and where they lead. So I took the responsibility to ask Krupp to meet with his peers, first in Geneva, then here, to preserve his Europe and ours from falling into chaos . . ."

Abruptly he tossed down his pen and crossed the room with angry strides, to seize the attaché case from the desk on which the security men had laid it.

"Your young colleague wanted this as evidence! And it is! I brought these documents to illuminate the dangers to Krupp. They contain precise dates, divisional designations, of the mutinies that have occurred within the French army within the last three months! We have been at pains to conceal our weakness from you, Colonel House, and even from our allies! Fifty-six mutinies in all. I took the risk of showing these to Krupp, to prove how quickly the rot would spread, from Russia, to Germany, to us . . . and how urgent it was for him to reverse the Kaiser's suicidal decision to let revolution loose in the East . . ."

His body shook with emotion as he whirled to Max and overturned his case, pouring the papers into his lap, letting them spill over to the floor.

Colonel House, for the first time, ceased to regard the plains of Texas and came sharply to the excited Foreign Secretary.

"You fear collapse?"

"Yes," Chardon said. He tossed the empty attaché case aside. "Would I have risked my career for less? Does anybody think Jules Chardon would throw away a painstaking lifetime for anything less than the paramount interest of France and Europe?"

Max looked down at the papers. Their covers were thick with stamps of their topmost secret nature. The language was the lifeless stuff of military intelligence, reducing to numbers the mutineers dead, mutineers wounded, mutineers jailed; notations also indicated how this information was to bypass regular channels for direct transmission to highest authority.

Colonel House broke the silence, still urbane. "Are we to infer you failed with Krupp?"

"Dismally."

Chardon threw himself back into the chair and took up his intricate pen work, admiring it as it proceeded to full flower.

"Those documents only inflamed his appetite for victory. He would agree to nothing. I was compelled by my solemn oath to him and his associates to let him leave . . ."

Chardon laughed harshly.

"And then you appear, M'sieu Maxwell," he said. "In the darkness. I wanted to kill myself, and you were anxious to spare me the trouble!"

He swung to Depardieu.

"Too late," he said regretfully, "did we see we had been taken in by a hoax, one carefully worked out by Abteilung Three. We feared the leak to your Maxwell was aimed at America. We never imagined Krupp himself was part of it, a desperate effort to keep you from aiding French democracy, by tainting it with collaboration. Our Krupp proved to be a true Junker!"

Depardieu came to where Max sat and slowly began to gather the papers from the floor, a tidy housekeeper. He seemed singularly devotional, stooping to his knees before Chardon's consummate performance.

"I must confess," he said, "we were victimized by this woman, Mata Hari . . . just like you, M'sieu."

Colonel House broke in. "Would that be Lady McLeod who called me, Max?"

"Yes, sir."

"The one who took you to that carriage?"

"Yes, sir."

"A dancer, is she?"

"Yes, sir."

Colonel House peered at Depardieu. "The one you say is a Boche agent?"

"Ours, we thought, Colonel," Depardieu said. "It was she who informed me that Krupp wanted to come to an agreement. It was she who went to Berlin and conferred with Von Jagow, the former German Foreign Minister, whom you know, Colonel . . ."

"Yes."

Depardieu went to the desk and shuffled a file and came toward Colonel House.

"We have these photographs." He slid one to Colonel House. "In Berlin, with Krupp, only three days ago. In a Swiss bank, receiving payment from the German consulate."

Colonel House took the photos and passed them on to Max.

"On the street with a young woman, D'Estrelles, an agent she recruited and planted as mistress to His Excellency. The one she used to be M'sieu Maxwell's informant. The one she had her Boch helpers eliminate, so that she herself could lead your young colleague to the railroad, just as her helpers previously had disabled his car, to strengthen his confidence in her . . ."

He produced yet another photo. "In the arms of some man during the air raid the other night. We believe him to be a Boche agent, whom she contacted in the Métro . . ."

A surging anger came up into his temples and Max could no longer heed the warning in the colonel's eyes. "But if you knew all this, why didn't you warn me?"

Depardieu's shrug was that of the hardened professional. "We knew she was a double agent. We encouraged her to be. Quite ordinary. When she told us something, it was like the way you accept a funeral sermon; untruths mouthed to the undeceived for the sake of the undeceivable. Only in this case, we were taken in by her eulogies of France."

"In short," Max said bitterly, "your story is, you were duped by her—just like me."

"Regrettably." Depardieu bent his head. "Though the affair has the stamp of Frau Eva Zeit, General Ludendorff's chosen instrument. And it's his policy, of course; revolution in the East, keep America out, fight a one-front war in the West. But we only heard the part they wanted us to hear and they knew we wanted to hear . . ."

Chardon swiveled in his chair to face Colonel House. "The responsibility was mine. Is mine." He jabbed the point of the pen into the blotter, and stood up. "In the event, Colonel, that you decide that this affair damages your confidence—not in me—but in France's solemn pledge to pursue early victory, I will resign immediately."

The colonel ran a forefinger along the crease in his trousers, and then rose. "We're grateful to Your Excellency." He came to Max and touched his hand to Max's shoulder, again a soft warning not to make their turf the arena of American dispute.

"I believe we've had an explanation," he said, with careful impartiality, "and we assume that the candor tonight will be a guide for the future . . ."

At the last moment, Depardieu overtook Max.

"Would you know where she is?"

"No."

"A pity," Depardieu said. "But we'll find her."

The colonel prevented any rejoinder, apologizing, "If I lose a night's sleep at my age, I lose a month."

In the limousine, Colonel House huddled, depleted, in a corner. His thin, handsome face was now almost bloodless, the bony structure pronounced; he seemed to be bending his whole attention to regathering his strength, shutting out Max, the city beyond them.

In the predawn light the ornate buildings were compressed into dark blocks, a predictable series. Empty streets presented themselves in their pristine scale. At this angular hour, Paris became what its planners intended: a thrilling abstraction.

"All that, Max, just for us, you think?"

"Yes, sir."

"Which one do you disbelieve?"

"Both."

"Both? The failed savior of Europe? The failed guardian of French security? How can it be both?"

"Yesterday, they said it was a Boche fiction, foisted on me. Now, though it turned real, it's still a fiction, themselves as victims."

"You don't believe in fiction?"

"Not that one."

"But those documents about army mutinies. That was the nub, I felt."

"If genuine."

House stirred from his corner. "But you yourself have been bringing me proof of disaffection and weariness on the home front. You urge me not to waste American lives here, to maintain our neutrality, until their weakness compels them to accept the just peace our President demands. Now, suddenly, you reject the proof that validates your own thesis."

"I do."

"Why?"

"Something she said."

"This Mata Hari?"

"Chardon told her this meeting was to arrange loans for their cozy cabal . . ."

"Loans?"

"From us, from the U.S."

"Well, they're trying."

"Chardon could have concocted those documents to show France's urgent need . . ."

"Could." House was unconvinced. "Isn't that conjecture?"

Max found himself sweating. "I saw Chardon at that railroad. He was in a panic. Now he's all confidence, smooth lies. That's not conjecture, Colonel!"

"But can't that be explained? Didn't you suddenly come on him in the darkness?"

"And I can't swallow the internal logic of their story! If Krupp had been playing a role for the Abteilung, why didn't he let me catch him in Geneva? And why would they let him go—once they'd discovered he had come only to keep us out of the war?"

"But their point is," House corrected, "that Krupp was the innocent victim of the Abteilung."

"But that means somebody gave orders to the Abteilung—somebody had to be willing to sacrifice Krupp. Who would dare give such orders? The Kaiser? Yes, but only the Kaiser. But I cannot make myself believe he would do it, no matter what the stakes . . ."

"I see that, Max," House conceded. "But this matter of the Russians ... the revolution ... supported by the Germans ..."

Max looked out the window. "A diversion. So you won't expose them and their internationale of plunder. So you won't call in the press and renew our President's demand for peace without annexations or indemnities, a peace without victory, a peace that's truly international ..."

The small body of the Texan shrank into itself and the cushions. "All to frighten me into immediate intervention, to save France from calamity?"

"Yes, sir."

"And you think I must denounce them?"

Max sighed. It came from deep inside. He had not intended to push so far, so far, with so little proof. The colonel valued him, he knew, not only because he was a friend of the President, but because he was a historian, pledged to examine each moment against the weight of enduring policies, forged by interest and tradition, an analysis that alone would provide the basis for the fateful American decision to enter the war.

"If we are to keep faith with our President and our country ..."

For a long time, House gazed out at the passing streets. The sweepers had come out, isolated in the bleak light, their long brooms metronomes for the approach of dawn, the hopeful intruder.

"Max ..."

"Yes, sir."

"About this woman ..."

"Yes, sir."

"Trust her?"

"Yes, sir."

"But she's an agent, twice over."

"Ostensibly," Max said. "But not really."

"Oh?"

"She was acting on her own, for a blind lover, to stop this war. I'm sure of it."

"You know how fond I am of you, Max." House spoke with great effort. "I respect not only your brain, but your feelings and intuitions. We are all heir to the flesh. Even your old mentor, the President, whom I admire above all men, has shown he is not immune, with this second wife of his . . ."

The streets rolled by; the silence was a barrier between them.

"You are a historian," House came back from his thoughts. "Do you reject the possibility of this Russian gambit by the Germans?"

"No."

"Those photographs?"

"No."

"And you have no proof to the contrary, do you?"

"No."

"Yet you'd have me call a press conference, provoke an international crisis, on the basis of the warmth of a young and virile male for a very attractive and undoubtedly persuasive actress?"

"Is that a question or a conclusion, Colonel?"

Again House drew within himself. "Let me sleep on it. Will you let me have that, Max?"

"But if they arrest her first?"

"I know, I know," House said wearily. "But would you risk that much for me? Will you say yes with your whole heart, son?"

His throat constricted. He knew that House was pleading for much more than this point. They were both bonded by their admiration of Wilson, and both had made of that bond a relationship they had thought to endure for the rest of their lives. Now House was begging him not to rupture it.

"Of course, sir."

"I appreciate that, Max."

The rest of the journey was wrapped in silence, and even their leave-taking was made up of small gestures of hands and bodies and the movement of their eyes.

Max watched the small upright man, who had effaced himself for his country, take his weariness into the house, withholding his decision for love, not for wisdom; and Max, who loved this man who had long ago taken the place of his father, wished him the surcease of sleep.

*   *   *

Time had become the presence of light. As he wandered from street to street he waited impatiently for the eastern sky to brighten, to bring in the new and decisive day.

At intervals he tried to reach Duchess Caroline by phone, at her apartment, at her office in British naval headquarters, only to find no response at the first, and to be told by some rather haughty voice at the latter that the Duchess never appeared before ten.

He had sought refuge at a workingman's café and slumped against the counter to drink some bitter coffee. Against all his inner warnings, he even risked a call to Tha's apartment, and though he let the phone ring interminably, there was no answer.

He came back, to swallow the dregs.

He could never explain to Colonel House, or Wilson, or his father or mother. He saw that what had happened during the night belonged to another, an alien mode of comprehension, to acceptance of uncertainties; in some way, he had passed beyond his beginnings, exposed himself to a different style, a different danger.

The sun had come up.

He found himself in a small street, telling himself he must call Colonel House, even if it meant disturbing him prematurely.

Ahead of him, a knot of people had gathered before the steps of a local post office. The postmaster had emerged from the building to stand on the top of the pedestal. He was in uniform, but hatless. His gray hair seemed disordered. He frantically waved a blue telegram above the heads of the crowd, crying out in consternation, as if the world had ended.

"A démissionné! Démissionné! Nicholas a démissionné!"

People came hurrying by Max to join the crowd gathering in awe about the old man, dazed like him, silenced by the sense that they were witness to an event that, though invisible and far away, had forever altered this street and their daily steps, and henceforth they would walk a new path.

"The Czar! The Czar has abdicated! Nicholas gives up his crown!"

Slowly Max pushed his way out. He felt his vision blur and automatically reached for his glasses and then remembered he had lost them. He began to shiver uncontrollably. By now, he knew, they would be waking Colonel House with this news; the great crash, so far away, had already set this quiet street atremble. Soon there would be a mighty uproar, and the warning he and Tha had tried to raise would count for no more than the feeble cry of an old postmaster on a back street.

ORPHANS OF WAR
15 March 1917

Across the top of the trolley barn a sign in bright tri-color announced the grand opening of a charity bazaar for the benefit of the orphans of war. Flags of the Entente hung at every post. A huge illustration, near the entry, put two children on duty, stretching out emaciated arms of entreaty, while behind them the ghosts of their mother and soldier father cast eyes downward in parental agony.

At the corner, Tha lingered until some lavishly dressed ladies descended from chauffeured automobiles and bunched at the ticket taker's booth, waiting their turn to yield their invitation cards. Gawkers of both sexes formed an aisle for the passage of the birds of extravagant plumage, and Tha, carrying her ermine cape, trying to efface her wine dress, made a wide circle to reach the kiosk unnoticed.

"Madame Zelle," she said, following the directions Caroline had given her on the phone. "A ticket has been left for me."

The man studied his list. "You'll find the duchess in Booth Twelve, Madame."

Madame Zelle. She stood momentarily lost in the steel-girdered vastness. A memory of her mother came up out of the shadows. The pale face assailed her from the pavement. Fallen half a block from the apothecary to which she had gone to purchase her "heart medicine." She had made the long walk through the gusty streets in order to save a few pennies, and lay writhing on the street, catching at her daughter's hand. Not much older than I am now, Tha thought. Banda! Does she know I exist? How can she? By now, I am a name; and one she will never acknowledge, even as a ruse.

The trolley barn made an endless vista of crisscrossed steel, the Eiffel tower toppled on its side. I am bereft of mother and daughter at the same time, she thought.

Two men in black silk hats strolled toward her, tricolor rosettes dangling from their lapels. Officials. Brothers of charity. She stooped again, fearing recognition, pretending to recover the stub of her invitation from the ground.

Caroline had been so terse, so ominously terse, on the telephone. "Heard from our American cousin," she had said. "I'm commited to this charity bazaar. I'll leave word. What name should it be in?"

The silken pair passed by, leaving behind a trail of worry about the Czar's abdication and the shortage of sugar and its volatility on the commodity exchange.

Booth Twelve.

She went rapidly down the aisle. Booths and displays lined both sides of the cavernous building, tended by only one or two guardians, while the bulk of the crowd gathered for an auction of rare china and objects of art not far from the entry.

At a high podium an auctioneer exhorted the magnificent to magnanimity. An assistant held aloft a jeweled potentate, astride his small marble kingdom, eliciting devotional gasps. On a table in the front there were tiaras from Italy, Spain, Austria, Greece, the resplendence of things; on a curtain there hung the prize, a canvas by Rembrandt, a portrait of an aged philosopher half withdrawn into his own gloom.

Suddenly, ahead of her, she saw a man in the midst of a display of books and manuscripts. He was moving quietly among these treasures, head down. He was gray-haired and sparer than ever, and her heart constricted in recognition.

Massimy, for one instant, lifted his head as she went by, then quickly lowered it again.

If he had seen her, he made no move toward her. She winced at how time had eroded his face. In that instant, she had seen an old man, hawk-nosed, eyes pouched, the fine chin lost in a sag of jowl.

Booth Twelve!

An ancient trolley, deprived of its wheels, had been curtained with lace, behind which a phonograph blared and female figures moved, loosing bursts of laughter, a stranded caravan of women.

Behind the trolley, a slender woman emerged and turned to her. "Tha! How wonderful! What a stroke! I didn't know you were back in Paris. We'll find a costume for you, the less the better, and you'll join us, of course!"

The Princesse de Noailles began to pull Tha toward the tent at the rear of the vehicle. Of all the beautiful women in Paris—and Paris had gathered the beauties of the world—she remained, at forty, the unquestioned prima donna: beauty, wit, uncowed sensibility, moving to no drums but her own, a free soul, unconstricted by any borders, geographic or spiritual.

They were putting on a tableau vivant: famous females of the past, undraped for the sake of charity. Tha's presence would, the princess was certain, bid up the price for a visit by the gentlemen and their gentle companions.

Caroline came out of the dressing tent to intercept them, nude and tan under an almost transparent silk robe, holding a large powder puff, her blue eyes bright in a chalk mask. Deftly she sent the princess on her way, assuring her that Tha would serve, ". . . but give us a few minutes to catch up on some absolutely epochal gossip!"

Escaping, they squeezed along a narrow space by the side of the wall. They could hear the princess announcing her to other wicked daughters of Lilith. "Mata Hari! Now we'll be history and make it!" The derailed seraglio began to buzz with a new sense of destiny.

Stacked animal cages barred their way. It was a random menagerie, mostly show dogs, with a sprinkling of wary parakeets and silent canaries. Beyond, in larger cages, there were rarer pets, monkeys, jaguars, a taut polecat, brown and black and unhappy.

From it all there came a discord, which only keyed Caroline up above her normal range. "Max wanted to come. Can't. He's being watched. I gathered it all went wrong. Somehow, they've decided you're to blame. They're out looking for you, to arrest you."

"The Bureau?"

"I think . . . yes."

She had prepared herself, ever since her call to Caroline; locked her fear inside her, feeling its edge pressing to her throat, but lodged there.

"And his Colonel House?"

"Seems."

A piece of the world fell away. During the hours of waiting, she had convinced herself that the fatherly American would listen to Max and come to succor them both, no matter what games Chardon or Depardieu might play.

"You haven't told Adam?"

"Only that it didn't work."

"But not about them wanting to arrest me?"

"No."

From the cages eyes watched her in suspicion. The polecat paced its cage, unconvinced of its captivity.

"Adam's here," Caroline said. "He's in misery, as you can imagine . . ."

Tha felt her being knot. "Here? Where?"

"Just beyond these . . . sitting out in the ring . . . waiting for you . . ."

Tha leaned against a cage. "He mustn't know . . ."

"Tha, can't you make a run for it, to Spain?"

"And give them a chance to make me into another D'Estrelles, and do the same for Adam?"

Caroline paced and came back. "He's damned depressed. I'm scared of what he'll do to himself if they take you—"

She remembered their wild ride from the ruined church, and the way he had reached for her as a shield against self-destruction.

"Caroline—couldn't you arrange to get him to England—to your place in Scotland?"

The Englishwoman half turned away, her eyes filled with tears. "I'm a bitch. If I take him now—I might never let him go."

"Will you?"

"Will he go?"

Tha kissed the powdery clownish face. "If I succeed, do it right away, leave at once, don't let him have a chance for second thoughts!"

Ragged, Caroline sank to a crate, holding Tha's hands. "My Tha," she said, "how I hate them all for this!"

On the other side of the barrier they had built a corral of sorts, the uprights made of trolley signs anchored in concrete, ropes joining them in a rough sort of quadrangle, fresh sawdust scattered in the center. Several thoroughbreds were being readied by the grooms and handlers to do their part in the care of child victims of war.

At the far side, Adam sat alone on an upended box, combing and gentling a golden setter. The nerves of the excited animal and sightless man seemed joined in defense against a universe of treachery.

Both sensed her simultaneously—the dog stiffening, and Adam, holding the animal's scruff, bending lower, waiting for her coming.

"Tha . . . all right?"

"Yes."

"Sure?"

"Yes."

She came close to him, but touched the setter.

"Botched?"

"Yes."

He stood up, trembling. "If only I had been there with you."

"Max was. Nobody could stop them."

"They don't know about you, us?"

"Of course not," she spoke lightly. "You know how good I am at shams. They're so impressed, they want me to stay and take on the American, until further notice . . ."

He was silent, bitter. "No option now. I saw to that, didn't I?"

"Oh, it won't last long, Adam. I'll make up some other fable, about how he detests me. But for the moment, I do think it would be easier for you and me if we separated for a time— I've talked Caroline into inviting you to Scotland . . ."

He held the animal next to him. "I've given the bastards another walk-over, haven't I?"

"I promise," she said. "A few months to clean up the loose ends, and I'll join you. But I don't think we should write to each other until then, until I can break away. . . . Adam, do this for me, so we can look ahead, find a way out of this plague . . ."

His hand came to her face and gently probed it. "Thought I'd hit the bottom of pain. Tha, will you come, come quickly?"

"Yes, Adam."

Abruptly he turned from her, using his cane, guiding himself along the ropes, until Caroline came from the other side and took his arm. The setter, released, followed Adam, his muzzle reaching for Adam's hand.

She took his place on the box, holding her hands together, as if he could see her, and she must give him an image of composure to take with him, to hold against a bitter awakening.

Dimly, she became aware of the footsteps.

Inwardly racked, she lifted her head.

Massimy came slowly toward her, flanked by two gray men whose function she knew at once. He did not try to avoid her eyes. His face was aquiline and stern; a reprise, almost a caricature, of that day in the garden by the river when he had relinquished her to preserve his country and his own roots in it.

"The Bureau, Madame," one of the men said.

She forced herself erect. Massimy turned away, as if in

that one gesture he had crumpled into old age. The two security men ranged themselves with her between them.

As they went past the bidders at the entry, she heard the auctioneer extolling an Aubusson tapestry, the gift of Louis XVI to Madame de Sévigné, so that the gentlemen and their ladies had a chance to acquire, not only imperishable art, but the even more enduring memorabilia of love.

In the car that took her away, she had a glimpse of the setter, searching for Adam among the crowds, whimpering and forlorn and lost.

PALAIS DE JUSTICE
26 July 1917

Several times he forced himself to remain at a quai and put his nose into a book, only to have the words interrupt his own interior dialogue and make him even more fretful and impatient.

From each temporary roost he observed the crowds in front of the Palais de Justice. Almost as dense as the day her trial had begun; the heat, though more normal, still oppressive. But this time the police were better organized. Not only had barriers been set up, keeping the crowds at bay, but spectators were being issued tickets that would entitle them to later entry to the courtroom to hear the verdict.

At least an hour prior to their rendezvous, Capel, the yardmaster, came marching across the bridge and then down to the river waving a green card at Max.

"They've changed it to a smaller chamber!" the old railroad man reported excitedly. "They don't want anybody to be there, the sneaky bastards! I was the last to get a ticket. They're having their hands full with the crowd. Most are just standing there to give them a bad time!"

They had debated a long time about whether it was worth taking the risk of drawing the attention of the security people to them once again, after the trouble they had taken to avoid surveillance.

Capel had cast the deciding vote. "I won't be in uniform. To them, that's what I am. Besides, for me to be on that line won't seem exceptional. They expect me to show an interest in her verdict, considering that night . . ."

During the trial, Max had surreptitiously made contact with Capel, hopeful that he might enlist the yardmaster as a witness for Tha. Capel had harshly refused. "I saw nothing that night. No Boche, nothing. Do not involve me, M'sieu. If I am forced to testify, I will provide nothing to her advantage, I assure you."

Obviously the old man had been reached and silenced by the Deuxième Bureau. He'd had the same result with all the others he'd circuitously approached through the union officials he'd known from earlier days. Many of the men who had been present that night had been transferred to other locations. Railroad employees were under constant scrutiny of the Minister of the Interior, their ranks infiltrated by undercover agents, seeking evidence of defeatism; people were arrested and jailed, pending a trial that never occurred; and with Malavy, the Interior Minister himself, now held incommunicado and accused of being a German agent, the yards were in the grip of almost hysterical suspicion. His friends finally advised Max to abandon his quest before a bullet ended it for him.

Grudgingly, he had backed off.

And though he had promised Ralph Beck that he would take no active part in the case, he knew the sleepless optic of the Deuxième Bureau was still upon him.

Often, in his inaction, it seemed to him that he had crossed the shadowy line separating the ruse of compliance, as a tactic of struggle, from the reality of accommodation. He gained some comfort from his two clandestine meetings with Maître Clunet. Without revealing to Clunet the substance of his testimony, he had offered to become a witness for Tha. On each occasion, she'd sent back word vetoing the move.

"She insists silence is her only hope," Clunet had told him. "To implicate others will only bring savage reprisal by powerful forces. I have advised the opposite. But I cannot impose my will. Perhaps she is right. In these times, which seem to preclude justice, all that's left is charity."

Nevertheless, all his circumventions had ended with him revolving on the same spot, cursing himself for describing a zero.

Major Beck had stopped hounding him. "I'm glad you came to your senses, Prof. There's lots of good stuff floating around. You give yourself a chance and you'll get over it toute and sweet."

Not long afterward a note had arrived from Colonel House, who had returned to Washington, to help prepare the President's declaration of war on the Central Powers.

"I'm pleased, Max. Your behavior affirms my confidence in you. You have been tested under fire. I have mentioned you to the President and he sends his warm regards. We are in this now, and the ideals which you and I share with him, which humanity shares with him, will bear fruit, not alone in victory but in the just peace that will follow."

And that he had a vote of confidence was soon made manifest by orders from Washington, doubling and quadrupling the size of his unit and conferring new authority on him. Each day brought new arrivals from the States, experts in various fields of European history and economics. Most were, like himself, academics. He found himself in charge of nothing less than the future of Europe, resolving its ancient knot of national enmities—and then, in the middle of a conference, he would suddenly imagine D'Estrelles lying in the middle of the carpet, while Tha, in chains, stood in the shadowy corner, the sound of iron mocking the collegium of dreamers.

More and more frequently he would go directly from his office to a bistro across the street. Alone at a table, he would study the Paris newspapers, hunting down items about Tha, which appeared almost daily, in spite of the official ban. They would be disguised as biographical feature stories, celebrating some triumph of hers as dancer or courtesan, but would slyly connect these with hints of additional treachery. Since the arrest of Malavy, his name would appear in these accounts, sometimes with little more linkage than that they had both been at some large gathering, yet often alleging that she had added him to her conquests and was the secret manipulator of his infamies.

By closing time, Max would have to depend on the proprietor to summon a cab and send him home. He would flop into his bed, more exhausted than drunk, to lie awake in the darkness, rehearsing some melodramatic appearance on the witness stand, his eloquence bringing instant acquittal; and then, when he went over this ground, sleeplessly, the prosecution would compel him to admit that the sequence of events, from the murder of D'Estrelles to his own homicidal anger against Chardon, had become confused in his own mind. He began to see how it had been possible for eyewitnesses in the Jaurès case to suddenly soften and waffle, though at the time of writing the monograph he had subjected those witnesses to scornful review. Frustration and attrition, he realized, had turned him into an unreliable witness, almost a despicable turncoat.

Two weeks ago, on an evening soggy with liquid and printed poison, old Capel had turned up outside the bistro.

"A moment," the yardmaster begged. "I know what you think. But hear me!"

Max sent away the cab. Together they walked the night street, hectic as always with the presence of the German Gothas.

"Of course the Bureau came to me. They said you were an agent provocateur, shielded by diplomatic immunity. Looking to get me into trouble. Then you turned up. I gave you the boot, because I knew they were watching. And for my skin. No doubt about it. I saw them chopping this woman to death. Maybe she is as bad too. But then, there must be those above her. Do you see one ratty word about them? Not on your sainted ass! Just her! One small hole—and a whole country falls into it. So, M'sieu American, before I testify, you must show me there is a chance—not a guarantee, but a chance—it can save her . . ."

Since then, bonded in their understanding of the fragility of their shared truth and the danger of its espousal, they had become fast friends. Quietly, Capel sought out other witnesses of the truncated battle at the yard and had found two or three who would, like himself, come forward if their testimony might alter the outcome of Tha's case.

"Not now," Max had said. "She doesn't want it. Perhaps after the court comes in with their verdict and Maître Clunet makes his appeal, we can supply new evidence."

With that, he felt a lift in his spirit. Though he still visited the bistro, the ratio of drink to print reversed. The announcement that the court had postponed its sentencing from the twenty-third to the twenty-sixth of July had given him a wild moment of joy, and he had read into it everything from a split court to the complete success of Tha's strategy of silence.

And with hope as a prod, the urge to be present at the court: the chance that he might see her; the remoter possibility he might be seen by her; all irrational, all irrepressible.

And Capel, his latest father figure, had pointed out that his presence in court might alert the Bureau to his devotion to Tha and the truth and evoke new counteraction.

"I must see her," Max had said.

Capel wagged his head. "I'll stand in line. But if you spoil her chances, on your noodle, Professor."

"Even so."

Capel sighed. "I'd never hire you as a trainman," he said and sighed again. "Let's have a coffee."

Despite all his fears and calculations, his entry into the court chamber was unobserved.

The security men, of course, were posted outside the door, as he had anticipated, but their attentions were devoted wholly to the notables, civil and military, representatives of both Entente and neutral countries. The international press made a noisy commotion and the shufflers with green cards proved to be beneath contempt and, fortunately, beneath inspection.

Two huge porters from Les Halles, still in their work aprons, half screened him. Both men were voluble about the guilt of Mata Hari, but saw the trial as only a precursor, a warning of the wrath of God that would surely fall on a sinning France, which had sacrificed its best sons in a useless and sinful war. Nevertheless, they were eager to lay eyes on the witch in her moment of reckoning.

They broke off their jeremiad as the military tribunal took their places on the dais. Unaccountably, the prisoner had not yet been led to the door. Twice Clunet, his black robe adorned by the medals of the war of 1870, went to the rear door to confer with some authorities, only to return to his seat at the counsel table.

Villiers, still presiding, took his seat, and the spectators did the same. But for several minutes there was an awkward silence and shuffling of papers and coughing, and the dock remained empty.

Clunet began to rise again, when a military escort appeared from the door at the rear, with Tha in their midst, surrounding her as they marched her to the prisoner's box.

Yet, in this very act of hemming her in, she became more conspicuous, towering above them, high heels adding to her height, her face clearly visible to Max even at the rear of the chamber.

But she had changed. There were streaks of gray in her long black hair, gathered into a severe knot at her nape. Her complexion, which he had imagined as permanently honeyed by her sojourn in Indonesia, had succumbed to prison pallor. Her lips, which he remembered as carmined and full of life, were stretched and pale.

Yet, for all these ravages, perhaps because of them, her dark eyes were more brilliant and compelling than ever, reminding him and all of them that her beauty had little to do with appearance, that its source was themselves and her awareness of their lives, that she seemed to draw energy from those men who, solemn at the bench, were about to judge her.

Even before she reached the box, the prosecutor began to rattle off the indictment, framed as eight questions, which were to be answered yes or no by the tribunal.

He waited for the eighth and final question, having been warned by Clunet that, unlike the others, it would be barren of specifics.

"Guilty of having had, in Paris, in 1917, intelligence with the enemy power of Germany, with the aim of furthering the enterprises of the enemy?"

Villiers did not lift his head from his papers. "Yes," he said dryly, "to all questions, unanimously."

Clunet rose, shaken, to support himself on the desk. His voice trembled with anger. "With deference to the court, I must appeal to higher authority."

Perfunctorily, "Recorded, Maître."

Villiers's pen moved for a moment.

"Does the prisoner wish to make a statement before sentence is pronounced?"

All during the prosecutorial drumfire she had fixed her eyes on Villiers. She studied him now. "I call on you to note"—her voice was low, weary with the repeating of a single simple truth to deaf ears—"I am a neutral, but my sympathies are with France. Since that does not satisfy you, do as you will."

Villiers rustled his papers, his voice their dry echo. "Execution, on the sixteenth day of October, by firing squad, at Fort Vincennes." He hurried to rise, then checked himself and settled back. "For the security of the Republic, the dossiers in this case are sealed for a period of one hundred years from this date. Court dismissed!"

Somebody bawled, "Present arms!" and the platoon held their rifles rigidly vertical as the tribunal, in their military uniforms, and in due order of rank, followed Villiers out of the chamber.

Sealed. For a century. A trial behind closed doors and the record dropped into a pit. Perdu, hidden from sight; the woman of seven veils, perdu; the casual cartel of plunder, perdu; the charmed circle of predation in a gilded carriage, perdu; but were not several million young lives also perdu?

He was on his feet, like all the others, eyes fastened to

the platoon that screened Tha and hustled her toward the door at the rear.

From the front part of the chamber there came a woman's intense cry, foundering in a crash of sobs. Tha's eyes sought to locate her. Her face was pale and her lips drawn. She seemed to want to offer assurance to the unknown woman that, though they were all forced to live in a time of pestilence, they must not cease to resist it.

After a moment she abandoned her search and let herself be led out. The platoon stood aside to let her go out the door alone, her blue cape billowed out by her natural dancer's stride, so that she took on an abundance, a sculptural richness, beyond the reach of any in the courtroom.

Beside Max, the market porters swore. They had come for an exhibition of torment. They wanted to see her submit to desolation, not celebrate her endowments. They had expected her to break down under the stress of the unknown woman's cries; instead, she had found a new strength in them. As she departed, her air of being a mortal among the mortally ill outraged them, and they howled curses at her.

From the door, Max glanced back. At his desk, Clunet wept into folded arms, close to collapse; her erect carriage, far from concealing her misery, had only made him more painfully aware of it.

On the street, numb with bitterness, he paused to recover his bearings. He had promised Capel he would rejoin him on the other side of the river and bring him news of the verdict and the sentence. Not that the old man had even for a moment shared his hopes of leniency.

But as he struggled to cross the avenue, his way was blocked. Dense crowds lined both sides of the street. At first, he thought them to be connected with the trial, but only after he had gained the edge of the pavement did he comprehend that he was now part of a throng lining the route of a march by recently arrived American troops.

These parades had become part of the Paris scene. Each arriving American contingent had to show itself to the public; they were put on display from Cherbourg to Paris, to bolster the national will to continue the war. Max knew, from his con-

versations with Beck and others, that these troops were mainly
National Guardsmen, hurried across the seas, lightly armed,
inadequately supplied; behind that urgency, the rumors of mutinies in the French army, which had now become a part of the
established belief as sacred as the flag, as safe from objective
scrutiny as the dossiers of the Mata Hari case itself.

From the pavements young women dashed out to the
middle of the avenue, to decorate the young Americans with
flowers, or to thrust bottles of wine into their hands, or to fling
themselves at these strangers, their kisses in gratitude for the
saving of sons and lovers.

A band sounded the familiar and homely "Dinah." In
spite of all his cynicism, his anger at the court, his grief for Tha,
he felt the hair rising on his body, moved, like the women, to
embrace the youngsters who were about to hurl their lives into
the pit of Europe.

"Maxwell," a voice said, "hold a minute."

Jules Chardon struggled through the crowd to reach
him. Despite the homburg and the formal clothes, he looked
sweaty, harassed.

"I saw you leave. Didn't you hear me call you?"

In his bitterness, Max began to turn away, pushing at
the crowd. "Go and celebrate with Depardieu and that pack. It
must be a big day for you!"

Chardon kept step with him. "But it had to be this way.
She had the wisdom to see that. Why can't you?"

"The great wheel of justice," Max grated. "Cogs in
God's machine."

They were both, in their obduracy, elbowing people out
of their path. Chardon was irritable and aggressive. "Surely—
as a historian—you know it's all a matter of timing and emphasis in these affairs—"

"And casuistry!"

"Why should you reject that," Chardon demanded, "if
it saves her life?"

"Is that it, today? That why you turned me from your
office? Why you refuse to answer my calls?"

The dark face, with its perpetual look of being unsha-
ven, became all jaw. "Do you think I'm here today because it

serves me? I've argued in the Cabinet to avoid the blunder of the Germans in taking Edith Cavell's life. I've been overruled. But starting today, they'll be vulnerable to a campaign for clemency—to save the life of a beautiful woman!"

They had pushed out beyond the crowd; two combatants beyond the main stream of conflict.

"Nothing to worry about?" Max demanded. "All going to turn out beautifully for her? That why you chased me?"

"Only pressure," Chardon repeated, ignoring his taunts. "She has many famous friends. And there will be many others who will respond to an appeal to save her life. All one needs to do is organize it, so that even opportunists like me can be comfortably merciful. And that, actually, is your function now, the only useful one, I think . . ."

"I'm an American, a scholar, an outsider," Max said scornfully. "Some chance."

"Perfect," Chardon said. "Made for it. Above suspicion. You only need an assistant who knows the nuances. I'd recommend somebody, only it must never be traced to me . . ."

"Oh, never . . ."

Chardon suddenly swirled on him, grabbing his coat. "Don't be a blind fool. I was compelled to do what I did. That meeting was a failure!"

"Oh, sure and that parade out there—a figment of my imagination."

"A failure," Chardon repeated. "Of course I wanted the Americans to come in, but only after we had been compelled to accept Wilson's terms for the peace—the only basis for a peace that can last. But you intervened—and Depardieu seized his chance to bluff his way past me and your colonel! Now the way is open for Depardieu—and the man he supports, Clemenceau—to dictate their own savage views. All we can do now, is, perhaps, salvage . . . her . . ."

Some dignitaries were coming out from the Palais. One of them waved his hat at Chardon. Resilient as always, Chardon pulled himself together, tipping his hat in reply. The anger left his face.

"Sixteenth October," he said, repeating the date set for the execution. "Go to Massimy. Play on his feelings. He'll find some one to help you. An opening, not debacle! Take advantage, friend!"

Brusquely, he swung away to rejoin the officials grouped at the entrance, waiting for their limousines. Stocky and short, he nevertheless bulked among them, a commanding figure.

Behind Max, the American servicemen had begun to sing the words of the song, powerfully playful.

> *Someone's in the kitchen with Dinah,*
> *Playing on the old banjo . . .*

Obviously, a campaign for clemency would serve Chardon: it would keep more explosive material, like the truth, safely out of sight. Yet it followed from Tha's own logic that her best defense was silence; now her life was in the hands of the individuals she had known—he among them.

> *Someone's in the kitchen with Dinah . . .*

He wondered if the French heard that exuberant chant in praise of cuckoldry as a sign of their future.

Probably, but not a barrier to fraternity. And if Chardon's invitation to continue silence violated his ethics, he must, like the applauding French, find his satisfactions in the imperatives of practice.

> *Playing on the old banjo . . .*

NEITHER SLAYER
NOR SLAIN
3 September 1917

"Lady McLeod?"

The whisper, in English, came to her from the adjoining cubicle.

"Yes."

"I'm Tess Morkan," the voice conspired. "A journalist. For the *Freeman*. Ireland."

"Where?"

"Dublin, Ireland."

Within the serpentine folds of the ancient prison, few things were uniform. The toilets, however, marched in dress parade against a wall. Doorless, they faced the corridor, where a nun was stationed at all times. In addition, Tha's own warder, the formidable Sister Lucille, had also taken up a post at the doorway. Though the pair were chatting, they might turn at any moment to examine their charges; for it was a universal truth that lavatories were the hotbeds of crime.

"Tell Depardieu," Tha said, "he's wasting his time."

"Who?"

"Oh, enough!"

The adjacent wall had a series of washbasins, some of tin, some of crazed porcelain, yellowed with age. Some had two taps, others but one, which variously gave off spurts or trickles of rusty, tepid liquid.

Tha laved her face, hands, arms. She liked to prolong this ritual, which had the virtue not only of keeping her from her cell but separated, if only by a few yards, from Sister Lucille, her constant guardian.

"The trouble it's been to get here!"

Leaning over the basin, Tha glanced sidewise at a tall, rawboned woman who ran both taps into a metal basin, setting up a din to cover her entreaty.

"Look," Tha said. "Tell Depardieu it didn't work with Leclerc and it won't with you!"

Not again, she thought. Two weeks after her sentencing, Leclerc had turned up to interview her. In the past, he had been a close friend. But to suddenly open the doors of her cell to a journalist, after she had been forbidden all visits of any kind except from those of Clunet, had been only too obvious a stratagem of Depardieu's. Poor Leclerc hadn't quite been able to carry it off, and she sent him packing. But he had published a story that she was making a candid confession to him, naming names of all those in high places who had helped her betray France. A yarn, she knew, calculated to doom her appeal to the Minister of Justice.

"Don't mix me with that lot," the Irishwoman urged. "Shoplifted my way in here. You've Irish friends. Like George Moore and Yeats and Lady Gregory and all the talkers. We've had it with the British doing in Roger Casement behind closed doors, when they weren't out of doors killing right and left to celebrate Easter. We've been signing petitions. And pennies have been collected, where pennies're scarce, to have me come and get your side of it."

"All that for me?"

"Oh," the Morkan woman said, "and twist the lion's tail, I don't doubt. But I saw you in court. A woman of her own. I know the jackboots have had a fair stomp with you, but not so much you won't make a fight for your own life . . ."

She consulted the woman's wide bony face. She had the fair skin and ruddy cheeks of a Frisian farm woman, milking and being milked, but never beyond the point of necessity. A sort of clumsy grace which Tha, as a town girl, had secretly envied and, with her schoolfriends, noisily parodied.

Behind, she heard a step. "Hurry up, Zelle. They say Clunet's come to see you."

Sister Lucille, stout and forty, bore down on her. Twenty years of prison life and prison food had made her lumpish and doughy. The peasant sturdiness, so evident in the Irish reporter, had disappeared into the nun's wadded flesh.

Tha dried her face, using the towel she had brought from her cell. Morkan angrily splashed the basin, uttering curses in a bewitching lilt.

"Call this water?" Morkan shouted at the approaching nun. "Tears and piddle. The Holy Father and all his miracles couldn't wash clean in such drool!" She turned fiercely to Tha. "Don't forget what I said, purgatory stinks from those who deny us hot water to clean ourselves!"

Sister Lucille, who did not understand English, turned to Tha in amazement. Was the Irisher totally out of her skull? What was all that shouting about? Tha nodded, smiling inwardly at Morkan's ruse, and followed her keeper from the room.

The corridors changed direction and level capriciously. Originally, the prison had been the home of the man who became Saint Vincent de Paul. He had turned it into a hospital. Later, the church had made it a sanctuary for the poor. Expanded haphazardly, it finally became a prison for women, called the St. Lazaire after the neighborhood, and, though still run by priests and nuns, had long since fallen under civilian jurisdiction. Legend had it that one inmate, trying to escape the prison, had succeeded only in losing herself for all eternity in this maze of halls, and at night one could hear her sighs of distress.

At the far end of a bridge that joined two annexes lay the death cell.

It had three iron cots and three battered chairs.

After her sentencing, Tha had had the company of another woman, condemned to the guillotine for the murders of her husband, lover, and three children. After the madwoman's dispatch, Tha had occupied the cell with only Sister Lucille, whose humorlessness constituted a torture worse than any cruelty.

Repeatedly Tha had pleaded for a cellmate. She had been rejected, always on the ground that any such companion might help her circumvent the ban on communications with the world outside. She would have to make do with Sister Lucille.

As Tha and the nun entered the cell, Dr. Speranti rose from one of the aggrieved chairs. The prison doctor, an overworked little Italian with dark circles under his eyes, came to see her daily, and these visits had come to be the bright spot of the day.

"I located the Nagarjuna book!" He waved a paper-covered volume that had turned brown. "In Russian. I bought it anyway. Do you know Russian?"

Unlike the nuns, who condemned her interest in Buddhism as almost a greater sin than having been born a Protestant, the doctor had supplied her with Buddhist texts. And though he was a scientific scoffer, he had engaged her in long discussions, reading the texts along with her, ignoring the frowns and the peevish interruptions of Sister Lucille.

Tha held the book in her hands. The Cyrillic letters brought a wave of desolation. Behind them she saw Adam, that night of the housewarming, bending at the fire, taking warmth and hope from the Russian redheads, forcing a path through pain and confusion, holding out to her a way of shared joy. Adam! Oh, Adam! She felt his fingers on her face once more.

There'd been so little news, and that little had to be filtered from letters of Duchess Caroline to Clunet, who always referred to them in circuitous language, knowing her fears of involving Adam in persecution by the Bureau. From these she had put together a picture of Adam, who had undergone an operation in Edinburgh, regained marginal vision, and was now trying to supervise Caroline's large sheep farm in northern Scotland. In that isolated place, Caroline had taken precautions to surround him with people primed to keep the news of Tha's trial from him, a ploy made easy by Adam's own bitter refusal to have anybody speak to him about the war.

But of course, he was still expecting her, from day to day, Caroline had written. That was what really kept him going.

"Excuse me—are you ill?"

Speranti had come to her side, frowning up at her.

"No, no."

Sister Lucille bustled in between them. "No time for that nonsense now. I have to get her dressed for Maître Clunet. Be good enough, Doctor, to let her be."

Speranti was not to be intimidated, even by a nun with the seniority of Sister Lucille. He took Tha's arm and reached for her pulse.

"It's this food," he said. "Bad enough before the war. An indecency now." He released her wrist. "I'll come back later. I'll bring you something by Bertrand Russell. It's like this Nagarjuna philosopher. It connects your search for eternals with mine for scientific absolutes. I don't have enough English, so you must go into it with me."

The nun began to make scathing remarks about the Italian as soon as the door closed. She thought he would do well to think about his wife and six children instead of making a spectacle of himself, trying to camouflage his infatuation for Tha with all this disgusting talk about Indian rubbish.

"Buddhist texts! He's been warned by the priests! It's only because there are no doctors that they have to let him carry on!"

Tha submitted to Sister Lucille's attentions. It was one of the few privileges of the death cell that she was allowed to change from prison smock into a dress when the lawyer visited her. And Sister Lucille doted on this moment. She had an obsession about high fashion and had collected magazine photographs of Tha in various costumes and wardrobes. She had suggested that Tha, when her time came, deed her clothing to her, so she could, in turn, give them to a niece. Of course, she would always manage to denounce this finery as sinful and her own interest in it as forced upon her by the necessity of being forearmed against the devil and his works.

"There!" Sister Lucille buttoned the last fastenings. "Now you can give the old lecher a thrill!"

Once more, the nun guided her through the labyrinth. Their destination was a small room on the lower floor. Yet, despite repeated tours, Tha had to rely on the nun to lead the way.

It was obvious to her and to Clunet that their conversations were being monitored. The rules of court did not proscribe discussing personal matters. The danger, of course, came from their giving Depardieu just the advantages he sought against her, new points of pressure and blackmail, to exact the confession he had repeatedly sought in the course of the trial, and which she and Clunet had as stubbornly resisted, knowing that to submit would end all hope for clemency from higher authority.

Each of Clunet's visits was a kind of torture. Sometimes they exchanged information by writing on a pad, which Clunet took care to carry away with him and subsequently destroy.

She kept longing to hear from Sita—and Banda.

Several times Clunet had written to Sita. A note advised him she had reached The Hague, and that with the help of Van der Gelder she had been placed in the service of a governmental family. But there were legal obstacles to taking Banda from her father, and these would take time to work out.

At the door, with the final pat of a wardrobe mistress ushering her on stage, Sister Lucille left her, to take up her vigil in the corridor.

Clunet struggled to rise.

Ever since the end of the trial, the mark of death had been on him. Always frail and vulnerable, he was held to life through her. If she lost, so would he. But unlike her, if she won some reprieve, he would let go his grip.

She prevented him from trying to rise, brushing her cheek against his. "Maître," she said, "how glad I am you came. I've finally made you see, good news or bad, anything is better than the tedium of waiting . . ."

But the old man's eyes were bright today. "I'm untrainable! Good news. From our friend, Maxwell."

"More signatures?"

"Not just more, Tha. This morning, His Holiness, the Pope, agrees to appeal on your behalf! He will make his own statement, of course, but Max is confident that it will turn the tide . . . force our new Prime Minister, Painlevé, to give in . . . at least to a stay of execution until the war ends . . ."

She held herself under control, not wanting to be trapped by hope. "And you, Maître, you think so too?"

"I'm elated," he said. "For the first time I agree with your way—yes, yes, it is wonderful, Tha! Max thinks he will surely get your Queen Caroline in Holland and Queen Sophia in Greece to speak out . . ."

"And Van der Gelder?"

It was their code name for Sita and Banda.

"Not yet," Clunet said. "But there's been a letter from The Hague, that's going forward."

"Now, you've convinced me, it's good news!"

"And," Clunet said, "I stopped by to talk to the Abbé and tell him the news from Rome. He's going to let you have a cell mate—no madwoman this time—and permit you to exercise in the yard with the other women!"

"Oh, Maître . . ."

She found herself unable to keep her eyes from filling with tears.

"That's too much for one day, you should have held some of it back!"

"Only because I am a coward," he said. He shuffled his briefcase on the desk and extracted a pad and pencil. "Only because I could not bring myself to tell you yesterday that the Minister of Justice has rejected our appeal and refused to stay the date . . ." His thin hand trembled in the air. "Their date . . ."

She forced herself, as before, to a dead neutral tone; it was the same shield she had used on the day she had been sentenced in court.

"I never expected him to. Max is right. They all need to hide behind somebody else's clemency before they can be French and chivalrous to a wayward woman . . ."

Clunet reached for her hand. "I beg you not to despair of the law. I've gathered some young men from the Sorbonne. We are researching the statutes. Even now it's not too late for you to have me declared senile and incompetent, as I urged at the start . . ."

She squeezed his dry hand. "Who would believe that, Maître?"

"I would be happy to have you do it, Tha. It may even be true."

"If you are, then I am, and I would deserve their sentence, their date."

"Another way," he said, "would be for you to become pregnant. The statute forbids execution of women prior to full term."

She stared at him. "And how would I manage that?"

She saw him scribble. He turned the pad to her. On it, he had written *"Speranti."*

Quickly she scrawled back. "Better you, dear Maître."

And then, seeing him flush, said, "But haven't we decided that just as with Banda, progeny constitutes the ultimate cruelty?" She leaned to him and kissed him, this time on the lips. "But I don't despair, Maître, tell Max I take hope from all your efforts—"

Outside, she found not only Sister Lucille but a small congregation of nuns. They stared at her as if she had been given a halo; apparently word had reached them, via the Abbé, of the Pope's action on her behalf, and it had served to remind them that the saints in heaven stood on the shoulders of sinners like herself.

In the cell, she found the Russell book on her bed, with a note from Speranti. He, too, had learned of the dispensation from Rome and was wildly hopeful. Surely, they would delay acting against her now that the Pope had spoken!

She tried to calm herself with her texts. Today, the sentences of the Bhagavad-Gita struck her as unhelpful and arid. "He who looks on the Self as the slayer and he who looks on the Self as the slain, neither apprehends aright. The Self slays not nor is it slain. He who knows the Self to be subtler than the atom, more glorious than the sun, beyond all darkness—how

can that person, O child of Pritha, slay or be slain or cause another to slay?"

Restless, tossing the book back on the bed, she went to
the narrow window. It looked out on a slender air shaft, at the
foot of which there lay a narrow entry to what had once been
the cloister and had now become the exercise yard. She had
passed that way for her examinations in Dr. Speranti's infirmary, envying the other women there, who had enjoyed the
sight of the trees and one another's gritty laughter.

No matter what the texts told her, she could not quench
her desire for this passing life, her own and Banda's, her own
and Adam's, her own and Max's; she could not empty their fate
and hers into the calm ocean of Om.

The challenge of the Morkan woman came back to her.
"Have they stomped the fight out of you?"

"No!"

But she had to fight in her own way.

Her silent prayer had been answered, by the Pope, now
by this woman from Dublin.

And she would contrive, with the help of that Irish reporter, to utter her reponse to the Pope. She would confess. She
would tell the world she had been a double agent, because
France had pressed her to be, and she had betrayed her German friends in order to serve France. But that had been only
part of the betrayal. The essential guilt was that she had helped
send the Adams on both sides to march to a processing plant, to
be vivisected, repackaged, returned, duly crossed or starred, relieved of the obligation to see their sons march along the same
glory road to the same destination.

She would ask the Pope to let her live, because she had
been both innocent and guilty, and both had turned out to be
crimes for a child of an uprooted century, who had matured as
a woman of storm, and who begged for survival as a paradox,
demanding not charity but wisdom.

Absurd? No. To die, that would be absurd.

She must let down her defenses and abandon herself to
hope. Let it come flooding in, awakening her parched nerves,
making her dizzy with wild expectation.

CROSSTIES
29 September 1917

Disturbed, Max left the gloom of the church for the windswept street. It wasn't like Capel to be late. If the yardmaster had any religion, it was punctuality. You could count on him to enter the church as the bells struck six; and then, after a precise interval of five minutes, having made certain of Max's presence on one of the rear benches, he would leave for the tiny restaurant, where he would have his soup in grave silence while Max unburdened himself of the frustrations and triumphs of his campaign for clemency.

Max made one last tour of the church. At this hour, people stopped by Saint-Germain-des-Prés to light a candle on their way home from work. Women, in black, were a living pageant for the casualty lists published each day in the newspapers; and their soft cries emptied the church of air, making it hard for him to breathe.

On the street again, Max hailed a cab, deciding to stop by the office he had set up to coordinate the drive for Tha's petition. Just possibly the old man had called there, though they had agreed to avoid using that phone, which Max was sure had been tapped by the Deuxième Bureau.

To his surprise, light came though the glass partitioned door.

Usually at this hour, the Baroness Bouvard was gone. In fact, at this hour, her day began. A portly lady in her sixties, who limped from an old hip injury, the baroness had by turns been actress, courtesan, wife, widow, grandmother of an enormous brood, and it was said of her that she could recite the Almanach de Gotha in its entirety, correcting its errors along the way.

Max owed her to Massimy, who had sent him to the Princesse de Noailles, who in turn had put him in touch with the baroness, whose adroit socializing, whose inner knowledge of a recondite pecking order, made it possible to woo the elite to support Tha; and from the elite, to seek the endorsement of the hoi polloi, in a subtle demonstration of the ways of French democracy.

Ralph Beck, teacup in hand, rose from the desk. "Hi, Prof. Thought I missed you. The baroness here had been feeding me tea, helping me celebrate!"

"Do join us"—the baroness gave him a soft jowly smile—"and congratulate our newest colonel."

The gold leaves, Max saw, had turned silver: the military reversal of the value of metals.

"Congratulations, Ralph."

Beck's whiskey flush turned a deeper crimson. "Hell," he said, "I had nothing to do with nailing this Paul Bolo Pascha, but they got so many raves, they passed some on to me!"

Max let the baroness pour tea in benison of his ignorance.

"Like I told the baroness," Beck said, "it's not just we got the goods on this Pascha. Now these froggies know we mean business, no more damn Boche payoffs. We came to win a war, not shovel Heinie francs around. Right, Prof?"

"Errorless."

"And let me tell you, Max," Beck said, "this Bolo isn't

just a cat. He's the number-one German paymaster. We made the Deuxième arrest him, and if they don't let the dawn into him at Vincennes, our soldier boys ain't about to get their asses shot off, and that's the straight from your old buddy, WW himself!"

Max made himself nod. "I see."

"Maybe you do, Max, and maybe you don't." Beck put down the teacup. "The champagne party's over, over here. And that goes for the Paschas and the Matas, the whole holus-bolus. And not one minute too soon."

He faced Beck directly. "That from you—or M-1?"

"Buddy-buddy." Ralph spoke without guile. "Asshole to asshole. I know you've been knockin' your brains out for her, so I thought I'll tell the Prof what's on the stove so he stops tearing out his guts for nothing!"

The big broad face seemed full of sympathy.

"Got it, Ralph."

"I hope so. No kidding, Max. I hope so, buddy."

Strangely, he was touched by the man's sincerity and directness.

"And I thank you."

Beck pummeled his shoulder. "How about we tie one on tonight?"

"Can't."

"One night soon?"

"Sure," Max said. "And congratulations again."

Only after Beck's departure was he able to take in the full weight of that warning. It accounted for the increasing difficulty in enlisting support at the very highest levels for Tha's appeal for a stay. During the last few weeks, there had occurred, over Tha's body, a new struggle for peace in Europe. All those who had, in the past, like the Pope, sought to bring an end to the suicidal struggle, had ranged themselves behind Tha's cry for life; and all those who wanted the war to continue, draining venom to the bottom, had poured abuse on the campaign for clemency. In Clemenceau's newspaper, the signatories were being vilified as "bathers in Boche filth, wallowers in enemy slime."

Now he could read Beck's warnings reflected in the wise

face of the old baroness. She had consistently tried to avoid en-
tangling the appeal in the larger struggle over Europe, to bring
it down to a person-to-person level, beseeching men and
women to suspend a fatal judgment on another human until
calmer times.

This last week, Queen Caroline of Holland had sent a
private message to Premier Painlevé, asking for clemency.
They had tried to make it seem a victory; but both had read
the signs: the queen was unwilling to have her name used publicly for Tha, who, after all, was a Dutch subject, an intimate of
many famous people at The Hague. And that difference between public avowal and private letter was the difference between success and failure.

"I think," the baroness said, "one can translate what
your friend said into what we've been feeling. Your State Department is bringing pressure, particularly among the neutrals,
not to endorse the appeal for Tha."

It explained, too, the resistance he had encountered in
the States. He had put it down to the climate that associated
the name of Mata Hari with European degeneracy. Now there
would be added the scandal of someone called Paul Bolo Pascha, a Turk who used German money to bribe members of the
French Chamber of Deputies. And though there was no suggestion that Tha had ever had anything to do with him, the
linkage had already occurred in Beck's condemnation of the
"Matas and Paschas" and would be taken up in just that sensational way by the yellow journals back home.

Sensing his despondency, the baroness tried to cheer
him up. "I'm on my way to a dinner party," she told him,
drawing on long gloves. "I've a new lead to Queen Sophia of
Greece. I've hopes of having her come out and declaring herself. Even though she's a Hohenzollern and a neutral, she has
great influence. I haven't given up, so don't you, dear boy."

Alone, Max tried to concentrate on the latest list. New
names had come in during the day, new contributions. Some
were from famous names, induced by other famous names to
become signatories.

In the correspondence was a note from Elaine Chardon,
refusing her signature because "my husband won't permit me

to sign." Often he had contemplated visiting her and exacting her support in testifying about that night of the railroad. But he knew that such testimony at best would be far from decisive, and that any approach to the woman would only antagonize Chardon, and could only do a great deal of harm to the clemency campaign, which the Foreign Minister had quietly and steadily supported.

After an hour with the lists, the work palled and Max, restless, pushed away the remaining pile.

At a dark corner, he found a phone kiosk.

A woman's voice answered.

"M'sieu Capel, please . . ."

"Don't you know?" The woman's voice broke. ". . . can you not have heard?"

"Heard?"

"An accident . . . in the yards . . . I am his niece, Geneviève . . ."

"An accident?"

"Oh . . . if you are a friend . . . we are all sitting here . . . come, but I cannot speak of this now . . ."

"Dead?"

"The funeral will be in the morning . . ."

The street was dark, no searchlights in the sky, just wind and autumnal unrest. Accident. A man who could sense every vibration in the web of steel with a spider's delicacy, whose bloodstream was the map of the yards of the Gare du Nord.

No accident.

Though he could never prove it, it was just too convenient to have his only witness to the traitorous meeting at the Gare du Nord wiped out. Now he alone could tell the story, though he no longer had corroboration.

Dear boy, the baroness had called him.

Don't be Dink Stover, Colonel House had warned.

And he had been both, in a war that was kind to neither juveniles nor Yale men.

But he had survived; and he knew the truth; and he could yet fight their jungle war in their way, and save her.

ANGELA
29 September 1917

> *Words,*
> *Gaston,*
> *Some words,*
> *Before you go.*

Angela Moulins, aged nineteen, convicted murderer, her incredibly long frame slopping over the prison cot, was drunk and singing and a joy.

Early this morning, word had come down from the Minister of Justice granting Angela an indefinite postponement of execution, and she had vowed to get wine and celebrate.

See the sun,
Fill my palm.
Lip a butt,
And exhale,
Some screwed up words,
Before you go.

Sister Lucille glowered from her chair, bent over one of her scrapbooks, pasting images of adornment on the cardboard. She had tried to interfere, but Angie had threatened her with reprisal by the prison's criminal sisterhood, and Sister Lucille had gone to her corner.

Bricks in a wall,
Birds in a cage.
Words in my head,
A twist of words,
You, Gaston.

It was a rule of St. Lazaire that those in death cells be given a carafe of wine with the evening meal. Thin, bitter red stuff, an aid to sleep, possibly, but never enough for flight in a cage.

Somehow Angie had sent word out to the criminal substructure, and when their large pails of drinking water had been delivered, Angie had poured out tumblers for Tha and herself. The yellowish wine easily counterfeited the color of what passed in the prison as aqua pura.

Sister Lucille hadn't caught on until they were deep in their buckets, but Angie's ferocity had forced her to acquiescence.

Words, Gaston,
Give us the words,
And then you can go.

Angie was off the bed, dancing.

She took Tha into her long thin arms and whirled her about. "Next—your reprieve! Because you are so important, they'll hold back until the last moment. End of the month, you'll have yours!" Almost as tall as Adam and even more boney, she dominated the cell. "How am I doing? Is this the way you danced, Tha?" She began to shed her smock. "Take a look. Will this get me some buttered buns?"

Sister Lucille bent to book and glue pot. Angie never lost a chance to deride the nun's shame of nudity, for which her interest in fashion was twisted evidence. Now she shook her scrawny and angular frame before the subdued nun.

"How about it, Sister? Honey for my croissant?"

Tha could feel the wine expanding the walls of the cell. It mystified her that Angela, with the body of a scarecrow, could have been a successful streetwalker. But she had been on the boulevards since her thirteenth year and had done well.

Her crime had been passionate, which customarily would have entitled her to leniency. But her victim had been a cop. A year earlier, the cop had sent Angie's lover, a thief, to prison, even though he had kept up his payoffs. The detective had moved in on Angie, beaten her regularly, and appropriated her earnings.

"Sure, I hated him," Angie had related, "but no more than I did half the men in Paris. And I didn't stick a knife in them!"

She had come home from her street rounds early one morning to find the detective snoring in bed. In the kitchen, on the stove, there lay a pan with some meat that had been burned black. Angie had picked up a knife, and in a burst of rage, attacked the man in the next room, unable to explain why that domestic offense had set her off and provoked murder.

"They'll let me off," she had confidently predicted. "They won't send me to the guillotine, any more than they're going to send you to Vincennes!"

At times, Angie would turn cruel and gibe at Tha. She took it for granted that Tha was guilty of treason, reserving her condemnation because Tha had let herself be caught. "Don't sing those Indian lullabies," she would storm. "You had a date with Vincennes before you were born—it's what you crave!"

But these outbursts served to keep Tha both sane and hopeful. In Angela's company, expectation was the furniture of adversity. Angela collected the newspaper clippings about Tha's clemency campaign and insisted on complete biographies of each celebrated person. A photograph of Robert Maxwell had sent her into rhapsodies. "There's one professor I'd be glad to take some lessons from, and give a few, on the side."

And of course, without her, there would never have been the link to the Irish newswoman.

Unlike Tha, whose movements were restricted by the orders of the military tribunal, Angela enjoyed some measure of freedom within the jail. She was permitted to exercise with the other women and to take part in various chores around the huge and gloomy building. And she made use of this mobility to establish contact with Morkan and become Tha's surreptitious go-between, aided by the prisoners' grapevine to steer clear of police who might turn over information to the Deuxième Bureau.

Under Angie's beanpole shadow, Tha and Tess had become fast friends, though they took care only to nod to each other. Their communication was always through Angie, sometimes verbal, sometimes written.

"I'm out of my depths," Morkan had once said. "I can't use soft crayons on this story. I need strong colors, harsh words, the eloquence of anger. I don't know whether I'm up to it."

Tess had only recently become a reporter, and then, by accident. She had been a schoolteacher and had seen two of her students gunned down by the British. She had written a letter to the *Freeman* about their short lives. Because of it, she'd been fired. Promptly, the *Freeman* took her on and assigned her to cover the Easter uprising. Her unpretentious, countrywoman directness had brought her fame. But it was only because the famous Maud Gonne had been otherwise employed that Morkan had been sent to Paris to seek the truth about Tha.

Slowly, the interview took shape. It began with an account of Morkan's frustrated efforts to reach Tha through official channels, only finally to have to resort to the crime of shoplifting in order to have herself sentenced to St. Lazaire. Tha emerged as one figure among the women prisoners of this ancient holy place, and their anguish had mixed with hers to make a portrait of France at war, so that all that Tha had dreamed of saying to the world was being told in the form of a story.

Angie, reading, had cried and laughed. "She's a clown, that one, but she's got us right—we're all poor saps in a nut house!"

Tomorrow, Tha thought, she'll be on her way out. How she would miss her, even though it would be to her benefit to have Morkan go.

"It's all set," Angie had reported after coming back from the exercise yard. "Tess'll leave tomorrow. She'll go to Geneva and wire out her story to Dublin, with copies to London and New York. You'll be heard, you old jelly roll, around the world. And then I'd like to see the farts do anything to you! A week, a week, and I promise, you'll have your reprieve, just like me!"

Angie flopped back on her cot, emaciated, breathless, laughing from her flapping dance.

> *Some words,*
> *Screw up some words,*
> *And then you go.*

She came to join Angie. "You make it sound so happy."
"No big thing," Angie said. "Just sing."

> *Wine in a bottle,*
> *Windows in a room,*
> *Dreams in a skull*
> *Give the word,*
> *And go, go.*

Tha was surprised that it was her voice, not Angie's, that took the grave words of the sad song of the faubourgs and lifted them above the abyss.

RUE FRANKLIN
7 October 1917

The official limousine drove at a stately pace through the quiet streets of Paris, and Max felt his nerves stretch to the breaking point. Beside him, Chardon chain-smoked, remaining pale and subdued.

"Let me be the spokesman," he had said as they left the Quai d'Orsay. "I know our Tiger. If we make him snarl, he'll feel compelled to pounce. Now, more than ever, since he will soon come to power."

A precious week had been lost, Max bitterly recollected. The first part in maneuvering Chardon into cooperation; the last three days in arranging this decisive parley with Clemenceau.

"If you go to the press," Chardon had reasoned, "you'll play your last card. And what will you accomplish? You will

348

force me to deny your allegations, lock me into the camp with Depardieu, who is no friend of mine, and Clemenceau, who is even less so. Hard as you may find it to believe, I am with you in this matter."

He had grilled Chardon, taking him over the steps that had led from Geneva to the Gare du Nord, and the Foreign Minister insisted again that he, like Max, had been a victim of a power play by Depardieu.

"Clemenceau will come to power because he wants revenge against the Germans and you Americans want victory. I myself am finished."

"Are you telling me that nobody can save Tha?"

"I am saying, we will go to the Tiger, together. I will tell him you threaten me with exposure, and that you will force me to go to the press with you. I will urge him to spare the life of this one woman until the war is over rather than embarrass France."

"And yourself?"

"To a degree," Chardon acknowledged. "I don't want you to go to the press. If you will agree, I will help you. Those are the terms. But no others."

A muddy, dishonorable bargain. Since making it, he had counted each hour. He had lived in a stupor of apprehension, watching the hours go by, hearing in the rustle of leaves from the park the approach of the sixteenth of October. And Chardon had called him each day, promising to bring about the showdown with Clemenceau.

The limousine crawled into a narrow street.

14 Rue Franklin.

Named in honor of old Ben, Max remembered. For the provincial from Pennsylvania who had whored it up in Paris with the castoffs of a tyrant, yet from whose funky sheets there had birthed a new age. Poor Richard. Poor Robert. But I am learning, he thought.

An aged servant in a pair of baggy pants and a stained and collarless shirt met them at the door and had them sit in a small anteroom. He poked his head into the next chamber, shouted their names, and shuffled away.

Chardon chewed on his cigarette and swallowed the indignity of being kept waiting. He examined the paintings on the wall. They were all by Manet, the impressionist, and a close friend of Clemenceau. Glowing scenes of park and picnic, of the early days of the century, of the effulgence of anticlerical republicanism, the era that Clemenceau, who said he was both anarchist and conservative, had made his soul's scene.

"So damn sunny," Chardon grumbled. "In my Thionville, we only saw the sun through the factory smoke. And in my father's day, they never even looked up."

The door opened. A very short man, with bristling white hair and white moustache, ushered out two guests, thanking them for their gift, a small piece of ancient Greek sculpture, which he fondled in his hands, misshapen by age.

"Jules"—he finally took note of Chardon's presence— "forgive me for not going to you, but the Quai is no place for anything but gossip. I saw the photo of you and Painlevé and the rest feeding the swans in the park, and I thought, who would fail to be reassured that our country is in firm hands?"

Chardon permitted the shot to pass over him. "Professor Robert Maxwell." He brought Max forward. "One who worked in Princeton with President Wilson, and who has been serving his government here . . ."

Bright eyes raked Max from under the beetling brows. "I hear you write books about France," he said. "But then I wrote books about America. I never read your strictures on what we did to Jaurès, but then you never read mine on your impeachment of President Johnson."

"On the contrary," Max said. "I even made it assigned reading for my students."

The hawkish, wrinkled lids opened wider. "Then I suppose you know I married an American woman and lived in your country, and that I was once accused by the French of being too American, as you Americans now accuse me of being too French. But I blame myself. It is the consequence of living too long, one comes a full circle . . ."

He led the way into a study. It had shelves filled with artifacts of ancient Greece and attested to his love of antiquity. Chardon had hinted that Clemenceau saw himself as a Demosthenes: a man come to denounce the world for its failure to uphold the tenets of civilization.

"I still admire America"—Clemenceau found an empty place on the shelves for his new gift—"even though I realized, after my first half hour there, while a dark man carried my bag, that your moralities were for export. But, alas, as all the world knows, we are an importing country . . ."

They waited until the old man, surprisingly agile, arranged himself on the couch. He lay stiffly against the cushions, neither lying down nor seated, but ready to pounce to his feet at any moment.

"Jules," he said, "I'm sure you are not here today to confuse politics with morality?"

"I envy your flair for turning the obvious into aphorism, Georges," Chardon said. "Nevertheless, morality is a factor of political life. Not only for our young American friend, but for me, as well."

"Meaning, your Krupp fiasco?"

"Mine," Chardon said. "But if I am forced to go to the press, then, not only ours, but France's . . ."

"What would you tell them?"

"What Depardieu told Colonel House," Chardon replied softly. "That Krupp manufactured a conference for peace, and I, in the interests of France, acceded."

"A dupe of Boche intelligence? How would you recover?"

"I take hope from your example, Georges," Chardon said. "I remember you yourself were once accused of receiving money for your newspaper from the Germans. And in spite of that, you are now about to return to power. Yet poor Painlevé won't even spare the life of a woman, because he fears you'll accuse him of being soft on German spies!"

"That was a long time ago . . ."

"Yes, and who knows, I may live to be an elder statesman, just like yourself."

The bushy brows took on a menacing life of their own, quivering with outrage. "You would allege," he asked, "that I knew of that meeting, too?"

"Yes, Georges," Chardon said quietly. "Not only allege—prove."

Clemenceau thrust his hands deeper into his pockets, his entire body stiffening into one plane, and then suddenly he sprang erect, swiftly moving on the balls of his feet, with a pronounced catlike tread.

"Come along, gentlemen!"

They followed in silence along a narrow passage that led to a solarium; roof and sides were of glass, and its entire area given over to benches and tables covered with plants and flowers, crowded minuscule aisles, with a long potting table against the rear wall, facing the outdoor garden.

Clemenceau lowered one of the hinged windows and called out to the greenery. "Depardieu, would you be kind enough to join us?"

The garden stretched back a hundred feet, and, like the solarium, attested to Clemenceau's greed for devoting every inch to yield some plant.

After a moment, Depardieu appeared on the twisty path, along with a short blond woman, plumply attractive, who wore a fleecy white cape. He stood with her a moment before answering the old man's summons. Max, looking out, was struck by the woman's clairvoyant smile.

Depardieu shut the glass door behind him.

"You know these gentlemen?"

"Of course." Depardieu bowed to Chardon formally, and nodded in Max's direction. "We have all met on this matter before."

Clemenceau busied himself with a plant at the potting table. "May I trouble you to identify your companion out there, as you did for me?"

"As you wish. She is Frau Eva Zeit, until recently attached to General Ludendorff's headquarters, in charge of intelligence."

"Certain?"

Depardieu smiled. "She is better known than me."

"She came to you voluntarily?"

"Yes."

"For what reason?"

"For several, no doubt."

"But the one she gave you?"

"Principally, for asylum. She fled the Abteilung. As a result of the Krupp affair and Mata Hari's double dealing, she had to run for it."

"You're not going to arrest her?"

"Not yet," Depardieu said. "She's too valuable. She offers to give us information on Ludendorff's winter offensive. She asks, as a token of our earnestness, that we carry out the sentence on Zelle; and, second, that you and I provide her with a written guarantee of asylum."

Clemenceau snipped off some unwanted growth with a pair of shears. "Should I believe her?"

"I don't know," Depardieu said. "She may be here on behalf of both Krupp and Ludendorff. To protect Krupp from having that meeting exposed and his own reputation in Germany severely damaged. And Ludendorff may want her to disclose half-truths to cover his real intentions this winter."

Max felt a pulse beat in his throat. "But—with all those alternatives—you're still going to send Tha to Vincennes?"

Depardieu nodded, but faced Clemenceau. "I'm asking you to give Zeit her guarantees, because she will have to tell me something we can confirm about Ludendorff. Even a half-truth would serve as a clue to the rest. We know Ludendorff is going to make the great German gamble of the war. I know, sir, you will soon be in the Elysée. And that is why, in view of our negligible risk, and the possible great gains, I unhesitatingly recommend your signature . . ."

Clemenceau gently carried the dripping roots of a plant to a moist bed. "I have told the Chamber of Deputies I will go to the Elysée only if I am given a free hand in the conduct of war and peace. I am seventy-six. Some call me a fossil of 1870; others, of an even more primitive eon. I have said for a generation we will have peace in Europe when Germany is crushed, and remain at peace as long as Germany remains crushed."

He patted the earth around the tender plant.

"If some among us work for Germany, they must go to jail or be shot. I will never relent. Not for a Malavy. Nor my old friend Caillaux. And not for you, Chardon."

"Much less this woman, Zelle?"

"Much less."

Chardon had become pale. He nodded at the old man's threat and turned back to Max. "In view of what we have learned, I do not see how we can but accept . . ."

Max moved past him, past Depardieu, directly to the ferocious old man, stooping over his plants with the air of a French peasant. "How can you do this? A German agent, motivated by spleen, or Krupp's fears, or Ludendorff's schemes— to put away the life of a woman who you know is telling the truth?"

The old man's head remained bowed for a moment, preoccupied with his work. He glanced sideways at Depardieu. "I think you owe it to our young historian," he said, "to put all the facts at his disposal . . ."

Depardieu shouldered his way between them, ranging himself alongside the old man, as if to physically protect him from Max's assault. "We know how much faith you have in this Zelle woman. But, regretfully, she has confessed. We are in possession of a complete document, which I will have her sign tomorrow in the presence of Clunet . . ."

He felt hollow, nauseated. "I don't believe you."

"Today," Depardieu said, "I confronted her with the evidence supplied us by Frau Eva. It verifies that the Abteiling engineered that meeting, and that Zelle was their instrument to deceive you and your country. Zelle broke down completely. I have asked Clunet to come to the prison to witness her signature as voluntary and unforced. With the permission of Monsieur Clemenceau, and His Excellency, I will be glad to let you examine it . . ."

He had a sense of suspension, of seeing himself and the others at a great distance, of a tiny Clemenceau shuffling among the plants, of Chardon rubbing his lips with the back of his hand, as if to wipe away a bitter taste, of Depardieu looking into the garden, linking himself with Frau Eva with an air of severity and pity.

"Tomorrow, in my office, at five, Professor?"

Somehow he managed to nod and stumble away. Chardon was at his elbow, guiding him through the rooms, waving away the old houseman in his grubby shirt, until they found themselves in the open, walking along the windy narrow street.

The limousine followed them, like a dog on a leash.

"Let me take you home, Max."

"I have to walk, just walk, by myself . . ."

Chardon waved to the limousine to come up, but he did not get in. "I'm going to sign your clemency petition," he said. "Not only for Tha, but for me. Clemenceau belongs to the past, to revenge and vindictiveness. Your President has the real vision, an international community, based on full disclosure, relying on the approval of the masses. I think that when the men come back, they will endorse that idea. At all events, I will take my chances with it as the way of the future . . ."

He squeezed Max's shoulder.

"Let us keep in touch."

Max heard the limousine roll away. Blind strides brought him to the avenue. The evening hour had come. Women were queuing up before the shops. Always he had taken comfort from their lively and pungent complainings and comments, eavesdropping to understand this country and its people.

She's not guilty, he thought. Even if they forced her to say it, I know better.

He realized he had spoken aloud and the women were staring at him. Let them. Every country is native to the mad. You have made me your compatriot. But until tomorrow at five, let me be excused from singing "La Marseillaise."

TWO WAYS
8 October 1917

Dr. Speranti stood waiting outside the infirmary. "Angie's asleep now, but I thought I better have you down. She wants to see you. She's very restless. Best thing, sit by her until she wakes up."

One of the nuns led Tha through the aisle of beds. Like all the other chambers in the prison, this one too was irregularly shaped, given to surprising alcoves. A crude wooden screen marked Angie's bed. A nun sat near the foot of it; yet another, within the screen, close to Angie's head.

Again, like all else in St. Lazaire, the sheets and coverlets were grimy and aged. Angie's face was turned away. Her curls were damp with sweat, and her hair lay in tangled disorder. From the pale, emaciated body there came long swooping sighs, like the night wind under the city bridges, as she fought to breathe.

The nun passed beads through her fingers and mouthed a silent prayer.

Who could say when it had begun?

Angie herself would insist that her mother passed the cough along with the milk. Sometimes she would boast about it, as if she were a Dumas heroine, making of her weakness a sign of a finer nature, a natural aristocrat among trotteuses.

The first signs of the attack had come during the night hours of their drunken celebration. Tha, awakening in the cell, had listened to Angie's racking cough and had hurried to her side, offering to get her some water.

Angie had laughed into the darkness, weak from coughing. "Unless it's holy water, don't bother."

Next morning, she had been on fire and Dr. Speranti had been summoned. He took one look at her face and gave orders to have the nuns remove her to the infirmary. Angie had protested vehemently. "I know your slaughterhouse. Bring me some garlic, a couple of strong men, and I'll sweat out the poison." She laughed and then coughed again. "At least two cods, but more will not be turned away."

Speranti had laughed at her jokes and firmly supervised her removal from the cell. He had ultimately replied to Tha's unspoken query: "Fever, possibly pneumonia, but that's a very general diagnosis."

The following day he had been even more evasive. He had come to continue their examination of the essay by the English philosopher-scientist who, having opted for science, acknowledged that both mysticism and science sought transcendence, the heart's will to conquer time; Atman and Faustus, locked in a thaumaturgical embrace, recognizing that their lies and truths were both dreams.

"Can I visit Angie?"

"Perhaps tomorrow."

She had forced him to deliver on that vague promise, only to find Angie in an incoherent state. Once, suddenly clear, she'd demanded, "Morkan get out?"

"I've seen nothing in the papers."

"Oh, I've lost track. It's today she leaves, isn't it?"

Tha forebore telling her that Morkan had been gone for forty-eight hours. Not a syllable had appeared in the Paris papers. But they were censored. She would have to ask Clunet, on his next visit, to bring her the English and Irish journals.

Angie, whirling in a fog, threw out disconnected phrases. Some about her boyfriend, the thief, who was serving time, and whom the detective said had regularly cheated on her; some about her mother and the various men who had succeeded Angie's father in the maternal bed; and many were orphaned images of her life, about which she laughed weakly, making a wine of her wounds.

But Speranti refused to make a dire prognosis.

"She's a street brat. I've seen others like her come in here and wait for the Abbé to shove the last wafer under their tongues before they jump up and announce they're cured. Forgive me, I've been in St. Lazaire too long to make predictions . . ."

Yet today, his cryptic neutrality at the door had delivered his verdict, echoed now by the nun's rapid clicking of the beads, keeping time with Angie's stricken shallow breathing, a mordant scherzo.

The resistance came from Tha. She knew the Minister of Justice was reexamining Angie's file. There were rumors that he was inclined to grant a shorter term as a Christmas gift. There was a general agreement among the nuns that Angie would not go to the guillotine, that she would cheat death.

Now this.

But she's too stringy to give in, Tha thought. And we are bound together. We agreed to live. I . . . I have yet to find the answer to the puzzle of my brief visit, of the limits to which I must be bent, so much remains beyond my comprehension, so unstrung am I.

"Zelle . . ."

A nurse, poking her head around the screen, beckoned with her forefinger. The other woman did not look up from her devotions, the small globes passing between her hands were substitutes for the world and its small hopes.

Tha, coming out to the aisle, had difficulty surfacing.

"Visitors!" the nun repeated. "In the exercise yard."

She made her way along the winding aisle, conscious of the envy of the sick, much as she had envied Angie, the one who had been reprieved, the one who must remain alive.

Across the yard, she saw Depardieu with Clunet.

But only the security chief moved toward her.

As always he carried some files beneath the clasp of his arm; weapons, she knew, far more deadly than a gun. What had Massimy once said about information? Something about the prop and prison of society, on which each man rested for his security. Words from Gaston.

"Good afternoon, Madame."

"Afternoon."

"I asked Maître down, so he could witness our transactions."

"I wasn't aware we had any."

"Oh, several," Depardieu said. He advanced a step, taking her elbow, leading her along the walk. "Tess Morkan, for example."

She hunched her shoulders against the blow. "What about her?"

"We stripped her at the border. Of her documents. She wound up in Geneva without a passport and we lodged a complaint against her. The Swiss will intern her, for how long, nobody can now say ..."

Tha raked her teeth across her upper lip, almost bringing blood. "You would not have bothered if you thought your case was strong. You deceive no one, Depardieu."

"Nor you, Madame. A jail is the last place one should try to avoid surveillance."

"I'll remember," she said, "the next time you put me away."

Depardieu was not amused. "Morkan we owe to our efficiency. I have to admit sheer luck handed us Frau Eva Zeit."

She did not give him the satisfaction of letting him see her inner shudder. "Congratulations."

"My alter ego," Depardieu said. "More precisely, your nemesis."

"A fabulous woman." Tha forced herself to be cool. "What fables has she brought you?"

Inside her, she saw Frau Eva's seraphic smile: the smile of one as didactic as death, beyond all wayward questions and ambiguous answers, both feet firmly planted in the grave.

"She testifies," Depardieu said, drawling, "you acted on behalf of the Russian revolutionaries. A plot evolved by Lenin, for the sake of stifling peace and creating a scandal preventing American intervention. The testimony is concrete, incontrovertible. I have given a transcript to Clunet. It is here for you to examine, even contest, if you care to . . ."

She moved along the colonnaded walk where once monks had paced in abnegation, serving the sick and the dying, in a pesthouse that could only take their lives along with those they served.

"Has he seen it?"

"Yes," Depardieu said. "I have brought a confession for you to sign. In the presence of your lawyer. I will deliver it to Monsieur Clemanceau, our next premier, who promises you will be granted a month's postponement until he comes to power and can review your case . . ."

"Another month?"

"Not much, yet all."

"But no other guarantees?"

"I urge you to accept," Depardieu said. "Not only for yourself, but for your American friend. In spite of everything, even Zeit, even the body of D'Estrelles, he persists. He threatens to go to the press with his wild talk. We have heard how much you think of the American, how grateful you are to him. Who would want an accident to befall him? Madame, bow to the evidence. Show us that your sympathies are really with France. Save your own life and his . . ."

The voice, so judicious and equable, brought a chill, as no animosity could have done. Depardieu was reading the signposts, telling her all the avenues of escape were blocked, leaving only this chink through which it would yet be possible to squeeze her life and Max's.

They had reached the other end of the cloister. Depardieu turned her back to complete the circle. They could see

Clunet, half sagging against a column, looking down at his feet.

"Maître begs me not to burden you with his emotions. He urges you to accept, not to risk your life for another hour. We both know his life depends on yours. For his sake, too, Madame, do as I say."

She shivered.

Dr. Speranti emerged running from the infirmary, calling across the quadrangle. "Angie! At once! Hurry, Madame!"

Strength came back to her cold body, and she sped across the yard, ignoring Depardieu's frowning impatience.

At the bed, the nun swung her beads away.

Only Angie's eyes moved. They were bright with anger. They had a child's shine in a face that disease had made seem childlike.

"See the Abbé?"

"No."

"I sent him away. No old man jawing at me! Tell them to fuck off!"

"All right, Angie."

The eyes filled with entreaty, burning. "Tha—tell me— it don't matter."

She stroked the girl's forehead, slick with sweat, above a face raw with fever.

"You and the doctor ..." Angie struggled to push the words past her weakened lungs. "... The dream lives, not us ..."

She reached deep into herself, wanting to give that assurance, and not only to Angie, but to herself, floundering and helpless in the void.

"I tried to believe that," she said. "But now ..."

Angie's hands feebly moved to take hers. "The doctor ... a visitor ... you made them give in, Tha?"

"No, Angie."

"No reprieve?"

"No."

"Bastards," Angie said. Spittle came to her lips. "What do they want now?"

"A confession."

Angie's laughter bubbled out past the dry lips. "I

watched you ... how the fat asses hate you ... but get even with them ... too late for butter on my rolls, but screw them ... do what they say ... screw them for me, Tha!"

In her anxious plea she had half lifted her head from the pillow, but the effort spent her last strength. She lay back, eyes closed, trying to smile.

"... I almost taught you to sing."

"You did, Angie."

"Give me a kiss, Tha."

She pressed her lips to the girl's. They were brittle and cracked. Her breath made only a faintness in the air, scarcely disturbing the universe.

Behind her, Speranti moved close to the bed. He took the girl's wrist, trying to catch the beat of life. He looked old and tired, his white jacket full of stains no amount of washing could make clean.

"Let her," he pronounced.

He helped her to her feet and walked with her all the way to the exit to the cloisters. They stood looking out into the yard. A wind had sprung up. The trees, which had been so fat with growth because of the early spring, were now almost denuded. Leaves scuttered along the cobbles and piled up in the corners, some turning a savage red, others curled into ashy gray submission.

"Fall," Speranti said. "I like this season best."

"Once you told me ... only viscera and a pulse ... do you still?"

The doctor nodded. "For me, that's all."

She walked away from his sigh, her eyes on Depardieu and Clunet. The wind pulled at her. It dried off her tears and sweat.

She went past Depardieu to the old counselor.

"Tha ..."

He took her outstretched hands.

"Maître," she said, "once more, I must reject your advice ..."

His frail body shrank within itself, and she felt his hands tremble in hers.

"Must ... must?"

She took his arm and linked it with hers, making him come away with her, past Depardieu's scowl. She knew that he had foreseen her rejection, and yet, he would never understand it, never approve.

Nor could she hope to still all the questions within herself, now that she had launched herself on the sea of paradox and contingency, rejecting the two ways of the Bhagavad-Gita—the way of fighting, because one had immortality; the way of relinquishing the world, to gain immortality.

"Please, Maître, will you take a message to Max?"

"Of course . . ."

"Tell me, if he loves me, as I should love him, not to throw away his life. Ask him to abide with a measure of truth and the margin of what can't be known, the edge of mystery, which I could never be content with . . ."

"To desert you?"

"To embrace me," she said. She saw the leaves swirl in a corner, drying away, dying away, the mixed colors of life. "As I am. I was always filled with malice against the world, seeking beauty and permanence where none can be, fearful of the singular dance of shadows. Tell Max, if I refuse to surrender to Depardieu's lies, it's to give myself to questions, without answer . . . the nothing that yet is everything . . . to which I ask him to hold open the door for me."

Clunet was heavy against her. "Tha, child, child of love, men can't live without answers . . ."

"Tell Max, I can and he must."

She left them both, the shaken old man and the defeated man of security, to stride across the quadrangle and its lacing winds and its incongruent trees. She would go back to Angie's bed and keep the vigil, waiting for Angie's anger to find liberation in death, and, for herself, losing herself to uncertainty, from whose inmost core she had always flinched, and which she must now make her own domain.

VINCENNES
16 October 1917

She had awakened in the dark, and beyond the cell the world lay behind a glass wall, out of reach. Again and again she tried to force her mind to cope with the present moment, but she could not breach the transparent barrier, leaving her cheated of her pain, of her existence.

Around her the cell was a black pit wholly occupied by Sister Lucille's braggart snores. From the corridor came the menacing scrape of the rats carousing on the bridge of sighs. Always before they had frightened her; now they meant nothing.

Her dream had drained her of emotion. It had been so happy, at the start. She had been walking along a road in Friesland, with the sun shining, every tree applauding her youth, her stride, her breath. She was on her way to pick up

Banda at a nursery school. Then the road suddenly lay under a black riptide. It was after all only a dead dyke and the sea had swept in, as if it had never existed.

But farther on, the road was dry. A sailor appeared. When he came to help her cross the water, she saw he was Max.

On the farther side, they made love. She protested he was not a sailor, but he continued his caresses and she gave in, anxious to reach Banda.

Atop a hill, Adam was guarding a fold of sheep. Banda was with him. But he carefully turned the child away so she could not see the act of love. He himself was sad about her betrayal; not angry, only sad.

She had left Max to run up the hill. It bothered her, because she knew the hill could not be in Friesland. She wanted to tell Adam that she had mistaken the American for a sailor she had once loved, and that Adam would surely forgive her error.

But when she surmounted the hill, both Adam and Banda were gone. And there were no sheep. Only large rocks. Some were malevolently sharp, like the stones of the shelled Saint Hilaire. A cold wind blew and she ran among the rocks, refusing to believe they were not sheep, touching one after another, until her hands were bleeding.

Awake, she tried to force herself to think of Adam, to connect the hill with Scotland, to make the terrain of her dream a corridor back to the present.

But instead of Scotland, she was back in Indonesia, during the days of her first pregnancy, her back aching as she followed a guide through the Borobudur temple, trying to understand what he was telling her about the mandala pattern of its construction, but oppressed by the heat outside, her burden inside. She had leaned against the wall for support, hearing the guide rattle on about the discontinuity of spiritual evolution, until one reached the seventh level and resolved all the contradictions within its own dome.

After the tour, they had given her tea. She could still taste it. She had been so grateful for the chance to rest. The child, too, had luxuriated in her womb. And for the first time she perceived the marvel of the temple's structure, which satisfied some secret fold of the brain and impossibly squared the circle.

Adam, she thought, let me see you again.

But she could only bring back the hill with its broken stones, changing color as the wind swept the rays of the sun; colored stones, without life.

A knock sounded at the door.

"Time to dress, Madame," a strange voice said.

Tha rose from her cot. "But it's so early."

"I'm instructed to accompany you to Vincennes," the voice said, "I am Lieutenant Flournoy. Be so good as to dress quickly, Madame."

Sister Lucille was up now. There was no electricity in the cell, but they had an oil lamp. The nun had trouble with the wick, but finally brought it to life.

"Can I select the dress?" Sister Lucille asked. "Would you do that for me, as a favor?"

She waited while the nun went to the rack they had improvised for the six or seven dresses they had let her have. Obviously Sister Lucille had planned this for a long time. She had chosen a gray cape with a red lining; a matching dress with red piping; and a hat with a broad brim, of soft gray felt with a dark rust ribbon.

Silence separated her from herself and the attentions of the nun. And when it was over, she said she was pleased with the selection and that she had left instructions with Maître Clunet that the Sister was to inherit the wardrobe.

The nun broke down, weeping, crouched on a cot, great ploughing sighs that broke harsh dry ground.

A dim light showed a young officer in the corridor. He averted his face, as if she had a dread disease. Behind him two soldiers held their rifles above stiff shoulders. They too were figures in a vitrine.

Their path, through the labyrinth, was completely unfamiliar to her. It led to a circular stair without a light. She had to hold to the sides of the wall. The lieutenant preceded her, the two riflemen at her back.

In the crook of the stairwell, a figure slumped in a straight-backed chair. He attempted to rise, and then crumpled back. "Tha," Clunet said, his voice a weak whisper. "I can't get up. I can't go with you."

She stood above him, watching him, herself unable to connect, the watchful lieutenant part of her decomposition.

"Does Max understand?"

"I'm not sure. Like me, he will do as you say."

"Say I love him, as I say it to you."

He put his head in his hands. "You gave me a new life. And I helped them take yours away. Under our rags and robes we know only violence. I would kill them if I knew where to strike."

"Will you tell him, tell yourself?"

He struggled to rise. "I will only have myself now."

She touched her fingers to his lips and then followed the lieutenant, hoping for pain to come again and rescue her from her glass prison.

The courtyard felt icy.

A van showed its lights. Their footsteps echoed along the cobbles and on the walls of the ancient buildings, but timed to steps that had gone here so many times before; the darkness needed to make no comment.

They rattled and bumped through the streets. In the van, benches lined each side. The lieutenant and his two men occupied one side, leaving the other entirely to her, as if her disease were not only dread, but catching. The rear doors of the van had two narrow windows, narrower than the judas doors of her cell, illumined only now and then when they passed a streetlight in the blacked-out city.

"I thought it was to be at dawn."

"We go by the meterological charts," Flournoy said.

"But how will they see?"

"I don't know, Madame. This is my first time."

"Mine as well."

But he was too young to laugh, too trimly turned out, a lieutenant in a shiny bottle. "They must know what they're doing, Madame."

Through the windows, the roofs of Paris began to appear as a faint diagram. She tried to remember the Sundays with Adam at Vincennes, to reconstruct the crumbs on the white picnic cloth. She could see the geometric cloth against the green, but as an abstraction. Adam eluded her. As did her pain, her existence; she was being robbed of life, and not yet dead. She cursed fear for blocking her nerves, but to no avail.

The van slowed, bumping over some uneven ground, and there was the sound of steel in heavy ratchets.

"Vincennes," Flournoy said.

A gate was swinging open, and now the van sped along on a smooth graveled road, tires spattering moistly.

People were shouting.

They were calling her name and a thousand voices made it into an indistinct chorus, merging the syllables into a universal chant.

As the truck drew away from the gate, she was able to see a portion of the crowd through the slit back windows on the doors of the van. The hooded street lamps gave the crowd a momentary garish identity. She knew Max would be there, but the van was going too fast to make it possible to recognize any one of them.

At the last moment, a small figure scrambled up the iron gate, reached the top, frantically waved a scrawny arm.

She was sure it was the boy who had staggered under the weight of his champagne, and that he was shaking a tiny fist both for her and his brother.

His figure slid down into blackness.

But he had restored her to life, to her present, to her fear and anger and misery.

The van stopped.

I'm going to die, she thought with great relief, I can stop hiding behind fear and disbelief, I who am I am going to die.

"Please come with me, Madame."

She felt the damp and the darkness and the decaying mossy walls of the ancient fort. They were in a kind of well, the detritus of centuries having raised the streets almost to the level of the top of the old fort, whose walls were cracking under the pressure of the present.

A wooden stake, planted in the rough field, was blackly there, firm, a terminal in the night.

The young man still could not look at her. "Do you wish to be tied?"

"No."

"Blindfolded?"

"No."

"Do you wish, according to the regulations, to say anything to me, Madame?"

"Nothing."

He brought her to stand beside the pole. He whipped off his cap and tried to look at her for the first time. "Please face them, Madame." He was shaking.

Against the light, the Zouave platoon were cutouts in a child's geography book: flowing white pantaloons, long-waisted coats, tall peaked caps, figures in a costume party, a masquerade party that had wandered into dawn.

Adam . . .

At last!

In the sun. Bareheaded. Standing there in the grassy dell where they had picnicked. His eyes, unmarred, full of anger and life. Telling her about the fortress and an ancestor of his who had been executed there. Gesticulating with a roll, in the Sunday air.

She'd bitten into it.

He'd been momentarily taken aback. Then dragged her down in their public Eden, to roll over in the grass, the old walls of the palace a peeling yellow, sour to their carefree tumbles.

Now those walls were black sheets against the faint light.

Like the alleyway, that night of the illicit lingerie show. She could suddenly hear Adam whispering to her, "What matters—makes everything matter—I love you, Tha." And then he had left her with Max while he had gone off with Caroline. Their laughter came to her, and pain burned along her nerves. She was jealous of their laughter, of all sound that would soon stop.

The lieutenant had moved away.

The muzzles lowered in the east and the soldiers were

like carved figures, their dark faces linked with Sita and Banda and her murdered son, welding her pain to every part of her.

A playful ray found a crack in the old walls. Eye of the sun. She had taken its name in her arrogant ignorance. In the east, the symbol of abiding life; here, the flaky agonies of a dying star. Now, remembering how both fancies had nourished her, she lifted her eyes above the Zouaves and gave herself to the volley of light.

AFTERWORD

The people and events come from the record,
but they are combined as fiction; or, redundantly,
historical fiction.

Dates, names of persons, and places
have been changed or modified out of respect for
the memory of the dead, the laws of libel, and
the rules of narrative economy.